The critics on Anita Burgh

'A blockbuster . . . an excellent reading experience'
Literary Review

'The mix of suspense, romance, humour and good old heart-tugging pathos is irresistible' Elizabeth Buchan, *Mail on Sunday*

'A blockbusting story of romance and intrigue'
Family Circle

'The perfect beach book' *Marie Claire*

'Its crafted writing keeps you hanging in there until the last page' *City Limits*

'Sharp . . . wickedly funny' *Mail on Sunday*

'Ambition, greed and manipulation add up to a great blockbuster' *New Woman*

'A well-written contemporary story that has all the necessary ingredients to make a great read – and it is!' *Oracle*

'Anita has the storyteller's gift' *Daily Express*

'Sinister and avaricious forces are at work behind the pious smiles . . . Gripping!' *Daily Telegraph*

'A sure-fire bestseller' *Prima*

Anita Burgh was born in Gillingham, Kent, but spent her early years at Lanhydrock House in Cornwall. Returning to the Medway Towns, she attended Chatham Grammar School, and became a student nurse at UCH in London. She gave up nursing upon marrying into the aristocracy. Subsequently divorced, she pursued various careers – secretarial work, a laboratory technician in cancer research, and an hotelier. She has a flat in Cambridge and a house in France where she shares her life with her partner, Billy, two bulldogs, three mixed breed dogs and two cats. The visits of a constantly changing mix of her four children, two step-children, six grandchildren, four step-grandchildren and her noble ex-husband keep her busy, entertained, and poor! Anita Burgh is the author of many bestsellers, including *Distinctions of Class*, which was shortlisted for the RNA Romantic Novel of the Year Award.

By the same author

Distinctions of Class
Love the Bright Foreigner
The Azure Bowl
The Golden Butterfly
The Stone Mistress
Advances
Overtures
Avarice
Lottery
The Cult
On Call
The Family

Tales from Sarson Magna: Molly's Flashings
Tales from Sarson Magna: Hector's Hobbies

Anita Burgh

BREEDERS

ORION

An Orion paperback
First published in Great Britain by Orion in 1996
This paperback edition published in 1996 by Orion Books Ltd,
Orion House, 5 Upper St Martin's Lane, London WC2H 9EA

Reissued 1999

A CIP catalogue record for this book
is available from the British Library

Typeset by Deltatype Ltd, Ellesmere Port, Cheshire
Printed in Great Britain by
Clays Ltd, St Ives plc

This book is dedicated to
Gertie and Gussie with love.

And in fond memory of:
Paddy, Brutus, Fanny, Sammy, Sappho,
Rita, Emma Dane, Kefti and Shin.
But especially Buttercup.

Acknowledgements

It was my agent, Mic Cheetham, who suggested that I write about the world of dogs, whereupon my editor Jane Wood enthusiastically agreed and has never wavered in her belief in the project. I'm grateful to my publisher, Anthony Cheetham, for liking big books and to everyone at Orion involved in its production.

The members of the Special Operations Unit of the RSPCA have been incredibly helpful in sharing their experiences. Officials of the Kennel Club supplied me with information and explanations about the frequently confusing world of dog shows. Elizabeth and Helen McCreath were so hospitable and patient with what must, at the time, have appeared to be a lot of stupid questions about dog breeding. Pat Brigden, Jenny Ziman, Alex Briggs, Andy Foxcroft, Don Balfour and Pauline Lockyer helped me enormously, as did the many breeders I talked to at Crufts '95. I shall always be grateful to Steve Glanvill MA, Vet MB, DBR, OVS, MRCVS, who, despite his busy schedule, found time to check various aspects for me. Rebecca Leith drove many miles meeting and talking to people when I was too crocked to do so. My thanks to David Macmillan and the real Bandage who was the inspiration for the fictional one. Gertie, Gussie, Portia, Marble and Hero helped in their own way. And Billy was always there.

Although many of those mentioned above helped in checking what I have written, if mistakes have been made then the responsibility is entirely mine.

Il y a aura toujours un chien perdu quelquepart
qui m'empêchera d'être heureux.
There will always be a lost dog somewhere that
will prevent me from being happy.

Jean Anouilh

We are alone, absolutely alone on this chance
planet; and amid all the forms of life that
surround us, not one, excepting the dog, has
made an alliance with us.

Maurice Maeterlinck

March

1

Fear was the dominant emotion in the speeding car. She sat, huddled, in the passenger seat, her breathing heavy with anxiety. He drove fast, far too fast for the atrocious conditions. He was angry. She had no way of knowing why, or what had caused this latest furious outburst. In the short time she had been with him she had learnt to be afraid of his temper, which could erupt at any time and over anything.

The heavy black Mercedes slowed. He did not stop, but with one hand still on the wheel he dragged her across him, opened his door and hurled her out on to the rain-sodden road. She fell heavily, grazing her chin. The car roared away into the night.

She tried to stand, but one leg collapsed beneath her. She attempted to drag herself to the verge, but the pain was too great. She sank on to the road, blood oozing from her damaged chin, her large dark eyes brimming with terror. Helpless and dejected, she lay awaiting whatever fate might bring.

Thomasine, driving slowly because of the foul conditions, decided that such weather was a fitting conclusion to an all-out awful day. She had overslept, laddered two pairs of tights in the mad scramble not to be late, had had her credit cards stolen, got divorced, endured dinner with a disapproving mother, and now this storm. Still, nothing much else could go wrong, she told herself.

The windscreen wipers clunked noisily, the black blades streaking in an hysterical rhythm back and forth, yet failing to clear the screen. Thomasine sat hunched over the steering wheel, clutching it firmly in her hands, as much for comfort as control, and wished she were anywhere but here, on this roadway, and on such a cold and stormy night – more like midwinter than the first month of spring.

She wished she were safely home in London – not in the present but three years ago, before her husband's betrayal, before all the anger and pain – not returning to an empty, strange house facing an uncertain and lonely future. It was hard to accept she was divorced when it was the last thing she wanted to be. Despite everything she still loved her husband with a painful longing. Over dinner with her mother, Di, she had tried to hide these feelings. And although her mother had said she was well shot of the deceiving bastard and the sooner she found someone else and stopped mooching about the better, Thomasine was sure her mother had seen through her and despised her for being weak and indecisive.

Thomasine sighed. It was easy for her mother; she was one of those dogmatic individuals who never doubted they were right and who seemed immune to hurt, as if they had an extra layer of skin. Di was puzzled and irritated by her lack of ideas and plans for what she wanted to do with this new, unasked-for, freedom. If this had happened to her elder sister, Abigail, she wouldn't be afraid of an empty future. No doubt she would already have enrolled in a mind-improving course, be working for an Open University degree, while doing a full time job perfectly. Abigail would never waste a moment dreaming about what might have been. But then, it wouldn't ever happen to Abigail with her orderly, busy life, a paragon of a husband who would never stray, and three ideal children.

Divorced, dinner with mother, and her credit-card wallet nicked. 'It isn't bloody fair,' she said aloud as a large black car overtook her at speed. It swung sharply in front of her, far too close, its fat wheels kicking up a dense cloud of rain and mud which impeded her vision even more.

4

'Inconsiderate bastard!' she shouted at him impotently, and peered, trying to make out his number, but registering only an A. She reduced her speed even further. The sudsy water in her windscreen washer, caught in a slipstream, slid in foamy tendrils across the sheet of glass, compounding the mess. The wipers faltered, made an agonised screech and stopped.

'Oh, no, I don't believe this!' Thomasine, with all vision totally obliterated, slowly stopped the car, not wanting to aquaplane on the wet surface. She flicked on her hazard lights, tied a scarf over her head, grabbed the cloth she kept in the glove compartment and, cursing under her breath, did what all women travelling alone are told not to do – she opened the car door and got out. The rain-drenched wind whipped around her, hugging her tight, tugging at her dress. About fifty feet further along the road, she saw what she thought was the culprit car. It was moving, even though its huge rear brake lights were glowing red.

Within seconds she was soaked to the skin, her hair, despite the scarf, hanging lank and damp against her face. She wiped at her windscreen with her cloth – it only made matters worse. The wind lashed at the trees on the roadside, shadows darting amongst them as the branches arched and bowed in a wild dance. Any number of maniacs could be hiding in there, she thought, and the risk she was taking raced head on to meet her. She quickly climbed back into her car, hoped the rain would ease and prayed that she wouldn't be shunted in the rear, but even that seemed preferable to the alternative of standing amongst those trees. Nervously, she double-checked the car locks. She was cold, scared and wished she was home.

The rain gradually began to clear the windscreen. She switched on the engine; the wipers, now there was no mud, worked again. With the headlights on, she eased into gear and set off at a slow pace.

She was still in third gear when she slammed on the

5

brakes, feeling the back of the car dance skittishly. In her headlights she saw the bedraggled figure of a small animal. 'Drive round it!' common sense whispered. 'What if it's hurt?' compassion replied.

'Call me St Francis,' she said aloud, and with a hefty sigh she climbed out of the car again. Cautiously she approached the creature, which was lying in the road, shivering from head to toe; two large dark soulful eyes stared at her and then looked submissively away. It was a dog.

Thomasine knew little about dogs, except that it would be foolish to touch a strange one, especially if it was hurt. She stood looking down at it wondering what to do next. If she left it in the road the next car to come along might not see it in time. She was aware that the creature was watching her with its expressive eyes, as if reading her mind. She shook herself at that, ridding herself of such stupid fancies – she was going to have to make a move or get run over herself.

She bent down, but it cowered away from her. If it was that scared, maybe it had no intention of biting her. On the other hand, perhaps a frightened animal was even more likely to attack. 'Here, have a good sniff.' She thrust her hand out, but the abrupt action made the animal lift its head, avoiding any contact with her. She waited patiently. The dog sniffed the air a good foot from her hand, paused as if registering what it smelt, and then wriggled slowly towards her on its front. Thomasine was unsure if she should talk to it or not, and decided to compromise by making a cooing, soothing noise, much as she had used to her daughter, Nadine, when she had been a baby.

The dog appeared to interpret these noises as encouraging, for it risked sniffing her hand intently. Thomasine gently patted its head. Round the massive neck of the dog was a black leather collar with large, wicked-looking metal studs on it. Feeling more confident, she looked for an identity tag, but there was none.

She looked at the dog; it studied her, head on one side. The beautiful eyes held hers for a moment but then were cast demurely down again, like a shy maiden. The animal was waiting, she was sure, for her to decide what to do. She returned to the car and opened the passenger door. 'Here, boy, girl, whatever you are.' She patted her leg encouragingly. The dog scrabbled desperately at the tarmac, its long black claws scraping on the surface, afraid it was about to be left. It heaved itself up using powerful shoulder muscles, but its back legs could not support it. The dog flopped back into the road. 'Hang on Buster. First things first, let's put this newspaper on the seat, you're a mite wet for the good of my upholstery.' She felt a bit self-conscious talking to a dumb animal, but she seemed to have got its confidence, so maybe the sound of her voice would continue to reassure it. 'Come on then.' She bent down and, putting her hands either side of the dog's stomach, with difficulty lifted it up into the car. 'Wow! You weigh a ton. You ought to be on a diet.'

Evidently used to car rides, the animal settled on the seat. A tip of pink tongue emerged between smooth, black lips, and the noise it was making sounded friendly.

Thomasine put the interior light on. 'What are you?' She registered the heavy muscles, the deep folds of skin, a pushed-back nose, and a massive jaw. 'I hope you're not a pit bull, I don't fancy a ride with one of them.' The dog made a snuffling, snorting sound and looked expectantly forward, as if waiting for them to move. A car overtook them at speed, blaring its horn, angrily flashing its lights.

'Roadhog!' she yelled, putting the car into gear.

As she drove along Thomasine, aware of the heavy breathing beside her, found the dog's presence rather comforting – it was not large, but heavy and obviously powerful; anyone would think twice before trying anything funny with you, she thought. It was nice, for once, to feel safe alone in a car at night.

7

Thomasine was on the Morristown by-pass. Despite the weather, she put her foot down, for joy riders from the Forest Glade Estate in the town were known to frequent this stretch of road. There was a large police station in Morristown and she supposed she should have taken the creature there, but she found the town frightening with its bleak tower blocks, badly-lit walkways and cavernous multi-storey car parks. There was too much violence in Morristown for anyone, especially a woman, to enter it at night with any degree of equilibrium. So she pressed on to the A road which would lead her to the pretty market town of Shillingham; it had a much smaller police station, but an atmosphere of security and well-being.

She parked outside the police station and, with difficulty, carried the heavy dog inside.

'What have we here then?' a constable asked her, opening a hatch in the wall and leaning over to peer out at them both.

Thomasine lowered the dog onto the floor where it stood, looking pathetic, on three legs. 'I found this dog on the dual carriageway ten miles the other side of Morristown. I think it might be a very large pug, they've got squashed in faces like this, haven't they?'

'That's a bulldog,' the constable said, peering down at the dog.

'Are you sure, aren't they usually bigger than this? There's one at The White Hart, that's huge – Butch, they call it.'

'This one's a female,' the constable said sagely, and pointed to the chart of dog breeds hanging on the wall. 'That's why it's that much smaller. I've never known a bulldog to be dumped before, they're too valuable.'

'Dumped? You mean, people abandon their dogs on motorways? But they could be killed.'

'Oh, that's the general idea, Miss.' He smiled knowingly. 'Poor things hardly stand a chance, do they, with all them articulated lorries?'

'But why?'

'Saves on the vet's bill – that way there's no need to pay to have it put down. Splat!' And he slapped one balled fist into the flat of his hand.

'That's awful! I'm not that mad about dogs, but how could anyone . . . ?'

'Takes all types,' the constable said, with all the sagacity of his profession, sucking through his teeth at the same time. 'I've dealt with all sorts,' he continued, as if glad of an audience. 'When the dangerous dog legislation came in we had a lot of pit bulls and Rottweilers. But I've dealt with a wolfhound, a St Bernard – could cause a nasty accident, a dog that size.'

'But why, if someone has gone to all the trouble to buy an expensive dog, should they do that?' she questioned, puzzled.

'Dad loses his job or docs a runner, dogs have to be fed. Or it's grown too big, or they're bored with it. It's easy, kick it out on the road, make a quick getaway and let a nice lorry do the dirty work for you.'

'I feel sick.' And she did, and had to sit down on the bench against the pale green wall.

'Great nation of animal lovers, aren't we?' he said sardonically, as he pulled his pad towards him. 'Best take your details.'

The paperwork finished, the constable came round to her side of the counter, a lead in his hand. The dog moved towards Thomasine and hid behind her.

'There, my lovely.' The constable put his hand out to grab at the collar, but the bulldog moved away as quickly as she was able to on three legs.

'Then you don't think this is a lost dog? His owner isn't going to come through that door saying "Fido, darling!"?'

'Unlikely. Possible, but unlikely. Did you have trouble with it? I mean, did it get nasty?'

'No, nothing like that. Here, give me the lead.' The dog allowed her to clip it on. She felt touched by its faith in her, but also guilty that she had tricked and betrayed it.

'Thanks,' said the constable, and began to drag the dog away.

'Its leg. It's hurt its leg,' she said, but he did not appear to hear. The dog pulled hard, looked back at her with those large brown eyes. Thomasine turned her back and hurried from the police station, away from their stare.

In the car, the newspaper the dog had sat on was crumpled and wet. She screwed it up and threw it on the floor. The car smelt of damp hair too. 'Horrible,' she muttered, switched on the ignition and swung out of the car park.

As she drove she kept thinking about the dog. She tried to put other thoughts in its way, to blank out the recurring memory, but the dog always won. Or, rather, the dog's eyes won. All too easily, as she remembered them pleading with her, begging her for help as it was dragged across the police station floor.

'For God's sake, woman, stop it,' she said aloud as she waited for a set of traffic lights to turn green. A lone male figure was walking towards her and she pushed down the central locking switch, felt the familiar tensing of her body at a possible danger, drumming her fingers on the steering wheel, urging the lights to change. She'd felt safe with the dog in the car, if it were here she wouldn't be reacting like this.

The green light shone. Still, she thought as she gathered speed, there was more to owning a dog than feelings of security. They were a pain, she'd heard friends who owned them moan often enough – even when they loved them. They messed up the house, chewed things, piddled, caught fleas, ruined the garden, you couldn't leave them, they smelt. No, she'd been wise never to have pets – one was freer without.

She was five miles the other side of Shillingham, two miles from her new house in the village of Middle

Shilling, when she abruptly stopped the car, reversed into a field gateway, and shot off again at speed.

'What will happen to her?' she asked as she burst into the police station, bringing the wind and rain with her.

The constable looked up. 'We'll keep her in the kennels here for seven days and then, if no one has claimed her –' He made a slicing action across his throat. She clutched at her own with her hand. 'No, that's what we used to do.' He laughed; she didn't join in. 'She might be lucky,' he said more soberly, aware she did not appreciate his attempts at humour. 'One of the lads might take a shine to her. And we get lots of people looking for their own dogs; someone might want her. Failing that, we give them to a refuge and they'll try to re-house her. If they're full, mind you . . .' He did not finish.

'Can I take her?' she said, interrupting him almost breathlessly, as if afraid of what she was saying, as if part of her did not want her to do so, and she might change her mind. 'I could look after her until someone wanted her. Just temporarily, you understand. Is that possible?'

'You'd be doing me a real favour, Mrs Lambert. The kennels are full to bursting, I blame those travelling people, you never see any of their dogs on leads. Should anyone want a bulldog, should I send them over to you?'

'Yes, fine.' She waited while he went to collect the dog. Alone, she doubted the wisdom of what she was doing. Should she just slip away? Her hand was on the door when the constable returned, dragging the dog along on its rear.

'Careful, it's hurt,' she said, feeling a surge of anger towards the policeman. She picked the dog up, and it licked her face. 'No!' she said, turning her cheek away. 'Just temporarily,' she said to the policeman as he held the door open for her.

Jim Varley was bone-numbingly exhausted. He felt like a deep-sea diver with his boots on as he walked across the cobbled yard at the back of the practice in Middle Shilling. He was cold as well; it was unusually cold for March which, according to the locals, meant a bad summer ahead. He swore to himself when, at the back door of his house, he had to go through the layers of his clothes searching in his various pockets for the keys. He could still remember a time, not so long ago either, when he had never bothered to lock a thing, certainly not his back door. But now it was like getting into Fort Knox – twice fools had raided the surgery for drugs, what were things coming to when they stole veterinary medicines? Last time it had happened he could only pray that they knew what they were doing, since they had stolen sufficient pentobarbitone to put an army to sleep, for good!

In the back porch he hung up his soaking Barbour to finish its dripping on the quarry-tiled floor, slung his cap on a peg and eased off his muddy boots. In thick-green-stockinged feet he padded into the warmth of the kitchen. His old mongrel, Castille, lifted her head from her basket and her tail beat a tattoo on the side. He bent and patted her head, telling her what a fine girl she was. She looked up at him with her rheumy eyes – time was running out for the old girl, he knew that, who better? Not yet, though, not yet. It was something he did not like thinking about, and very quickly put out of his mind. He turned his attention to the pine table. There was a note, there always was, propped against a pretty arrangement of dried flowers – Beth's hobby. From the beams hung huge bunches of flowers and grasses, which she had picked and dried herself. *Supper's in the slow oven. Pudding's in the fridge. EAT! Beth.* He smiled; poor patient Beth, how many suppers had she prepared and left in the Aga, only to find them still there in the morning? He'd do better tonight.

From the rail in front of the cooker he took the duck-shaped oven glove and retrieved his food, but seeing how dried up the chops were, he decided to eat only the pudding. He sat at the pine table and began to eat. Beth had left him a wine glass along with an unfinished bottle of red wine. He pushed it aside and instead collected a bottle of Glenfiddich from the work top, poured himself a lethal measure, and drank deeply before returning to his pie.

'You've got to eat, Jim,' a voice said from the doorway.

'I am eating,' he said, hurriedly spooning up a mouthful of pie.

Beth, a flower-sprigged dressing gown wrapped round her full breasts, her long, naturally curly, brunette hair swinging loose on her shoulders, joined him at the table.

'Whisky?' he asked, indicating the bottle.

'I am honoured,' she laughed, since he guarded his malt jealously. 'But no thanks. I'd prefer a small glass of wine.'

'You're pushing the boat out tonight,' he teased her, for Beth rarely drank. She said nothing, merely smiled her thanks.

Seeing the chops, she grimaced. 'No wonder you're not eating, they look grim. Let me make you an omelette? Bacon and eggs?'

'I'm fine with this. I think I'm past a proper meal.'

'You look tired, Jim. Was it a difficult foaling?'

He brushed his hands in front of his eyes as if pushing the fatigue away. 'You could say that. A breech. The trouble with Ben Luckett is he thinks he knows all there is to know about nags. He should have brought me in hours before he did. He may know how to ride the bloody things, but that's about all.'

'Maybe he didn't want to disturb you on a night like this,' she said reasonably.

He hated it when she was so tolerant, especially when she was right, for that was exactly what Ben had said to him tonight. He poured himself another measure and

13

she frowned imperceptibly, but refrained from comment.

'What was it? The foal.'

'Oh, a filly. Pretty little thing. Were there any calls?'

'Nothing that appeared urgent. I've put them on your desk. Let them wait until morning.'

'I'd better look now – just in case.' He stood up. 'Thanks for supper,' he said like a polite little boy.

'You're going to have to get a partner, you know. Your workload's impossible. It would kill even a younger man.'

'Thanks, dear Beth, I'm not *that* old.' He laughed good-naturedly. 'Good-night, sleep tight,' he said at the door and, carrying his glass and bottle of whisky, left the room. Beth stayed where she was, staring at the door. Then she sighed deeply, gathered up his dirty plate and loaded it into the dishwasher.

Jim sat in his study, though study was really too grand a word for the chaotic room where he did his accounts, kept up with the latest in the professional journals, and did a lot of thinking. He never let anyone in here to clean. He liked the muddle, knew where everything was and could lay his hands on it in a second; if anyone tidied it then the filing system of a lifetime would be lost. Give Beth her due, she was the only woman he had ever met who accepted the room as it was. Even Ann, his wife, had not understood, and had often suggested decorating the room and getting new office furniture in. It had been his father's study when he had been the vet here, and when the old man had retired, he had taken over the practice and the room.

He sat in his battered Captain's chair and lit a cigarette – he was down to five a day and proud of it. He riffled through the telephone messages Beth had stacked neatly on the desk; she was right, nothing that couldn't wait until after surgery in the morning.

Beth had been a godsend. For two years after Ann's

death he'd muddled through, and then a year ago, his friend Fee Walters had taken things into her own hands.

'You look a bloody mess, my dear Jim, like a vagrant. I know just the person to help you out.' She had told him about Beth Morton and he had grudgingly agreed to meet her. What Fee had failed to tell him was that Beth came with Harry – five years old and with a permanently running nose. As soon as he knew this he had every intention of turning her down. But there was such a look of desperation in her eyes, like a cornered doe, that he had found himself saying 'yes' instead. He'd never regretted it, though he could have wished for fewer of her dratted dead-flower arrangements. Still, he'd never said, she seemed to get so much pleasure from them. He had even got to quite like Harry. Once the child was plugged into his Sega games he was no trouble to anyone, though Jim did have twinges of guilt that something else should be being done with him.

Beth had made life almost bearable again. She seemed to understand his pain, but without the need to say anything about it, nor to pry. He topped up his whisky. She was right of course, he did need help. The last three years had been hell. He was permanently tired, since there was no one to share the night calls with. And he was stressed too, he knew that – he might have cut down on the smoking, but he knew he drank too much, all to relieve the bloody stress. Times had changed, people had greater expectations for their pets these days than his father had ever known. New techniques, new medicines, made it possible for animals to live longer when, even ten years ago, they'd have been put to sleep. But such advances made for extra work, extra outlay on equipment, extra time to learn about developments, and all of this combined led to the extra stress which in turn led him to the whisky bottle.

He couldn't remember when he'd last had a holiday. With locums charging up to a hundred and fifty pounds a day – if you could find one – a holiday was out of the question. He couldn't just shut up shop, not when he was the only vet in the area. What would happen to the animals then? No wonder vets had the highest suicide rate of all the professions.

He was aware of all this, but he also knew why he hadn't looked for an assistant or partner. It was irrational, he could never explain it to anyone, the persistent feeling that if he got a new partner he would be betraying Ann's memory. They had met at college and worked side by side since they qualified, he treating the large animals, she taking care of the small-animal side of the practice. He was pretty sure that behind his back people were saying it was time he got over his wife's death, but he knew he had a long way to go yet. Too often, as now, the memory surfaced of that last morning as he'd watched her lithely swing herself into the saddle of her hunter and wave him goodbye. He didn't hunt, didn't like it. He'd never seen the point in spending his life patching animals up to go out on a Saturday and try to kill them. So he wasn't with her when the large horse had tripped as it jumped a fence, failing to see a wire. Ann had fallen and then the horse had crashed down upon her. She was dead by the time she reached the local hospital, and he'd not been able even to say goodbye. He'd sold the horse immediately, he'd had to, for part of him wanted to kill it there and then. But reason had prevailed and he'd known it was the last thing Ann would have wanted him to do.

He often wondered whether, if he'd been with her, he'd feel differently, if things might be easier. But now he'd never know.

It was past midnight before Thomasine carried the dog into her kitchen and put it down on the floor. It looked up at her expectantly, head on one side again, as it had in the road. She checked its leg. There was a nasty cut, and the underside of its large white chin was badly grazed.

She filled a bowl with warm water, bathed the wounds and patted them dry with kitchen towels.

'You want something to eat? I haven't got any dog food, you realise that? You'll have to make do with last night's lasagne. Do dogs eat lasagne?' She put some in a soup bowl, and poured water into another. Dogs did eat lasagne, and with gusto. 'I should have asked you if you wanted more parmesan.' She laughed and poured herself a glass of wine, which she sipped as she watched the dog, still on three legs, eating with noisy enjoyment.

On the roadway she had thought the animal was black, but that had been the rain darkening her coat. She was drier now, and Thomasine could see she was fawn with a slightly darker saddle. Her ears were black, and when Thomasine had touched them in the car, she had found them softer than the softest velvet. Her nose was like a small black button beneath eyes of darkest brown. Thomasine was aware it was those beautiful eyes which had made her stop thinking straight.

'I don't want you, you know. I should have thought about this, not jumped in blind. What if no one claims you? You can't stay, you do realise?'

The dog put down her injured back leg as if testing it, and finding it felt better, then put her rear in the air, her forelegs parallel to the floor, and rested her head on her paws. Then she stretched her whole body and farted mightily.

'Well, that's a case in point. Phew!' she exclaimed, amused.

In answer the dog rolled on its back, kicked four legs in the air and spun round and round like a top, another trick that made her laugh. Was she doing it on purpose, she wondered? To amuse her? To get attention? When the dog finally finished this game she stood up and pointedly turned her back on the blanket which Thomasine had found for her in the laundry room and had placed in front of the wood burner.

'Well it's that or nothing. You'll just have to sleep on

the floor then. I'll sort a box or something out in the morning. Now, I'm going up to bed. You're perfectly safe here, no one will hurt you.'

She bent down and began to undo the large, ugly collar. 'I don't think we need this, do you? Horrible aggressive thing.' She opened the cupboard housing the Hoover and threw the collar into the back. 'There, it's hidden well away.' This was madness, talking to a dog, she told herself, as she crossed the kitchen. Before she turned off the light, she blew the dog a kiss. 'Good-night,' she said, for all that.

As she undressed, she thought how much she had dreaded returning here today – divorced, official, rub-ber-stamped, new status. She had lived alone in the London house for over a year, so she should be used to it by now, but everything there had been familiar and comforting, now all was new – house, neighbours, even the shops. She had moved last week in time for the divorce; she had probably clung on to her old home too long and should have come here sooner.

She climbed into her brass bed, lay back on the lavender-scented pillows and began to think those thoughts which she knew were futile, and yet which, most nights, she thought anyway. Thoughts of when she and Robert had been happy together, when he was content with her and their marriage. For the umpteenth time she wondered why she had lost him, worried about how she might have played things differently.

The memory of the evening he'd told her he had met Chantal and wanted a divorce was bitterly clear, even now. She'd gone to pieces. She shuddered at the dreadful scene she'd made, crying out in disbelief. Then ranting at his duplicity. Then begging him to return to her, getting onto her knees, clinging at his trouser legs, pulling at him. Coldly he'd prised her hands away, retreating from her in horror and contempt. He had left that same night.

Thomasine had cried for three days non-stop, but then had begun to plan and scheme. With a superhuman

18

effort she'd pulled herself together and forced herself to play it cool. She had turned herself into such a calm, patient and understanding wife that she'd marvelled at the performance she'd put on. Rational meetings took place, plans were calmly made, though all the time she was shrieking with pain inside.

As a strategy it had failed. The idea had been that he was to see her as such a wonderful wife that he would not be able to let her go, that he'd ditch Chantal and return to her. What an idiot she had been!

'But you must have known something was afoot?' her mother had said at dinner this evening.

'No, honestly. It was a bolt from the blue.'

'Then you must be either blind or stupid,' her mother had said with her characteristic lack of tact.

'Both, probably,' she'd replied, demoralised to the point of resignation.

She half sat up, aware of a snuffling noise from the kitchen below. At least finding the dog had kept her mind occupied for the last couple of hours. She wondered what it was called. She smiled into the darkness. This was something new, she'd begun to think of something other than Robert and all the sad and wasted past.

Half an hour later she could stand the barking and scratching from the kitchen no more. In her pyjamas she ran down the spiral stairs from her mezzanine bedroom. 'What on earth's all this racket?' she asked angrily, an anger which disappeared immediately when the dog's rump waggled back and forth in welcome. 'Come on, then. Just for tonight,' she said, not realising that those were the most fatal words a dog owner could say.

The dog settled happily on the floor beside her bed. What did it matter that it was in her room? She could get a basket for here too. 'A two-basket dog, there's luxury for you,' she said, forgetting she'd earlier promised it a box. But the dog was asleep, judging by the wiffling noise emerging from the small, black, button-like nose.

*

In his weekend hideaway two miles outside Middle Shilling, Oliver Hawksmoor tossed and turned. He had a bad cold, which he'd convinced himself was 'flu and which he'd been nursing carefully for several days. He felt as miserable as sin, and wondered if it was being ill or the new situation in his life which was making him so. Christ, this bed was bloody uncomfortable! He moved his rear only to discover the problem, a swathe of crumbs from the toast he had made himself this evening. He clambered out of the bed and stripped off the offending under-sheet. He bundled it into the dirty washing basket and opened the linen-cupboard door.

'This I do not believe! The bitch! How could she!' In front of him was a cupboard, empty, except for one bath towel, two hand towels and a pile of embroidered tray cloths. 'Oh sod it.' He slammed the door shut angrily. In the bedroom he dressed in jeans, a black silk polo neck and a pale blue cashmere jumper slipped over the top. He splashed some cologne on his face to wake himself up, stuck his tongue out at himself in the mirror and, not liking what he saw, popped it back into his mouth. Downstairs he scribbled a note, which he left propped up against the kettle, apologising to Grace White, his cleaning lady from the village, for the mess.

He drove at a sedate speed for him, only a maniac would drive fast in these stormy conditions. He shoved a CD into the player and Sutherland's voice filled the black leather cocoon of his BMW. Sophia should not have taken all the linen; the cottage and its contents were not part of their agreement. Everything in Bishop's End was as it had been the day he had inherited it from his great-aunt Phoebe. Dear old Phoebe, he wished she were alive now. He wondered what she would make of the state of his life. She had not liked Sophia – 'Why can't she call herself Sophie? That "a" makes her sound suspiciously foreign to me. Was she baptised thus, that's what I'd like to know.'

'English born and bred, Aunt Phoebe.'

'Trade, are they?' Phoebe had asked with a sharp incline of her aquiline nose, which always reminded him of a face he had once seen on a Plantagenet tomb in France.

'What on earth makes you say that, Aunt?'

'She studies the furniture a little too closely for my liking, as if she's a shopkeeper stock-taking. A well-brought-up girl would never do that. I think you might be making an unfortunate mistake, Oliver, my dear.' Phoebe had said it totally without malice, merely stating the facts as she saw them.

Aunt Phoebe, if not pleased to know how upset he was, would have been pleased to know she was right about the furniture. Sophia had insisted on Sotheby's being brought in for a valuation of the contents of his London home. Not nice, not nice at all. They had agreed on who was having what, but after the linen incident, could he be sure she had kept to it? It had seemed a simple enough division; she had agreed that if she could have the farmhouse in France and a property in London, then he could keep the Holland Park house and Bishop's End. This cold could prove more expensive than he had realised. She had planned to move her stuff out of their London base yesterday. Perhaps he should have been there keeping a beady eye on things, instead of feeling sorry for himself in his bed at Middle Shilling.

He drew up outside his smart house – another reason to thank Aunt Phoebe, whose legacy to him had bought it. Phoebe had had the ability to churn out romantic fiction by the yard, for which she was paid handsomely. She had amassed a large fortune, judiciously invested, all of which she had left to Oliver, her favourite great-nephew. Such good luck had not endeared him to the rest of the family, but it was something he had learnt to live with – not, after all, too hard a task.

It was three in the morning when he let himself into the house. The first thing he noticed was that the console table and mirror had gone. He entered the drawing room to find it bereft of virtually everything. She had left him a sofa, a coffee table, a side table and one armchair. The pictures that remained, he was gratified to see, were his most valuable; no doubt her nerve had failed her at taking those. Still, he knew he would mourn the loss of the less valuable just as much. He sat down on the armchair, looked about the denuded room with a doomy expression, and lit a cigarette.

What the hell had got into the woman? How could one be so wrong about someone? He had loved Sophia the moment he had set eyes on her at the varnishing dinner at the Royal Academy. Oliver collected paintings and she had been a student of art at the Courtauld – they had so much in common. She was pretty and delightful in the way of a young woman who had never wanted for anything in her life and to whom it had never been anything but sweet. When he learnt that her father had recently bought an estate near Middle Shilling, Oliver reasoned that fate had intended them to meet one way or the other, and he'd rushed out and bought the LP of Kismet. Her father was enormously wealthy from his property development company, which he'd man-oeuvred skilfully through the various recessions and collapses of the past thirty years – not that Oliver had ever let on to Aunt Phoebe where the money came from. Sophia's divorced mother, Constance, was the daughter of an earl whom Ben Luckett had snapped up to give him a bit of social cachet. She now lived in the South of France off her alimony and had been perfectly adorable to Oliver. Mind you, come to think of it she had warned him not to marry her daughter which, at the time, he thought was a bit odd coming from a mother. Sophia loathed her mother only slightly less than she loathed her stepmother, Cora, whom she regarded as a vulgar gold digger. He liked Cora, which had annoyed Sophia no end.

He supposed he should go right through the house, check the lot, see his lawyers. Would he? He doubted it,

22

come the morning he probably wouldn't bother. It was the hassle he hated, the letters that would fly back and forth. It was only money, after all. He might have no wife and no children, but he'd plenty of *that* to see him through, since Phoebe's books still sold in their thousands. Amazing how money helped one recover from most things.

He put out his cigarette and wearily climbed the stairs to bed. Wonder upon wonders, he thought, as he entered the bedroom, she had left it very much as it had always been – her dressing table had gone, but then if it hadn't he would probably have thrown it into a skip. He sat on the edge of his bed and began to remove his shoes.

What had gone wrong? Was it having no children? Was it that simple? But then it wasn't his fault they hadn't had any, the quacks had given him a clean bill of health on that little number. And he'd spent enough money trying to sort out why she could not reproduce, she'd been everywhere for treatment. He had felt genuinely sorry for her over that, she'd certainly seemed to long for children, though how they were going to fit into her busy social calendar would have remained to be seen. He would have liked a son, carry on the name and all that drivel, but when nothing happened he had merely regarded it as his bad luck, something that was not to be.

Basically he had wondered if she was just bored with him. He had suggested this to her, but she had screamed at him for making her sound shallow. He could not have blamed her; he supposed he was boring. He had his work – in which he was not a high flyer, since he lacked the necessary ambition. But Oliver nursed a strong work ethic, and so he worked in a firm of brokers in the City and made a reasonable living from that also. Since he did not feel passionately about the career he had chosen he rarely mentioned it to Sophia. In fact, come to think of it, he couldn't now remember what they spent their time talking about – certainly not his fishing. Even their shared interest in art had waned, now that Sophia was enraptured with the avant-garde, which Oliver cared nothing for. Nor did she share his love for Bandage, his bull terrier.

'Bandage,' he called. He stood up and crossed the room to his dressing room where Bandage's basket normally stood. It was not there. He checked his bathroom. Bandage had an endearing habit of standing in the corner of a room if he was depressed, worried about something, or sulking. All emotions Oliver knew for sure his dog felt. Bandage could often be found, his back to the room, his chin supported on the wall, and there he would be sometimes for five minutes, once for over an hour. But this time there was no sign of him. He ran down the stairs two at a time and into the kitchen, where Bandage often lurked and where he had a second basket. The basket was there, his toys piled neatly in it, but there was no dog. 'Bandage,' he shouted. He bounded back up the stairs calling his name as he went.

'Wimpole, where's Bandage?' he asked the sweet-faced, grey-haired woman who had appeared on the landing, still putting on a shabby, blue wool dressing gown. Wimpole was his nanny, who had lived with him since the first day of his life and would remain with him until the last day of hers.

'What the fuck's all that row?' she demanded angrily.

'Wimpole! Language!'

'Well, you gave me a fright. What's the matter?'

'It's Bandage, where is he?'

'Your dear wife took him,' she said sarcastically. 'Said she was taking him to her father's. She wouldn't listen to Wimpole.'

Oliver slumped against the wall of the staircase, half-registering that the Hockney had gone too; so much for his theory of her being afraid to remove the best. 'She took that painting of the swimming pool you liked so much, as well as some from the drawing-room. Rapacious moo, isn't she?'

'She can have the bloody paintings, I don't care about them; she can't have Bandage.'

'That's what I said. She said she had bought him so he was hers.'

Oliver sighed. 'That's true, she paid for him, but he was a present to me.'

'Some present. You can't go around giving presents and then taking them back when it suits you, can you? No class, that family, I always said, so did your Aunt Phoebe. Good job the old trout isn't here to see all this. Fancy a drink?'

'No thanks, Wimpole, but you go ahead. I've got to think.'

'You should never have gone to Bishop's End. You should have been here – then it would never have happened. Or taken the hound with you.'

'I usually do take Bandage. But, I remember now, she said her father wanted to show him to a friend and she'd take him to the Lucketts'. But he should have been back by now.'

'So what are you going to do?' They were back in the drawing room and Wimpole was busily pouring herself a very large Scotch on the rocks.

'If she's planning to keep Bandage she can forget it!' he said, with conviction.

But later, alone in his bed, Oliver did something he had not done in years; he covered his head with his pillow to keep the bogey man at bay. He could take anything but the loss of his dog.

At Oakleigh Kennels, far enough outside the village of Middle Shilling so that the barking of the dogs would not be a problem to anyone, Eveleigh Brenton was finally going to bed.

What a day it had been! She doubted if she would sleep, the excitement was almost too much for her. Crufts. She had returned that evening without winning a prize, she hadn't expected to this year. It did not matter. Just being there had been enough. Meeting the other owners and breeders, talking to the judges, being surrounded by people who knew what it was like to have dogs who were the most important creatures in your life. It was a joy not having to explain this love she felt. And she'd spied a fine St Bernard dog; already she was imagining the puppies that he and her Brünnhilde might produce. The dogs were excited too, and had taken a long time to settle in their kennels.

No doubt about it, she said to herself as she turned to switch off the light. There was nothing in the world like Crufts.

The lights were on in every room of the smart Georgian terraced house in Shillingham, and outside the carriage lamp shone above the bay tree in its white wooden tub. Viewed through the windows, its predominantly peach decoration made it warm and welcoming. The house was artfully perfect. The hall had a black and white marble tiled floor – shush, tell no one, Gill tended to say with a laugh, but it's Amtico's best. The carpet in the sitting room was palest cream, the sofas and chairs were covered in a rust-and-green-striped silk fabric – or rather it looked like silk but was, in fact, sixty per cent polyester, just another of those little secrets. The secretaire was Chippendale. The Canterbury music stand, filled with the latest glossy magazines rather than sheet music, was Georgian, as was the slender nest of occasional tables. Chippendale, Georgian and Hepplewhite, all the best reproduction furniture that Brights of Nettlebed sold.

The two bedrooms were white with the merest hint of peach. The bathroom suite, Edwardian with reproduction brass taps, and the Provençal pine kitchen, were wonders thanks to MFI.

It was a veritable palace and Justin and his friend Gill – pronounced with a hard 'g' as in fish, as he was fond of saying – had scrimped, saved and worked their little arses off for seven years to achieve the effect.

There was only one jarring note in the whole house, and that was in the sitting room. Tucked in one corner was a shabby, fawn, dralon-covered chair. Slung over it was a kelim which had also seen better days, but its orange, scarlet and brown design toned in reasonably enough.

This chair belonged to the third member of the household – Sadie. Sadie was her pet name but officially she was known as Saradema, Princess Light of Snippers, offspring of Champion Felix, Prince of Darkness of Barton. She was a white miniature poodle, with coal-black eyes set in a pretty and intelligent face. She was important and knew it, for she always sat in her chair with her snout in the air and the regal expression of one who expected to be waited upon.

Sadie was the love and joy of Justin and Gill's life. They doted upon her in the way that only the almost middle-aged and childless can. Both of them were certain it would be impossible to love a human child more than they loved their canine one. It was a theory never to be tested. Since they made no secret that they did not believe in God and regarded children as noisy and messy but, if mankind was to continue, necessary evils, they found it odd they'd both been invited, countless times, to be godfathers. Sadly, they reached the conclusion that their heterosexual friends were moved by matters fiscal; since they would never have children of their own, a godchild might cop the lot when they went to the great hairdressing salon in the sky. So they always refused.

They knew they were cynical. Life had made them so. It was harder being gay in the small market town of

Shillingham than in cosmopolitan London. So they had grown carapaces against the whispers, the funny looks.

On the rare occasions clients asked them to parties, it was, they sensed, more for their entertainment value than for friendship. They camped it up, especially Gill, a bit like singing for their supper, for they knew that was what was expected of them – sad no one wanted to know them as they really were, but they could handle this.

But in the last six months something new had come to haunt them – a group of louts who congregated by the fountain in the market square. It was not what they said: as Gill recited often enough, 'Sticks and stones . . .' No, they were genuinely afraid of them, and with reason. Their salon was just off the square in a chic little cul-de-sac of shops, but the only way home was across or round the square. On Saturday evenings when the yobs were to be found lolling around the Cromwell fountain they had to run the gauntlet of the oafs, who screamed abuse, spat at them and accused them of being HIV positive. As if this were not enough, what upset both Justin and Gill further was the way the noble, honest and true citizens of Shillingham looked embarrassed, lowered their heads, and en masse appeared to be deaf.

Of the two Justin was the more sensitive, and thus the more upset. It was understandable, for as a child he had been cosseted in Upper Shillingham vicarage where his father was the incumbent, followed by the sheltered life of a chorister in Norwich. A choral scholarship had taken him to Kings College, Cambridge, like-minded friends, a lot of fun and a poor third class degree. He had spent a miserable year working as a trainee manager for a large company making chocolate until he had met Gill in a bar in London and had become a hairdresser instead and now only sang in his bath.

Gill's route to Shillingham had been rougher and harder. Born to a hard-drinking, wife-beating bricklayer and a valium-distanced mother, he had survived, just, on a council estate in Morristown. The place reeked of despair and neglect. The walkways were filthy, the graffiti beyond a joke. The lifts rarely worked and had become latrines instead. Burglaries were commonplace, though there was little to steal. Muggings were too frequent to be anything but the norm, and rape went unreported. It was called, ironically, the Forest Glade estate, but not one council-planted tree had survived the attentions of the bored unemployed youths who swept through the place like locusts.

Gill realised early in his life that he was different from his neighbours. He was brighter, cared about his appearance, and liked nice things. As a result he was bullied at school and beaten up out of school on a regular basis. He lived in a society which ruthlessly rejected the unfamiliar. He knew that the hatred was based primarily on jealousy, but knowing that was not much comfort when the boot was going in.

From his bedroom in the high-rise flat, he could look out and see in the distance green fields, and far beyond that was London, to which he longed to escape. In view of his father's attitude, he could forget any dreams of university and a degree. So Gill found a job as an apprentice hairdresser in the shopping precinct. He washed hair, swept up, stood and watched, all for a pittance which he squirreled away for three years until he could get to London and the life he knew was waiting for him.

Meeting Justin was the best thing that had ever happened to him. He had been in London for six years and done well, was already a stylist at Frederico's of Mayfair, building his own list of clients. He had had lovers galore and, at twenty-six, had reached that point in life when he longed to settle, to find someone with whom he could have a steady relationship. He found him in a smoky bar, and he got to him before anyone else could. It was love at first sight and they'd been together ever since – ten years in all.

It was Justin's father dying and leaving him a legacy that had enabled them to look around and find a permanent base. Seven years ago they had come to Shillingham. Neither could explain satisfactorily why they should choose a town close to where both had spent their childhoods, for neither would have thought their roots mattered to them. 'There's nowt so queer as folk . . .' Gill often said in his good imitation of a north country accent, which always made Justin laugh. Shillingham was pretty, relatively crime-free, but most importantly they were able to afford the Georgian house of their dreams and still have enough to buy the lease on a shop and open their salon, which they had called Snippers.

If the house was all peach and charm, then Snippers was slick and efficient. Black, white and chrome. It was state of the art and they loved it as they loved their house, as they were later to love Sadie. There was constant music, Vivaldi, golden oldies, that sort of thing – they would have preferred Mozart and Manilow, but they had to think of their mostly middle-aged customers. They both wore black, and Gill had taught Justin everything he knew.

Sadie had entered their lives three years ago, when they had decided how nice it would be to have a pet. Books on breeds were bought, dog magazines studied, but since they were both hairdressers a poodle was a foregone conclusion. Choosing Sadie from a litter of six had been difficult – they would have liked them all – but there was something about Sadie that made her stand out, an air of aloofness, as if she knew she was different, and it struck a chord with them, a memory was rekindled, and Sadie it had to be.

Sadie was different from your run of the mill poodles;

she won prizes. For a bit of fun, they had entered her in the dog show at the local church fête one summer day. She won the prettiest dog category. Then just as they were leaving the woman judge had found them and told them they had a corker of a dog there, and they should show her. At that point they were not to know that everyone in the dog world listened to Eveleigh Brenton, champion breeder of St Bernards, show judge, and passionate advocate of dogs' rights.

Eveleigh had been right. Sadie did win. They had bought a glass-fronted cupboard to display the silver cups, glass bowls and rosettes which she had won while climbing the show ladder until she had won sufficient qualifications recognised by the Kennel Club to be eligible for showing at Crufts. That was a day of such excitement that neither of them would ever forget it; Sadie missed being Best Poodle Bitch by a whisker, though Gill to this day was convinced it was fixed. On Sundays they cleaned the trophies and Sadie had a major grooming. They took it in turns to trim her. She returned their devotion a thousandfold. On the days they did not take her to work with them she welcomed them back with a joy bordering on hysteria. Through her they experienced a love that demanded nothing; she accepted them as they were. No one had ever loved them like that except each other.

Tonight the men were in a state of dither. Sadie was whelping or, at least, she was due to whelp. But Sadie appeared to be taking no interest in the fact that it was long past three and she should have whelped yesterday.

'Do you think we should call the vet?' Justin asked anxiously, for at least the twentieth time. 'He said we could call him any time if there was an emergency.'

'I don't think being three hours late amounts quite to that, Justin.'

'Gill, you're always so calm and sane.'

'It's not that, remember what Jim Varley said, that sixty-three days is the average, that she could go to seventy-one. And she's shown no inclination to build a nest, and look how she turned her nose up at the one we made.'

'My God, I couldn't stand the strain of another eight days.'

'Open that Chardonnay in the fridge, it'll help us relax.'

As Justin rummaged in the kitchen, Sadie suddenly stood up, slid from her chair, walked behind the sofa, let out a soft whimper and collapsed into a heap on the carpet.

'Justin, come quick, I think she's started!' Gill shouted.

Justin appeared, bottle in hand, a tea-towel in the other. 'What should we do? Oh, where is she?' Gill pointed to behind the sofa. 'Oh, no, the carpet, the mess!' Justin waved the tea-towel impotently.

'Drat the carpet, we can get another. If that's where Sadie wants to have her babies then that's where she shall have them.'

The next few hours, instead of being a trial, were some of the most beautiful and exciting of their lives. At twenty-minute intervals, with the minimum of fuss, out popped another puppy. Sadie elegantly licked away the membrane that covered each of them, gave them a good rough washing, put them beside her teats and got on with having the next one. In the end they had five puppies, and both Justin and Gill were in tears at the sight of their Sadie, a new mother, knowing exactly what to do.

'Champagne, we should wet the puppies' heads,' suggested Justin, and when they had poured the wine into their flutes, they gave a saucer of it to Sadie, who much appreciated it after all her hard work.

*

In the countryside outside Shillingham the rain continued, and as the night progressed the wind rose and was soon battering senselessly at the corrugated iron roof of an outhouse on Tom White's smallholding, Primrose Acre. As the storm intensified, from within the shed an agitated rustling began. At first it was a few growls and then there was a bark and then another, and then one dog started to howl, followed by the rest.

The shed stank of faeces and urine and now, as the rain poured through in several places, to those smells was added the smell of wet pelt.

In the far corner of the shed lay an emaciated bitch. The elbow joints of her front legs were suppurating with sores from the endless rubbing on the concrete floor of her pen. There were no blankets, no straw, just a few urine-soaked rags which she had pushed into one corner, for she was a clean dog. It would be impossible to say what breed of dog she was, for she had lost much of her coat from a bad attack of mange; what little hair was left was crawling with fleas. Her teats sagged beneath her. She was a large dog, and her enclosure was too small for one of her size to lie down comfortably.

It was noisy in the shed, for the other dogs, some in boxes standing piled one on top of the other, were unable to sleep and moved restlessly. A large wave of muscle rippled down the bitch's side. She had a resigned expression as she lay on the floor, the pain ripping through her body. She struggled, panting, but there was no water to ease her thirst. It took longer for the first pup to appear than it had in the other eight whelpings she'd had in her five-and-a-half years. She was exhausted as she licked it, cleaning it. Her body shook as muscle after muscle contracted until one muscle in particular contorted deep within her and she sank back on the concrete as her heart fluttered and faded. With waning strength she scooped at the newborn puppy with her paw and guided him to her nipple and then sank back. Within her, six puppies kicked and fought in their effort to escape her dying body.

In the morning Tom White came and cursed the sight of the dead dog, and one dead puppy, as if it were her fault. He kicked the corpse of the Old English Sheepdog; they were a popular breed, he could not afford wastage like this, he thought, as he threw her corpse onto the rubbish tip.

2

When Oliver was a child, putting a pillow over his head to keep the bogey man at bay had always worked. It appeared that now, although he was an adult, and very tired at this late hour, it was not going to. He could not sleep, he felt insufferably hot, so he gave up the effort, sat up with the pillow propped behind him, lit a cigarette, and spent the small hours re-evaluating his life. He had heard of friends who did this at frequent intervals. Oliver had never felt the need; he had merely drifted amiably and contentedly through life. No doubt he would have continued to do so if Sophia had not put a stop to it. She had gone; she had taken most of his possessions with her; his marriage was irretrievably over, so now what? What did he want to do with the rest of his life – that really made him shudder, for if he said 'rest' then he had to think of it ending also. No, he didn't want to think about that, he'd stick to the immediate future.

He could easily afford her allowance, so was there any need for him to continue with his work? Perhaps he could find something else to do? This was a rather pleasant thought. Here he was, forty-five next birthday – happily a good six months away yet – maybe it really was time for a complete change. He looked at this thought from all angles because it was a new one to him. In Oliver's world, men went to work at nine in the morning, returning at six o'clock at night, if not later. Their aim was to make as much money as possible to give their families the luxuries of life and a secure future. But with no wife, only himself to consider, what were the luxuries he wanted?

Should he stop work entirely, or might that be a mistake? He knew that inside him was a great band of idleness which, if indulged, could swamp him. He could well imagine himself content to lie on his back in a water meadow, a piece of grass stuck between his teeth, watching the clouds scud by. A slight exaggeration possibly, but seductive all the same; he did find the prospect of idleness perhaps a little too attractive. Why not? said a voice inside him, one he had not heard before. 'Why not?' he said aloud. 'I can do what I bloody well want.'

He lit another cigarette. He could work at something else. Make a complete change. But what? He found himself thinking of Aunt Phoebe's house and how contented he was during the weekends he spent there. What if he should sell this London house and move lock, stock and barrel to the country? In the recesses of Oliver's mind was a secret which he had never told a living soul. Oliver had a sneaky idea that he had inherited slightly more from Aunt Phoebe than a house and money, that maybe he had some of her genes too. He thought he'd like to try to write – nothing serious, something that was fun and gave people pleasure, very much as the old girl had. Bandage would like it there, dogs were happier in the country with a big garden to roam; here in London one had to use the park with all its restrictions.

How would Wimpole react? She was a game old bird, but would she accept life in the country? She liked the city. He never really thought much about what Wimpole did when he wasn't around. He supposed she must have friends, and therefore maybe would not want to come with him. He would sound her out in the morning.

He felt enormously happy now. Happy for the first time in weeks, he realised. Not that he'd known that he'd been particularly *unhappy*. When Sophia had announced that she wanted a divorce he had admittedly been rather suprised. But on the other hand, once she'd said the words, 'Oliver, I've decided this isn't working, I want a divorce,' he had thought, yes, of course, how logical. So he hadn't really known that he'd been a bit miserable about the break-up of his life. It only registered now, when he had decided to reorganise himself. Now he knew that perhaps he'd been unhappy for a very long time but, with his nature, had decided not to acknowledge it.

At six he got up, padded downstairs to the kitchen, prepared not to look at Bandage's empty basket, and made himself a pot of tea.

'What's got into you?' asked Wimpole, as she bustled in in her blue woollen dressing gown. 'Not like you to be up this early, lazy bugger like you.'

'I couldn't sleep.'

'Told you last night you should have had a drink,' she said. She crossed to the long pine dresser and took down her mug, which said *Meg* on it, although Oliver was never quite sure why, and wondered if perhaps Meg was her name? She'd always been Wimpole to him. He didn't ask her if Meg was her name, it would have seemed too much of an impertinence somehow. Wimpole she was, and Wimpole she'd stay.

'Enough in that pot for me?' she asked. He replied by pouring tea into her mug for her.

'So, what *are* you doing up so early then?' she said, taking her tea from him.

'I've been re-evaluating my life.'

'Sounds like hard work in the middle of the night. Doesn't sound like you at all, Oliver.'

'It was a bit of a shock coming back and finding most

of my things had gone, I couldn't sleep and I thought, well, maybe she's done me a favour. Maybe I should start looking at my own life.'

'Was it the picture or Bandage that upset you?'

'Why should I be upset about Bandage? I'll go and pick him up this morning. No, the picture doesn't matter either, saved me more moving costs.'

'Moving costs?' Wimpole pounced on the words.

To delay his answer, he busied himself topping up his own cup of tea. 'Have we got any biscuits?' he asked.

Wimpole shuffled across to the dresser, and came back with a biscuit tin. 'Moving? What's that mean?' she said.

He spent a few seconds rooting amongst the biscuits; looked up at her sitting opposite him, saw the anxiety on her face, saw how suddenly she looked old and afraid. Oliver realised in that moment something that had probably been so all his life and which he'd never thought about because it had never been necessary. Suddenly he realised that he loved her.

'It's just an idea, Wimpole. I wondered how you felt about our going to live at Bishop's End? I don't need this large house any more.'

'Why there?' she said, and stirred her tea. 'If anything it's bigger than here – rambling old thing. How many bedrooms has it got?'

'Six, I think. Maybe seven,' he said vaguely.

'And then there's that blooming draughty hall with all those rotting rafters exposed. What did your aunt call that?'

'The Great Hall. It was her work room, where she wrote all her books. I might hang the pictures in there. What do you think?'

He hoped that his voice did not sound as anxious as he felt. He watched as she sat concentrating on her tea, which she was still stirring rhythmically, irritatingly. She sipped the tea, and finding it not to her taste, added more sugar and began the stirring ritual again. 'So?' he asked, impatiently. 'What do you think?'

'Well, I've never been much of a one for the country-side. I've never actually trusted it, get what I mean? You know where you are in the city, don't you? You know what you got to look out for. Muggers, pickpockets, rapists, traffic. But the countryside, well, that's a creepy place, I tell you that.'

Oliver laughed gently. 'Wimpole, you are funny. If someone bangs you on the head in the city, who's going to come running? People just don't care.'

'You've never said a truer word, Oliver.' She sipped her tea with the same rhythmic action as, he realised, she always drank her tea, as if her arm were a metronome, taking two sips, down on the table, up, sip, sip, down . . .

'Mind you,' she said. 'Who's going to bloody *hear* you in the countryside if some bugger comes along and hits you on the head?'

'It's just that it's less likely to happen, Wimpole, that's the point.'

'Maybe I've been watching too much *Eastenders*. Maybe all that's gone, really, that friendliness in the street, that I knew when I was a kid.'

'I think it might have. I think you might just be able to recapture it in the country. I hope so, anyway. But, Wimpole . . .' He put his hand out and covered her small work-worn hand, worn from working for him, and squeezed it comfortingly. 'Wimpole, there's no question of me doing this unless you want to come with me. If you don't like the idea, I won't go.'

She grabbed her hand from under his, fumbled in her dressing-gown pocket, came out with a man-sized handkerchief and trumpeted into its folds. 'You see, Wimpole, I love you,' he said, and coughed because it wasn't a word he used an awful lot.

At that Wimpole cried, tears she did not dab at, as if unaware of them. She certainly wasn't ashamed of them.

38

'Oh, Oliver, you've never ever said that to me, ever.'

'Well, you know, didn't think I needed to,' he said, and wished he had.

'It means a lot to me that, Oliver. I mean, you get to my age, I'm sixty-three next birthday, and okay, I'm fit and able and I can find plenty to do and I help those useless Filipinos Sophia insists on employing – thank God they've gone with her. But I do sometimes wonder, what when I'm seventy and I can't get around so much, what happens then? What's to become of me?'

'Wimpole, I should have said, I mean, I just thought that you understood. I'd look after you, I will always look after you, I promise. And if you don't want to go to the country, we won't go. We can sell this and get a smaller house, one that won't be so difficult to run. I don't expect you to decide now, it's a big decision to make, I realise that. You think about it, and let me know what you want to do.'

'I did a good job on you, didn't I?'

'Sophia wouldn't agree,' he laughed.

'Bah, what would a stupid moo like her know? Nothing.'

An hour later, at just past seven-thirty, Oliver pulled the BMW into the car park of a Little Chef and went in and ordered the American breakfast, an orange juice and a cup of coffee. His 'flu was definitely on the wane. He had set out far too soon to see his father-in-law who, although an early riser, probably would not appreciate him clattering into the house at this time in the morning. He dawdled over his breakfast, smoked three more cigarettes, got back into his car, and arrived at Ben Luckett's half an hour later.

He paused in the driveway, as he invariably did, for the house always gave him immense pleasure. It was a beautiful, stone Elizabethan house, the outside of which Ben Luckett maintained to perfection.

Inside was a different matter. Ben and his wife Cora's

taste did not marry happily with the age of the house. Dralon-covered sofas, green onyx coffee tables, huge paintings of wildlife charging across the veldt, and Cora's almost bordello-like fixation with ruffled curtains didn't quite suit the starkly beautiful Elizabethan interior. Oliver admired Ben's self-confidence, to have exactly what he wanted in his house. The enormous television set in the linenfold panelled drawing room might scream out that it was an anachronism, but to Oliver, it was a statement. *I, Ben Luckett, can afford the biggest, largest, most vulgar television set on the market, and I shall put it in my beautiful house, so there.*

Cora had, according to Ben's daughter, been a bit of a mid-life mistake. Oliver wondered if this was so, or was it just jealousy speaking? For if Ben felt Cora to be a mistake, then he managed to put a good face on it. Cora had once been a pretty, dim, peroxide blonde. Such looks had not travelled comfortably into her mid-years. She wore too much make-up, her hair was over teased, lacquered and coloured and she ate so little, in order to maintain her slim shape, that it was a miracle she survived. Her dimness had, of course, accompanied her. In her youth it had been girlishly attractive, but it did not suit a mature woman nearly as well – at least, according to Sophia it didn't. Oliver, however, found it rather endearing and certainly more relaxing than Sophia's rapid, sharp mind. Maybe Ben hadn't been so daft after all.

Ben Luckett, like many self-made men, had all the accoutrements of a successful country gentleman. On the immaculately raked forecourt, with its pristine flower beds in front of the large house, stood the four-wheel-drive Range Rover, dog guard in the back. Snuffling around on the forecourt were two fine black labradors and a Jack Russell, which charged at his car in hysterical welcome. Before Oliver even got out of the car, on the steps appeared Ben Luckett himself, his face glowing claret red, in his tweed plus-fours, and already sporting the sheepskin wrist-warmers that he wore for shooting.

'You're early, Oliver,' he said, holding out his hand in welcome. Oliver wished that people would stop making remarks about him being up early for once.

'I've come for Bandage,' he said. 'I gather Sophia's brought him here.'

'Sophia's not up, not yet.'

'Oh, I'll just pick up the dog and go.'

'Have some breakfast.'

'No thanks, I already have.'

'You'd better come in now you're here. You might have a long wait, Bandage is upstairs in Sophia's room – unhygienic, I say, but she won't listen.'

'Bandage sleeping with Sophia! In the same room! God Lor'.' This information made Oliver feel unsettled. Why should Sophia do that, when she'd made such fusses about Bandage sleeping in his dressing room?

Oliver allowed Ben to lead him back into the house. In the hall he paused. 'Where's the oak chest that stood over there, Ben?'

'Cora said it was a dust trap. She sold it. Sophia's a bit miffed. Said we should have let her know, she'd have liked it.'

Oliver did not wish to make any further comment on Sophia's current acquisitive nose for furniture, and smiled to himself instead. Cora and this house were a trial to Sophia, who had such exquisite taste that she worked as a consultant on a new magazine which was taking the British public by storm. It was the sort of magazine town dwellers loved, full of glossy photographs of tarted-up Tuscan farmhouses and tatty English cottages, with collections of old, junk-shop bottles arranged artistically to look like a display at the V & A. The loss of the intricately-carved chest would have pained Sophia; he was grateful to Cora for selling it.

Ben Luckett had been in the middle of breakfast, and Oliver accepted the cup of coffee he offered him.

'I haven't said anything, you know, about you and Sophia.'

Oh God, thought Oliver, here it comes – heart to heart time. 'I appreciate that, Ben,' he said, craftily he thought.

'Of course, I'm sad. And I don't understand. I like you, Oliver, I hope we keep in touch.'

'Well, thanks, Ben. Me too.'

'Don't get me wrong, Oliver. I love Sophia deeply. But I can see she's not the easiest of people to get along with – and to live with.' He added this with such feeling that Oliver realised that Sophia's visit had obviously been a great strain on him too. 'But why, Oliver? Why?'

Oliver felt suddenly sad for his father-in-law's obvious confusion. 'Well, I guess I haven't been much of a husband. Perhaps I should have been a bit more romantic – all that stuff. I'm the first to admit Sophia ran our house like clockwork, and I guess I took it all for granted. And with no kids it's been hard for her, a disappointment really. No hard feelings though, Ben, you realise?' he coughed, and found he felt quite emotional.

'You've been very generous, boy.'

This touching little talk ceased as the door opened and in walked the subject of it. Oliver jumped to his feet. They might be separated, they might be heading for divorce, but he could still acknowledge that Sophia Hawksmoor was a beautiful woman. And even now, fresh out of her bed, hurriedly dressed in slacks and silk shirt, with no make-up and the brush just raked quickly through her hair, she looked stunning and belied her thirty-five years.

'I couldn't believe it when I saw the car,' she said in the clipped voice which was the only thing that marred her. It was a little too abrupt, a little too sharp.

'I've come for Bandage.'

'Well, you can't have him,' she said, pouring herself coffee.

42

'What do you mean, I can't have him? Is he ill?'

'No, but you didn't expect to keep him, did you? How can I live alone in London without protection? I'll need the dog.'

'You've got the Filipinos.'

'I want Bandage.'

'But he's mine.'

'He's *ours*.'

'I thought he was a birthday present to me.'

'He was a present to both of us, and I've decided to keep him.'

At this, Oliver's heart lurched, and Ben interrupted. 'Sophia, come on, that's a bit hard. You can always get another dog.'

'I don't want another dog. I want Bandage,' she enunciated carefully.

Oliver banged the table. It was a tactical error, and as soon as he had done it, he realised it. But it was too late. 'No,' he said. 'You've got every other bloody thing I own – you're not having the dog.'

'We'll see about that,' she said and, pushing her coffee cup aside, she stalked from the room.

3

Thomasine woke just after eight and was immediately alert, which was unusual for her, for she was one of those people to whom waking, each morning, was a rebirth. The reason was obvious. There was a heavy weight in the crook of her elbow. In the night the dog had abandoned the floor and was not just on the bed, but in it with her. She stroked its soft coat, liking the feel of it against her bare arm, looked down at the sleeping bulldog and realised, with a start, that she had not felt this protective towards a small object since she had held her daughter, Nadine, when she had been born, sixteen years ago. Dangerous notions, stupid ones to pursue she told herself, and promptly thought of Robert. What would he think of this? She, lying in bed, cuddling the dog beneath the duvet. She was smiling, for, as she well knew, Robert would have been apoplectic with disgust.

Why, when she relaxed, did Robert always pop into her thoughts? It wasn't surprising, she supposed; after all, she had been married to him for twenty-two years, and for twenty of them she had thought that she was the be-all and end-all of his life, as he was of hers. She had loved him, she had tried to be a good wife to him – whatever that meant, she was none too sure any more. And in any case, being a satisfactory wife hadn't always been easy, not with Robert.

Thomasine remembered the conversation she'd had with her mother when she had first told her that she wanted to marry Robert.

'What birth sign is he?' her mother had asked immediately.

'Virgo, I think.'

'Dear God, Thomasine, you can't even consider it! Never *ever* marry a Virgo. I did, and look where it landed me.'

'So what's so very wrong with being a Virgo?' Thomasine asked.

'I'll tell you. They're pernickety, they're precise, they're exact, they're critical – hypercritical – and they're tidy. All the things you're not.' Di Haddon spoke in the bald, brutal way that some mothers have.

She had thought her mother wrong, of course she had – mothers were, in her youthful experience, always wrong, they knew nothing. But with the passing years she had had to acknowledge, grudgingly, that her mother possessed the gift, awkward and often inconvenient, of being invariably right.

The first sign that Robert might be the Virgo her mother had described occurred on their honeymoon night. He had been markedly irritated at finding one of her court shoes on one side of the bed and the other on the other side. Not that he'd said anything. It was the exaggerated way he had picked them up between thumb and forefinger, as if he was saying to her, 'Look what I'm doing, I'm putting your nasty, dirty shoes away. I'm putting your shoes away neatly and tidily as they should be.' She'd been irritated for a second or two, and thought of a smart-arse response, but had controlled it and, wanting to please him, she had thanked him instead and had never left her shoes like that again. Nor did she scatter her undies or talcum powder around the bathroom, or leave her clothes on the chair waiting to be hung up in the morning as had been her way. Overnight she began to tutor herself to be better, to be tidier, until their house was exactly as Robert wanted it. A model of efficiency. A place that anyone could come to at any hour of the day or night and not find it in a pickle.

It was because of her mother that she had embarked on this sea of compromise, for another of Di's wisdoms, trotted out blithely, completely ignoring the fact that she herself had failed in the institution, was that marriage was all about give and take. It had crossed her mind once or twice over the years that, discounting the money he gave her and the mortgage he paid, Robert was taking a lot more than he was giving. However, Thomasine had also learnt that life was a lot less stressful if she did as he wanted, and she regarded it as a small price to pay for happiness.

Thomasine, however, was not merely being a Goody Two-Shoes. In that first flush of determination to make her marriage work, she had discovered a wonderful thing. With order and system, everything ran far more smoothly than it had in the past. Housework, which she had always abhorred, could be sped through in a tidy house, whereas her jumbled-up flat had always taken a day, at least, to clean. This way she had more free time. She had used this time to attend cookery classes, and discovered she had a talent for it and that what could have been another chore was, in fact, a pleasure; she'd done an A level in History of Art; she helped a friend out in her boutique and did alterations for her; she'd resurrected a small painting talent and worked hard to make it a larger one.

While Robert congratulated himself on how well he'd trained her, Thomasine congratulated herself on the number of skills she was accumulating. Skills which, one day, might come in handy, and which gave her a welcome sense of security.

It was almost, she later realised, as if she subconsciously knew the marriage wasn't to last, that she would need to be able to do other things some time in the future.

Robert had been generous. He'd kept their London house for himself, but had given her the money to buy this converted school house in Middle Shilling. She had an adequate allowance for their daughter, Nadine. Thomasine, whilst accepting gratefully the money to buy the house, had refused all other assistance; she wanted to support herself. It was a point of honour with her – that door had closed, she must open another. It was not something her mother understood and she'd had long arguments with Di, who felt no inhibition in calling her 'stupid' – though what business it was of hers, or anyone else's, Thomasine could not understand.

Thomasine was confident she could support herself. Several years ago she'd illustrated a friend's children's book. She had enjoyed the challenge, but when the editor of the publishing house had told her to keep in touch in case they found other work for her, she hadn't. With her family to care for she did not have the time to become a professional. Everything was different now, she could start again. She was good, she knew she was. She had already been in touch with the self-same editor, who had promised to keep her in mind.

She shifted position and the dog snuffled, annoyed with the movement which disturbed her sleep. Sometimes she marvelled at the way she tried to fool herself. How could one hide the truth from oneself? Why, after all that had happened, did she still dream of the day he'd return – she'd even planned the meal she would cook. 'Fool!' she said aloud. 'Stop thinking that way.' Oh, she wished she could. Wished it was that simple.

Think positively, she told herself. Now she had a new house in a strange area, new friends to make and life was about to become an adventure. It was time for her to begin living her life. Her way.

The dog in her arms stretched languorously. Now this, this dog. She mustn't become attached to it, it would be gone soon, she was sure. For a second she allowed herself to think of keeping it, but smartly rejected the idea; she did not want the responsibility nor the restrictions that it would impose upon her. The dog's eyes opened and looked at her.

'I can't keep calling you Dog, that's for sure, too precious for words. How about . . . how about Luna? I mean, if it hadn't been raining last night the moon would have been shining on you. Yes, Luna.' The little black tightly-curled tail twitched, as if acknowledging that such a name was to her liking. Or so Thomasine liked to think. 'I suppose you need a pee.'

She released the dog from her arms, slid off the bed, put on her dressing gown. 'Come on, Luna,' she said. But Luna didn't budge. Luna sat in the middle of the duvet and stared at her in a very disgruntled manner. 'Come on, Luna, what's the matter? Come on,' she said, encouragingly. Still the dog didn't move. Maybe she couldn't, maybe she'd stiffened up.

'Is that your problem? The old joints are stiff after last night's catastrophes? Come on then, I'll try and carry you.'

Try was the operative word. She didn't know how much the dog weighed but she guessed it must be fifty pounds or so. Gingerly she manoeuvred her way down the spiral staircase into the drawing room below, which had once been the main schoolroom. Now it was delightfully furnished in chintzes, a cliché, she knew, but then she didn't mind what others thought, it had been what she wanted. Cream Greek rugs were scattered on the highly polished plank floor. She opened the casement door into the garden and stepped outside, putting the dog down on the red-brick path. The dog stood and looked at her balefully. Thomasine stared back.

'Well, I've got all day. It's up to you,' she said.

There was a raw nip in the air, despite the early morning sunshine, but it looked as if it was going to be a lovely day. She took deep breaths of air, fresh from the downpour of last night, and felt very pleased with the world as she looked around.

Thomasine had not been alone in wondering if she was going to settle in the country, never having lived there before. A city girl she had been, born and bred. But something in her, deep down inside, had wanted to live in the country. She had promised herself that, when she had time, she was going to start delving into her own family history to find out where she had come from, why she had such a feeling almost of returning. Had her family once been of yeoman stock? Was that why she had this strong conviction that happiness would be found in the peace and solitude of the countryside?

Peace and solitude, she smiled to herself at that. Whoever said that didn't know much about the countryside. She only had to stand here now, at half past eight in the morning, listening to the racket which was the countryside. Birds, returning in droves now that spring was almost here, were making a twittering din. Cockerels were cockadoodling, cows mooing, two cats were fighting, dogs barking. She could hear the clatter of as yet unknown farm equipment, a tractor was whirring up, a plane was flying overhead. Had it not been a Saturday then the noise of children waiting outside for the school bus to take them into Shillingham would have been added to it all. She did hope that her living in what had once been the village school was not going to cause problems. She had heard that there had been a big petition to try and keep it open; she sincerely hoped that she wouldn't be blamed for its closure.

She looked down. Luna was still standing in the same place, looking angry, as if whatever was upsetting her were Thomasine's fault. 'Luna, my love, you do seem to be in a bad way. It's the vet for you after breakfast, I think. Come on, maybe the long grass will be more to your liking.' She manhandled the dog across the lawn to what she liked to call her wilderness patch – in truth it was one buddleia tree and a load of weeds that she planned to let run riot in the hopes that in the summer her garden would be full of butterflies. She placed the dog down on all four paws, but held onto its tummy.

'Luna, this isn't ideal, but it's the only way. You're going to have to pee. Come on, girl.' Maybe it was something in the tone of her voice, for the dog looked at her, lifted one leg elegantly into the air and piddled.

'That's odd. Why are you cocking your leg like that? You're a bitch!' She guided her back into the house and into the kitchen, mixed her some Weetabix and laughed at the folly of warming the milk for her. She didn't think she ought to add sugar, it couldn't be good for dogs if it wasn't good for humans, so she broke an egg on the top.

While she waited for the kettle to boil, Thomasine took out the Yellow Pages and looked up Veterinary Surgeons. She was in luck, there was one right here in Middle Shilling. She would call him after she had had breakfast.

4

Unusually for him, Jim Varley had overslept. He blamed it on the Scotch he'd drunk last night and made a mental note, admittedly one of many in the last two years, that he must control the amount he was drinking. It was an odd thing about such resolutions, he realised with a wry smile, that he only ever made them in the mornings, never in the evenings.

It was eight before he left the house, rejecting the enormous breakfast that Beth tried to press upon him, as she did every morning. With only coffee slurping about inside him, he climbed into his battered old Land Rover. He wanted to check Ben Luckett's filly before his morning surgery.

He regretted he was late because, in Jim's opinion, there were two times that were best to visit a stable. One was at twilight, as the horses were bedded down for the night and a sweet tranquillity descended upon the stables; the other, very early in the morning, as the horses and the grooms prepared for the new day and there was a briskness and excitement in the air. And now, by oversleeping, he'd missed it.

As he swung the Land Rover onto the forecourt of Ben Luckett's house the front door opened and a man dashed down the steps, climbed into a large BMW, slamming the door angrily behind him. He crashed the car into gear and with a spray of gravel set off down the drive at a ferocious speed. Oliver Hawksmoor, Jim thought, and in a fine temper. The car had just started when a very angry-looking Sophia appeared on the steps also. Jim vaguely wondered what the fuss was about, but not wanting to get involved in other people's dramas, he thought it politic not to acknowledge her. Instead he continued round the corner of the house, past the kitchens and the kitchen garden to the fine red-brick stable block, and drove into the immaculately kept yard, complete with clock, stable cat and a few chickens pecking idly about.

He hoped that, intent on their own problems, no one in the house had noticed him arrive, for he really hadn't time to stay long. At the sight of him, Amanda, one of Ben Luckett's overworked but devoted girl grooms, came running towards him. Girls like Amanda always amazed him, the way they worked for a pittance just to be close to the creatures they adored. All was well, she told him. The mare was fine, the foal suckling well, both a picture of contentment. He was just about to get back into his vehicle when Ben Luckett himself appeared.

'I thought it was you I heard. I expected to see you earlier than this, Jim,' he said, rudely.

'Busy morning,' Jim lied.

'I suppose animals don't take weekends off,' Ben laughed.

Jim laughed back politely, even if he didn't think it much of a joke. 'Filly's fine, nothing to worry about there, and mum also. I'll pop back again this evening if you want, but I don't really think it's necessary.'

'Better to be safe than sorry, Jim. She's an expensive horse.'

'Fine, as you wish.' He put his bag of medical supplies on to the passenger seat and began to climb in.

'Doing anything tomorrow morning?' Ben Luckett asked.

'It's always difficult to say in my trade,' Jim replied cautiously, not wishing to commit himself.

'Just a few people in for pre-lunch drinks, if you fancy it?'

'Thanks for inviting me,' Jim said. He really didn't want to go, he hated drinks parties, or any party come to that, but perhaps he should accept Ben's invitation, the man was a good client and was always asking him, and he always turned him down. 'I'd like that,' he found himself saying.

'Well, that is nice,' said Ben, obviously as surprised as Jim by his acceptance.

Jim took the short cut back to Middle Shilling, which took him past the Oakleigh Kennels. He glanced at his watch. Had he got time to pop in and see Eveleigh? She was concerned, and with reason, about a St Bernard dog of hers. Visiting these kennels always gave him pleasure. They were immaculate. So many he'd seen were little more than a collection of sheds, dirty concrete runs, and God alone knew what was contained in the offal, stored in the fly-infested barrels, waiting to be stewed up later. But Eveleigh had neat rows of brick-built kennels, well fenced, with an outdoor run and an indoor sanctum. The water bowls were always full of clean water – how was a mystery to him. She had heat lamps for poorly dogs, a special whelping room, and hanging baskets outside each kennel. Beyond was a large, securely fenced paddock where the dogs were exercised regularly. He wished all breeders could be made to inspect her set-up and improve their own. She was a caring breeder, and although successful in her chosen field, he very much doubted if she made a penny out of the enterprise, so great was her concern for the well-being of her dogs. Breeders were an odd breed, he smiled at his own lame joke. Money could be made, he knew, if one were ruthless and had no concern for the health of the dogs and overbred from a bitch, doctoring the forms to hoodwink the Kennel Club whose rules for registration stipulated, rightly, that a bitch must not be whelped over the edge of eight and then have only six litters in her lifetime. But there were still those who bred dogs because they loved them, and one breed in particular, rarely making a profit. Even the winner of Crufts, Eveleigh had told him, only won a small cheque, got a cup and, if they were lucky, some dog food for a year.

He beeped the horn of the Land Rover. There was no point in going to the front or back door, for by seven each morning Eveleigh was out tending to her dogs behind the house.

'Jim, have you come to see Siegfried?' Eveleigh asked as she appeared round the side of the house.

'Just passing,' he said. He liked to keep Eveleigh's bills down as much as possible. He would only charge her for any treatment today, no call-out fee. And, after all, it was true, he had been passing.

'This way,' she said, taking the lead. She was a tall woman whose body was lean and taut from hard work, though it would be hard to see today, dressed as she was in cords, tucked into her wellies, and a baggy jumper which reached almost down to her knees. She had a wide, open face, an honest face. Her blue eyes were surrounded now by a fine network of lines, and her nose, which when young, had been the bane of her life, was of a noble proportion which suited an older face. Her hair, once blonde but now greying, was invariably tied back into a pony tail – a mite incongruous in one of her middle years, but which, when socialising or judging, she wound into a neat bun or sometimes had set. She was a fine-looking woman who carried herself well and had several admirers, even if none of them had dared make an approach, for she had a natural reserve about her. Rumour was that even if they had spoken up, it was unlikely that they would have received a response for, it was said, Eveleigh still grieved too much for her dead husband, Reggie, killed five years ago by joy riders on the Morristown by-pass. Eveleigh was aware this was said, and felt sad, for she was lonely. Secretly she longed for someone to replace Reggie, but did not know how to let others know it.

'How many dogs have you got at the moment, Eveleigh?' Each time he came there seemed to be more than the last time.

Eveleigh paused as she counted silently in her head. 'Well, I suppose eighteen St Bernard adults, six puppies and my King Charles.'

Jim smiled. 'Still taking in the waifs and strays?' he asked kindly. He was aware that of the eighteen St Bernards, only four bitches were used for breeding; the others were her own retired dogs, and those that other people did not want. Eveleigh, it seemed, always had room for just one more.

'A new one arrived last week; a dear sweet year-old St Bernard bitch. One of her front paws twists in very slightly and the owners didn't want her any more as she wasn't perfect. As you know, I have a return-if-not-suited policy.'

'But after a year? I mean, didn't they notice this before?'

'I'm sure it was not there when I sold the puppy. I wouldn't have sold a puppy as being perfect if I'd noticed anything wrong with it, I would have reduced the price. I've my name and reputation to consider.'

'Of course, Eveleigh. And I've seen all your litters and I never noticed one with a twisted foot, it must have had an accident since.'

'That's what I think. But how filthy, how absolutely filthy – what a way to treat a dog! Just because it has the slightest of limps, it's rejected. It's disgusting.'

'You'll never eliminate irresponsible dog owners, Eveleigh. Sometimes I wish people had to apply for a licence and pass a test to be allowed to own a dog. Still, when you think what lousy parents humans can make, is it any wonder? Let's go and see that old brute of yours, check him over. And I'll look at the one with the bad paw.'

Champion Siegfried Nibelungen of Oakleigh was sleeping heavily, as old dogs do. He finally deigned to raise his head and peered at them from under the wrinkles that, in the way of St Bernards, sagged, giving him a mournful expression. A steady stream of slobber dribbled from his mouth and Jim, knowing St Bernards of old, hoped he wouldn't shake his head and cover him with it. The old dog stretched conveniently for Jim, as if inviting him to listen to his heart. It was slowing down, just a little bit more each time he came. He knew what Eveleigh was praying for, what every dog owner prays for; that the dog would die by himself, so that the awful decision to have him put down would not have to be made. Jim hoped especially with this one that Eveleigh could have her wish.

He checked the dog with the twisted paw. The malformation was barely detectable. Far more likely that, once the dog was fully grown, the owners had tired of its size – a common happening with the large breeds. Eveleigh invited him for a coffee, as she invariably did, but looking at his watch he reluctantly refused. He enjoyed nattering to Eveleigh, she always made him feel relaxed. They had known each other for nearly twenty years and so there was never any need to explain themselves to each other, to pretend. It was an honest relationship, similar, he presumed, to having a sister to talk to.

By the time he reached the surgery he was running seriously late, and as he rushed in Beth met him with his telephone messages.

'What's the surgery looking like?' he asked.

'Not too bad, four people, but there were lots of phone calls. Those hairdresser blokes called; their dog had puppies in the night.'

He glanced up. 'Really? And they managed OK?'

'They were so excited, it was lovely to hear. They were bubbling with happiness and sounded just like proud new parents.'

'Good. I'm glad all went well for them. Do you think I've got time for a cup of coffee?' He looked at her questioningly.

'I'll bring it in. But after surgery you're sitting down, Jim Varley, and you are going to eat some breakfast.'

'Please, Beth, not bacon and eggs. Something light.'

'Toast, with a scrambled egg.'

'Do I have to?'

'Yes you do.'

For the sake of a cup of coffee he agreed, and went into the surgery. On Saturdays he was on his own – his veterinary assistant only worked five days a week – so a light surgery was a relief, for it would mean less sterilising and general cleaning up afterwards. His first client was in and out in a matter of five minutes, a man who was planning to move to France and wanted to arrange for rabies vaccinations for his dog and cat. Then a cat with a nastily cut paw, which was soon bandaged and away. A pet rabbit which was off colour he hospitalised for observation; he was suspicious it might have an ulcer, caused by the stress of not being able to get to the doe in the next cage. He'd seen that before.

He was drying his hands on a paper towel as he turned to welcome the next patient with its owner. Standing rather shyly in the doorway was a woman who made Jim's heart lurch in a way it had not done for ages. She was tall, not too slim, with long brown shining hair, and she smiled a greeting with a generous mouth.

'Good morning,' he said, and suddenly felt as gauche as a schoolboy.

'Good morning. I'm Thomasine Lambert. I'm new around here. I moved into The School House in the village last week.' She said this in an attractive, low voice, but rather as if she spoke by rote, as if she were saying it a lot at the moment.

Jim introduced himself and they shook hands; he registered that hers was cool to the touch, with long, finely tapered fingers, like those of an artist. 'Ah, what

56

have we here?' he said to cover up how flustered he felt, and knelt down to introduce himself to Luna. 'I like bulldogs. My grandad had one, you don't often see them these days.'

'I found her,' she said simply. 'She's not mine. I'm just looking after her till we find someone to take her on.'

'Found her? What, a stray?'

'Yes, on the by-pass. But she's not a real stray. Some ba –' She grinned. 'Bastard, yes, that's the word. He was a right bastard. He threw her out of his car in the storm last night. Abandoned her. She could have been killed. Fortunately for the dog, I was just coming along behind.'

'Did you inform the police? Perhaps she fell out of the car.'

'I don't think so, neither do the police. The kennel there was full and there was something about the dog, something appealing, so I said I'd take her home until somebody wanted her.'

'You don't?'

'Well, no, not really. I mean, I've enough to do at the moment without a dog as well.'

'Right, so what is it you want me to do? Examine her? Is she hurt?'

'Yes, her chin is grazed and she seems to have done something to her leg and it's stiffened up overnight because she's having awful trouble walking. In fact, when she peed this morning she cocked her leg like a dog and she's a bitch.'

'Have you got another dog?'

'No, I said I hadn't time for dogs.'

'Then she was marking her territory. A dog can pee high up and aim its scent further; so by not squatting she was spreading her scent, marking your garden as hers.'

'How clever of her,' she laughed. 'I just thought she was being fastidious.'

Jim picked Luna up and sat her on his examination table. 'You're a weight and a half, aren't you?' The dog looked at him, then at Thomasine, and then lay down.

'Well, she's not scared of vets. Either she hasn't seen too many vets or has been so often that she's resigned to us. Let's have a look.' He checked the graze on her chin, gently moved her legs. 'Nothing broken there, I think you're probably right, it's just a bad sprain. I'll put some antiseptic cream on that chin and we'll give her a jab just to be on the safe side and . . .' He stopped speaking as he ran his fingers down the dog's flank. 'Ah, I think here's the reason why she got thrown out of the car. Not obvious at first because she's naturally so stocky.'

Thomasine leant forward eagerly. 'Why?'

'I'm afraid she's pregnant and, since she's been abandoned, probably not by a bulldog, probably a little mistake.'

Thomasine looked at the dog. 'Oh, Luna. What were you up to?' As always when she spoke to the dog the little tail waggled excitedly, making her whole rump wriggle with apparent pleasurable anticipation. 'So the father could be anything, I suppose.'

'Exactly. I mean you wouldn't ditch a bulldog in pup to a bulldog, their puppies sell for a lot of money. They're probably mongrels, and the problem with bulldogs is they're very bad whelpers, the puppies' heads are big and can get stuck in the birth canal, which, of course, is dangerous and might lead to a Caesarean. Any operation is a risk to a bulldog, they are difficult to administer a general anaesthetic to, so there is always the possibility of complications. In other words, Miss Lambert, I think you've got a bit of a problem here. You could land up with a large litter of mongrel puppies – half bulldog, God knows what they'll look like. You may not be able to get rid of them and, I have to warn you now, there could be considerable veterinary expenses as well.'

'What do you recommend, then?'

'I know of a dog refuge near here, who will do their best to care for her and hopefully find homes for the puppies afterwards. The only other alternative I'm afraid is to spay her, but then, as you say, she isn't your dog.'

'No, and what about the risk from the anaesthetic you mentioned?' Thomasine leant against the examination table and stroked the dog protectively. 'How many dogs are at this refuge?' she asked.

'It varies. Close to Morristown, it gets its fair share of abandoned, unwanted dogs. She has a lot of greyhounds in, you know; when they can no longer win races, they're abandoned. There's a lot of irresponsible dog ownership around, so that on average she has two to three hundred dogs at a time. No matter how Betty tries, this dog wouldn't necessarily get the attention she's going to need.' He looked with sympathy at Luna and patted her; she licked his hand in response.

Thomasine looked at Luna too. If she was going to have a bad time, if it was all going to be difficult, no matter how kind the refuge owner, it wouldn't be the same as being just one dog being cared for. 'I think I'll keep her for the time being and look after her. I'll face the matter of the puppies when that arises.'

'The time being?' he queried.

'When she's had the puppies, then I'll find a home for her, it shouldn't be too difficult, a pedigree dog like this.'

'Maybe it'll be more difficult than you think.'

'Why?'

'Perhaps you'll love her too much.'

'Me? Not a chance.' Thomasine shook her head and he noticed how the overhead light shone on her hair. 'I don't even like dogs. It's just that I hate cruelty to any animal. I don't think a dog should be treated in this way.'

'Fine. I'd say she's halfway through her pregnancy. I can arrange for her to have a scan if you like, to see what's going on in there or, to keep the cost down, I could just keep an eye on her. I'll give you a diet sheet for her, some vitamin pills and a wormer. Do bring her back if you're at all worried. If she begins to whelp, give me a ring. It doesn't matter if it's in the middle of the night – it invariably is.'

'You're very kind, thank you so much.' Thomasine looked down at Luna, who was so relaxed she looked as if she had fallen asleep. 'You know, I think she's a witch. As soon as I decide one thing, she looks at me and I find I decide something else.'

He smiled. 'Some dogs have that effect. She's a good bulldog, though. Once back to normal she'll be one to be proud of.'

'You think so? There, did you hear what the man said?' Thomasine asked Luna as she bundled her into her arms.

As soon as she was out of his surgery and in the car she immediately regretted what she had taken on. It was the combination of the dog and the vet – it was all his fault. His 'poor bulldogs suffering' routine, plus Luna and those eyes, had made her lose her senses. And what if Nadine wanted her to keep it? No, that was unlikely, Nadine liked cats, not dogs, and was always nagging her to buy her a Siamese. Thomasine had read somewhere that a cat lover rarely became a dog lover.

'That's your lot, Luna. You can stay until you have your babies and then that's it – out into the big world with you after that.' Luna gently butted her with her large forehead. 'I mean it,' Thomasine said sternly as she put the car into gear.

5

Since Kimberley White's bedroom was over the kitchen at Primrose Acre it was warm, benefiting from the heat generated by the solid fuel Rayburn which was never allowed to go out. The small room was in need of decoration, and new curtains would not have gone amiss, but Kimberley was resigned to nothing ever being done to improve it. Tom, her father, was at pains to tell her what a lucky cow she was to have her own room and not to have to share as he had had to. She sighed inwardly whenever he said so, for it meant that he was about to embark on a long description of his own deprived childhood when, as the youngest of eight, he hadn't even had shoes. She knew the saga off by heart. After so many repetitions, she had acquired the ability to switch off and think of other things. In any case, she didn't believe a word of it. She had asked her Nan before she had died if what he related was true. 'Nothing of the sort,' the old lady had snorted indignantly. 'We weren't rich, but my hubby made sure we never went without. My Tom always was a bloody little fibber.'

The room looked over the fields of Chris Walters' farm at the back of the house. A pleasant view compared to the clutter of broken machinery, defunct fridges and washing machines, which cluttered the front and were part of her father's scrap dealings, one of his many sidelines. In winter the wind whipped over the flat field as if coming straight from Siberia, so she could not have her window open at night, for then it was too great a battle for the Rayburn to keep the room warm.

The wind had died from last night's storm. She pushed back the curtain, which was now just a faded memory of the riot of bright-coloured flowers it once had been. She saw the sun glinting on the furrows of the next-door field, registered that, despite that, it was cold, and dived back under her blankets. She had no idea of the time, she did not have a clock and wasn't wearing her watch. She did not need either; she could rely on her mother to call her. If she was unlucky then her father would be bellowing up the narrow stairs with its frayed runner, yelling for her to get up and give him a hand.

Kimberley had fantasies about the runner on the stairs; she hoped that one day her father would catch his foot in it, tumble down the stairs and hurt himself – a twisted ankle, or, when really annoyed, she'd dream of a broken leg. However, such thoughts tended to be treacherous, for sometimes she found herself hoping he would fall and break his neck. When that happened she shut her eyes tight, trying to shut the idea from her mind. It was wrong to think of a parent in such a way, wicked. Something bad would happen to her if she let such a thought escape. But for all that, it lingered there and, much as she scolded herself, it would never quite go away.

Kimberley had other dreams which she liked to unlock, polish and improve. One was of getting a job and having enough money to leave home. She dreamed of a nice flat with decent furniture, and how she would buy ready-made lined curtains like the ones she had seen in Marks and Spencer's in Morristown. She thought about it so often that if she closed her eyes she could almost see it, with its Habitat sofa-bed, the white shelves she'd seen in Texas for the books and CDs that she would one day buy. Yellow and white she wanted, with striped rugs in blue and cream on the floor which, of course, she would have stripped and polished.

The only way such a dream would ever become a reality was if she worked as hard as possible to get her A Levels. She was good at maths, but had rejected any idea of going on to university, for that would mean being dependent upon her father for too long. Her ambition was to work in a bank and one day become a manager. Not her father's bank in Shillingham, that would never do, for then he would come in, loud-mouthed and unwashed, and embarrass her.

Years ago, when still quite young, she had become aware of her mother's life – worn to a frazzle with hard work and never enough money, frightened to death of her husband and his moods, and seemingly with no mind, or opinions, of her own. Kimberley had no intention of ending up like her. That she was still at school was an example of the contrariness of her father's nature. He had so often told her how much he loathed her that she now did not even register it. Whatever she did was never right for him. He shouted abusively at her, occasionally hit her – and yet took a perverse pride in her achievements, and so her education continued.

The way her mother lived angered Kimberley, for she was certain that her father made far more money than he let on, that somewhere there was a stash of it hidden away. She had watched him doing deals often enough; he never accepted a cheque, always cash. Frequently he said to her, tapping the side of his nose with his finger, 'Mark my words, Kim, deal in notes whenever you can, then there's no proof of nothing.' If he did have money hidden away it was so unfair to her mother, and it would be one more reason to loathe her father.

After the treatment of her mother, she most hated him for the treatment of the dogs. It shamed her now, that it had taken her so long to wake up to what went on in the big sheds outside, and to realise it was cruel. The sheds and the dogs had been there all her life and since, in the way of children, she knew no better, she had not questioned anything. She had assumed that it was normal for dogs to be raised and kept in such conditions. Two years ago she had woken up to all the hideousness of it, and still despised herself for being so thick.

Until then she had helped with the dogs, cleaning them out, feeding them, playing with the puppies. But after the row, and what a row it had been, she had never been in the sheds again.

She could still remember every detail of that particular argument. It had started calmly enough. Rarely for her, she had stayed overnight with her only friend, Liz. Rarely, since her father did not like her going into other people's houses – she might see how other people lived and get dissatisfied. That visit to Liz's had been allowed because he knew Liz's father hadn't two halfpennies to rub together, and because Liz and her family were moving away to Durham. Liz, who loved animals, had insisted they watch a film on Channel 4 about puppy farming in Wales. At first she wasn't that interested, but as she listened to the impassioned commentary and saw the tears that Liz was shedding for the poor dogs, it was as if the scales had fallen from her eyes. She realised that that was exactly what was going on at Primrose Acre, and that it was wrong. Now she knew why she had never been allowed to bring any friends home. It was why her parents also had no friends. It was why any callers at the smallholding were promptly dealt with and sent packing.

She had been excited as she described the film to her parents. She explained how she felt as if, since she had discovered how wrong it was, they must also, and then they would agree that it must stop.

'Stop!' Tom had bellowed. 'Don't be such a stupid cow! Where the bloody hell do you think your keep comes from?' He banged the kitchen table with his fist, making the plates jump and jangle. 'Where the fuck do you think this food came from? Not from the veg we sell, not the eggs, from the fucking dogs. Wake up, you stupid bitch.'

'But it's cruel.'

'Of course it isn't – they know no better.'

'Perhaps if you had less, perhaps then we could care for them better. Improve the conditions. And this programme said that the bitches, like ours, are over-breeding and it kills them, and . . .'

She did not finish what she was saying; instead she saw stars as Tom's fist whammed into the side of her face.

'If I hear any more of this stupid claptrap, you don't get a penny more from me, and that's straight. You say another dicky bird and you can go and get yourself a fucking job and leave here, is that understood?'

'But Tom, her education . . .' Sue, her mother, began,

but the fist landed square on her mouth and any further speech was lost in the spurt of blood from her loosened front tooth.

'Don't you hit my mum like that!' Kimberley was on her feet, but her mother waved a hand at her in weary resignation. 'You can bully me, and blackmail me, but I can promise you one thing, I'm not going to help you with the dogs ever again.'

'Watch it, miss.' Her father waved a forefinger menacingly at her.

'I mean it!'

To shut her up her father had hit her again and she had run from the room and up into her little bedroom, slamming the door noisily behind her, for she was determined not to let him see her cry.

By taking such a stand Kimberley had, inadvertently, made matters worse all round. Her mother, who was already overworked with her tasks in the house and on the smallholding, now had to do all the chores for the dogs that previously Kimberley had done. Her father, cantankerous as always, refused to allow Kimberley to help her mother with the chickens and the pigs – she worked, but only at what he told her to do, invariably on the vegetables, weeding, sowing, digging, harvesting – probably because he knew she loathed the job so much.

She had certainly made things worse for the dogs, for without her no one ever played with them, talked to them or gave them even a modicum of comfort and human contact. Kimberley had not realised that not only did her mother not like dogs – she was frightened of them, having been bitten as a young child. She did the minimum of work possible, and was out of the shed as quickly as she could.

As if things were not bad enough, worse was to come. Last year her father had been introduced to dog fighting, and had taken to the sport with zeal. He'd his own fighters now. These dogs were not neglected, but fed the best muscle-building food. One shed was set aside for them and there they were trained on a treadmill he'd devised from a conveyor belt he'd picked up at a clearance sale. Tied on to it, the two pit bulls he'd acquired ran for hours at a time to nowhere. They were trained to pull ever-increasing weights attached to a harness, building strength and muscle all the time.

And then, because of the isolation of the smallholding, Tom allowed the odd dog fight to take place there. Sunday lunchtime was quite a favoured time or, occasionally, late at night cars with no lights bumped up the drive from the main road. In the house, Kimberley and her mother could hear the shouting of the men, their blood lust up. These nights they turned the television up loud.

'I hate this, Mum, it's cruel.'

'It's what your father wants,' she answered.

And because of it all, Kimberley suffered pangs of guilt and self-loathing. Not just because of her mother's lot, but because she knew about the dogs and did nothing. Most of all she despised herself that she did not walk out but had hung on, living under his roof, eating his food, allowing it all to continue just so that she could work in a bank and have a pretty yellow Habitat sofa-bed. She felt she should go, but lacked the courage to do so.

'You getting up or do I have to come and turf you out?' her father shouted.

'I'm up,' she lied. 'Doing homework,' she compounded it, and hugged herself with glee beneath the covers.

'There's some early potatoes to be dug. And the last of the cabbages.'

'It's too soon for potatoes.'

'You do what I fucking tell you.'

'I've got to go into Shillingham.'

'Not until you've done that, you don't.'

She had planned today too, she thought as she quickly dressed in jeans and thick woolly jumper. She'd not had school yesterday and had, she thought, done all her chores so that she could get away this morning. She looked at her watch. Eight. She'd have to rush if she was to catch the bus as well as dig up his bloody potatoes. She flounced down the stairs and passed him without saying a word, flung a heavy winter coat over her shoulders, collected her boxes and marched out to the vegetable patch. To get there she had to pass the dog sheds; she could hear them barking and generally rustling about as her mother quickly tended them. At the rubbish pile, she stopped dead in her tracks. Her father had only half covered the body of the Old English Sheepdog with rubbish, its head was protruding. It was a head Kimberley recognised, it was Charlotte – she had christened them all, she always had. Now they were all nameless, she supposed.

'Oh Charlie, not you. I should never have left you to him.' Gently she stroked the dead, unfeeling head. She had to get away, she must; getting her A Levels wasn't worth having to see things like this.

Two hours later, Kimberley was in Shillingham. She shopped quickly for her mother. Her pocket money was on the meagre side, but she had an agreement with her mother, unknown to her father, that whatever she saved by judicious shopping she could keep. Rather than lug her bags about with her, she had an arrangement with one of the stallholders that she could put them safely under his stall. She would collect them when she caught the late afternoon bus home.

Just after eleven she was sitting on the rim of Cromwell's fountain in the middle of the market square, waiting for the gang to appear. It was a large and ornate fountain where, it was claimed, Cromwell had stopped and drunk the water which, it was also alleged, came from an underground spring thousands of feet below the town. The truth was somewhat more mundane in that the water came from the reservoir on the outskirts of town, and the fountain was Victorian rather than pre-Cromwellian. But the local council, aware of the revenue that any association with Cromwell attracted, happily allowed the legend to remain uncorrected.

As she waited for the others Kimberley knew that people were staring at her: the fountain gang had a reputation for hooliganism, and by sitting here, on a Saturday, she was proclaiming herself one of them. They were a lot of yobs, she was fully aware, but what else was she to do? She had to meet up with people her own age, and these boys and girls accepted her as she was, asking no questions. She knew she was cleverer than them, that they had little in common, but she was lonely at home and at school. After Liz had left, she had tried to make other friends, but without success. Friendships had been forged earlier in school careers, and because she had been content just with Liz, there was no room in the various groupings for her now.

She would have liked a boyfriend. Several of the fellows in the fountain gang fancied her, she knew that. But what they offered, clumsy fumblings and quick couplings, was not what she wanted or expected. She had seen the other girls handed from one gang member to the next and had kept herself aloof. It was surprising they put up with her, but they did – she was never sure why, but had a sneaky idea it might be because they felt sorry for her. She wore her poverty with dignity, and maybe they respected her for that.

Perhaps, one day, when she could smarten up, when she had a place of her own to invite him, then someone special would enter her life. Until then she sat waiting for the friends she had. Her blonde hair was tied back in an elastic band. Her old duffel coat, that had once been her mother's, was clutched firmly about her against the cold. Her jeans were tucked into black wellington boots instead of the Doc Martens she dreamed of. And she watched the bustle of market day swirling about her.

6

Oliver, eventually realising the danger of driving so fast, slowed down and pulled into a lay-by. He might be as furious as hell with Sophia, he might be upset about Bandage, but he did not want to kill himself. He sat for a while smoking. He did not want to return to London, he hated weekends in the city, with everyone he knew away in the country. It was an odd contradiction in Oliver that he could not abide being alone in London, and yet enjoyed it in the country. He was so near to his holiday home he might as well go and hole up there, lick his wounds and plan his strategy over his dog. '*My* dog,' he said aloud and with emphasis. Cheeky bitch, how dare she think she could nick back a present just like that? She'd never liked the dog, in fact invariably ignored it, and Bandage loathed her too, so what was the point? Spite, sheer unadulterated spite, no more, no less. He was well shot of her, that was for sure, he told himself as he started the engine again.

He parked the car outside Bishop's End, something he had done so many times before that he had become blind to its familiarity. This time, when he got out of the car, he walked slowly round the entire property and looked at it in a different way. A house that he used purely as a weekend retreat was a different matter from a house in which he intended to live permanently. Minor inconveniences which might be overlooked in a holiday home could turn out to be insupportable in a main one.

He paused in his tour of inspection outside the bow-fronted dining-room window. It was a pretty window, tall and wide, with the panes reaching almost to ground level. The problem here was that a row of macrocarpa was shutting out too much light; they were not his most favourite trees, but he had been too idle to see to them. The dining room was rarely used since they preferred country kitchen eating on their weekends. But, this could change. He could just imagine Sunday lunch in the pretty room, with his best silver – if Sophia hadn't nicked it. If those trees came down there would not only be more light, but a clear view of the magnificent Cedar of Lebanon on the far lawn, which had been planted by Aunt Phoebe's Bishop grandfather, who had built the house and given it its name.

He looked up. The guttering on this side of the house was in need of repair, and, he thought, one of the chimneys was looking a bit dodgy. The house was watertight. However, the woodwork round the doors and windows, which had once been crisp and white, was now a flaking greyish-green from neglect.

He had worked his way around to the front again. The steps leading up to the extraordinary Gothic porch needed prompt attention; they were cracking and covered in moss, since the front door was never used. If he moved in, perhaps the front door would once more come into its own. These were all minor things to do, but they had their uses in that already they were calming him down, making him begin to think of his future and not his past.

In the porch was a wooden bench on which Aunt Phoebe's trug and gardening gloves had invariably sat. He wondered what had become of them and resolved to search for, or replace, them. He stood on the top step, surveying the front garden. Phoebe had been a manic gardener, and one of pure genius. She had made it appear as though the garden had evolved effortlessly and by accident, not design; whereas, of course, such gardens involved an enormous amount of work and money. Since her death the wondrous garden had become seriously wild. That anything still bloomed was a credit to the plants' tenacity, not Oliver's care. This was something he would have to attend to, and quickly.

He began to list the other things he had already seen that needed attention, adding that the house was in need of a coat of paint. It was just his luck, when every other house in the area was made of the pretty grey, local stone, he should end up with the Bishop's concept of a Strawberry Hill Gothic house rendered and painted pink. It was an unpleasant candyfloss sort of pink, from which he had always averted his eyes and tried to divert his friends' remarks. Perhaps if he could get the colour toned down a little it would look better.

It was odd what divorce did for you, he thought. Last night, he'd lain in his bed thinking long and hard about himself, a totally new experience for him. And then made the spot decision to move. And now this morning, just look at him, wandering about his garden, looking at his house dispassionately in the way a surveyor or an estate agent might do.

He put his hand up and felt along the rafter of the porch, wondering if the spare front-door key was still there. Covered in cobwebs and rusty, it was. The key turned reluctantly in the lock. He pushed at the door with his shoulder until, with one last heave and an agonising creaking sound, it swung open. He battled through the folds of a heavy brocade curtain which hung, against draughts, over the door on the inside in the hall. He would get the floors here sanded and polished, buy new rugs. He would ask Grace White if she would clean every day, and if not to find him someone who would, and then the hall furniture would be buffed and shine and smell of beeswax and lavender and he would have large vases overflowing with fresh flowers. It would be just as it was in Aunt Phoebe's day. He would bring the house back to life. He felt such excitement at the prospect, such pleasure in his incomplete plans. Goodness only knew what other ideas he would come up with – enough, no doubt, to fill his notebook. New curtains, chairs re-upholstered, books bought, his paintings up. Still – he stopped the frantic scribbling in his notepad – he must not overdo it, he didn't want the house to lose its slightly faded charm, most decidedly he did not want to end up with a house that shrieked of the tarting-up typical of Sophia's designer buddies. Perfection of her sort the house did not want; perfection of Phoebe's it would.

From the hall he wandered along the stone-flagged passageway with its original William Morris wallpaper, still more or less intact, to the kitchen, still in need of Grace White's attention. This was the only room he had renovated. It was doubtful if Phoebe had ever ventured as far as the kitchen, leaving the nether regions of her house to her servants. In consequence, it had been dark and forbidding. He had had the lot ripped out, an oil-fired Aga put in to replace the fearsome range that his aunt's cook had battled with, and had the furniture replaced with built-in oak units. The purists might shriek, but it was now a comfortable room to be in. Not that Oliver knew much about cooking; when they had guests, and Sophia had deigned to join them, she brought hampers of food from Fortnum's. When here alone he stocked up from the local Sainsbury's and Marks. If he moved here he would have to sort something out about food; Wimpole happily admitted she couldn't cook and had no intention of learning. Perhaps he could find a gem in the village.

He looked at his watch and found it was nearly noon. He crossed to the Mickey Mouse telephone he had given himself one Christmas and which had appalled Sophia so much she had banned it from the London house, dialled his number and listened as it rang and rang. That was odd, where was Wimpole? She so rarely went out.

He replaced the receiver. 'You've earned yourself a pint and a pie, Oliver, my lad,' he told himself.

Ten minutes later he was in the Duck and Thistle, downing a pint. They knew him in the pub; they had respected his aunt enormously and because of her there had been a welcome, if on the tepid side, for him. They were always polite, but he realised early on that they were telling him, subtly, that he might own a house here, he might weekend, but he did not belong. Because of this attitude, understandable though it was, he rarely popped in.

This time, propping up the bar, listening to the chatter of the other drinkers, he decided to change all that. He took the bull by the horns and confided in the landlord that he was thinking of living here permanently.

The change in the landlord, and in the manner of the locals when he excitedly passed on what Oliver had said, was dramatic. No one grabbed him and hugged him physically, but it almost felt as if they had. That would be grand, the assembled company assured him. Bishop's End was a sorry sight, empty most of the time. No one liked second-home-owners here. As if to compound their approval the landlord offered him a drink, something that had never happened before. Things were looking up, life in the country would be an improvement on the city. He even found himself talking gardening and crops, putting out feelers for a permanent gardener – his friends would never recognise him.

7

It was no hardship for Kimberley to sit and wait for everyone. She liked Shillingham and had known it all her life. Compared to Morristown it was small and not so threatening, for Shillingham was a market town which had managed to escape the fate of others of a similar size when decisions had been made to enlarge them and to turn them into dormitory towns.

Each Saturday, and on quarter days, a thriving market was to be found in the main square – admittedly it tended to have more cheap clothes, handbags, and ethnic tat stalls than farm produce these days but, nevertheless, it gave the town cohesion. It was this market which attracted Kimberley's friends, less for the reasonable cost of what was on offer but for the ease with which they could nick the stuff.

Not that Shillingham was without shops. Because it had no giant hypermarket on the outskirts, shops still stood a chance of trading. And these shops worked like a magnet on the gang. Whatever could be stolen they took, and not necessarily covertly. The owner of the off-licence had been enraged when they had walked in one day, lifted a bottle of Scotch, and had the audacity to say 'ta' as they walked out. He had a large Alsatian behind the counter now; it had never been known to go for anyone, but the group were not giving it the chance to prove itself. They were more interested in the stealing than the goods. When the shoe shop had a display outside on the pavement – only one shoe of each pair – the urge to pinch was so strong that they lifted the lot. They had long been banned from the Spar mini-market, and the police were called if they as much as popped their heads in the door.

Kimberley was not part of the thieving. She had no desire to acquire a police record and mar her chances of working in a bank. But also, when she had got to know the gang about six months ago, it had been decided that she should not risk being caught, for then she might have to leave school. In fact it was Butch, their leader, who reached this conclusion, much to the annoyance of the others, especially the girls. When she had first joined them, Butch had made a pass at her, but it was a somewhat half-hearted attempt, as if he didn't really want to and when she had shoved him and told him to 'piss off' he'd seemed almost relieved. In an odd way she felt she had become their mascot. For some reason, which he never explained, Butch, a classic non-achiever, had enormous respect for Kimberley's intelligence and almost a pride in her achievements. She had often wondered why, and worried that it might have something to do with her ambitions to work in a bank, and his ambition to rob one.

Their presence every Saturday was a shame, for it marred the reputation of Shillingham as a law-abiding town. Not only did they steal, but they had targets which they considered legitimate – they particularly hated the homosexuals who ran the hairdressing salon and enjoyed hurling abuse at them. And they loathed the travelling people with even greater venom, and chased them away at every opportunity. Nor were they keen on the disabled or the old – so they terrorised a lot of the population. They were, however, careful never to aggravate anyone male, fit, and young.

One by one, the others joined Kimberley. They did not kiss each other, shake hands, or clap each other on the shoulder. Rather their greeting was a grunt, though occasionally one pushed another as if trying to shove them into the water at the base of the fountain. It was obvious to any observer that to show pleasure in each other's company was forbidden.

There were seven of them today, four boys, two other girls and Kimberley. It was probably the cold weather keeping everyone away, for on a good day there could be as many as twelve. The other girls were unemployed, and always had been, and had no desire to find work. They were both seventeen and, although she was a year older, Kimberley felt nervous of both of them, for they were loud-mouthed and tough and were best friends to the exclusion of any other females. Shelley was the girlfriend of Butch, who, though never elected, took the role of the leader, primarily because he was the biggest, he was eighteen, and he had a motorbike.

Kimberley did not envy Shelley her role as Butch's girl, for there seemed to be few advantages to the position. She rarely rode on the back of his bike, but took the bus with the others. It seemed Butch thought it made him look soft to have a girl on his pillion. There was no affection between them, no soft words or lingering looks; if anything, Butch was ruder to her than anyone else. Having a particular girlfriend did not stop Butch occasionally taking one of the other girls to the dark corner at the back of the Rialto Cinema where he could quickly screw her and be back at the fountain, all zipped up, in five minutes flat – Kimberley knew, because she had once timed him.

All the other boys were underage and all they possessed of the bikers' world were their leathers. In these they strutted around trying to give the impression that they had a Harley Davidson around the corner rather than a mountain bike, which was the case.

Most of them came from Morristown and had been to school there, or rather had played truant there. It was a mystery to the inhabitants of Shillingham why they plagued them each weekend. The truth would have cheered them immeasurably – they were too scared to swagger about in their own town, for there was a fearsome tooled-up gang on the Forest Glade Estate, who ruled the roost and had ordered them off their patch. So they were, in a way, serving their apprenticeship here in the smaller town. All, that is, except Butch. He liked it here, liked to be top dog and knew that if he joined the Forest Stags, as the Morristown gang was known, he would be a mere nobody. But the others lived in hope that they might be invited to join, which made Butch despise them all and treat them even worse than he would normally have done.

'Christ, it's bleeding cold, you all right, Kim?' Butch asked her while Shelley sulked.

'Fine thanks,' she said, hunkering further into her coat.

'Aren't you ever going to get some decent clothes? You let us down,' Shelley's friend Amber sneered, rubbing her hand up and down the fine black leather of her fringed jacket, which Kimberley envied her more than she would ever let on.

'Leave her alone, you don't know her circumstances.' Butch jumped to her defence.

'And you do?' Amber dared to ask.

'As a matter of fact, I do,' Butch said, but to Kimberley's relief did not elaborate.

They sat around for a bit smoking, joshing, being rude, being obstructive, and then Butch told the girls to go and get them something to eat.

'Your dad breeds dogs, don't he?' Butch asked her as soon as the girls were gone and the other boys, Snotty, Greaser and Ginger, were engrossed in their own conversation.

'Who told you that?' she asked, looking up sharply.

'I saw him at the service station the other side of Morristown, unloading a pile of puppies from his van into another bloke's. That's what they do, don't they? Puppy breeders sell 'em on to pet shop dealers, that sort of thing.'

'I don't know.'

'Course you do!'

'You saying I'm lying?' she demanded, with more spirit than he had ever seen before.

'Nah. It was just . . . I wondered if he bred any fighting dogs?'

'No,' she said.

'You sure?'

'I just said.'

'Only a mate told me he did – pit bulls, that sort of thing. He'd planned to take a bulldog bitch he'd nicked from someone's front garden to your dad's to be mated with a pit bull. But he never got there. Some bugger nicked the bloody dog from him.' He laughed. 'Tell you what, you can't trust no one these days, can you?'

'Not my dad.' She looked away from him and hoped she sounded convincing. After all, it was more than likely Butch was right. It was ages since she had been in the sheds to see what he was up to. In the time she had helped out it had always been the popular breeds her father had bred – King Charleses, Dulux dogs – he always claimed that advert had done wonders for his sales – Yorkies, poodles and whatever had won at Crufts that year for, sure as sure, there would suddenly be a demand for it.

'Why?' she asked Butch suddenly.

He looked to left and right and leant forward. 'Don't breathe a word or I'll fucking screw you witless, but there's a dog fight most Saturday evenings round about here. You can make a lot of money on bets. I just thought I might like a dog of my own. Might be interesting.'

'I'll ask him,' she said, not intending to do any such thing. What her father did was bad enough without this.

The girls returned with some chocolate and coke they had nicked, and the evidence was quickly devoured. For the rest of the day they loafed around, idling about the town, making themselves annoying, returning to their fountain and then wandering off again. A pretty useless day, as usual.

Kimberley was not happy here today and wanted to go, though when she said she was off, Butch stopped her, and said he'd lam her one if she went. She was pretty certain it was because of the dogs.

Gill was alone in the shop. He and Justin, unable to decide who should stay with Sadie, had, in the end and after much good-natured bickering, tossed for it and Justin had won. Without his partner it had been a ghastly day, as Gill had had to do the work of two. He had planned to try and rush home at lunchtime to see how they were all doing but had had to content himself with a phone call instead. He could have kissed his clients a dozen times over for, when he told them why there was such chaos and why he was all at sixes and sevens, no one made a fuss or complained. Even better, two clients had gone out and bought presents for the puppies – squeaky toys from one and a super padded basket on short legs from the other. Gill could not wait to get home and show them to Justin.

One of his last customers was Eveleigh Brenton, who had come in for a rare hairdo since, as she explained, she'd been invited out for drinks at the Lucketts' – what Gill would give to be invited there.

'Mixing with the smart set are we, then? Lucky you! But you're heaven sent and no mistake,' said Gill as he wielded brush and dryer. 'Our Sadie had her pups last night – no I tell a lie, this morning. Five little sweethearts.'

'That's a relief for you. It's always a worrying time with a bitch's first whelping. It could go either way.'

'We'll never let her go through that again, poor love. I tell you, Mrs Brenton, Justin and I felt every pang. It was awful.' He shuddered dramatically. 'We both looked at each other and guess what, we said it in unison, "Never again," we said. Isn't that extraordinary?'

'You will be careful when selling the pups, won't you? Make sure they go to good homes?'

'We shall inspect them ourselves, we've already decided. Mind you, three of them are spoken for already and we'll keep one, so that only leaves one. This time we're determined to win Best of Breed. And to think it's all thanks to you, we'd never have thought of showing or breeding from Sadie if it hadn't been for you. How do we choose the one we'll keep? I promised Justin I'd ask you.'

'Honestly, I can't help you there. At this age it's almost impossible. But even a few weeks on it's difficult. It's an instinct, I suppose. I look at a litter of my St Bernards and I just know which one it is, I feel it here.' She clutched her cardigan to her bosom.

'Bet you're never wrong.'

'No, never,' she answered, modesty making her bow her head.

His last client gone, the shop shut, Gill cashed up. He had seen the fountain gang lurking about during the day. He did not fancy walking alone across the market square to the bank's night safe with the day's takings. As a precaution he slipped the cheques, notes and cash into a handbag he had bought once in Italy, and which he had given up using here in Shillingham because of the comments it caused. He wound the strap three times round his wrist before locking up and setting off, loaded with the puppies' bed and toys.

The gang were just about to go; the last bus to Morristown was due in ten minutes.

'One of the poofters coming, on his own!' yelled Ginger.

'Get him,' called Butch.

'Too fucking right,' shrilled Amber.

Gill heard them and felt his guts turn to water. He put his head down and walked quickly, hugging the walls of the perimeter of the square. One jumped him from behind, two from the front and another tugged at the bag. He hung onto the strap for grim death. But the puppy bed got stamped on and the contents of the bag of squeaky toys were kicked all ways.

'Fucking let go or I'll kick your bleeding poofter head in,' Butch snarled, sounding his most ominous. To help, Ginger stood on Gill's hand and Snotty kicked him in the side. Gill let out a shout of pain.

'Go boil your balls,' he yelled with foolhardy courage, and then paused for a split second for dramatic effect. 'That is, if you've got any!' He was rewarded by another vicious kick in the side.

'Leave him alone, for God's sake!' a girl shouted and Gill, through the pain which was distorting his vision, saw a young blonde-haired girl in jeans and a duffel coat.

'Wet cow!' Shelley shouted.

'He's never done anything to you lot,' Kimberley retorted. She could turn a blind eye to the shoplifting, she couldn't watch this. They had never physically attacked anyone before, bar the odd shove and punch. This made her feel sick.

'He's a sodding queer,' Greaser sneered.

'You a fag hag?' Snotty asked.

'Gay, if you don't mind.' Even as he said it he knew it was stupid of him, but somehow it had just slipped out. Gill tried to curl himself up to protect himself against another kick. Instead Butch laughed. Not a small laugh, nor a sinister laugh, but a loud and happy laugh.

'You've got to hand it to the geezer – queer as he is, he's got guts. Leave off Ginger, Snotty, Greaser. Come on . . .'

Butch ran off and the others followed like lemmings. Only Snotty and the girl remained.

'I'll get you, don't worry, you disease-ridden shitbag,' Snotty spat at Gill before he, in turn, ran away.

'Thanks, miss,' said Gill, as he got painfully to his feet. 'You probably saved my life.' He picked up the broken bed; she helped him collect the squeaky toys.

'Don't be silly, they wouldn't have done that, they're not all bad, you know. They don't usually . . .'

'Beat up queers?' At least she had the grace to look embarrassed. 'Not bad? You could have fooled me,' Gill said with feeling, but grinning at her.

She smiled back, but she wasn't smiling later in the bus when both girls attacked her, pulling her hair, spitting great gobs of phlegm on her and splitting her lip into the bargain, telling her never to turn up at the fountain again, or they'd really dust her up. The other passengers sat huddled in their seats, studiously looking out of the windows at the dark night. The bus driver ignored the noise coming from behind. Kimberley stumbled off at her stop, the jeers of the two girls ringing in her ears. She limped along the road into the turning for Primrose Acre. At least she now knew how the homosexuals must feel. Although the square had been crowded with shoppers returning home, no one but she had come to his rescue, as no one had come to her aid on the bus.

When Gill eventually managed to hobble home, he tried to minimise what had happened to him.

'Don't fuss, Justin. I only walked into a bloody door.'

'You expect me to believe a door did this to you – just look at you, your jacket's torn and look at the state of your trousers!'

'I banged into the door and then fell down some stupid steps. Okay?'

'What door, what steps?'

Justin helped him out of his black coat, which was muddy and torn. 'I can do that,' Gill said sharply, having to fight the urge to cry out, for the pain was not being helped by Justin's tugging at the sleeves. All he wanted was to be left alone to soak for the rest of the evening in a hot bath.

'No, you can't. Whatever next? You didn't answer, you haven't said where you fell.'

'Christ, you sound like a nagging wife.'

'How would you know? Keeping something from me?' Justin looked at him, and then laughed with the confidence of one who knew all there was to know about his companion.

Gill's mind seemed not to be working. He tried to think of something to say to reassure Justin, but he felt as if his brains had turned to porridge. He felt dazed and muddled.

'There was no door or stair, was there?' Justin asked gently.

'Yes, there was – the store room . . .'

'Two tiny steps a mouse couldn't fall down – oh, my God, just look at those bruises!' Justin exclaimed as he removed Gill's Snippers T-shirt. Where he had been

82

kicked showed bright angry red, already beginning to discolour from the engorged blood. 'Stay put, don't move an inch!' Justin raced from the room, up the stairs two at a time to the medicine cabinet, found the witch-hazel and was back in a minute, kneeling, tending the bruises.

'I think we should go to the hospital. What if something's broken?'

'I'm pretty sure nothing is. Honest. It's worse than it looks. You know me, how fragile I am, bruise like a peach.' Gill started to laugh but had to stop because it hurt too much, and he wondered if a rib was cracked, but decided not to say anything.

'Come on, Gill, love. You're telling me porky pies, aren't you? Protecting me. It was those filthy louts, wasn't it? You were alone, they jumped you, didn't they?'

'Something like.' Gill felt too weary to continue to try to cover up the truth.

'I'm going to call the police.' Justin jumped to his feet.

Gill put out a restraining hand. 'No, Justin, don't. What would be the point? You know the police, they'd probably reward the little sods with medals for doing it.'

'But this is Shillingham.' Justin looked distressed.

'What sympathy are we likely to get from the fuzz? I don't care where they're stationed, they're all homophobes. Forget it. The yobs didn't get the money, thank God. Sad thing is they broke the puppies' present from Mrs Greenslade.' He nodded at the now very battered cardboard box which he had managed with difficulty to lug home.

'Maybe it can be mended. I'll try – the wonders of Superglue,' Justin said. 'A right one you are, you haven't even seen the little ones yet.'

'I'll make it up to them, promise.' Gill grinned weakly, stood up shakily and, with Justin for support, made his way to Sadie's nest behind the sofa. Sadie wagged her tail, with its pompom on the end, glanced up at him, gave a gentle bark as if to say she was happy to see him but she hadn't time for him just yet, and went back to grooming her puppies. 'Beautiful sight,' Gill said softly, smiling at the blind, snuffling little bundles. 'They don't even look like dogs yet, do they?'

'What a thing to say!' Justin admonished. 'Jim Varley popped in this afternoon to check them out and said they were all perfect. In fact he said they were the best litter he had ever seen,' he reported proudly as he poured Gill a large brandy. This wasn't strictly true, Jim hadn't said that, but it didn't stop Justin saying he had, for he felt that was what Jim *should* have said.

Justin pulled two chairs up and they sat, side by side, nursing their brandies and telling Sadie at regular intervals what a clever girl she was. Later Justin cooked them an omelette which they also ate, sitting on the chairs, beside her.

8
——

Thomasine woke to the sound of church bells. She lay in bed feeling very satisfied with the noise, for wasn't this one of the very things which made the countryside attractive to her? This was England, this was what expats dreamt about, and here it was, just up the lane, the bells ringing as if just for her. Ten minutes later, she was less sure and wished that there were a volume control button on the belfry. Further sleep was impossible, and even though she had planned a Sunday lie-in, she got up. Luna, who was moving more easily this morning, slid off the bed unaided and was able to negotiate the stairs herself.

Thomasine let the dog out on her own for the first time. While she waited for the kettle to boil she kept watch out of the window, afraid the dog might run off, but after a lengthy inspection of the garden, Luna returned and stared at the door imperiously. When Thomasine opened it she waddled past her and took up position beside her bowl, looking aggrieved that her breakfast was not yet prepared.

'So this is a dog's life, is it?' Thomasine smiled at the small creature as she mixed Weetabix and milk as if bidden. That done, she sat at the table with her tea and wished she'd something to read. She'd asked in the village shop if it was possible for the Sunday papers to be delivered and had been met with amused and somewhat condescending looks, as the woman behind the counter informed her she would have to go into Shillingham itself for those.

Later, in the bathroom, she studied herself intently in the mirror, wondering if the dramas of the past months were written on her face for all to see. She thought she looked much the same, but she was probably the last person to judge. She made a moue of her mouth to see if any lines had appeared since she had last checked, but there were none. She made her lips smile and was pleased that they were still well defined. The fine network of lines around her eyes she'd had for some time, and she accepted them, for what more could she expect at forty-three? But her eyes bothered her, for she was sure they sparkled less, had a wary look to them which had not been there before. In her misery she had eaten a mite too much and she knew she had put on two kilos, but did it show in her face? She turned this way and that, but couldn't decide. She relaxed; Nadine hadn't said anything, and she would be the first to comment if she thought her mother was getting fat.

Her appraisal finished, she decided that physically she had weathered the emotional storm reasonably well – then why did she feel so unattractive? She was aware she was still licking her wounds and that her self-confidence had taken a severe knock, but would she ever recover? On chat shows on television she'd often heard the expression 'lack of self-esteem' bandied about and had thought it meaningless. She didn't any more. Now she knew what it meant only too well; she felt as if she was nothing and of no interest to anyone – how could she be, when within her she knew she was a total failure? As a child she'd had a rag doll and one day, out of boredom, she'd removed the kapok stuffing – that's how she now saw herself, a husk of her former self.

'Find a lover,' her mother had advised glibly. It would be an impossible task for her – how could she search for a lover when, for a start, she was still in love with Robert and feeling about herself as she did, how could she expect anyone to be the least interested in her? It was an idea she did not even entertain.

She picked up a hank of her thick, dark-brown hair and wondered if perhaps the time had come to have it cut. There was nothing worse, she thought, than a woman hanging on to the past with a too-youthful length of hair and the same make-up she had worn when young. Maybe she'd find a hairdresser and have the lot off and restyled, maybe even have a fringe – after all, a new life required a new image. Yes, she'd do that next week. Meanwhile there was today to get through. She ran a bath.

With no husband to cook breakfast for, she could have a long leisurely soak in the bath. There were some advantages, she told herself as she soaped her arms. Positive thinking, that's what she must do a lot more of. The house was so quiet, she thought, as she lay back in the water and closed her eyes. She had wondered how she would feel with the quietness after the bustle of London, she had not dared hope she would find it as restful and calming as this, since everyone had said it would drive her mad – her daughter included. She smiled broadly at the thought of Nadine and her reaction to Thomasine's plans to move to the country. She had been adamantly against.

'You needn't expect to see me every holiday. I'd miss my friends.'

'Of course, darling,' Thomasine had said, but it did not stop her secretly hoping that after a visit or two Nadine would find new friends and interests here – that was a fond hope. In the way of such hopes lay problems – Chantal, Robert and the delights of London. Nadine and Chantal got on well. Thomasine knew that for Nadine's sake she should be pleased, but in reality she felt a jealousy which, no matter how much she reasoned with herself, refused to go away. One resolution she had made, and was determined to stick to, was that she was not going to make an issue over whether Nadine stayed with her or with *them* on her half-term and holidays from boarding school. That would be a recipe for disaster where a sixteen-year-old was concerned.

She'd never wanted her daughter to go to boarding school but had been defeated not just by Robert, but by Nadine herself. She had told her daughter it wasn't all fun and midnight feasts in the dorm and that she'd be homesick. She couldn't have been more wrong – Nadine loved her school from day one. Thomasine had felt hurt that she didn't miss her; not that she'd told anyone, she knew it was childish and selfish of her, and that she should be pleased for the child. But now she was glad Nadine was so content at school – not only had she missed the worst of the trauma between her parents, but, more importantly to Thomasine, there was no tussle over where she was to live full-time. Thomasine had a sneaky idea that Nadine would have opted for life with Chantal and Robert, and the humiliation of that would have been intolerable. Then the world would have known that she had not only failed as a wife, but as a mother too.

Everyone she knew had urged her strongly not to move to the country. To hear some of them talk, one would have thought she was moving to another planet. But she had stuck to her plans; she had felt it would be wise to get away from the area she'd lived in with Robert, surrounded by their many friends. She didn't want any of those friends feeling they had to take sides, as she herself had done too often in the past with other couples. She knew what it was like to be torn between 'him' and 'her'. Far better not to be around, far better to be Thomasine in the country. Those who were true friends would make the effort and visit her, and the others would send her Christmas cards. That way, friendships that mattered to her were likely to be maintained.

These same people had told her how lonely and miserable she would be, how making friends in the country was an impossibility. Well, they were wrong. The very day she had moved there had been a telephone invitation to drinks, which boded well for the future.

Now that day had arrived and Thomasine felt as nervous as any debutante. She wished she hadn't accepted; she was certain it was too soon; that she wasn't ready to meet new people; that she would clam up and make a fool of herself. Still, she had said she'd go and manners forbade her not to turn up.

Thomasine took some time deciding what to wear, unsure what people in the country wore for pre-lunch drinks. She finally chose a long, biscuit-coloured cashmere skirt to wear with highly polished brown boots, matching waistcoat and a rust-coloured silk shirt with a high collar. This expensive outfit always gave her confidence. She pinned a small topaz brooch at the neck, and out of habit put her engagement and wedding rings on her finger, then spent some time looking at them, wondering whether she should or shouldn't wear them any more. The trouble was that if she didn't her hands looked completely naked, as if there were something wrong with them, since the rings had lived there for so long. She tried them on the other hand but that didn't look right either. She got out her small jewel box and delved into it. Somewhere she had a topaz dress ring; it was large and would easily cover her wedding band.

Downstairs she found a contentedly sleeping Luna. What was she to do with her? She could hardly take her to a stranger's house, but she didn't like leaving her. She might wake up and find herself alone and get frightened. She supposed she could put her in the back of the car and leave her in it, but then she might get cold and catch a chill. She put a blanket in the dog basket she had bought yesterday in Shillingham, and one eye looked at her and closed again. 'Luna, it's for your own good,' she said. 'It's not a good idea to be sleeping on the floor in the draught in your condition. You should be in the basket in the warm, by the fire here, now come on!'

Ten minutes later she left, pleased that Luna had finally condescended to use her new bed. What she did not know was that as soon as her car had left, Luna slid out of the basket, pattered through to the sitting room, hauled herself up into Thomasine's favourite armchair, turned round three times and then curled up in comfort and was quickly snoring noisily and contentedly.

Thomasine stopped at Shillingham on the way and bought her newspapers. The weather was holding crisp, sunny and dry; if it wasn't for the dog, she would have gone out for a pub lunch. What a pain, she thought. Still, it wouldn't be long and she'd be free to do such things; as it was she had some nice pâté in the fridge and some white Mâcon. As she drove along she grinned at the idea that now she was alone she could eat a whole tin of fruit salad all to herself if she wanted. Robert would never have allowed the tins into the house, he would have thought her childish to want it. But she loved the feel of the slippery maraschino cherries sliding down her throat, and one of the first things she'd done when he left was to go out and buy a supply of them.

She found the Luckett house easily but, at the sight of half a dozen cars parked on the forecourt, she had to stop herself from bolting. In London once or twice she'd forced herself to go out alone, and that had been difficult, but here, to venture out among strangers was a terrifying prospect. However, there was to be no escape for her as her car stopped.

Ben Luckett came out on to the steps to welcome her. She admired his house and he said 'thank you' in the laid-back way of someone who was used to having his house complimented and was perhaps finding it all a bit of a bore. His wife, Cora, tripped towards her in an immaculately pressed, turquoise silk trouser suit. Costume jewellery clanked around her neck and on her ears, but the real thing was on her hands. Thomasine would have bet that Cora's underwear matched – she looked the bandbox type. Robert would have approved of that, for try as she might, Thomasine always ended up with mismatches – her knickers always seemed to wear out long before her bras. What a bizarre thing to think, she thought as she took Cora's hand in greeting.

'Mrs Lambert, I'm so pleased you could come. It's never easy moving into a new area, and I said to Ben as soon as I'd heard you had moved in, we must have that poor woman over and introduce her to some local people,' she said kindly, though Thomasine could not imagine why she should be regarded as 'poor'. But she smiled nonetheless and thanked her. 'Now, come along in,' Cora said. Her high-heeled strapped sandals, scarlet toenails peeping out of the front, click-clacked across the ancient flagged floors of the Elizabethan house. 'They're all in here – everyone's slurping away, and they're dying to meet you.'

They entered a large, beautiful room. In the fireplace, the surround of which was ornately carved stone, Tudor roses in both spandrels, was a roaring log fire. Cora flitted about her guests like an exotic bird, busily introducing Thomasine, bracelets jangling, diamonds flashing. She introduced at such a rate, so quickly, with the confidence of someone who knew everybody there, that Thomasine feared that she would soon have everyone in a muddle – except of course for the vicar, whose collar was a useful means of identification. She had a flash of guilty embarrassment that she hadn't been to matins, and then wondered why – she never went to church. He was a quiet, rather ineffectual man, in stark contrast to his wife who, for some inexplicable reason, she had expected to be dowdy and plain, but who had an intense expression on her intelligent, rather attractive face. She was as smart as a button and ran a consultancy business in Morristown, she told Thomasine.

'Consultancy in what?' Thomasine asked.

'Man-management,' said the vicar's wife, Charlotte, with a snapping of jaws which would have put the fear of God into any man, Thomasine thought. Asked what she did, she 'Ahhd' and dithered a second too long and the vicar's wife, impatient with her uncertainty, swung smartly about and left Thomasine still wondering if it would be presumptuous to say she was a book illustrator.

'I'm Fee Walters.' A woman about her own age, who had witnessed Thomasine's discomfort, approached. She explained she was a farmer's wife from the other side of Shillingham. 'Don't take any notice of Charlotte, she's an arrogant bitch. But her husband's rather a sweety, if terrified of her,' she said quietly. Thomasine introduced herself. Finding someone smiling, open, and apparently interested in her, she felt herself relaxing sufficiently to say she 'hoped' to illustrate children's books, even though she said it in a whisper so that the others couldn't hear. Fee, also whispering, confided that she'd written one.

'Just for my kids at bedtime, you understand,' she said, looking flustered.

'The best ones often are. I'd love to see it, if you wouldn't mind.'

'Mind . . . ? I'll bring it over tomorrow before you change your mind,' Fee laughed as Cora grabbed hold of Thomasine's hand and dragged her away.

'This is my step-daughter, Sophia. You've pots in common, she's a Londoner too,' said Cora.

'I'm not a Londoner, Cora dearest, I happen to live there,' Sophia said, her teeth very slightly bared. Thomasine, who had started off for this drinks party feeling pleased with her outfit, began to feel not necessarily untidy, but not as smart as she had thought. Sophia was immaculately dressed from head to toe in muted grey. She was beautiful, with the fine-boned, fine-skinned, fine-haired litheness of some English beauties, and, glossy with confidence, made Thomasine feel immediately inadequate.

'I hear you've bought the old school house, absolutely charming *little* building, I do envy you it.' She smiled such a ravishing smile that Thomasine wondered if the emphasis on 'little' was deliberate or whether she was being a twinge paranoid. 'I do hope you are very, very happy here. My father, I know, will go out of his way to make your time here as pleasant as possible. It's a wonderful place, absolutely wonderful.'

Thomasine, though wondering if she wasn't over-selling the Shillings a little, was at the same time completely thrown by Sophia's high-wattage charm, and mumbled a sort of 'thank-you'.

Sophia introduced Thomasine to a tall woman who, at first sight, looked rather on the fat side, but in fact wasn't. It was her hairy tweeds that made her look far larger than she was; tweeds of an alarming mustard colour.

'Mrs Brenton,' said Sophia. 'Eveleigh is a bit of a celebrity around here, she's one of the dog world's most prestigious judges.'

'Oh really, Sophia, please. You go too far.' And the woman looked gauche and embarrassed, which did not marry well with her height, nor the tweeds.

'But it's true, Eveleigh.' Cora interrupted. 'If you've any problem with your dogs, phone Eveleigh – don't bother with old Jim Varley here, he's only the vet.

Eveleigh knows far more than he does, don't you, Eveleigh?' And she playfully pushed Jim to show him it was just a joke.

'Oh for goodness' sake, Cora, what a thing to say,' said Eveleigh, looking bothered. Jim, standing beside her, laughed good-naturedly.

'Hello, Mrs Lambert, we meet again,' said Jim. 'And Cora's right, if you've got a St Bernard or a King Charles, Eveleigh is the person for you. Breeders tend to know the intricacies of their particular breed of dog, as much as the vets do.'

She didn't think he was being defensive, but she looked at him again to check. He smiled at her and she decided he was not, he was just being patient. 'How's the little bulldog?' he asked.

'Asleep. All she seems to do is sleep.'

'You have a bulldog?' Eveleigh's face became animated with a genuine interest. 'You don't see many of them about these days – I love a good bulldog, my grandfather had one, you know.'

'Really? Everyone's grandfather seems to have had one.' Thomasine laughed, looked at Jim and smiled. He longed to be able to grab the smile and take it home with him.

'Mrs Lambert acquired this one by accident, and it's pregnant, probably not by another bulldog.' Jim explained.

'Do you think that's going to be a problem for her?' Thomasine asked Eveleigh, just making conversation. And then realising how rude she must sound to Jim, apologised with a tentative smile towards him. He shrugged his shoulders as if he understood. She hoped he did – she liked him.

'Well, not necessarily,' Eveleigh paused, seemed to rock on the heels of her sensible shoes, took a deep breath, paused again and then launched herself into the explanation. 'If she mates with a Great Dane she's not going to produce Great-Dane-size dogs, she's a bulldog so nature would have to adjust the size of the puppies to fit a bulldog's uterus, or they would not go to full term. There's a problem once they're born, oh dear me, yes. How do you get rid of them? I do sincerely hope it hasn't been mated with one of the banned breeds. So reprehensible. You see, the original pit bulls were the result of a bulldog being mated with a terrier. With a bulldog you have enormous strength, tenacity and, above all, courage – you'll never hear a bulldog yelp or whine. But pit bulls, by law, are neutered so that they will eventually die out as a breed. What is to stop an unscrupulous breeder trying to create a new fighting dog? Say, breeding pit bulls back with bulldogs and then the result with another breed – an Alsatian, say, or a Staffordshire – to confuse the authorities. A dog which doesn't look anything like a pit bull, but has its characteristics – I mean, the consequences are quite terrifying, especially when you think of the damage already done in dog fights. A dreadful world we live in!' she said with deep feeling, and then put her hand over her mouth. 'Oh, dear me, I do apologise, but get me onto the subject of dogs and I do tend to go on.'

'We're quite used to you and the subject, Eveleigh dear.' Sophia, though smiling as she spoke, did not put sufficient warmth into it to remove the sting of her words. Thomasine felt sorry for the woman as she visibly blushed with confusion.

'But what will the puppies look like?' Eveleigh, concern for dogs overcoming confusion, looked anxious at the prospect. Not as anxious as me, thought Thomasine.

'Dog fighting? But not round here, surely?' Thomasine asked tentatively.

'Everywhere, I'm afraid. Wherever there's man there's cruelty,' said Jim. Sophia linked her arm in his in a proprietorial manner.

'Now please stop all this dog talk, Jim. I absolutely

forbid it. I tell you, Mrs Lambert, whenever these two get together it's all they talk about.'

'I suppose Oliver took Bandage,' Eveleigh said, bluntly, unaware that she might be stepping on toes.

'No, of course not! I couldn't let darling Bandage go, he's like a child to me – it would break my heart to lose Bandage,' said Sophia, managing to look beautiful and tragic at the same time. Eveleigh looked up sharply.

'I'd have thought it would have broken *Oliver's* heart, more like. He adores that bull terrier.'

'The one thing you can say about Oliver is he's not selfish and he realises I need the dog more than he does, for protection you understand.'

'I didn't realise you even liked the dog, Sophia. I thought you said it was ugly,' Eveleigh persisted.

'Well, it is ugly, isn't it? You can hardly call a bull terrier a beautiful object.'

'Oh, I don't know,' said Eveleigh. 'He's got a fine head on him, and I particularly like Bandage's eye, a good set to the eye there, a cunning mischievous eye he has.' She laughed at the thought of the black dog, which she'd always rather liked. 'But what is ugly to some is beauty to others. Take Mrs Lambert's bulldog, now. I've heard people without number find a bulldog ugly, and I think they're one of the loveliest-faced dogs in the world. Don't you agree, Mrs Lambert?'

'I haven't given it any thought,' Thomasine said lamely.

'Oh, I couldn't agree with you, Eveleigh, bulldogs are monstrous compared to Bandage,' Sophia said blithely.

And Thomasine felt an illogical surge of anger with the woman, and wished she'd defended Luna's looks instead of sitting on the fence.

'Well, anyway, who owns Bandage is settled and that's it.' She clung harder to Jim's sleeve, and Thomasine found herself very confused about all this talk of an Oliver whilst she so obviously belonged to Jim.

'Well, you could knock me over with a feather, that's

the last news I would have expected about Bandage,' said Eveleigh, apparently unprepared to drop the subject.

'It would have to be a very large feather, Eveleigh.' Sophia trilled a laugh, and quickly recovering the slip she had made, removed the very slightly spiteful expression from her face, and replaced it with her expert smile. 'Oh that was rude, Eveleigh, do forgive me.'

'Nothing to it. It's the truth,' said Eveleigh gruffly, though Thomasine was pretty sure she was a little upset.

'Anyone fancy seeing my new foal?' Ben had joined them.

Glasses were drained and coats retrieved as they obediently trooped out after their host into the yard. Thomasine was lagging behind; she had no interest in horses. Even less interest than she had in dogs, she told herself wryly. Jim waited for her to catch up.

'Don't like horses as well as dogs?' he asked, and the tone of his voice told her that he was teasing her.

'Not really. Years ago we went to stay on a farm of some friends of my mother and there was a Meet and I got kicked by a big brute, which then reared up, bolted, threw the rider, jumped a fence and fell over with a crash I'll never forget. I've never felt the same about them since. I don't mind watching them at a distance but I don't like to get too close.'

'I know exactly how you feel,' he said. 'There's no need to get too close, they're in their stables. It's a pretty little foal, you'll like her.'

They fell into step, dawdling behind the others, but they were not alone for long, for Sophia turned back and joined them, once again linking arms with Jim.

'Oh look, there's darling Bandage.' She pointed to the far end of the yard where a black bull terrier was on a lead held by a heavily-built man with grey hair and piercing blue eyes. The man was having to drag the reluctant dog towards them. 'Oh, Rudie, has he been naughty?'

'Not what you'd call co-operative, miss,' the man replied. Sophia did not introduce them.

'Darling Bandage,' she gushed, bending down to the dog who reversed smartly from her outstretched hand. 'Sulky thing,' she said, laughing.

'Bandage, here.' Jim patted the side of his leg and, with tail awag, the dog went to him gladly.

9

Gill lay under the goose-feather duvet and thanked God it was Sunday, because he felt he had been hit by an articulated lorry. Moving gingerly, he lifted his pyjama jacket and inspected his bruises, which were turning lurid purple and green.

'My, you look like a living Turner,' Justin said, also inspecting the gang's handiwork, as he placed Gill's breakfast tray on the bedside table. Justin had insisted Gill have breakfast in bed with the Sunday papers. In fact, they had lain arguing about where Gill was to eat for a good half an hour, and Justin had finally won. 'See,' he pointed to the tray. 'That's the first sprig of forsythia from the garden, blooming just for you. Poor dear.' And he patted the pillows up fat and comfortable. 'Now you take your time.'

'But I want to be downstairs.'

'You owe it to the puppies to get well quickly,' Justin insisted. 'Now rest!'

He didn't. As soon as he had eaten, he hauled himself out of bed. He'd have liked a bath, but quickly realised that that might be too difficult for him to climb into, so he took a shower instead. He dressed in his designer jeans and tasselled loafers, put on his Simpson's cashmere sweater in navy blue, a birthday present from

Justin, and creaked his way down the stairs, hanging onto the banister for grim life.

After a quick inspection of the puppies, who were all asleep, Gill found Justin preparing lunch in the kitchen, and sat on a stool and watched him, offering too much advice, and being told so. It was to be a special lunch, a celebration lunch of smoked salmon, a cheese soufflé, which was Justin's *pièce de résistance*, a crisp green salad and a perfect Brie, to be washed down with chilled bottles of Tokay. It was a celebration because their friend Martin was coming with his new friend Stevie, whom neither of them had yet met and whom they were agog to know. It was Martin's dog, Bubblegum, who had mated with Sadie.

When Martin had brought Bubblegum to the house to mate it had been a shade touch and go at first. They had let the dogs out onto the patio to make friends, but they might have guessed that their classy Sadie wasn't going to give herself too easily. At first she had appeared not to be interested in Bubblegum.

'It isn't going to work,' Gill had said, not too sure if he wasn't rather pleased.

'Give them time. You get some bitches like this. After all she doesn't know what to do, does she?' Martin said confidently.

'Of course she does, she's not thick. She just doesn't fancy him – it's obvious,' Justin had blurted out without thinking. It was as well that Sadie chose that moment to raise her tail rigidly in the air and turn her rear end to Bubblegum in a gesture of invitation. Otherwise Martin, having a very short fuse, might have taken the huff and removed his dog forthwith.

As it was it was not to be easy, for every time Bubblegum got close to her, Sadie snapped at him and stalked off, only to repeat the dance a moment later. It was frustrating – but then, both Justin and Gill later admitted to each other, they were rather proud of Sadie playing hard to get.

Then suddenly, there was a great flurry and it had happened – Bubblegum had mounted Sadie, they turned and were locked, and Justin couldn't watch and had to rush indoors and busy himself in the kitchen to take his mind off what was going on outside.

The mating successfully concluded, Martin had opted to take the pick of the litter in lieu of a stud fee. He did not normally do this, he told them, but he would in this case. For one, Justin and Gill were old friends from the London days. The other reason was he too had just missed Best of Breed with Bubblegum, at Crufts, the year after Sadie's failure. The three friends were now determined to breed the perfect miniature poodle puppy to win not only Best of Breed, but the championship too. Now the litter was here, and today, therefore, was a momentous celebration.

Their guests arrived. Stevie was not at all what they expected – he was on the lean side, when Martin normally liked them quite butch, and was taciturn, bordering on boring. Perhaps he was thick, Gill thought.

After the flurry of welcomes and a quick peep at the puppies, they sipped their Kir Royals as Justin set the table and Gill played down the events of the night before.

'Shall I get Dad in to see his puppies?' asked Martin.

'Should we?' asked Gill. 'Sadie might not like another dog too close – it's too soon.'

'She seems calm enough,' Martin said. 'And she's always struck me as being a placid sort.'

'Oh, let's!' Justin said. Martin went out to collect Bubblegum from his car.

While they waited for him to return, the contentment and happiness of the day became somewhat marred. Whereas Sadie had not minded Justin and Gill near her puppies and had been very polite to Martin as well, she took an instant dislike to Stevie when he bent down as if about to pick up one of the puppies. Sadie let out a low rumbling growl that grew in volume, like the sound of distant thunder getting nearer.

'What's your problem, old girl?' Stevie said cockily.

'I don't think you should try to touch the puppies,' Gill advised.

'I've been handling dogs all my life. And in any case . . .' But they were not to know what it was he intended to say for Sadie stood up, puppies tumbling from her nipples. Her hackles rose, her lips stretched back tight, her teeth bared as she stood guard over her family.

Stevie decided that he was not going to be beaten by a dog, and put his hand down again towards the pups. Sadie flew for him in a snarling, growling, spitting flash of white. Her teeth sank into his arm and although both Justin and Gill ordered her to let go, she was deaf to their calls. Stevie was screaming blue murder when Martin, all smiles, entered the room with Bubblegum – off the lead.

At sight of the male dog, Sadie let go of Stevie, who lashed out with a kick at the passing bitch. Enraged, Justin swiped him, hard. Martin bellowed with anger at Justin and Gill told him to shut up. It was at this point Sadie, a typhoon of fury now, made contact with Bubblegum. The two white dogs were a welter of flailing legs, snarling, spittle was flying and the noise of growling was awesome.

'But, Sadie, that's your husband!' Justin cried ineffectually. 'You'll get hurt!'

'Hurt? Hurt?' Martin shouted. 'What about my dog? Vicious bitch!'

'It's your fault, I told you not to bring that brute in here,' Gill said, raising his voice above the racket.

'Bugger the dogs. What about me?' Stevie wailed.

'Oh, shut up!' the other three said in unison.

The dogs rolled around the room. The men raised their feet to protect themselves. Tables were knocked over, lamps fell and short-circuited, pictures, nuts, knick-knacks rolled hither and thither. The jug of Kir went flying.

With the three men shouting in panic, Stevie howling, and the dogs fighting, it was difficult to say who was making the most noise. The racket did not stop until Bubblegum, larger by half than Sadie, rolled submissively onto his back, waving his legs in the air.

Sadie, a shade wet from Bubblegum's slobber, but without a mark on her, gave one more growl as if making certain he wasn't shamming. Then, with amazing dignity in the circumstances, she stalked back to her litter. There she nudged the puppies with her nose, making room for herself, lowered herself carefully amongst them, allowed them to suckle again and looked as if nothing untoward had happened.

The room was in chaos, the soufflé had collapsed, Martin was beside himself with rage and Stevie was crying after Martin had told him not to be such a wimp. Gill, limping, escorted them to the door.

'If my dog's damaged you'll pay the vet's bills, and you'll be hearing from my solicitor.'

'Don't talk such rubbish, Martin. You shouldn't have brought the dog in, I told you. He's not hurt,' Gill said.

'He's limping.'

'So am I, but I'm not croaking it.' Gill, exasperated, turned his back on the guests and exaggeratedly hobbled back into the house.

'What about that then?' said Gill as he entered the room. 'Wasn't Sadie magnificent – defending her family, that's what she was doing. He didn't even get to choose a puppy.'

'Too soon really,' said Justin, trying to create some order from the shambles which was their drawing room. 'Jim said it would be too early to choose, I asked him. A good month needs to go by, he reckoned. Oh, Gill, I feel all shaky.' He sat down with a bump. 'I was so frightened she would hurt herself.'

'Not our Sadie, she moves too fast. The way she flew

at Stevie! I always said that dog had good taste, I didn't like the look of him one little bit. Trouble with Martin, he always liked a bit of rough.' He laughed, trying to cheer the shivering Justin. 'Mind you, I've never been that keen on Martin either. I think he's out for all he can get.'

'You never said before.'

'Well, you know me, Justin. I don't like gossip or spite, but I reckon Sadie recognised him for what he is.'

'The lunch is ruined,' Justin said miserably.

'Nonsense, there's still the smoked salmon and cheese, and we've got another bottle of Tokay.' Gill bent down to touch one of the puppies. 'Just checking you still trust us, Sadie.' Sadie licked his hand in answer.

April

10

Alan Farmingham stood at the French doors of the semi-detached house on the edge of Morristown and looked at the overgrown garden with a sense of satisfaction. If the sale went through then putting it right would be the responsibility of somebody else, not him.

He turned and, still standing with hands in pocket, looked thoughtfully at the room he'd known all his life. It was shabby, even more than he remembered. In one corner the dado was detached and hung loose. On the far wall he could see the stain made by the coffee when his mother had hurled her cup at him in a drunken rage. He could remember the cup hurtling towards him and his ducking, but not what the argument had been about – how could he remember, there had been so many rows that they had melted into one great sense of unhappiness.

He crossed to the red-brick fireplace. The mantelpiece was stepped: on the bottom matching shelves stood two brass candlesticks, on the next shelves two china dogs, the head of one detached and lying beside it. On the top, in the clutter, his mother's pride and joy, the skeleton clock her husband had given her one birthday, stopped now and covered in dust. Behind it were stuffed a pile of envelopes. He carefully removed and glanced through them – mainly bills and circulars, and a couple of letters from him.

He looked at the furniture: an ugly bulbous table and matching sideboard; two armchairs, one either side of the fire, one barely used, the other worn and torn and with a grease mark where his mother's head had rested. He shuddered. He'd keep the clock, the rest could go.

He crossed the room and entered the kitchen, found

himself some instant coffee and made a cup. He supposed he'd have to steel himself to go through her things, sort out her papers, her clothes, when his instinct was to burn the lot.

He sat at the tin-topped kitchen table and wondered where he'd find the energy to do any of it. He was still recovering from septicaemia, picked up while on undercover work in Spain – he'd been involved in a scuffle and had cut his hand deeply, allowing the invading bug to enter. While he was in hospital in London, his mother had suddenly died. He had made it to the funeral – the only mourner – and was now convalescent. Some convalescence! He was here because, unexpectedly in the current market, the house had quickly sold. He'd reasoned he could convalesce here just as easily as in his flat in Horsham while he packed up his mother's possessions.

What he hadn't been prepared for was how sad being here made him feel. Last night, when he'd arrived, it was odd not to hear his mother call out. Too many memories came flooding back, and not happy ones either – there'd never been many of them.

He'd go out today, no need to begin packing up immediately. It was a lovely April day, he could have a pub lunch, relax a bit.

Upstairs, he wandered into his old back bedroom. He looked down on the garden next door; neat and tidy, not a rabbit hutch in sight. He wondered where Mr Humphrey was now – dead probably. It was, he supposed, thanks to the old boy he was doing the work he did. He'd only been eleven when he had anonymously reported Mr Humphrey to the RSPCA for neglect of his rabbits. He'd watched, from this very window, when the inspector, who'd called in response to his tip-off, told the neighbour off in no uncertain terms, and then gently placed the rabbits into clean boxes and put them into the back of his van. 'You'll be hearing more about this,' the man had said to the neighbour, who was so frightened and guilty he'd not even bothered to protest at his rabbits being removed. And at that moment Alan had known what he wanted to be when he grew up – an RSPCA inspector.

There was no stopping Alan after that – any dog tied up and left howling; any cat up a tree; any badger at risk from baiting; any donkey with rotting feet: all had reason to be grateful to Alan's eagle eye as he toured the area on his bicycle, searching out animals in need.

'Bloody little St Francis of Assisi, aren't you?' his alcoholic mother had sneered at him. 'Pity you don't care as much for your poor old mum as you do for those sodding animals,' she added wistfully, as she invariably did when in her cups.

Alan, as always, ignored her. He felt no responsibility for what had happened to her, though she often tried to blame him.

'If it hadn't been for you I'd have been the one to leg it,' she often said. He often wished she had.

He was dutiful in that he shopped for her – she'd long ago given up venturing out to the shops in the local precinct. When he came home from school he cooked for them both – if he had not, he would have starved alongside her. He always checked at night to make certain her cigarette was out and she would not harm herself, and to prevent her burning the house down in the night he removed her lighter and matches and took them into his own room. So befuddled was her state that she never worked out where they'd gone if, in the small hours, she fancied a ciggy. Each morning he put them by the cooker, and she always presumed she'd left them there.

There had, in the past, been a succession of 'uncles', none of whom stayed long. When very young he'd fantasised that one of them might stay and be a real dad to him, but it had not happened and so he had resigned himself to being fatherless. But as his mother's looks had faded, and she had become more unkempt, even the 'uncles' ceased.

He often wondered about his father and where he was, what he was doing. Of course Doris blackened his name at every opportunity, but Alan had learnt to ignore her. Stuck as he was he could not blame his dad for one night saying he was going out to buy a packet of cigarettes and never returning. He'd been eight then, eighteen years ago, but he could still remember the hysteria of his mother when her husband didn't return. He'd begun to regard his father as a wise and lucky man, and held no grudges against him.

Wishing to escape did not stop him feeling sorry for his mother. Sometimes he'd worried about the future and what they'd do if he fell in love and wanted to marry. But this had all remained a worry only, since he'd not met the right woman yet.

What had changed everything was when his mother became obsessively jealous of him and began to interfere with his life outside the home, for all the world as if she were his wife. She didn't like his friends. She nagged if he was late home. She insisted on knowing where he was, who with, and had even begun to phone his local to check he was there. She was making his life intolerable.

Everything had come to a head one Saturday, when he had planned to go into the centre of Morristown to do some shopping.

'I'm off, Mum, anything you need from the shops?' he called out to his mother.

'Nothing,' she called back. He supposed she was about to settle down to watch the wrestling on television, which she did every Saturday afternoon.

As he stood on the pavement outside Bata, talking to Gina Angelino, he was unaware that his mother was on the other side of the street about to go into Boots. He made a date with Gina, a girl he'd long admired but who was always seriously involved with someone else. He hadn't been able to believe his luck when he'd chanced upon her between affairs.

He rushed home to put his new jeans inside out in the washing machine to shrink and to look less new. He then had a long bath and a careful shave, wanting to look his best for Gina. He hadn't registered that his mother was not in the house when he returned. He was lying on his bed anticipating the evening to come when the slamming of the front door made him jump.

'Is that you, Mum?' he shouted.

'Whose else would it be?' she called back.

'I didn't know you weren't here,' he said, surprised since she never went out.

'It's not as if we live in blooming Blenheim Palace, is it?'

'What's that mean?'

'You can hardly bloody lose me in this rabbit hutch, can you?'

He heard her clatter into the kitchen and bang something on to the tin-topped table. Now what had he done wrong? he thought. He ran down the stairs in stockinged feet, into the kitchen, and went over to kiss his mother on the cheek. Not that he particularly wanted to, but it was a ritual that she liked. But this time she jerked her head sharply away from him. 'Surprised you've got any kisses left for your mum,' she said icily.

'I was only trying to say hello,' he said.

'Been busy saying hello today, haven't we?'

'What's wrong, Mum?' he said patiently, knowing full well something had annoyed her and that she would not rest until they had it out. 'What have I done?'

'How am I to know what you've done? I can't keep an eye on you all the time, can I?'

He glanced at the bags. There was a Tesco carrier bag and another from Boots.

'You've been into town?'

'Evidently.' She too looked at the bags.

'So? Why didn't you say? I told you I was going in. I

could have given you a lift, instead you carted all that lot back on the bus.'

'I don't like to ask. People should volunteer without being asked. I'm independent, I don't want to beg.'

Alan sighed inwardly. There was no point in sighing outwardly, for he knew his mother would pounce on that immediately as being a criticism of her. 'Mum, to ask your own son for a lift is hardly begging.'

She leant forward with a spiteful expression on her thin-lipped face. 'But you didn't ask me, did you? That's the whole point. It's always left to me to ask you, when all I want is for you to offer.'

'Sorry, Mum, I should have asked you.' He wasn't sorry, but what else was he to say? 'I just presumed –' But he was unable to finish the sentence.

'Presumed?' She leapt on the word. 'Well, maybe you shouldn't presume so much. Maybe *presuming* is the same as taking for granted.'

He sat down, took a cigarette out of the packet on the table and lit it slowly. 'Look, Mum, I don't want to row with you. I was thoughtless. I'll always ask you in future, I promise. Okay? I won't be in for tea, I'm going out.'

'Going out with that little wop tart, are you?'

'If you mean Gina, yes.'

'I hope you don't catch anything.'

'Oh for Christ's sake, Mum, I've known Gina since I was fourteen years old. We went to school together, remember? We're just going to the flicks.'

'Hm, and the rest no doubt.' She was busily and noisily unpacking her shopping, slamming the unit doors. 'I don't want you seeing that little whore.' She had stopped her task and stood looking at him defiantly, hands on hips as if daring him to disobey.

'Mum, don't push me,' he said slowly.

'You think you know it all, don't you?'

'No, Mum. But I know what I want and you can't stop me.'

110

'Oh yes I can. If you insist on whoring around, you needn't think you can stay here with me.'

He stood up, leant his hands on the table and looked her straight in the eyes. 'You don't mean that.'

She laughed. 'Oh yes I bloody well do. Test me.'

'There's no need, Mum. If that's how you feel, I'll go.'

'And where will you go?' Her voice was shrill but confident; she'd trapped him.

'To Horsham, if I'm lucky. There's a position in Special Operations open. I'd thought not to apply, that I shouldn't leave you, but thanks, Ma, you've made the decision for me – I'll go for it. If I get it, I'll move there. If not, I can ask for a transfer to another town.'

'No, Alan,' she shrieked his name, her voice hard with fear. He watched as the defiance changed to fright, her face seemed to sag, as if her flesh were melting. 'Don't leave me.'

'Sorry, Mum, you've gone too far this time. I choose my friends, not you.'

And he'd turned and walked out of the kitchen and out of the house. That which he had thought impossible had been made easy for him. Best would have been if, at the same time, he could have walked out of her life there and then. He couldn't. Nothing was ever as simple as that.

He'd applied for the job at Special Operations at the RSPCA headquarters in Horsham, had his interview, and then had to wait while other applicants were considered. Now he'd made the decision to go, the delay seemed to last for ever before he heard the position was his.

During this time his mother had waged a relentless campaign on his conscience, never for one day letting up. She cajoled, pleaded, screamed abuse at him. But his mind was made up.

'Just like your bloody father,' she screamed, her parting shot as he finally left.

He'd driven off and had had to stop the car a mile away from home for he was upset, far more than he had dared let her see. He was not like his father: for eighteen long and bitter years he'd cared for her, to the point of putting his own happiness second. At twenty-six, he'd looked at his future, seen how empty she could make it for him. Saw a lonely bachelorhood stretching ahead. No, he'd done not only the right thing, but the only thing. He'd restarted his car and moved on into his own future.

That had been over two years ago. After six years of conscientious work as one of the two hundred and eighty-seven local uniformed inspectors in England and Wales, daily investigating complaints of cruelty, enforcing the many laws relating to animals, sometimes successfully making the case that could bring the abuser to court, he had achieved his dream. He'd been selected to join the Special Operations Unit, a plain-clothes, often undercover group, regarded as the front line against cruelty to animals.

Set up in 1977 with four officers, it now had nine, and Alan was proud to be one of them. When he'd first joined he had enjoyed the seven-month training course, which had been hard and arduous. To all the learning and knowledge he'd acquired he had had to add new techniques. How to remain undetected, how to follow suspects and blend with the crowd, how to use all manner of modern surveillance equipment. He'd been taught subtle interviewing techniques; new legislation caused by entry into the EEC. His driving had, of necessity, to be more professional, more advanced, since often they were called upon to tail vehicles. He'd learnt to deal with boredom as, with a colleague, he pounded up and down the motorways chasing suspects. He'd learnt to control a slight feeling of claustrophobia when doing surveillance work in the cramped van with one-way windows they often used. He'd learnt to do without sleep and his stomach had become accustomed to getting food, and too often junk food, at irregular hours. Hardest of all, he had to learn to control, and to somehow distance his mind, when witnessing cruelty to the animals he loved. When working undercover they must not by a grimace show any disgust, anger or sadness at what they were seeing.

He'd trailed sheep to Spain, helped uncover a cock-fighting ring, worked with those trying to end the trade in exotic birds. More mundanely, in plain clothes, he'd patrolled markets the length and breadth of the country. Wherever there was a rumour of cruelty Alan and his unit would be hot on the trail. It was a bit like being a soldier, he reasoned: hours of planning, hours of boredom, and then a few minutes of exhilarating excitement when a raid was on.

The only change in him in the past two years was knowing that he wanted to settle down. Never having had a normal family upbringing, he wanted a family of his own. He wanted someone to love as well as to love him. He had a rented flat in Horsham, close to the RSPCA headquarters, which he'd never quite succeeded in making 'home'. He'd like a place of his own. He'd reached that age when he wanted to plant his own roots.

Now here he was in Morristown again. He didn't want to stay in the town, he'd made that decision easily. Still, in an odd way he liked being back in the area – it was pretty outside the town, especially the Shillings. Maybe, while here, he'd look for a cottage by the river Shill to buy from the proceeds of this house. He could always rent it and maybe retire to it. At this thought he laughed: at his age, the very idea of retirement seemed light years away. Still, he reasoned, it might be a good investment.

Despite being on sick leave, in a roundabout way he

was working. There had been a spate of rumours of a new dog-fighting ring that had started up in the Morristown area.

Dog fights were numerous anywhere – in garages, farms, even in suburban back bedrooms. Normally only two dogs were brought to a venue to be matched. The size of the meeting depended on the ability and reputation of the dogs. Dogs who had proven their courage and skill could attract punters from as far afield as Ireland and Holland, with large sums of money changing hands in bets. The fights in the Morristown area were not, as yet, in this league and, as far as the inspectors could make out, it was a fairly amateur set-up, with several dogs being matched at one meeting. Given this, they had presumed it would be the easiest thing to uncover. The opposite had been the case. As soon as they'd received a good tip, then everyone, dogs included, seemed to disappear like morning mist.

Everything had gone quiet, and everyone hoped the ring had been disbanded. But just recently the rumour machine had begun to work again. As yet there was nothing sufficiently concrete to warrant the expense of the Special Operations Unit moving in.

'Still, Alan, since you'll be there anyway perhaps you could snoop around, see what you can find out,' Don, the Chief Superintendent and his boss, had suggested to him when, out of hospital, he'd popped into the office to check on his mail, and of course he had agreed. He'd said goodbye to Indy, the Jack Russell terrier who belonged to Jane, the Unit's intelligence collator, who was always in the cramped office at their headquarters. He wouldn't dream of going without patting the little dog like a talisman – it was superstitious of him, he supposed, but he still did it.

Alan looked at his watch. Most of the morning had passed with him lost in thought. He collected his keys and wallet. He'd go for a drive around the villages outside Morristown, he'd decided. Maybe he'd find the cottage of his dreams, rose-bowered and owned by a little apple-cheeked old lady who'd give it to him for nothing. 'Chance would be a fine thing,' he said as, whistling, he let himself out of the house and onto the unfriendly streets of Morristown.

11

It amazed Oliver that what at the outset seemed a simple solution could become such a complicated muddle.

What could be simpler than deciding to sell his house, give up his job and move to the country with his dog? Oh dear me no, he sighed to himself.

The past month had been a series of frustrations.

Wimpole had decided she wanted to go with him, then had second thoughts. Then decided again to go, and then went off the idea. Such vacillation would have tried anyone's patience to the limit, he told himself. When she changed her mind once more, Oliver flipped.

'For God's sake, Wimpole, you're like a bloody Yo-Yo. Make your mind up.'

'Do you have to be so bloody impatient? It's a big step I'm taking.'

'Impatient! Me? I've been positively saintlike with you, but even I'm reaching the point of having had enough. Either you come or no – it's make up your mind time.'

'Oh yes, and what happened to all that – *I won't go without you, Wimpole. Take your time. I love you*? Load of old cobblers, wasn't it? Just as I suspected. You only said it to bribe me.' She sniffed audibly.

'It wasn't. I meant it. But for heaven's sake, Wimpole, I've got to know one way or the other.'

'You're going then?'

'I'd like to.'

'I'll think about it,' she said, with infuriating smugness, and sailed out of the drawing room with head held high.

Oliver hadn't had much luck with estate agents either. It was an odd thing, but the house he'd bought from the self-same estate agent who had assured him what a highly marketable property it was had, in the five years he'd been here, become a difficult property to shift and not nearly as valuable as he had fondly hoped.

The worst hurdle, he'd anticipated, would be the one at work. He had spent many an hour in his bath, gin and tonic to hand, composing exactly what he'd say to his partners about wanting to opt out. He'd honed his speech to perfection.

Their reaction to his news came as a complete shock.

'We've been expecting it,' said partner number one.

'Amazed you've held on as long,' said partner number two.

'And of course you'll want your share at valuation paid out – no problem,' said partner number three, knocking the wind out of Oliver's sails.

'If you could give us a month of your valuable time before leaving, we'd appreciate it.' Partner number two swiftly dealt with what little wind was left.

His ego deflated, Oliver thought that at least his secretary would be sad to see him go. Instead she said it couldn't have come at a better time for her since, she announced with glowing pride, she was pregnant, and since she'd had a couple of miscarriages was taking no chances and was leaving immediately.

He'd not had any success over the return of Bandage either. The telephone rang and rang at Sophia's new house in London. Then he remembered she'd said she was staying with her father until the decorators had finished. But Ben said she wasn't there when he telephoned; he wasn't too sure whether to believe him or

116

not. He'd tried to make an appointment to see his lawyer, but he was away and he had to make do with his junior partner, a chap he regarded as a total prat. He wanted to know if he could file for custody of a dog, or was it only children one was permitted to fight over in law? This lawyer irritated Oliver immediately by saying that unless Oliver had written proof that the dog was his then it might be a little difficult to prove. Since Sophia had paid for the dog with her own personal cheque and the receipt had been made out to her, the litigation could be lengthy and expensive. He had looked at Oliver as if he were barmy, and Oliver had decided it was pointless pursuing the problem with him, since he was obviously not a dog owner and would, therefore, never understand the anxiety and urgency Oliver felt.

This interview depressed Oliver more than anything else. The furniture, pictures and household goods she had taken could all be replaced; their removal had been an irritant more than anything. But Bandage was something else. And he had to face the fact that if he could feel this devastated over his dog it only pinpointed how empty their relationship had become. He'd loved Sophia once, and she him. So where had that love gone? And why had they allowed it to escape and die? It saddened him that his marriage should end in the importance of who'd written what cheque and who was in possession of which receipt.

Finally, today, frustrated by it all, and feeling he was no longer needed by anyone, he'd decided to go home.

Upon opening the front door it was to find that, with Wimpole away, he had been burgled. He stood in the even more denuded drawing room and lit a cigarette and found he wasn't in the least surprised, at this point in his life he should have expected it. What little Sophia had left the burglars had taken, except for the larger paintings. Suddenly a strange lethargy had taken over, and wearily he climbed the stairs to his bedroom knowing full well that his several pairs of gold cufflinks would have been lifted and, no doubt, his Patek Philippe watch. At least he had the satisfaction of knowing the watch had stopped and needed to go back to the makers. He entered his bedroom: it was in chaos, the contents of his drawers littering the floor. In the bathroom he found written in lipstick on the mirror, 'What's happened to you, mate? Hardly worth the bother. But thanks all the same. Your friendly thief.'

If it was meant as a joke, it fell on very barren ground. All it did was to underline how impotent he was in handling his life at the moment. Other forces had taken control of him; he was like the toy soldier standing in a paper boat, being swept along a gutter to a drain, as in the fairy story, which had frightened him rigid as a child. That's how he felt, bobbing along and everybody else messing his life up for him. He knew he should call the police, but he couldn't even be bothered to do that. What was the point, with their abysmal success rate with burglaries? He wanted to get right away. He quickly packed an overnight bag, left a note for Wimpole to tell her where he was, and drove to Bishop's End, wanting to put space between him and London, in the hope that he would find a measure of peace and equilibrium there.

Grace White, his cleaning lady, was in the kitchen when he arrived. 'Since you haven't been here for the past three weeks I was sure you'd turn up this weekend. I thought I'd best pop up and dust round a bit,' she said, putting the kettle on instead.

'Sorry to disturb you,' he said.

'I was just finishing. I always brew up when I've done.' She poured two cups of tea. 'They said at the pub as you're thinking of moving in, permanent like.'

'Well, yes and no. I'm not sure.'

'Ah, I see. I just wondered in the circumstances . . . Your wife gone, like. . .' Her voice trailed off. 'That'll be a pity if you don't. When the house is empty it looks sad – as if it's missing your Aunt Phoebe. How she loved this house. I can hear her now – "Grace," she would say, "when I'm dead and gone you look after this place for me. Oliver means well, but he's useless about the house, like them all." She didn't go much on men, your aunt.'

'Didn't she?'

'No. All, that is, except for you. Real soft spot she had for you. She told me – I can hear her now, "you mark my words, Grace, he'll be here. He'll come here to live one of these fine days." And there was me hoping her prophecy had come true.'

'I didn't say that I wasn't, just that I haven't completely made my mind up.'

'Ah well. That's different. If you're thinking of moving back and you're wondering how you'll manage, like, I could give you another two days a week. I couldn't do no more than that because I already do for the vet over at Middle Shilling.'

'Could you? That would be very kind indeed.'

'That's settled then,' she said, sipping her tea contentedly, and Oliver felt again he was being controlled by others. 'You look right down in the dumps, Mr Hawksmoor. Since I'm here, would you like me to make you a nice little casserole or something for your supper?' she asked kindly.

'Mrs White, you're a wonder. Is the village shop open today?' he asked.

'It's early closing day today, Thursday. You'll have to go into Shillingham itself if you want anything.'

'I'll do that. Get some supplies in. Anything you need, Mrs White?'

'Well, if you're doing a shop, I would really appreciate . . .' Before he knew where he was, Oliver was armed with the longest shopping list it had ever been his responsibility to deal with.

Thomasine was running late. There was nothing unusual in this, Thomasine was often running late. In fact, if she thought about it, she seemed to spend most of her life chasing herself, never quite managing to catch up. She was in Shillingham a good two hours later than she had anticipated, doing a frantic last-minute shop, since Nadine was finally coming to stay for the run-up to Easter. It wasn't until she had opened the store-cupboard door and looked into the fridge that she saw that she had let the catering side of her life slip rather. And what little she had Nadine would not deign to eat. A year ago Nadine had suddenly announced that she had become a vegetarian. Thomasine, sensibly, had not battled with her over this, hoping that it was just another teenage phase which would disappear with time. But it had not, and Nadine was at pains on the telephone last night to remind her mother that she was still vegetarian and not to try to *trick* her. Thomasine had thought it was an odd choice of verb, but had chosen to ignore it.

She was also in a panic because her husband was coming too. She knew she should think of him only as Robert or her ex, but she couldn't – he was her husband. She doubted if she would ever be able to think of him in another way. She wanted everything to be perfect, just in case he accepted her invitation to stay to dinner. After all, she told herself, if she was lucky and he decided to eat with them, anything could happen later.

In her hurried shop she had stocked up with fruit, vegetables, lentils, eggs and cheese, as well as a couple of steaks for Robert and herself. Now she was relaxing in the black leather swivel chair at Snippers.

'Here on holiday?' Gill asked, as he stood behind her.

'No, I've just moved here. I've bought the old school house in Middle Shilling.'

'Pretty, the Shillings, aren't they? I often think that with the river Shill meandering through them, the way it does, and each village straddling it, they're like pearls and the river's the string.'

'What a nice idea.'

'So, what do we want done here?' And he picked up a hank of hair and held it up to the light and scrutinised it. Thomasine felt herself go rigid, waiting for the criticism to come. Waiting for the question that all hairdressers invariably asked: 'And who cut this last?'

'Wonderful condition,' he said instead. 'Good cut, too. London?'

'Yes. Do you know Frederico's in Bond Street?'

'Know it? I was virtually born there, my dear. Everything I know Frederico taught me.'

'If you could trim the ends – just a little off the bottom. I think I'd like it cut and restyled, but I'm in a bit of a rush. Another day, perhaps.'

'It suits you like this.'

'I've been wondering if I'm not a bit too old for long hair.'

'You?' Gill laughed. 'You've got the face for it, love. Look, Gill here promises.' At this, he dramatically put his hand on heart. 'When I think you've gone over the top for long hair, on my life, I'll tell you.'

Gill had been working for a few minutes in silence, which in itself was unusual for an hairdresser, when another client came up, smiled apologetically at Thomasine and patted the deeply concentrating Gill on the sleeve. 'Gill, any chance of buying one of your puppies?'

'Well, Mrs Prentice, there could be, and there could not. Maybe yes, and maybe no.'

'Thank you, Gill, that's very, very clear,' Mrs Prentice laughed.

'We've got a bit of a problem; the man whose dog mated with our Sadie, well, she took an instant dislike to him and chased him out the house, and we've no idea now whether he wants to claim his pick of the litter or if we're going to get a whopping bill. Do you see? So, if he doesn't want the puppy, yes we could quite possibly have one for sale, but if he wants it, I don't think so. But I'll let you know as soon as possible.'

'How many puppies did she have?' Thomasine asked as Gill returned to cutting her hair.

'We had five. Lovely they are. We're taking it in turns, my partner and myself, to stay home and look after them. You know, just in this early period. We want to make sure each gets its own share of food and what have you and that nobody sits on somebody and kills them. That would be awful, wouldn't it?'

'How old are they?'

'A month – it's gone by in such a rush.'

'I've just acquired a dog,' she said.

'Acquired? That's a funny word to use.' He stopped cutting and stood with scissors poised.

'Not really.' And she explained how Luna had come into her life.

'And she's pregnant too?'

'Yes, but because of the circumstances the vet thinks that probably they're not bulldog puppies, that they're, well, we used to call them mongrels, didn't we? Now they're cross-breeds.'

'You keeping her?' He was wielding brush and drier expertly.

'I didn't mean to – it's difficult,' she replied. She'd had Luna for a month now and had reached the point – dangerous, she knew – of not being able to envisage what life would be like without her.

'I couldn't imagine being without our Sadie. Lovely girl, she is. Light of my life. We have such fun with her, especially after we found out about showing and the time to be had there. We've met some lovely people, you wouldn't believe how wonderful dog people are. Kind, helpful. We love the shows, we've missed them since Sadie's been pregnant, you know. Once or twice we went, just to look-see, but it wasn't the same as when we had Sadie competing. But we'll soon be back. You ought to come along one day, you know, you'd enjoy it. Meet a lot of nice people. Takes you out of yourself.' He held the mirror up so she could see the back of her head.

Five minutes later, her bill paid, packages in her hand, she opened the salon door, stepped onto the pavement and crashed into a man, dropping her shopping bag as she did so.

122

'I'm terribly sorry,' she said, bending down, chasing and scooping up the oranges she'd bought. 'I wasn't looking where I was going.'

'Please, neither was I,' Oliver replied, stooping down to retrieve the apples and carrots for her. 'I see you like fruit,' he grinned.

'It's mainly for my daughter, she's become a vegetarian.'

'I did that once, so I could face the cows in the morning without feeling guilty,' he said, thinking what a lovely smile she had.

'I know what you mean. I think emotionally I'm a vegetarian, it's just that I love meat so much . . .' She looked down at the pavement, thinking how odd he must think her nattering away to a complete stranger.

'Exactly!' And he handed her back the carrier bag.

'Thank you so much,' she said, and walked hurriedly towards the car park.

Oliver watched her. What an attractive woman, he thought. Beautiful hair.

12

Jim Varley had always thought of himself as a calm man, but he was finding great difficulty keeping so this evening. The subject of his irritation was standing the other side of his examination table, on which cowered a pretty Blenheim King Charles spaniel.

Jim had explained to the man that the discharge the dog was suffering from was because it had an infection of the uterus. 'It's more common when a bitch gets older and hasn't been spayed,' he continued. 'But it can occur in a young dog like this one.'

'Spayed? What's that mean? Taking it all out, I suppose.'

'Well, yes.'

'If that was done, then she wouldn't bleed and make a mess on the carpet a couple of times a year?'

'She is a bitch – bitches come into season.'

'Yes, but my missus doesn't like it, neither do I. I mean, it's not nice, is it, on the carpets and on the floor? I've locked her in the shed before, 'til it was over.'

'I see,' said Jim, anger beginning to seethe in him. Poor little bitch, living in the house and then banished to a cold shed, no doubt she thought she was being punished for something. No wonder she was so nervous, he probably hurt her too. 'Still, poor girl can't help it, it's only natural. We can treat this infection, but I do strongly recommend that she has a hysterectomy, then it won't recur, so then the carpets will be safe.' The irony in his voice was completely lost on his client.

'And how much would that cost, this here hysterectomy?'

'Well, she's a small dog. Seventy-five pounds, say somewhere between seventy-five and a hundred pounds.'

'You must be joking!' The man blustered.

'No I'm not. It's a major operation for a dog. Major operation for a woman.'

'Well, I'm not bloody paying that!'

'Then the infection will probably come back again and could lead to a very unpleasant death. Of course, the decision is yours, but if you take into account repeated visits to me and my fees, the cost of the antibiotics required to clear up the infection, you'll very soon be looking at the same sum of money,' he said as patiently as he could.

'Oh no, no I'm not. Put it down.'

'I beg your pardon?'

'Put it to sleep. I don't want it, neither does the missus. It's the last bloody bitch we have, I tell you that, the trouble it's been.'

'I don't like putting down healthy dogs,' Jim said.

The man stepped forward as if to pick the dog up. 'Then I'll find a vet who is a bit more obliging.'

'Hang on. Let's calm down here a minute.' Jim put a restraining hand on the man's arm.

'Calm down? I'm perfectly calm.'

'Would you have any objection to me taking the dog and rehousing it?'

'I don't give a damn what you do with it, I don't want it.'

At that, Jim scooped up the dog, carried it out of the surgery, placed it gently in a cage in what he referred to as his hospital ward. 'Don't worry, I'll be back.' He patted the small dog on its head, and noticed that it had stopped shaking with fear. So he had been right, it wasn't him, it was her owner she was afraid of.

He returned to the surgery, where the man was still standing. 'I forgot to ask you, what's she called?' Jim asked.

'Amy,' came the reply.

'Fine, thanks.' Jim turned, as if to conclude the interview.

'There's just one thing, if you're keeping her, I mean, like, it's my dog, it's a valuable pedigree dog that.'

'You needn't think . . .' Jim interrupted, his fists balled with angry frustration. 'You're not suggesting that I pay you for the dog?' he asked.

'I don't see why not, if you intend hanging on to it.'

'That's no problem then, Mr . . .' He glanced at the notes. 'Smith.' A likely story, he thought. 'I'll put her down tonight after surgery, if you'll just sign this consent form giving me the right to dispose of the dog. I'll send you the bill. I presume you've given my receptionist your address?'

'Yes, sure,' said the so-called Mr Smith, looking shifty, as he grabbed the pen. He paused, ever so slightly, before writing his name, as if he had to think what to write, Jim noticed with quiet satisfaction.

'Well, that's fine then, isn't it? No problem,' Jim said,

willing the man to leave his surgery so that he didn't have to look at him. He had an almost uncontrollable urge to hit him hard in the face.

As soon as the man had gone, Tessa, Jim's assistant, came in.

'Who was that? He was so unpleasant.'

'Called himself Smith. Wanted me to put the dog down rather than pay for an operation.'

'Oh, I hate people like that. I want to kill them.'

Jim laughed. 'I know what you mean.'

'What're you going to do?'

'I told him I'm going to put the dog down.'

'Oh no!' she wailed.

'If you promise not to tell a living soul, I'm going to do a hysterectomy on her, once we've cleared up this infection. Highly unethical, probably.'

'I'd love to have her.'

'Tess, you've got five dogs already.'

'I know, but I often think there's room for one more.'

'No, Tess, it's not fair. You must spend all your wages on dog food.'

'My mum gets a bit fed up with it, but then she's an old softy too.'

'You needn't worry about this one, I might even keep her myself. I've always had a soft spot for King Charleses.'

13

Thomasine had promised herself that when Robert and Nadine arrived she would open the door after a decent pause and with a serene smile on her face. Instead, at the first ring of the bell she raced pell-mell towards it, skidding on the parquet.

'Nadine!' she said, opening her arms wide.

'Hi!' Nadine ducked under her arms, entered the hall and wandered off through the open door of the drawing room.

'Come in, do,' she said to Robert who was on the doorstep. 'Don't stand there. It's very kind of you to bring her, Robert.' She spoke in short, breathless bursts of excitement. Her heart pitter-pattered its betrayal. She wondered if she should proffer her cheek to be kissed, and wished he'd take the decision from her and kiss her himself. 'I'm sure she'd have been all right on the train, I'd have gone into Morristown to pick her up. It's no distance.' She knew she was prattling.

'I felt happier driving her. The trains aren't safe these days for young women,' Robert said, stepping into the hall, carefully removing his driving gloves and looking about him.

'But she's so sensible,' said Thomasine. She held out her hand for his coat, and mindful of the fuss he made of his clothes, hung it on a hanger in the small closet.

'I care about her,' Robert replied.

'And that means I don't?'

'You haven't made much contact with her,' he said accusingly.

'I've tried to. You know they don't like us phoning the school – I didn't want to make things difficult for her. But I've written.' She knew how defensive she sounded.

'You didn't call during her exeats.'

'She's welcome to come here any time – heavens, she's only had one weekend free of school.'

'That doesn't explain why you didn't telephone.'

'It was – I didn't –' She could not quite bring herself to tell him that she hadn't called because she could not face Chantal answering *her* telephone in *her* house. 'I didn't mind her going to you. She had things to do in London – I understood.' Thomasine took a deep breath, needing to control herself; it would be silly to start fighting again.

'You don't ask, you insist with children.'

127

'With children, yes, teenagers – no.' She managed to laugh, if only a small one. 'Still, she's here now, at last.'

'I had to bring her. There was no guarantee she'd have stayed on the train.'

'What does that mean?' She had been leading the way into her sitting room, but swung round to face him.

'She didn't want to come. I had to force her.'

It was as if he had hit her. 'Did you have to tell me that?' she asked.

'You always were incapable of facing reality, Thomasine.'

'I don't know, I think I've been doing rather well at that,' she replied, aware of the familiar constriction at the back of her throat which was always a prelude to tears.

'What are you two talking about?' Nadine appeared in the doorway.

'Just saying hi!' Thomasine replied gaily, and knew it sounded hideously false. 'Would you like a drink before you go back? Or some supper?'

'No thanks.' He glanced at his watch; she noticed it wasn't the one she'd given him years ago, but an expensive-looking gold one. Aware of her glance, he quickly shot his cuffs to cover it. 'Chantal will be waiting for me. It'll be a good hour and a half before I'm home.' She knew that her disappointment was etched on her face, but it was no good, she couldn't pretend. 'I'll have a small Scotch, though,' he said, in a more kindly tone, as if he'd registered her expression.

They joined Nadine, who was prowling around the sitting room. 'It's a bit small, isn't it?' she said.

'It suits me well enough on my own.'

'But you won't be on your own when I come and stay, will you?' the girl said sharply.

'We're hardly the size of elephants, are we? I'm sure there's room for both of us to manoeuvre around in here.' She ended the sentence on an upward tone, trying to lighten her voice, trying not to sound too irritated.

'You've made it look nice,' Robert said.

'Thank you.' She went into the kitchen to get some ice. Luna lifted her heavy head, sniffed the air, registered that there were other people in the house, and with a weary sigh, hauled herself onto her legs and padded through to the drawing room. Thomasine followed with the ice.

'Good God! What on earth is that?' said Nadine.

'It's Luna. She's a bulldog.'

'She's gross!'

'She's pregnant, that's why.'

'What on earth induced you to get a dog.' Robert looked with displeasure as the dog lumbered towards him, moving his position sharply as soon as Luna reached him and began to sniff.

'I like dogs,' Thomasine said emphatically.

'Well, that's news to me. All the years we lived together, you never said you wanted a dog.'

'What would have been the point? You wouldn't have wanted one, too messy. Both partners have got to want a dog.' She realised that she was beginning to speak slowly, as if to a child, but was, in fact, controlling her temper. She laughed so that he wouldn't take offence, and then wondered why she bothered.

'Couldn't you have got something that's prettier than that?' Nadine said.

'I think she's lovely. She grows on you, you know.'

'It would take a long time for her to grow on me,' said Robert.

'I thought you liked animals, Nadine. That's why you're a vegetarian.'

'I respect animals. I don't have to share my space with them.'

Robert tipped his glass, finishing his drink. 'I'd better be going.' He kissed Nadine's forehead and stroked her hair affectionately. 'Now let me know what you decide, as soon as possible, young lady.'

'Yes, Dad,' she said, smiling sweetly at him. Robert

did not kiss Thomasine goodbye, merely thanking her again for the whisky as she held the door open for him. Such coolness made her feel empty, almost as if she did not exist.

When she got back into the drawing room she meant to ask Nadine what her father wanted her to decide, but she didn't have time for she found Luna stalking her daughter around the room.

'Would you get her to stop doing that?' said Nadine, shoving the dog away.

'It looks as though she likes you.'

'I don't like her. I wish she'd stop it.'

'Oh, Nadine, don't be so silly. You're new, she just wants to get to know you. She's a very determined dog, you might just as well say "hello" to her and get it over with, then she'll leave you alone.' Quickly Nadine struck out with her foot, catching Luna on the underside of her large jaw. 'Nadine! Don't do that. Don't be cruel.'

'I didn't hurt her,' Nadine said.

'You wouldn't have to hurt her physically. You can hurt her feelings very easily, she's a very sensitive dog.'

'Oh, Mum, really!' said Nadine with exasperation. 'She's a dumb animal. What's for supper?' she asked abruptly, as if bored with the subject of Luna.

'I made a quiche. I thought you'd like that.'

'I don't eat eggs.'

'Oh, Nadine, you didn't say. It was supposed to be meat you didn't eat.'

'Well, I've stopped eating eggs, cheese and fish.'

Thomasine sighed with exasperation. 'What's left then?'

'Plenty. There's lentils, all the vegetables. Fruit. Nuts.'

'Quite honestly, Nadine, if you're going to be this difficult about what you eat, then I suggest that you get it for yourself.' Thomasine poured herself a large drink, her second, unusual for her this early.

Nadine sat down. 'What?' she asked, with an expression of surprise on her face.

'I didn't mind when I thought I could use cheese and eggs as well as fruit and vegetables. But now . . . I mean, I would have to buy a cookery book to do things for you, I'd have to learn how to create a balanced diet for you.'

'Chantal doesn't complain.'

'Chantal's new to the job and is still full of masses of enthusiasm. She'll learn,' Thomasine said with feeling, and immediately regretted it. 'I suppose I could knock up a ratatouille or something like that, would that do you? And some bread.'

'Fine. Where's my room?'

'That door over there.' Thomasine pointed and Nadine crossed the drawing room and opened her bedroom door.

'Ugh! Laura Ashley wallpaper.'

'But you like Laura Ashley. You room in London is done like this one.'

'Not any more, it isn't. Chantal agreed it was too twee. She said I should do what I want. I'm more sophisticated now. I don't like this sort of crap.' She waved at the pretty blue and white room dismissively. 'You should see my other room now, I've had it done in silver and black.'

'Sounds wonderful,' Thomasine said sarcastically. 'You might have told me you'd changed your taste so dramatically. Why does it have to be a state secret until you suddenly plonk it on me?'

'I didn't know you were going to decorate my bedroom all girly-girly, did I?'

'You might have guessed that I would, since that's what I thought you liked.' Thomasine could feel the anger welling up inside her again.

'This is a great new homecoming,' said Nadine, rolling her eyes to the ceiling.

'You can say that again. How do you think I feel?'

They looked at each other. Nadine looked petulant and now, removing her school duffel coat, Thomasine could see that the change in her daughter wasn't just in

131

her taste in interior design. It was difficult to pin down, most of the clothes were the same as before – jeans perhaps a little more frayed; a cropped jumper well above her waist rather than a sloganned T-shirt; a backward-facing baseball cap. The biggest difference was that instead of the Doc Martens she had begged and pleaded for, she now wore the sort of tan coloured, heavy lace-up boots a forester would have happily paid for. But change there was, and Thomasine suddenly realised it was in attitude – there was a pouting defiance to her that had not been there before. Thomasine wearily pushed her hand through her hair, forgetting she'd had it done especially for this evening. Well, that was a waste of time, she thought and sighed audibly.

'I'm sorry, Mum. I'm being a bitch, aren't I?' Nadine said, as if the sigh had made her suddenly guilty. For a second she glimpsed the strong-minded but sweet daughter she had known.

'Yes, you are a bit. It's your room, and you must have it any way you want. I've always said that about your room, no need to change now. I'd be a bit iffy about silver and black though.'

'We could go to the local town tomorrow and get new stuff.'

'But I've just put it up.'

'You mean I've got to live with that until it needs replacing?' Any guilt she'd felt seemed completely negated, judging by her belligerent expression.

'I'd have thought that that would be the reasonable thing to do, yes.'

'I see,' said Nadine, in an ominously ill-humoured voice. 'I'll unpack, then, whilst you get supper.' She did not leave the room but flounced out of it, slamming her bedroom door.

Thomasine, in the kitchen, began the supper. She collected her cooking utensils, banging a saucepan down, snapping a door shut, the racket expressing how angry she felt. Why on earth had she hoped for Robert to stay? What for? To listen to him lecturing her? – she kicked a cupboard door shut. How smug he'd been, how censorious. And she'd let him. Why hadn't she let rip and told him the truth – she hadn't wanted to uproot, to change their lives. It was far more his doing than hers. So why had she been so mealy-mouthed with him? She ran the water in a gushing torrent into the sink. God, she despised herself, as no doubt he did too. Her reaction tonight had been humiliating – well, she thought as she lined up the vegetables on the chopping board, I won't be like that again, ever! With such a decision made she could feel herself calming. She pulled the kitchen stool towards her with one foot and sat herself on it.

As she worked it did cross her mind that having to prepare strict vegetarian food for the whole of the Easter holiday was going to be a pain, and how simple life had become *without* her daughter around.

'What a thing to think, Luna,' she said, looking down at the solid dog, who was, as always, sitting at her feet in the hope something interesting might fall from the worktop. 'What a way to think about my own daughter.' And Luna's small, black tail wiggled in reply.

14

Since it was Saturday, Kimberley was sitting with the others on the wall of the fountain in Shillingham. As usual the talk was of nothing in particular, mainly of the motorbikes they all dreamed of one day owning. She swung her legs back and forth. Why did she persist in coming here, what had she in common with the rest? As long as she hung around with them, how was she to meet anyone else? She knew what she meant by that – a boyfriend, that's what. A decent bloke, not one who nicked things and despised love.

Butch yelled with raucous laughter, a 'look at me' kind of laugh. She didn't dislike him, didn't despise him, in a way she supposed she felt sorry for him, for suddenly she saw how it would be for Butch in five years' time – he'd still be here, with another group around him he could control. The others would all have moved on.

'I'm going for a piss,' Butch said, loudly enough for the passers-by to hear and be shocked.

Yes, she thought, he was sad.

The market was busy with Easter week. The Council, or was it the stall-holders, had erected a large tableau of a cardboard chicken in an artificial garden. She had stopped Butch and the others from throwing stones at it. 'Leave it alone,' she'd said. 'Let the kiddies enjoy it.' And, give them their due, if there was one thing about the gang, they did like children and were nice to them. And so they had stopped.

Kimberley opened the bag she was holding and peered at the gaudy Easter egg she had bought for her mother. When she'd been little her mother had always bought her a chocolate egg, and some years had dyed hard-boiled eggs pretty colours and patterns, but she hadn't had one for several years now. She supposed her mother thought she was too old, but inside she still felt young enough for one. Maybe she should buy another and give it to herself.

'Mind if I sit here?' a man's voice asked.

Kimberley looked up to see a tall, broad-shouldered man with thick blond hair, dressed in jeans and a blazer – posh, she thought.

'Suit yourself,' said Kimberley, and swung her legs again, like a metronome, as if not caring, but she shifted slightly to give him room. She would have liked to sneak another look at him, to see if his eyes were as blue as she thought, but she didn't dare.

'It's a lovely day, isn't it?' he said politely. 'I hope it holds for Easter.'

134

'Yes,' she replied, and could not understand why she blushed slightly as she did so.

''Ere, you! Buzz off.' Ginger jumped up from his place two along from Kimberley. 'This 'ere's reserved,' he said, bristling with aggression as he took control of the situation in Butch's absence.

The man looked at Ginger – all five and a half feet of him – and slowly reached into his pocket for a packet of cigarettes.

'Pardon,' he said eventually. 'Did you just tell me to buzz off?'

'I did,' said Ginger, with a half embarrassed jerk of his head.

'Thought that's what you said.' He offered a cigarette to Kimberley.

'No thanks, I don't.'

'I'm trying to give up.' He lit the cigarette.

'You don't seem to be having much success.' She found the courage to smile.

'No, I'm not, am I?' He grinned and threw the remains of the cigarette on to the cobbles and ground it out with his heel.

'You shouldn't have done that.'

'Why not? You're right. Stupid habit.' He smiled again, turning to face her, and Kimberley could see his face full on. It was a square-shaped face, and yes, his eyes were blue, and with his blond hair she thought he looked like a Nordic warrior. He thought how pretty, how innocent she looked.

Butch, still zipping up his flies – again to shock – approached them, the buckles on his large boots clanging like the spurs of an ancient knight as he clomped across the cobblestones.

'Who are you?' He glared belligerently at the stranger.

'I told him to piss off, Butch,' Ginger said excitedly.

'Didn't you hear what my mate said?'

'I did.'

'And?' Butch asked in his most menacing way, hands

135

on hips, standing with black-leather-clad thighs wide apart.

The man looked at Butch long and hard. 'And what?'

'Move when you're bleeding well told to.'

The man squared his shoulders and sat up straight, and Kimberley wasn't sure if she wanted him to move safely away or to make a stand; she feared he might be hurt if he did.

'No, I don't think so,' he said finally. 'I rather like it here. Pleasant, watching the crowds, isn't it?' He spoke to Kimberley.

'Yes, it is,' she said, looking nervously at Butch, and then down at the cobblestones.

'Well, this is our pitch, and we don't like you here, mate.'

'I'm sorry about that. I'd no idea that this was private property. I assumed the fountain belonged to the citizens of Shillingham.'

'Well, if you were a citizen of Shillingham, you'd know that every Saturday we sit here.'

'Every Saturday?' he said with exaggerated amazement, and Kimberley giggled.

Butch looked none too pleased. He saw Kimberley was giggling and smiling, and realised he didn't seem to be getting very far in this conversation. 'Off,' he barked, gesticulating with his thumb over his right shoulder, and then, for good measure, waggling it in the air.

'When I'm good and ready.'

Butch seemed to think about this for an inordinate length of time; if he allowed the man to stay he would lose face. 'I don't think so,' he said, glowering in his most menacing way. The man started to rise from the wall of the fountain. 'Ah, that's better. Seeing it my way, are we?' Butch looked smug. But as he stood to his full height the man towered over Butch by a good head. Butch made the tactical error of taking one step back.

'I'm sorry my presence bothers you so,' he said. 'But I

intend sitting here awhile yet. So, why don't *you* buzz off.' He leant forward aggressively.

The members of the gang looked all ways but at each other, their eyes darting left to right, each taking a sneaky look at their leader's discomfort, each finding they rather enjoyed seeing him ousted.

'He's a big bugger, Butch, I wouldn't if I were you.'

'Shut up, Ginger,' said Butch. 'Leave this to me.'

The man had sat down again. From his pocket he took a brown paper bag. He offered it to Kimberley. 'Jelly baby, miss?' he asked pleasantly.

'Thank you,' she said. And even as she said the words, she knew that one small thank you was her resignation from the gang, that Butch would never forgive her now.

'Sod the lot of you,' said Butch, turning on his heel, and clomped off down the market. After a pause and a few startled whispers, the others ran behind him.

'Were you with them?' the young man asked.

'Yes and no,' she said, non-committally. 'I mean, I know them, but I'm not one of them, not any more.'

'I'm glad. A gang like that could mean trouble.'

'Yes. I know what you mean.' She looked at her hands and wished they weren't so rough. His glance followed hers.

'Are you cold?'

'No. It's my hands, they're always cold.'

'You know what they say – cold hands, warm heart.' She felt herself redden. 'I've got a pair of gloves, somewhere.' He felt in his pockets and produced a pair of leather gloves. She'd never touched leather that felt so soft.

'Thanks.' She put them on. The fingers flapped this way and that.

'My name's Alan Farmingham. And you're – ?'

She looked nervously at the cobbles. 'Kimberley.' She dared to look up. 'Kimberley White.'

'Nice name. Are you from round here?'

'Yes. My father's got a smallholding out the other side of Lower Shilling, on the Conniestown road.'

'You came in on the bus?'

'Yes, that's right. There used to be one every couple of hours, but now there's just the one in the morning, then you have to wait until the afternoon to get back.'

'Long wait.'

'Oh, I don't mind. I like watching people.'

'Yes, I do too. I like to imagine what they do, what their houses are like inside, are they happy or sad, that sort of thing.'

'So do I,' she said, astonished. 'And sometimes I make stories up about them, silly things,' she laughed.

'Me too.'

'Do you live here in Shillingham?'

'No. I've been packing up my mother's house in Morristown. She died.'

'Oh, I am sorry.' Kimberley felt flustered, not sure what to say in such circumstances.

'We weren't close,' he said, as if sensing her confusion.

'Does that help?' she asked, thinking of her relationship with her own parents.

'It must do, I suppose. I didn't think I'd ever want to come back here but, funny thing is, I've been wondering whether to buy a cottage in the area.'

'Why not keep the house?'

'I prefer the country.'

'Me too. I'd hate to live in a town – too noisy and claustrophobic.'

'Exactly.' They both sat a moment in silence, liking how much they agreed.

'What do you do?'

'Nothing at the moment – I'm on sick leave,' he said, neatly skirting the question. When investigating, as he was now, even if only semi-officially, he didn't want strangers to know he worked for the RSPCA, you never knew who you were talking to. And yet, oddly, this girl didn't feel like a stranger to him. 'What do you do?'

'I help my parents,' she replied, pleased that she hadn't had to say she was still at school. She'd be mortified if he knew. She liked him and wanted to stay talking to him, and a man of his age – mid-twenties, she reckoned – might run a mile if he realised he was talking to a schoolgirl. 'Vegetables and things,' she added, non-committal.

'What do you do in your spare time?'

'Me? Not a lot. Best of all I like to walk up into the hills, up beyond the Shillings and hide in the copses, pretend I'm the only person left in the world.'

'I like to do that too. I like to get in the car and drive to the sea and walk miles along the beach, away from the bathers, then flop in the dunes and watch the birds and pretend the same.' He looked at her, his face alive with excitement. She felt it too. Oddly, she felt she knew him, that she liked him, that she would always know him. It was an almost overwhelming sensation.

She mustn't seem too forward, she would frighten him away.

'Do you mind if I sit here?' said a new voice. Kimberley turned to see a young girl dressed from head to toe in black.

'Please do.' And she laughed.

'What are you laughing at?' said the girl, somewhat aggressively.

'I'm sorry. I'm not laughing at you, but how odd things can be. I mean, I sit here every Saturday, come rain or shine, and I think this is the first time anybody else has ever come up and said, "Do you mind if I sit here," all polite, like. Now it's happened twice. It's funny. I'm Kimberley, this is Alan.'

'Nadine,' she replied, completely ignoring Alan and speaking to Kimberley. 'Does anything go on in this dump?'

'Not a lot. There's sometimes a disco on Saturday nights. There's more goes on in Morristown.'

'A disco! They went out with the ark. No clubs here? No raves? Do you go?'

'No, I can't, I live too far away. There's no late bus, and my mum won't let me hitch-hike,' Kimberley answered, puzzled about what the difference was between a disco and a club.

'I fancy trying a *disco*.' The girl giggled, as if finding the word funny. 'At least it gives a little glimmer of hope. My mum's just moved here, I don't know what she's thinking of, choosing a place like this.'

'Where does she come from?' asked Kimberley.

'London, Islington. Then she suddenly, without consulting *me*, decides to bury herself down here, it's madness. I told her, she'll go stark staring bonkers. If she expects me to keep coming down here, she's got another think coming.'

'Where does she live?' asked Alan, thinking the mother would probably be better off.

'One of those Shilling villages, I don't know which one. Stupid names, Upper, Middle and Lower.'

'They're lovely houses there, though,' said Kimberley dreamily. 'I do envy her. I'd love to live there one day.' She smiled at her own silly dreams.

'Maybe you will,' said Alan kindly.

'I doubt it, not now, they're too expensive. None of us locals can afford them.'

'But the problem is it's the locals who sell for the ridiculous prices in the first place,' said Alan.

'Well, how about this disco, let's go, shall we?' the girl interrupted, bored with the theme of the conversation; lack of money had never been a problem in her life.

Kimberley looked up at her. 'I'm sorry?'

'I'm inviting you. I'll pay. Come with me, you can stay the night at our place, we've got a spare room. Then you needn't worry about the buses and my mum can run you home in the morning.'

'Can anybody go?' asked Alan, leaning forward.

'Of course. Don't be stupid.'

'No, I meant with you two.'

'If you must,' Nadine said.

'I can't go. I've got nothing to wear, and I can't go home because that's the last bus and I wouldn't get back again.'

'Get your dad to run you in or something.'

Kimberley snorted with amusement at the very idea.

'It's not just that. I've got chores to do at home. And my mum will want her shopping. I don't think my parents would let me, actually. But thanks all the same. Maybe we could see each other some other time?'

'Fine! Okay by me. I'll give you my number. So it looks as if it's just you and me,' Nadine said to Alan.

'Perhaps another time. Take a rain-check, hey?' he said, standing up.

Nadine shrugged. 'Suit yourself. You might live to regret it,' she laughed.

'If you'll excuse me, I've got chores to do myself.' He smiled at Kimberley, and she felt her heart turn turtle. 'See you next week?' he queried tentatively.

Kimberley looked down again, taking great interest in her hands. 'That would be nice,' she said.

'Fine then, okay. Bye.' He waved and was gone.

'Oh my goodness,' said Kimberley. 'I've got his gloves. I must . . .' She jumped up. Nadine grabbed the sleeve of her coat and pulled her back down again.

'Don't be silly. He won't need those. Is he your bloke?'

'No, I said, we just met.'

'I'm starving, are you? Any chance of finding a hamburger joint?'

'No, but there's a mobile van over there, he does them. And hot dogs too. But count me out,' she said.

'What? Got no money?'

'Something like that.'

'I'll get them, I've got plenty.'

'Oh, I couldn't. I couldn't possibly.'

'Don't be so daft. Those that have should give to those

that haven't, that's my philosophy. That and don't be cruel to animals, that's my most important philosophy.'

'And mine,' said Kimberley. 'I hate people who are cruel to animals,' she said, but looked away as into her mind's eye flashed an image of the dog sheds at her father's smallholding.

'Come on, then.'

Thomasine, shopping for yet more fruit for Nadine, fifteen minutes later, was more than perplexed to see her daughter sitting on the wall of the market-place fountain, happily chatting with a sweet-faced girl beside her, and munching, with relish, a large hamburger.

Thomasine sat at a table in the bow window of the Copper Kettle coffee shop waiting to be served. She looked about her, at the gingham table cloths, the polished copper pans hanging on the walls and the mainly middle-aged clientele chattering contentedly over their coffee and cakes. She thought, in the unlikely event of her owning such an enterprise, that she'd call it something more original, and she'd sling out the gingham for sure.

She moved the sugar bowl and pepper and salt pots into a huddle, and them moved them again, realigning them in a straight row like china soldiers. She drummed her fingers on the table and kept glancing at her watch, as if she were in a hurry. She wasn't. She had another half an hour before she was due to meet Nadine. She was restless because she was shaken.

Had anyone asked if her daughter was truthful, she'd have answered with confidence that Nadine would never lie to her. But now? Why tell her mother she was a vegetarian, why make all that fuss about food, why put her mother to so much extra trouble in the kitchen, when all the time it was just a game she was playing?

It was just that, a game, a joke. A joke she was finding difficult to understand. It couldn't be as simple as just another indication of how difficult and unpleasant her daughter had become.

And why had she changed?

The answer to that was inescapable – the divorce. The salt and pepper pots were moved around the table yet again.

Was claiming to be a vegetarian a way of getting attention? Too old now for temper tantrums, was she manipulating the adults in her life to take notice of her in this roundabout way?

If so, how sad. What had happened to their ability to communicate with each other? Had it ever existed? Had Thomasine, in the past, been kidding herself when she thought that she, Robert and their daughter were so close they could often guess what the others were thinking? Or did it just mean that Nadine was awkward and difficult? Perhaps it was a phase. Just because her daughter had reached sixteen was no reason to presume that the times of 'going through a phase' were over. Were they ever?

Still, even if it was not a cry for help but merely unpleasantness, who was to blame for that? There was no escaping the answer – her and Robert. She sighed, remarshalled the salt pot and inadvertently spilled some salt. She automatically picked up a pinch. What to wish? She looked out of the window at the shoppers milling about the market. She could wish for Nadine to be pleasanter; she smiled to herself as she thought that that was probably expecting too much of a pinch of salt. She could wish to get a good illustrating commission. Or she could wish for some romance in her life.

As if in answer to this, she suddenly saw Jim Varley striding along the pavement opposite. Ridiculously, she felt her heart quicken and she was half standing, about to rap on the window to attract his attention, when a young boy ran along the pavement towards him. He ruffled the child's hair in a practised way and swung him onto his shoulders. As he did so, a pretty, dark-haired woman appeared, and she was laughing at them both. Thomasine subsided into her seat feeling foolish, disappointed and, suddenly, very lonely. How foolish of her, of course he'd be married, an attractive fellow like him. But if he was, then where did that brittle Sophia woman fit in?

She realised she still held the pinch of salt. She flung it over her left shoulder and concentrated on wishing for a commission from a publisher instead.

'Do you mind?'

Thomasine looked up at the sound of the voice. 'Cora, how nice. Please do.'

Cora ordered her coffee and a plate of cakes. 'I shouldn't really.' She patted her very flat stomach. 'But what the hell?'

Thomasine smiled, but bleakly. Cora was as slim as a reed, probably never had to diet in her life, whereas Thomasine, to keep as slim as she was, had, out of necessity, to watch what she ate. She felt irritated by the Coras of this world.

'Hello, gorgeous.' The two women looked up, and Oliver bent to kiss Cora noisily on the cheek. 'Mind if I take a pew?' he asked, and sat down opposite Thomasine.

'Do you two know each other?' Cora asked.

'Not formally. We bumped into each other a couple of nights back, quite literally. Oliver Hawksmoor.' He held out his hand and smiled winningly.

'This is Thomasine Lambert,' Cora explained.

'Do people call you Tommy, or Tamsin?' Oliver asked.

'Neither,' replied Thomasine shortly. She had never liked people who asked if they could 'take a pew', and people who called her Tommy or Tamsin even less.

'Ah! Pity.' He smiled again and she felt he was the sort of man who was used to getting his way with that smile.

'So you've decided to move here?' asked Cora.

'If Wimpole approves.'

'Oh, really, Oliver. It's about time you got rid of that old crone. Honestly, a man of your age still clinging onto his nanny. It's wet.'

'That's right, that's me!' He shrugged his shoulders expressively and Thomasine was amazed at how unconcerned he appeared to be by the criticism, or was it an act? 'How did you know I was thinking of moving?' he asked, picking at the plate of fancy cakes Cora had ordered.

'Oliver, if you live in the country you can't burp without people knowing.'

'How's Bandage?' he asked suddenly, looking out of the window as he did so, as if he didn't want people to see his expression. But he hadn't been quite quick enough, Thomasine had caught it. She felt a quite illogical urge to make him less sad.

'Sophia's gone to visit friends in the Lakes,' Cora answered.

'Poor sods,' he said, with feeling. 'Fancy making up a party to rent a villa this summer? Tuscany, South of France, somewhere like that. You too,' he added to Thomasine. She wondered why he kept changing the conversation so abruptly, convinced it showed a very confused and floundering person. 'Do you know Sophia?' he swung round and asked Thomasine. 'Or are the saints preserving you?'

'I'm sorry?' Thomasine knew she sounded flustered. 'We met at Cora's.'

'Ah! Sad you weren't spared.'

'Oliver, you make her sound like an ogress.'

'As she is, Cora my love. As she is.'

Thomasine, seeing the time, got to her feet.

'Oh, you're not going already, I've only just got here.' And again, he flashed the practised smile.

'I must. I'm pleased to have met you, Mr Hawksmoor,' she said, formally. 'Bye, Cora.' And collecting her bags together she weaved her way across the coffee shop to the door.

'Pretty lady. What did I say to frighten her away?'

'Sometimes, Oliver, you're a little bit too smooth for your own good.'

'That's what Wimpole says. But what's a chap to do?' He grinned impishly at her.

'I like it myself,' Cora giggled, flirting lightly back.

Thomasine found Nadine still sitting on the wall of the fountain's basin.

'This is Kimberley, Mum.'

'Hello, Kimberley.'

'Can she come home with us, stay the night?'

'Of course, if she wants, but what about your parents, Kimberley?'

'You can ring them,' Nadine ordered.

'It's very kind of you, Mrs Lambert, but I must get home, my mother will be expecting me. The bus leaves in five minutes.' Kimberley smiled warmly at Nadine, who smiled equally warmly back, the first real smile Thomasine had seen since she had arrived. What a nice girl, she thought.

'Then we'll run you home, won't we, Mum?'

'Of course.'

'Then you can ask your mum if you can stay and you can pick up your toothbrush.'

'No, really. I'd best catch the bus.' Kimberley suddenly looked anxious, Thomasine thought.

'If Kimberley wants . . .' she began.

'I want to take her back,' Nadine said expansively. 'We've got plenty of time. Mum doesn't mind, do you, Mum? And I want to see where you live,' Nadine continued, with all the finesse of a Centurion tank.

They were soon bundled into the car and driving through the twisting lanes towards Primrose Acre.

'If you could drop me just along here.'

'But it's the middle of nowhere,' said Nadine, peering out of the window into the gathering dusk.

'No. My house is over there, see.' She pointed, and

about a hundred yards off the road they could make out the outline of some buildings.

Thomasine halted the car and Kimberley climbed out.

'I'll come with you.' Nadine made to get out too.

'No, no. You stay here. It'll be better,' Kimberley said hurriedly.

'No, I'll come . . .'

'Nadine, stay here. Kimberley doesn't want you to go.' Thomasine intervened. They sat in the car and watched as Kimberley, carrying two shopping bags, entered a ramshackle gate and walked quickly up a driveway. They sat and waited. And waited.

'God, this is boring,' said Nadine, twiddling the knobs on the car radio.

'That radio was pre-set. It took me ages to do,' Thomasine said with exasperation.

'If you had some halfway decent cassettes, I needn't have tried . . .' Nadine said, with a smart Alec expression which, to Thomasine's horror, made her hand itch with longing to swipe her one. 'Let's go to the house and see what's going on.'

'She didn't seem to want us to.'

'Oh, come on, Mum. We can't sit here all night.'

'That's true.' Thomasine switched on the engine. They turned into the rutted lane and bounced uncomfortably along.

The front of the house looked like a junk yard, scattered with old fridges, cars and washing machines. To one side stood two large, closed sheds with corrugated roofs. Suddenly the front door of the house opened and Kimberley stood on the step, a white plastic carrier bag in her hand. A man, with equal suddenness, emerged from the shadows of the long, dark sheds. Thomasine wound down her window to greet him.

'Fuck off! We don't want your sort here,' he yelled.

'Charming,' said Thomasine.

'What a nerd!' Nadine added.

Kimberley ran down the steps. 'You shouldn't have

come up here. He won't let me come, now. Please go,' she pleaded. 'Please.'

Thomasine put the car into gear and swung round, needing no second bidding.

'You're not going to leave her there?' Nadine protested.

'Too right, I am,' Thomasine said with feeling as she drove too quickly down the unmade drive.

'But she looked as if she was going to cry.'

'I know.'

'We've got to go back.'

'No way. Didn't you see? That creep was holding a shotgun!'

As they drove home, Thomasine still felt shaken up; it wasn't every day she was sent packing like that. But her paramount thought was – what had the man got to defend that needed a gun?

'Who the fuck was that?' Tom White lowered his gun, prodding his daughter into the house.

'A friend.' Kimberley wiped her feet on the doormat, trying to fight back her tears.

'You don't need friends.' Tom stepped over the mat. 'Who says?'

'I say.' He clattered across the living room in his heavy boots, leaving a trail of mud behind him, and locked his gun away in its case. Sue White hovered nervously at the table, carrying a dish in her hands, looking anxious and unsure if people wanted to eat or not.

'You can't decide my life like this. I've every right . . .'

'You've no bloody rights, not while you're living here under my roof, you haven't. I don't want no one snooping around here, isn't that clear enough? And stop that bloody snivelling.'

'They weren't snooping.' She wiped the tears from her face with the sleeve of her jumper. 'They invited me to stay the night. They were waiting for me,' Kimberley said, almost with pride, and placed the carrier bag she had been holding, containing her pyjamas and tooth-brush, onto the chair.

'You don't stay with people, you know I don't allow it.'

'Allow it? I'm eighteen, I'll decide myself.' She swung round and faced her father.

'You'll do as I say.' Tom banged his large fist on the table.

'Oh, no,' sighed Sue, and collected her dish and put it back on top of the Rayburn. Her anxious expression deepened as she looked from her husband to her daughter, waiting for the row to really ignite.

'No, Dad. Not any more. It's time I began to lead my own life.' Somehow she spoke in a normal-sounding tone, but she sat down as she did. She had to for her legs would not support her.

'You what? You cheeky cow . . .' Tom leant menac-ingly across the table, his large face looming an inch or two away from hers.

'You're not scaring me, Dad. Not any more. I'm going to have friends, whatever you say. You needn't worry, I won't invite them here to find out your little secret.'

'What you mean, my secret?'

Kimberley jerked her head in the direction of the sheds. 'The dogs. If the authorities found out about the conditions of those dogs, you'd be closed down, fined, go to prison. And it's illegal not to have pit bulls spayed – you'd get done for that too.'

'Oh no! Don't talk like that, Kim,' Sue wailed.

'Shut up, you stupid slag,' Tom shouted at his wife. 'You threatening me?' he asked his daughter.

'No. Just stating facts.' Kimberley felt calmer now, surer of herself. So she was unprepared for the fist when it hit her on the side of the face, making her head whip from side to side, making her teeth rattle. She put her hand up. Tears of pain spurted into her eyes, tears she

149

blinked away, determined not to give him the satisfaction of seeing her cry again. 'Don't you dare hit me!' She jumped to her feet.

'I will if I fucking well want, who the fuck do you think you are?' And he punched her again. Kimberley looked pleadingly at her mother, but Sue lowered her eyes and turned her back and put her hands over her ears so that she could not hear the sound of her husband's fist connecting with her daughter's flesh.

15

Was it cold in her room, or was it her? Kimberley felt ice cold. She lay fully clothed under the blankets and shivered. She ached from last night's beating, her head was sore, she knew her face must look an unholy mess. No room, no matter how pretty, how yellow and blue it would be, was worth this. She turned awkwardly and painfully and looked out of the window and across the flat field.

Gingerly she touched her face. It was as well it was Sunday and the Easter school holidays, so there was no chance of bumping into Alan in Morristown. He had told her where his house was and she had planned, despite there being no school, to think up some excuse to go into Morristown, to amble out that way, just on the off chance – not now, though, not looking like this. Her fingers gently explored her face; she felt the softness of the swelling, and winced with pain. She did not check herself in a mirror, she did not want to see the damage. But from what she felt, it was unlikely she could go out for several days.

A sense of isolation overwhelmed her. She could feel it behind her breastbone, a great aching lump of loneliness. Last night her mother had looked away from her agony. How often in the past had she done that? Times without number.

She lifted herself in the bed, doubled up her pillow for support, pulled the blanket up close to her chin and hugged her knees, making a ball of her body to conserve heat. She knew that it was her father's abuse of her, his assurances she'd never amount to anything, which made her work at school – to prove him wrong. But why should it matter so much to her to prove anything? He didn't love her, so why did she care? She owed him nothing – the work she did for him not only added to the abuse but negated the cost of keeping her, exonerated her from any feelings of gratitude. She should be working for herself, not for him. She should be proving to herself how good she was, and sod him.

And then there were the dogs. She inadvertently jerked her head at the thought of them, as if to remove it, but the pain of the movement merely made the thought more concrete. She had shouted at her father how cruel his neglect of the creatures was, but wasn't she just as bad? By ignoring them, pretending they weren't there, was she not just as guilty? They were there day in, day out, in their misery, and she could help them and didn't – she was as despicable as him.

Things would change. She swung her legs over the side of the bed and dug out some clean clothes from the chest of drawers. In the bathroom she switched on the infra-red heater on the wall, knowing that would annoy him into apoplexy if he knew. She washed and dressed, put witch-hazel on her bruises and avoided the mirror. She grabbed a cup of tea and then ventured out into the yard.

In the barn she found her mother. 'I'll see to the dogs,' she said.

'Would you?' Her mother smiled, but did not look at Kimberley, no doubt too ashamed to see her bruises. Kimberley ignored the smile as she took the large-headed broom from her.

'It stinks in here,' she said.

151

'The floor needs a good sluicing. I've been meaning to do it – but you know me and the dogs . . .' Sue's voice trailed off in apology.

'I'll see to it.' She leant over one of the concrete-floored enclosures and patted the head of a ginger-coloured corgi. 'You're new,' she said, and the dog, unsure how to respond to a kind tone, looked at her solemnly and then slowly allowed its tail to wag.

Thomasine had cooked scrambled eggs.

'I can't eat these. No eggs, I told you,' Nadine said.

'Eat toast then.' Thomasine scraped the egg into a bowl for an ever-expectant Luna. 'Who's a lucky girl, then, eggies for breakfast.' She placed the bowl on the floor, and Luna noisily began to lap them up.

'That dog is gross. Listen to it. It's making a disgusting noise.'

'She can't help it. If your face was squashed up like that you'd have trouble eating too. More tea?'

'And it's ludicrous, the way you talk to it – *eggies*. Really! Gross.'

'Is that the only word in your vocabulary? It's becoming tedious,' Thomasine said sharply. 'And what's wrong in talking to a dog?'

'You'll be talking to plants next.'

'I already do.' Thomasine began to scour the scrambled-egg saucepan.

'I hate it here,' Nadine said, morosely, staring out at the garden.

'So I gathered.'

'I make a friend, then her nerd of a father threatens us with a gun. I tell you, it's . . .'

'Gross! Yes, I know.' Thomasine grinned at her daughter, who did not respond. Oh, suit yourself, she thought, and would have liked to say it, but sense told her it would only make matters worse. 'What would you like to do today? I've got to drive into Shillingham to get the Sunday papers. We could have lunch at the Duck and

Thistle.' Thomasine made herself sound bright and cheerful.

'Do they do vegetarian?'

'I expect so.' She turned away from her daughter, still confused at the game she was playing, the lie she was living. Perhaps she should have it out with her, tell her she'd seen her with a hamburger, but she decided against it. Nadine might be confusing and annoying her, but she loved the girl and did not want to embarrass her. 'Then we could go for a walk, take Luna across the fields, she could do with the exercise.'

Nadine looked down at Luna, who was now sitting beside her bowl in expectation that some other morsel might land there. 'No thanks. I wouldn't want to be seen dead with *that*.'

Thomasine sighed. 'Look, darling, is there something you want to discuss with me? Talk about? Is anything bothering you?'

'No.'

'Then why be like this?' Thomasine's face was screwed up with concern.

'Like what?'

'So unco-operative.'

'I'm not.'

'You are.' Thomasine shook herself: how easy it was to slip into childish tit-for-tat when arguing with her daughter. She sat down at the pine table. 'You're obviously bothered by something. It's not like you to be so offensive.'

'How would you know, you're never around to know what I'm like.'

'Nadine, don't be unfair. We discussed my moving here months ago. We talked about it ad nauseam. You agreed, you said it would be better for me to get right away from home.'

'Better for you, what about me?'

'You said you wanted to stay with your father if you had a free weekend, to be near your friends. That you

153

wanted to stay at that school and not move to one nearer here. That you liked Chantal.' Thomasine condensed the weeks and months of discussion and worried debate into a few short sentences.

'I had no choice, did I?'

'That's not fair. Had I known you were going to be like this, I'd have stayed in London. I can move back, if you want?'

'I don't want.'

'Then what *do* you want?' Thomasine said with exasperation.

'I want to go to France with Dad and Chantal for Easter, that's what I want.'

Thomasine sat back in her chair, surprised at the sudden statement. Then the hurt came rushing in to take over from the surprise. 'You must do as you want,' she said, her voice shaky.

'I will.'

'That's all right then.'

'What will you do for Easter?' Nadine asked after a pause.

'I'll go to my sister's – as we planned,' she couldn't help adding.

'Good. You're welcome to it. I wouldn't want to go there, that's for sure, not to your sanctimonious sister's.'

'She's not that bad.'

'She is too. I shall have a lot more fun with Chantal – she's great. She understands me. After all, she's nearer to me in age.' On that parting shot, Nadine stood up and left the room, slamming the door behind her.

Thomasine felt she had just taken part in a conversation that had been pre-planned. That her responses had been part of a trap. That Nadine had purposely made herself unpleasant in the hope that Thomasine would happily let her go to France.

'Manipulative little bitch,' she said to Luna, who had been across the kitchen by her bowl at the beginning of the exchange, but had then moved and sat on Thomasine's feet, as if protecting her. 'Sorry, that's not very polite to you, is it?' She leant down and patted the dog. Oh, what of it, she thought, she'd probably be better off without her when she was like this. Perhaps her father's new set-up was all an exciting novelty. Perhaps if she fell in with Nadine's plans she would become disillusioned, that much sooner, with life with her stepmother.

It was best to think along those lines. After all, what alternative was there?

And she still had the rest of the day to get through with her recalcitrant daughter. 'Oh, hell!' she said aloud.

Jim Varley returned from the Duck and Thistle in Middle Shilling, where he had had his usual Sunday lunch. It upset Beth that he ate there, but he ignored her objections. She already did too much for him, and he insisted that from after lunch on Saturday until Monday morning, she was free to come and go as she wanted. That was the theory, but soon after she had come to work for him, he realised that she never went anywhere. Her time off was always spent about the house – often alone, for her son was a gregarious child who frequently stayed overnight with various little friends. These were the times she caught up with her ironing and made the dried flower arrangements which seemed to be her only interest, apart from her work. The sad fact dawned on him that there was nowhere for her to go. He wondered what it was in her past that had left her friendless. He didn't even know if she'd been married to Harry's father. Was it something about young Harry's birth that had caused problems in her life? After over a year of not asking, he felt he was most unlikely to ask now; he had an abhorrence of people who pried.

He went in by the surgery door, through to his hospital ward, and checked the little King Charles spaniel. The antibiotics were working well; the dog had a more alert expression in her eyes and she scrabbled at the bars of the cage, pleased to see a human being – another good sign.

'You're looking a lot better than you did the day before yesterday, young woman. In fact, so much better, I think we can let you out of there and you can come into the house. Would you like that?' He unlocked the cage and lifted the dog out. He put her on the floor where she scratched her ears for a moment or two, and then looked up at him expectantly. 'Come on then.'

Her claws clicking on the linoleum, she followed close at heel as he led her through the door. In the kitchen, Beth was sitting at the table, her flower arrangement paraphernalia spread out in front of her, and Harry was building a Lego space station beside her.

'Nice lunch?' Beth looked up and smiled at him.

'Yes, thanks. Oliver Hawksmoor was there, he was on his own too. I nearly suggested that we ate together, but didn't quite like to.'

'Why ever not?'

'I'm not sure. I don't know him well. I wondered, if by the time we'd had the starter, I might find I'd made a mistake and we'd got nothing in common. Then we'd have had to sit through the rest of the meal making polite conversation.'

Beth laughed. 'That's logical, I suppose. Still, if everyone thought like that no one would ever meet anyone new. I thought you knew him.'

'Oh, I know him – seen him about for years, but I don't actually *know* him.'

Beth looked puzzled. 'What a dear little dog. What's she called?'

'This is Amy.'

'I think Amy's a silly name for a dog,' Harry ventured.

'You think of a name for her, Harry, and we'll call her that. Something nice and short.'

Amy had climbed into the basket with Castille, Jim's old mongrel bitch, who was busily licking the new dog's

156

face. How wonderful it would be if Amy gave her a reason for going on, he thought. He dreaded the day she was no more, for Castille had been chosen by Ann and was one of those links between the living and the dead that neither time, nor other people, can ever break.

'I hope you don't think I'm presuming . . .' Beth said diffidently, smiled, and paused as if marshalling her words. Jim felt himself stiffen fully aware that when people said that, they undoubtedly had presumed.

'What have you been up to?' He tried to sound interested rather than wary.

Beth rustled about in some papers in front of her. 'Here,' she said, handing him a sheet of his headed notepaper. 'I thought Tessa could type it up on Monday.' Neatly written was an advertisement for an assistant vet or partner. 'I put both, I wasn't sure what you wanted – a partner or not.'

He read the advert and then re-read it, not because he had not understood its content but to give him time to compose a response.

'You're cross with me, aren't you?' she asked, anxiously looking up at him.

'I'm quite capable of drafting an advert myself,' he replied shortly.

'I was only trying to help.'

'I'm aware of that.'

'You work too hard. You need some help. Ever since the vet in Shillingham retired you've been worked off your feet.' He laid the paper on the table, but did not reply. It was true, he worked too hard, but then he wanted the work, when he was busy from dawn to dusk he didn't have time to think, and that suited him – he'd learnt to be afraid of thinking too much.

'I'm sorry, Jim. You think it's none of my business, don't you?' She was standing now, working one hand in the other as if washing them with invisible soap. 'Please.

I'm sorry,' she repeated. 'Do you fancy a cuppa? I've made a wonderful chocolate cake.'

'No thanks.' He turned to leave the room, not wanting to get angry with her.

'Are you cross with my mum?' asked Harry, looking up from his space station.

'Nope.' He had reached the door.

'I was only trying to help,' she said.

'Then don't,' he snapped, and walked out of the room, inadvertently slamming the door behind him, not seeing Beth slump at the table and put her head on her arms. Harry, leaving his toys, stood beside her, his small arm about her, trying to comfort her as best he could.

After Nadine's behaviour, Thomasine had no regrets about putting her on the train for London the following Wednesday. To be honest, she derived a certain amount of satisfaction from doing so; it might be spiteful and petty of her, but that was how she felt. At least she had the satisfaction of seeing that Nadine was obviously put out by this new resolve on her mother's part.

Thomasine let herself into her house, leant her back against the front door and let the peace of the empty rooms wash over her. Not for long, however, for there was an imperious banging upon the kitchen door – Luna demanding to be let out and disgruntled, no doubt, that she'd been left behind.

The welcome over, Thomasine picked up the telephone. In the night she'd realised that there was no way she could go to her sister Abigail for Easter – not with a pregnant dog who might soon go into labour.

As usual, when she telephoned, Luna sat almost on her feet. Thomasine accused her of being nosey, but all the same, she liked it and found it surprisingly comforting.

'Abigail? I've a bit of a problem. Well, a rather rotund problem actually.' Thomasine injected a carefree note

into her voice whilst explaining about her new acquisi-
tion, Luna.

'So you're not coming? I must say, it's a bit late in the
day,' her elder sister said in such an annoyed tone that
Thomasine had no difficulty in imagining the cross face
that would go with the voice.

'I'm sorry, I didn't think until last night. I'm not used
to owning a dog. But I did wonder if you couldn't all
come here?'

'We couldn't come. Not with the children. Not with
dogs about.'

'Really, Abigail – I could understand that attitude
when they were babies, but the girls are teenagers now
and Fred's eight, for God's sake. I hardly think that
they're going to go crawling about in the grass catching
toxocariasis.'

'It's no laughing matter, Thomasine. Dogs are filthy
creatures, God knows what they might pick up.'

'Did you know that you're more likely to pick up that
eye infection from cat shit than from dogs?'

'Do you have to be so vulgar? I just don't want my
children exposed, is that understood?'

'You know, Abigail, I feel sorry for your children.
They haven't even had a normal upbringing, with your
fanaticism about dirt.'

'And Nadine has? At least I've stayed with my
husband.'

'That's a really bitchy thing to say.'

'Good, I meant it to be.' And not giving Thomasine
the chance of another word she slammed the receiver
down.

Thomasine, sighing, replaced her own. Luna put her
head on her knee and looked at her sorrowfully.

'Oh, Luna. What a week I'm having. First Nadine,
and now my sister. Still, I didn't really want to go
anyway. How about you and I go for a –' She did not say
the word, merely thought it. This was her new game with

159

the dog, and sure enough, Luna lifted her head from Thomasine's knee, waddled towards the cupboard where she knew her lead hung and looked expectantly at her, as if saying, 'Come on!'

Oliver had finally decided to let the house in London. In the present market he'd wait forever to move to the country, if he persisted in trying to sell it. He was surprised how quickly tenants were found, and after that the move from London went more smoothly than he had dared hope. He had to thank Sophia, and the burglar, in some part, since they had removed so much from the house that one small pantechnicon was quite sufficient for what was left.

He found sorting through his books and papers a sobering task. He sat cross-legged on the floor of Phoebe's Great Hall, the one he was turning into his own writing room, sorting through his life. From his baptismal certificate, school reports, old love letters from girls he could now barely remember, the order of his wedding service to a copy of Aunt Phoebe's will, there it all was – his life. Houses bought and sold. Cars pranged. Tailors' bills and bank statements galore. All rather boring really. Not what a member of the SAS would collect together, or a captain of industry, or a mass murderer even. He sat back, leaning on a sofa for support. It was all quite frightening; forty-five next birthday, over half his life gone almost without him noticing. He was physically fit, mentally alert, he'd a full head of hair, his own teeth, and so the years had slipped by without his body warning him that time was zapping past. He really must be a thoughtless prat, he decided, not to think about it before, and to need boxes of old papers to tell him.

It made what Sophia was up to easier to understand. Had she opened a box and viewed her life and thought this isn't right, I'm not as happy as I might be, I'm going out on my own to see what I can find?

If she had, it was brave of her. Would he have had the courage to do the same if she hadn't pushed him into a new existence? He felt in his pocket for his cigarettes. He looked at them – well, there was resolution number one, if he gave up the weed perhaps he'd have longer to enjoy this second chance. Yes, that was what it was he was being given, a second go at living.

He'd never liked making decisions, always preferred them to be made for him; on that score he was changing already. He'd decided to move, give up his job, start writing and give up smoking. He was quite proud of himself, if quite surprised also.

While in this mood, perhaps he'd better think of what other decisions he would like to make. He had all the material possessions he could possibly need, so what could he decide on? Success. He wanted to become well known as a writer so that he had something to leave behind when he died; since he had no children his books would take their place. He'd always been disciplined in his job, so working out a routine for writing would not be difficult.

It was sad he'd not had children. When with Sophia he had accepted the situation unquestioningly. It was odd that he should think about it now he was on his own. Odd after all this time that he should be saddened by it.

Did he want to get married again? No! He shuddered at the very idea. Imagine if it all went wrong again and he had to go through this sort of upheaval another time. He'd take things as they came; if a woman should happen into his life, he'd go for it, but he'd explain that he didn't want to get too involved and that marriage was not on his mind. And if someone came along he hoped she'd be disorganised and reasonable, instead of capable and bossy like Sophia.

'What on earth are you doing sitting in here in the dark?' Wimpole noisily entered the room.

'Thinking.'

'Dodgy thing to do – thinking. If you're not careful it'll give you the heebie-jeebies.'

'Maybe I haven't done enough of it in the past. Perhaps if I had I wouldn't be having to start over again at my age.'

'Your age? You're a spring chicken. Don't you go talking like that – you sound like a menopausal old crow. Where did you put the whisky?'

'Box – kitchen. I'd like one too.'

'It's too early for you.'

'You're as bossy as Sophia.'

'Do you have to be so rude?' She grinned at him before disappearing to get a drink.

He'd been surprised at how enthusiastically Wimpole, once she had finally taken the decision to move into the country, had thrown herself into the preparations. She'd even been to the local bookshop and bought a pile of gardening books, declaring she was going to grow her own vegetables, and he needn't laugh at the idea.

All he needed was to get Bandage back and all would be well. He'd try to get hold of Sophia later this evening, threaten her with legal action if she didn't return the dog. She'd had him nearly six weeks now, it was a ridiculous state of affairs. And then, for no apparent reason, he found himself thinking about that nice woman Thomasine, and if she was married and to whom and, if not, what her telephone number was?

Jim felt wary of Beth. Her wanting to organise his life had, in some strange way, changed everything. As he drove along he argued with himself, back and forth. It was kind of her to be concerned for his well-being and to suggest he needed a second vet – that was one argument.

The other was that *he* would decide if he needed assistance, and it was none of her business.

He tried very hard to latch onto the first argument, but kept coming back to the second one and finding he felt happiest with that. Happy he might be, but not comfortable with it, for Jim was not an unkind man and would crawl a mile rather than hurt anyone.

He did what he often did when upset and needing peace and a chat. He drew up in front of Oakleigh kennels. Eveleigh invited him in, as always, with a welcoming smile, and the malt whisky bottle was produced from the sideboard without her even asking.

He sat in the wing chair, its seat comfortably sagging, its arm-rests worn bare from use, and looked about the untidy room and felt at home in it, as he always did. His own home was too tidy, he often thought. So tidy he could waste hours of precious time looking for things if Beth was out. When Ann had been alive they'd had a friendly clutter like this, they'd both been far too busy in their work to be houseproud.

'Thanks, Eveleigh, you always have a malt ready.'

'What sort of friend would I be if I ran out?' She raised her glass to him. 'What shall we drink to?'

He thought a while. 'Dogs and friendship,' he replied.

'The two most important things in the world.'

'Good Lord, that isn't –' He pointed to the top of a corner cupboard.

'One of Beth's flower arrangements? Yes. She turned up here the other day with it. Rather sweet of her I thought.'

'I loathe them – dead things.' He shuddered.

Eveleigh's laugh was one of relief. 'I couldn't agree with you more, but what could I do? I had to accept it – but I put it right up there out of the way. She's a nice woman.'

Jim didn't answer.

'Is there something wrong, Jim?'

He looked at the whisky in his glass long and hard before speaking. 'Have you got over Reggie dying yet, Eveleigh?'

'I don't think I ever will. Does one? We were together for twenty years – I was only nineteen when we married, I'd grown up with him, you see – that is if one ever does, grow up I mean.'

'How long has it been?'

'Five long years, Jim. Does it get better? In a way, yes – you don't stop mourning or forgetting, but you get used to living with it. It's like a backdrop of sadness to my life, and I can't remember any longer what it was like to live without it. That, of course, is a blessing.'

'People say I should be over Ann by now.'

'Who are they to say? What do they know? It has to be different from person to person. It must depend on what your relationship was like. There can't be a chart that says your heart is mended this month in this year. What rubbish people say.'

'I just feel – well, if I met someone else at the moment I'd feel so guilty. I know I would.'

'I understand that, but such feelings pass,' she said, a shade wistfully, and looked up at him, but he was looking down, studying his hands.

'She was so young. Such a shock. I mean, one minute she was vibrant, alive, the next –' He slammed one hand into the fist of the other.

'I think a sudden death, as we have both had to bear, has to be harder. The shock of it alone. I had always assumed Reggie would die before me – he was, after all, twenty-five years older. I'd imagined he would one day be ill and I would care for him and that I would be given time to adjust to the concept of being without him, and then the crash – I didn't expect that. So cruel.'

They sat either side of the fireplace, both deep in

thought, both locked mentally into their own private sadness.

Then Eveleigh wondered if the 'people' he spoke about had been Beth. She had long ago sensed that Beth was in love with Jim; nothing had been said, but when she spoke about him Beth's face became more animated and she who rarely smiled did so. Others might think it a suitable match, but Eveleigh was not so sure. Beth, she believed, tolerated animals but would never be involved with them as Jim was. There was always the risk that as a one-parent family she was searching for security and not love. And lastly, Eveleigh thought her far too dim for Jim. At this she shook her head to stop such reasoning – it was not becoming.

'I'm glad you came by today, Jim. I've had the most extraordinary letters.' She stood up and from behind an ornament on the mantelshelf she took down a stack of papers. 'My filing system,' she said half laughing. 'Look, this is the first one, you see. It's from a firm of solicitors offering to buy this place.' Jim took the letter and quickly read it. 'Of course I replied saying it was not for sale. Then I received this one.' She thrust that forward too.

'They've upped the price by ten thousand pounds. Good God! And they don't say why they're interested? How odd.'

'Isn't it? I must say I'm a bit concerned – the land the other side of the fields behind was sold a couple of months back, I'm wondering if it's something to do with that, but I can't think what.'

'Have you replied to this one?'

'Not yet, I thought I'd talk to you first.'

'Then I suggest you write something along the lines of – you cannot proceed with any further correspondence unless you know firstly, who is offering, and secondly, why. At least then you'll know what it's about.'

'Bless you, Jim.' She accepted her letters back and

smiled at him with deep affection, but he did not notice, since he was getting to his feet and saying he must be off.

And so he left without saying what it was he'd come for. He'd wanted Eveleigh's advice about Beth; was he imagining she was taking over his life? Should he get rid of her? If so, how? But when it came to it, for some odd reason, he found he couldn't raise the subject. As he drove home he wished he had.

16

On Easter Saturday Sadie sat upright in a large basket, watching her puppies frolicking on the floor around it. The imperious expression on her face would have made anyone think twice before touching them. Justin had erected a barricade of sorts around the area to keep them from wandering into the main part of the salon and, heaven forbid, getting trampled on.

'We're rushed off our feet with Easter bookings. There was no way we could leave them at home on their own and we both needed to be here,' Gill explained in a somewhat bored tone of voice. He had repeated the explanation at least a dozen times that day – so far.

'What are they called?' his client asked.

'We haven't named them – just numbers one, two, three, four . . . If we gave them names we'd never let them go to their new homes, for sure! Except for the one we're keeping, and that's Sukie.'

'Sweet.'

'Blissful, isn't it?' Gill waved his comb in the air, finished his teasing of her hair and with the dexterity of a magician, flashed a mirror to show her his handiwork at the back.

'Next,' he called as, with a click of his fingers, he indicated to their new assistant she should tidy up from the last client. 'Mrs Brenton. Just the person,' he said as Eveleigh, her hair already shampooed by Gill's assistant, took her seat.

'It's kind of you to fit me in. I know how busy you are, Gill. But I didn't know until yesterday I'd been invited out.'

'For an old friend, no problem.'

'Did you sort out the stud fee with the owner you were having problems with?' she asked.

'What, grumpy old Martin? We did exactly what you advised – wrote a cheque for the amount you suggested and popped in a covering letter saying that it was in full and final settlement – tickety boo. Worked like a charm. And we haven't heard a word from him – right scum bag.'

'That's a lovely pup you've chosen from the litter.'

'You think so? Honest?'

'That one especially. Have you thought about entering her for the Spillers Puppy of the Year?'

'No. Should we?'

'Why not?'

'You're our dogs' fairy godmother, Mrs Brenton, make no mistake. Of course we're aiming for Crufts again once the showing season gets going. Are you?'

'I've a good St Bernard bitch, Brünnhilde, and dear Lohengrin of course.'

'In with a chance?'

'One's always in with that, Gill. But you can never be sure. There's such a large element of luck involved. It all depends on the day and how the dog is feeling – the weather affects some dogs and makes them frisky or grumpy, just like humans. And then there's the judge – what side of the bed did he get out of and what's his preference.'

'Or who was he in bed with, you might ask?' Gill laughed. 'I thought judges weren't supposed to favour one breed over another. That they just judged best of.'

'Sometimes it's easier said than done. After all, we've

all got soft spots for our own particular breeds. Would you swop your poodles for my St Bernards?'

'No offence, but –'

'Exactly.'

He worked a minute in silence. 'Just think if our Sadie or Sukie became Supreme Champion at Crufts!' he said.

'And why not?'

'Dreams, dreams! Justin says I'm a fool with my dreams.'

'We all need those,' Eveleigh said, rather sadly.

'Now don't you get all gloomy. Think positively, I always say, and it might just have a chance of happening.'

'Next,' he called, once he'd seen Eveleigh on her way. A tiny woman with red hair slipped into the seat she had vacated. 'New here?' he asked politely.

'We've just moved to Lower Shilling. We lived on the other side of Morristown but –' she paused, her expression seeming to crumble from the bright, smiling face she'd first presented him with. 'We had to move –' Her eyes filled with tears. Gill, sensing a confidence was about to be spilled, flicked his fingers and ordered the assistant to get them coffees.

'Tell Gill,' he said comfortingly, turning back to his new client.

What always annoyed Jim Varley was that on Friday nights, and the eve of any big holiday, the surgery was nearly always empty. Yet come Monday, or the day after a holiday, it would be crammed – just like a GP's surgery, he'd discovered when he'd confided this phenomenon to his doctor. No patients, canine or otherwise, were ill when it would be inconvenient, they decided. Of course that didn't mean that on Easter Sunday, Christmas Day, or the vet's birthday, just as they sat down to eat, they'd not be called out. He could even lay bets on what it would be – a dog sick from gorging. On Easter Sunday it was invariably chocolate

168

eggs. They should carry a health warning that chocolate was bad for dogs. On Christmas day it was nearly always a turkey bone stuck in its gullet. And on his birthday – well, it could be anything.

Here it was, Easter Saturday, and Jim was driving back from Ben's. He wondered what the next two days would bring. He was also feeling disgruntled. Not because he'd been called out to the hunter Ben was worrying about – convinced it had colic, unnecessarily it transpired, all that was needed was a minor adjustment to the horse's diet. No, it was Sophia who had put Jim in this mood.

When she had appeared, he'd looked at her admiringly: she was certainly an attractive woman, especially in her riding gear. She was, however, the type of woman who made Jim feel uncomfortable. He was not used to dealing with women, he'd been married too long and too happily to maintain any skill at flirting. And he'd been in mourning too long even to want to. But he was not so stupid as to be unaware that Sophia was flirting with him; but was it just games she was playing, or did she mean it?

Jim was watching her leaning on the gate, her backside pertly outlined in the skin-tight jodhpurs she wore, rubbing herself against the gatepost very suggestively. He longed to tell her it reminded him of a cow scratching its rear against a hedge, but refrained. She ran her long-fingered hands slowly up and down her thigh. And her hand rested just a second too long against his on the top bar of the gate. Once she'd have been called a prick-tease; he supposed that was politically incorrect now.

'Penny for them?' She smiled at him.

'What? Oh, not a lot – just thinking about a cow.' He grinned.

'How bizarre.'

'Hardly. It's my job.'

Later he could not remember how, as they talked of

this and that, the conversation had got on to the subject of Thomasine Lambert.

'Oh, that woman,' Sophie spat out. 'You know she's set her cap at Oliver? He can't move without her mooning about after him.' There was not so much to find attractive in her face now, spite had wiped it all away.

He felt anger at her for speaking of Thomasine in such a dismissive way, but it was swamped by disappointment that Oliver had got there first. He should have plucked up the courage to call on her, to invite her out for a drink, and now it would be too late.

This was not the only thing making him fed up. He was not looking forward to getting home. The atmosphere there had changed. He realised he had been short with Beth over the advertisement she had wanted to place in the journal, but he felt her reaction to his reaction was over the top. She did her work just as before, he had no complaints about that. It was the way she did it that bothered him; there was a lot of banging and crashing of pots, pans, brooms and Hoovers which reminded him of how his mother had indicated noisy displeasure with his father. Her work appeared to be done more quickly and, he noticed, some things were no longer done – his sock drawer, which she always arranged for him, was now a terrible muddle. She no longer cleaned his boots nor washed his hairbrushes. She was telling him something, but what? After all, it was finally his decision whether he took on a partner or not. And why was he so bothered? Was his reaction a sort of smoke screen? Was it, perhaps, he didn't want to share his practice with anyone now Ann was gone?

The last thing he expected to see as he walked into his kitchen was Beth in tears.

'What is it, Beth? Do you want to tell me?'

'I can't, I'm too ashamed.' She was sitting at the kitchen table, tears pouring down her cheeks. He'd never seen her cry before and suddenly felt awkward and clumsy, unsure what he should do or say. He didn't have the practice, he couldn't remember ever seeing Ann cry. So he stood, wondering if he should do something. Then a particularly loud sob made him put his arm about her, which only seemed to make matters worse as an even greater sob shook her body.

'Beth, it can't be as bad as all that,' he said kindly.

'It is, Jim. It's worse. I'm so afraid.'

'Then I think I should know why, don't you?' He crossed to the dresser and took down his bottle of malt and poured two large measures. 'Here, that is what you need.'

'I hate whisky,' she managed a watery smile.

'Then pinch your nose and pretend it's medicine – it'll calm you. Your friendly vet is telling you.' He sat down and placed his large, capable hand over her small but equally capable one. 'What's up, Beth?'

She took a deep breath and looked wildly about her, as if checking that no one else was listening. 'It's my husband.' She gulped. 'He's out of prison – been let out on parole, for good behaviour.' She snorted derisively at that. Jim sat stunned as he assimilated all these facts. He had not known Beth had been married, let alone to a jailbird.

'Is that bad?' he asked, and thought even as he spoke what an asinine question it was.

'Oh yes. He's vowed to kill me.' At this dramatic statement she began to weep again, but in earnest now. If Jim had thought she was crying before, he'd seen nothing compared with this. There seemed nothing he could do but let her cry, so he sat, patting her and stroking her hair until the storm had passed.

'Harry's not his, you see,' she finally said.

'Ah!' said Jim, for want of any other word, but reeling now and wondering how many more shocks Beth was about to deliver. She sat for some time gazing into space and then, almost with a jolt, launched herself into speech.

'He raped my best friend, you see, and to get back at him, I slept with his best friend. And got myself pregnant.'

'Are you sure Harry's not his?'

'Oh yes. I waited until he was inside.'

'Ah, well.' Jim looked wildly about the kitchen, hoping for inspiration.

'I had a letter from my aunt – she says he's going to find me and kill me.'

'Will he? I mean, people say stuff like that and don't mean it.'

'He does.'

'How does he know about Harry?'

'I told him. That was the whole point of sleeping with his friend, wasn't it?'

'I'm a bit out of my depth here, I'm afraid.' He tried laughing, not altogether successfully. How simple his own life with Ann had been, compared with a web like this. 'Can he find you? Would your aunt tell?'

'I don't think so.'

'Then don't worry. He'd have to get past me first.'

'Jim, you are a love.' Beth blew into a piece of handy kitchen paper. 'I know you've been angry with me. I know you think I went too far over organising you.'

'I wouldn't go so far –'

'Yes, you do. I've been so scared you'd ask me to go.'

'What on earth made you think that?' he said, having the grace to look embarrassed.

'I wouldn't have blamed you. I'd have understood – but now, with this hanging over my head . . .'

'Don't worry, Beth. It'll be all right. No one's going to hurt you,' he said, and as he did so he had the feeling that he was rapidly getting into problems he could well do without.

'Bless you, Jim. I'll do anything for you – anything.'

'That won't be necessary, Beth. Please!' He felt confused as he disentangled her arms from around him.

*

For the last few days Luna had had trouble climbing the spiral stairs to Thomasine's bedroom – her stomach was now so large she rolled like a drunken sailor when she walked. Not only was the effort too much for her, but it was too dangerous. So Thomasine had been sleeping on the sofa in her drawing room with Luna beside her in her basket – even getting to the comfort of the sofa was now too much for the bitch. It seemed as if she needed to be as close to Thomasine as possible at all times. She'd been told that when the time came Luna would become restless and would start to build herself a nest. Thomasine smiled as she looked down at the sleeping bitch. There was little activity there.

They were both in a small room that led off the kitchen, which, with its large windows, tiled floor and shelving had been intended as a conservatory, but which instead made an ideal workroom – Thomasine did not like to call it a studio, that seemed to be far too pretentious. The table beside her and the desk with its sloping top, like an architect's, were both covered in open books with illustrations of dogs. Thomasine was drawing a St Bernard. Or rather Thomasine was failing to draw a St Bernard. For several days she'd been occupied with this task, but each attempt looked wooden and insubstantial, and the wastepaper basket was full of this morning's rejects. She was trying to draw for Fee Walters' manuscript which, at her suggestion, she had sent to the one editor Thomasine knew. The woman had immediately shown interest in it and suggested Thomasine submit a couple of full-page colour illustrations. If she was successful, it could be the lucky break she needed, for this would be a lavishly illustrated children's book about a group of St Bernards. As she sketched she could not stop the dreams of becoming another E. H. Shephard to another A. A. Milne from floating about in her head. She'd enjoyed reading the book, and with her new-found interest in dogs, she felt she was in a better position to try to illustrate it than she might have been before Luna entered her life.

The latest effort was screwed up. This was hopeless, she could not get it right, perhaps it would be better to pack it in for this afternoon and try again tomorrow, she thought. She'd her household accounts to do, long overdue.

The paints set aside, she took down the shoebox in which she kept bills and receipts – how Robert would sneer at her filing system!

Luna moved onto her back so that her huge stomach rose like an inflated balloon. Thomasine watched her stomach, saw the rippling effect made by the puppies kicking inside.

'It must be hell in there, poor lady,' she said softly, and one large brown eye opened, regarded her for a second, and then closed. Luna had such a contented expression on her face that Thomasine could almost believe she was smiling.

Thomasine returned to her figures. An hour later she wished she hadn't begun. Maths had never been her strong point, but one did not have to be a mathematician to see that she was heading for a financial crisis.

Economise, but where? she asked herself. She did not live an extravagant life, rarely going out, only the odd pub lunch, and she'd bought no new clothes for ages. The move had been expensive, but still, where was the money going?

She began to break the figures down and made columns of sums – household, utilities, car and, at the last minute, she remembered to add a column for Luna's expenses.

Further into her calculations she reached the uncomfortable conclusion that she did not have enough money coming in to keep going as she was. She had written down an approximate figure of what she hoped to earn from her illustrations. The numbers jumped off the page as the realisation dawned that she would have to be producing illustrations like a conveyor belt, and far more than the market would ever demand of her, to make ends meet. It would take years for her to be recognised and be top notch – if she ever was. Maybe Robert had been right all along when he referred to her 'pin money'.

What other alternatives did she have? To get a job was the obvious, but doing what? She faced, bleakly, the prospect that there was little she could do – she had a minor painting talent, she could cook, sew, clean a house. That was all. She couldn't type, so office work was out; she had difficulty enough adding these figures up, so she wouldn't be much good in a shop. All she'd ever been was a housewife, she was trained for nothing else. She felt panic beginning to rise. Calm down, think logically, she told herself.

There was Robert, of course. She could pocket her pride and tell him she'd been mistaken and that she needed his help after all. But that meant confessing she'd been stupid in the first place, not working out a sensible budget – he would have. She looked up sharply – he no doubt already had! He'd have known exactly what her shares earned. He'd have asked publishing friends what she could earn with her illustrations. He'd already know she couldn't manage! The bastard! She mouthed the words. But why? To prove himself right yet again? To show he was still important to her? God knew. Well, she wouldn't give him the satisfaction. She'd find something to do. She was fit and strong – she'd do *anything* before she went begging to him.

And then she suddenly thought of the puppies. If she sold them, that would help. But what if they were ugly mongrels? Be optimistic, she thought, pray for bulldog pups.

The front door bell rang. Luna stirred, but showed no inclination to accompany her. Thomasine patted her head before walking from her workroom and through the kitchen, shutting the door behind her.

'Good afternoon?' she said enquiringly to the middle-aged couple on her doorstep. The woman was small of body, and features too; her face – which might have been pretty if her expression were not so strained – was surrounded by beautifully styled, naturally red hair. Her husband stood ramrod straight, white-haired and moustached, and so smartly turned out that Thomasine would have bet what little she had that he was ex-Army.

'Mrs Lambert?' he asked.

'Yes, I am,' she replied in the unsure way of one who, while knowing who she was, was unsettled as to why these strangers should enquire.

'I wonder if we might have a word?'

Thomasine stood holding the door, uncertain how to proceed. These people looked far too respectable to be burglars or mass murderers, she thought. The wife was far too nervous, the way she kept clutching and unclutching her gloved hands. But on the other hand, why was she so nervous? One could never be sure these days . . .

'I assure you we mean no harm,' the man said, as if reading her thoughts, and Thomasine felt ridiculously embarrassed at being caught out.

'I was thinking no such thing,' she laughed, perhaps a little too heartily. 'Come in, do.'

She ushered them into her drawing room and smilingly accepted their fulsome admiration of her house.

'Amazing what these architect chappies can do, isn't it?' her male visitor commented.

They all agreed, and Thomasine wondered if she should be offering them something to drink, but decided to wait to see what it was they wanted.

'Ronnie, you haven't introduced us. I'm Sally Tregidga, and this is my husband, Major Tregidga.' Sally spoke in a soft, pleasant voice.

'Cornish?' Thomasine asked. 'My sister lives near Penzance.' This was a mistake, for it encouraged the major, who was not as soft-spoken as his wife, to launch into an explanation of his Cornish antecedents. Thomasine could hear the clicking of Luna's claws on the kitchen quarry tiles.

'Ronnie, I think we should explain to Mrs Lambert . . .' Sally's voice trailed off, and she glanced at the kitchen door, at which Luna was now scratching.

'My dog,' Thomasine explained. 'She's dreadfully nosey.'

'It's like this, Mrs Lambert. It's difficult to know where to start, but . . .' He took a deep breath, as if in preparation of a long speech to come.

'Is the dog a bulldog?' Sally interrupted.

'Why, yes.'

'A fawn one?'

'Would you like to see her?' Thomasine asked, realisation dawning. No doubt they'd heard Luna was about to have puppies and perhaps they wanted one. She cheered up enormously at the prospect of a sale.

'No, Mrs Lambert. Not for the moment. I think it's best if we explain first.' The major held his hand up, palm towards her, like a traffic policeman. His voice rumbled on and Luna continued to batter at the door.

'We think, or rather we hope, you might have *our* bulldog,' Sally explained abruptly, interrupting her husband's flow.

Thomasine felt her stomach contract and had to sit down quickly. 'Yours? But I . . .' She wanted to say *I love her*, but stopped herself.

'You found her, we were told,' Sally continued anxiously. 'Abandoned on the by-pass by some brute.'

'That's right. But I'd need proof.'

'We have photographs.' Sally began to delve into her handbag, which she immediately dropped on the floor, the contents spilling everywhere. Flustered, she went down on all fours scooping up her possessions.

'Sally, darling, try to calm down, do. Let's explain a little more to Mrs Lambert, shall we? Our dog – a bitch – was stolen from our front garden in March.'

'It was all my fault. We never let her out the front unless one of us was watching her. We'd been warned by her breeder that bulldogs are so often stolen, they're so valuable and – oh, I can't even think about it, let alone say it.'

'Unscrupulous breeders,' the major explained for her.

'But the telephone rang and I left her – less than five minutes. But when I went back, she'd gone –'

'We posted rewards and put adverts in the papers –'

'We drove and drove around searching. It was such a desperately sad time –'

'But we had no luck, not one sighting, until this morning when my wife went to a new hairdresser – Snippers, I think it's called, and the young man said you had found one.'

'Gill,' Sally explained, nervously patting her hair. 'And he said it was about March time.'

'That's right.'

'Obviously you'd need proofs. Well, we've been listing them. She's got one crooked front tooth.'

'The vet said that was common in bulldogs,' Thomasine replied sharply.

'She's pregnant. The puppies are due Easter Monday,' Sally said. Thomasine was clutching her cardigan to her, for she felt suddenly cold in the heated room. Luna continued to scratch at the door in a demanding tattoo.

'Her nose, she's a little dip in the black pigment on the right nostril – a bit of skin fell off last summer. I always said it was sunburn,' Sally said, desperately trying to smile.

'I haven't noticed,' Thomasine answered honestly.

'She has an odd number of teats. Five pairs and then one on its own – eleven in all.'

Thomasine clutched the cardigan closer. She had noticed that. She often counted them to make sure she wasn't mistaken. Hadn't she counted them only this morning? Luna was, by now, hurling herself at the door.

178

Thomasine stood and walked towards it, afraid Luna might harm herself, but aware what the battering meant.

'Here, I've found them, the photographs!' Sally was holding them out to her.

'Somehow I don't think they're necessary,' Thomasine said, opening the door and Luna, despite her size, despite her swollen stomach, raced into the room, scampering across the parquet, skidding this way and that, yelping, barking, and with frenzied leaps jumped onto the sofa and hurled herself onto Sally, who disappeared under a hail of long, pink-tongued licks of welcome.

Sally was in tears, the major found it necessary to blow his nose, and Thomasine watched the reunion as ice settled around her heart. There was no doubt, she did not need the photographs, but they proved conclusively that the Tregidgas were Luna's rightful owners.

Now Thomasine heard that she was two and a half, had been mated with another bulldog – no mongrels for Luna – and that her name was Fengie.

'Short for Fengari – the Greek for moon,' the major explained. 'It was a full moon the night she was born.'

'Isn't that extraordinary, I called her Luna – Latin for moon,' Thomasine managed to say, her throat aching with crushed tears.

Luna, having licked Sally, was now reintroducing herself to the major, who Thomasine noted with approval did not, despite his immaculate suit, seem to mind. From the shopping bag they had with them, he produced a threadbare cuddly toy which might once have been a bulldog, but which now was difficult to identify.

'Her comforter, she's had it since she was a puppy,' the major, with a hint of embarrassment, explained.

Now Thomasine learned that so great had been their sense of loss that they had had to move house to get away from the memories.

'Weren't you worried she might one day return? Don't dogs travel great distances to get home?'

'Our daughter and her husband took over the house so we knew there would be someone there. Sally could not stay, not with the memories.'

'We even had to sell the three-piece suite – I kept finding her hairs and every time I did . . .' Sally flapped her hand at the horrific memory, though now tears of happiness were rolling down her cheeks.

The major searched in his inside pocket and produced a cheque book. 'We were offering a reward,' he explained as he took the top off his pen.

'No, please, I couldn't.' Thomasine put her hand on his to stop him. 'It's been a pleasure, she was a joy to have with me.' She stopped speaking for the simple reason she was too choked to continue.

'There must have been expenses – the vet, baskets, food.' The major waited patiently as Thomasine took a deep breath before she could continue.

'I haven't had the vet's bill yet, he was waiting until she whelped. The rest was nothing.'

Luna now lay contentedly sprawled half across Sally and half on the sofa. Thomasine wanted them to go now, this was more than she could bear.

'She's got some toys she's used to and a lead.' She hurried into the kitchen and leant against the sink, taking deep breaths, trying to calm herself. You never wanted the dog, this is the perfect solution, she tried to tell herself, but with little success. She didn't want Luna to go, she loved her, she needed her. She wouldn't let her go, what was that saying? 'Possession is nine tenths of the law'. They might be nasty about it, but she'd say 'see you in court' – though how she was to afford that would remain to be seen.

She returned to the drawing room with resolution. Luna slid off the sofa and waddled towards her and, with difficulty, jumped on her hind legs and pawed her. Thomasine bent down and nuzzled the dog's massive head. Luna licked her ear, nudged her as she often did and turned and lumbered back to Sally and sat at her feet, resting her back against her shins and looking as if she was smiling.

Thomasine felt as if the dog had just said goodbye to her. She looked at Luna, at her obvious happiness, and knew she could not part her from her family again.

Sally, as if sensing her distress, got to her feet, crossed the room and put her hand on Thomasine's shoulder. 'Thank you so much for caring for her for us,' she said. 'We're only in Lower Shilling, you can come any time you want to see her and the puppies.'

'I don't think I could do that.' Thomasine stood rigid.

'Do you want us to go?'

'Please,' she said bleakly.

The major did not bother to clip on Luna's lead as Sally collected her belongings and they moved towards the front door. 'If you're sure . . .'

'I'm sure,' Thomasine said, knowing she was losing the battle with her tears.

The front door opened and shut. Thomasine, who had felt rooted to the spot, suddenly rushed to the door and opened it as the couple, with Luna waddling between them, walked down the path. They turned and waved, almost apologetically. Luna did not look back.

May–June

17

Sophia returned late one evening from her visit to Yorkshire and swept into her father's house in the proprietorial way which always irritated Cora.

'You will stay, won't you, Sophia dear?' Cora asked, all smiles, for Cora was an expert in covering up how she really felt.

'Thank you, Cora, but no,' she said, but her returning smile was a quick, slick, professional one, a mere twitch of the bright scarlet-glossed lips. A smile which anyone else but Cora would have realised was only a polite tic.

'Are you sure? Well, have some supper before you go.' Cora continued to beam as she invited her, and such apparent generosity of spirit made Sophia seethe.

'No thank you. I've just come to pick Bandage up and I'll get straight on,' she managed to say in a reasonable tone. 'You eat too much in this house,' she added, as if she couldn't help herself, allowing a little of her edginess to show.

'Do we?' said Cora, puzzled, since she ate like a bird and constantly watched Ben's diet, since there was little she could do about his alcohol intake.

'I don't like the idea of you out in that car on these roads late at night,' Ben said to his daughter benignly, totally unaware of the undercurrent of unpleasantness Sophia had managed to build up in five minutes.

'Don't be silly, Daddy. You fuss too much. As if anyone's going to do anything to me with Bandage on board! Isn't that so, Bandage?' Bandage, who was lying contentedly in front of the log fire, appeared to be asleep, but one eye was very slightly open, sufficient to monitor the scene, but not enough to be noticed. His white socked paws did not move. His black, shiny chest rose and fell rhythmically.

'That flaming dog does nothing but sleep,' said Sophia. 'I can't think why Oliver wants him so much. He's so boring. He could at least have a dog that does something interesting.'

'Sophia, what a thing to say! Bandage is an absolute sweetheart. I've grown very attached to him. I said to Ben, if Sophia or Oliver don't want him, we'll have him.'

Sophia swung round and looked at her stepmother with an exasperated expression. 'I explained to you both, I want the dog for my protection in London. There is no question of my giving him away. If I'd given him away to anybody, it would have been Oliver, wouldn't it?'

'But I thought you already had?' said Cora, the fount of all innocence.

'Cora!' Sophia said, teetering close to losing her temper. She resisted the urge; she was fully aware how besotted her father was with this stupid woman.

'You owe me one, Sophia. I lied to Oliver for you.'

'What lie, Cora?'

'I told him Bandage had gone to Yorkshire with you. That you'd be gone two weeks. He kept calling.'

'I didn't ask you to lie for me.'

'What else was I supposed to do?'

'What do you want from me? Eternal thanks?' Sophia asked. 'Come on, Bandage.' And she kicked Bandage on his rump with her boot. Bandage leapt up, turned, and seeing it was Sophia, sat down. 'Bandage, come along, we're going now. Where's its lead?'

Ben fetched Bandage's lead, which Sophia clipped on to the choke chain round his neck. 'Thanks, Dad. Bye, Cora, *dearest*.' Again they went through the ritual of the smiles and Sophia pulled at Bandage's lead. The dog, not wishing to leave the fire, pulled in the opposite direction. 'Bandage, do as I tell you,' she said, crossly. But Bandage had no intention of doing what she said. He pushed his front paws into the Turkey rug and resisted with all his might. And all his might was far too much for Sophia. 'Dad, help me, will you? Kick him up the backside, or something.'

'He doesn't want to go, he likes it here,' said Ben, with a degree of satisfaction.

'He's not staying here, Dad, is that understood? He's coming with me.' Whereupon she took a copy of the *News of the World*, which happened to be lying on the coffee table, rolled it up, waggled it under Bandage's nose, and Bandage, frightened of nothing in the world except a rolled-up newspaper, stood up and followed her like a little lamb, out to the hall, click, click, click, his nails echoing Cora's high-heeled shoes clicking on the stone floor. Bundled into the back of the car, he lay down and promptly went back to sleep.

An hour and a half later Sophia parked outside her new house. She prodded Bandage awake and dragged the reluctant and still sleepy dog inside the house. In the hallway she opened a side door which led into the garage, littered with the remains of Oliver's furniture, for which there was no room in the house.

'Your days of sleeping in the house are over,' she said. 'You sleep there, is that understood?' She pointed at his basket, which was already in situ in a corner. Bandage looked at it too, but did not move towards it. She filled his water bowl and shook a few biscuits into his other bowl, switched off the light, slammed the door shut and locked it.

Bandage sat for a while, then crossed through the dark and nudged the door with his nose and then hit it with his paw. It did not budge. So he scratched it, and then harder and harder until the door was rattling.

'Shut up! Settle down.' Sophia banged on the other side, making Bandage jump back with fear. He sat in the dark listening to the silence and then he raised his snout in the air and howled.

Sophia, preparing for bed, heard but chose to ignore

him, putting in her ear plugs instead, blocking out the noise. Bandage howled on, but when no one came to fuss him, he slipped into his basket and collapsed on to his familiar-smelling blanket and was soon asleep.

The next morning Sophia was up early. After a healthy, but frugal breakfast, she began to unpack the tea chests stacked in the drawing room. She had an appointment at the *Design Today* office, but had planned to unpack two chests now and six in the evening. Methodical as always, she had worked out that in five days she should have the house organised to her meticulous standards. She would return after lunch, when a man from Sotheby's was coming to appraise the furniture in the garage.

Just as the first case was unpacked, and its contents unwrapped and sorted out on the sofa table, she remembered the dog. His hysterical welcome after his lonely night was not to her liking, and she spoke sharply to him before letting him out of the garage and into the small walled garden. She was even more put out when she noticed him crouching, and shuddered at the resultant pile of mess. She would need a dog walker, she made a mental note to phone an agency. There was no way she could allow the dog to defecate in her garden, it would have to be taken to the park. Bandage refused to come when she called, so she left him sniffing the small area. In her haste to get to her shower and dress she did not completely close the door to the garden, and was far from amused on her return to find Bandage contentedly asleep on the sofa in the drawing room.

'Off!' she ordered. Since there was no response, she grabbed some of the newspaper wrappings and waved them at the dog. Bandage jumped quickly to the floor, ran around the room as if in confusion until he found a corner and stood in it, facing the wall.

'Oh, for God's sake, don't start that stupid game. I haven't time.' She flicked the newspaper across his snout, grabbed hold of his collar and dragged him back through the hall into the garage, and slammed the door shut. After this exercise, she checked in the hall mirror that her make-up and hair were still intact.

In the kitchen she scribbled a note for her new cleaning lady. Unbeknown to Oliver, she had sacked the Filipinos. The house was far too small for live-in staff. She smiled in self-congratulation at her smartness – part of her separation agreement with Oliver was that he would pay the staff salaries. So with no staff she would pocket the money. She propped the note against the kettle; it told the woman what chores she wanted done and warned her that Bandage was in the garage. She added a PS, reassuring her that he was placid and wouldn't hurt a soul, but not to disturb him.

When the cleaning woman arrived the dog heard first the key in the door, then her footsteps in the hall. He was on his feet in a trice, pounding at the door, whining loudly. When it did not open immediately, he began to howl. The cleaning lady loved dogs. And the one thing she could not abide was to hear one cry, so she opened the garage door and let Bandage out.

'Aren't you a fine specimen, to be sure?' she said, and patted him as he welcomed her effusively. 'Do you want some milk, or something? Some Weetabix? My little Cassie loves a Weetabix for breakfast. You come with me.' And Bandage, secure in the tone of her voice and her smell, padded along behind her into the kitchen and waited patiently, tail wagging a tattoo on the tiled floor as she prepared the Weetabix. Liking the woman, he followed her round the house as she worked. He spent a busy hour sniffing and checking the furniture and objects in the rooms, recognising those familiar to him, having to inspect more closely anything that was new. That done, he sat in the hall and watched the door.

'You waiting for your mum?' she said as she passed him to answer a knock on the door. But when she opened it to the delivery man, Bandage was on his feet and through it in one swift movement. A mighty leap, his

189

muscles rippling beneath his shining black coat, and he cleared the gate and was up the road in a flash.

'Bandage, come back,' the cleaning lady cried. 'Oh my God, what do I do now?' she pleaded with the delivery man. 'Will you chase him?'

'Not me, I've got work to do. Call the police,' he advised unhelpfully, and climbed back into his van. Bandage was already out of sight.

Bandage ran along the unfamiliar pavement, his nose close to the ground, nostrils splayed wide, allowing the air to flow freely up his long snout and across his sensitive olfactory organ. Several thousand different smells swirled about his nose. Amongst them he was searching for the one which was most important to him, the smell of security, the familiar smell of Oliver and home.

His four paws beat a rhythm on the pavement. Neatly skirting people, never lifting his nose, never deviating from his task – the instinct that led him home. He crossed Kensington High Street, not pausing for the traffic. A Volvo smashed into the back of a BMW, but he was long gone when the enormous row that he had caused erupted in his wake. With each step the scent he had searched for increased in strength. He moved faster until in the end he was running, swifter than he had ever done before, down his street, through his gate and to his door. He scratched at it and waited, but it did not open. He snuffled at the crack at the bottom of the door, whining, but still it did not open. He tired of trying and lay down. What was left of the morning passed, the afternoon slipped by, evening came. The dog, at intervals, whined and scratched the door. As night set in, and still no one came, Bandage pointed his black head to the sky, opened his large mouth and howled again.

A window next door opened sharply. 'Stop that bloody racket,' shouted a man. Bandage, frightened by the anger in the man's voice, crept back to the door, curled up on the basement step and finally went to sleep.

The arrival of the milkman woke him. It was not the usual milkman, but Bandage still stepped forward to welcome him as he clattered down the basement steps. 'That's odd, look at that. That's Saturday and Sunday's milk there, not touched. Have they gone out and left you? Poor dog.' Bandage wagged his tail in response. 'Gone away for the weekend, I expect. Forgot to take you with them, did they? Rotten buggers. Still, if that milk isn't taken in tomorrow, then I think I ought to call the police, don't you, boy?' He patted Bandage on the head, and carefully closed the gate behind him.

Bandage was very hungry. He sniffed at the milk bottles, licked with his tongue at the silver tops, but couldn't get them off. The postman arrived. 'Bandage? Is that you? What are you doing here? You don't live here no more,' he said, as he put the post through the letterbox. And, whistling through his teeth, was on his way, leaving the gate open. Bandage scratched at the door again. It remained firmly closed. He climbed the area steps, slipped through the open gate, and padded off in the direction of his favourite place, the park.

It was a large park, which Bandage had visited most days with Oliver, with a special dog area, where dogs were allowed off their leads. Bandage trotted through the gate and made straight for the other dogs. He spent a sociable hour playing; there was no aggression, since they all knew each other from their morning walks. Several people patted Bandage and asked him where Oliver was. These dogs were walked before their owners went to the office in the morning, and so by nine they had disappeared and Bandage was alone in the park, since the dogs that were walked by their mistresses after breakfast and before morning coffee had not yet appeared. Becoming restless, he moved into an area where he never normally went.

He was trotting along when a park keeper began to

shout aggressively at him. Bandage stopped, flattened his ears and looked sideways at the man, who was waving a fork as he advanced upon him. With a sudden jump, Bandage was facing in the opposite direction and running quickly away from the shouting voice.

Ahead of him, sitting on a park bench, was a fat child eating an ice cream. Bandage was always attracted to children, and ice cream: the combination was irresistible. The dog bounded up, his tail wagging, jumped up at the child, at the same time as his long, pink tongue licked the ice cream. The child screamed, dropped the cone onto the dirty path, and Bandage immediately gobbled it down. The child's screams were augmented by those of a woman who rushed towards them and scooped the large child into her arms. The boy was now crying bitterly at the loss of his ice cream, but his mother, misinterpreting his cries, shouted and yelled for help. 'My child's been bitten! My child's been bitten.'

A group of people began running towards them. 'It's a pit bull,' one shouted. 'Get the police,' another called. Bandage sat on the path looking up at the people, his tongue lolling.

'Filthy dogs, I hate them.' A man spat in his direction.

'Where's that bloody policeman? Bloody dogs!' A man shook his fist at him.

'There, there, love. Should we call an ambulance for the little one?'

Bandage's tail ceased to wag; there was anger around him. A man, older than the others, approached him. He held his hand out to Bandage, palm upwards. 'There, boy, have a sniff of that,' he said, as he steathily lifted his other hand to grab at Bandage's collar. With a quick movement the dog stood up and crashed into the small crowd, passing between the legs of an elderly woman, who went flying, banging her head on the ground. Legging it across the grass, he sped towards the large gates which would take him to the road that ran parallel with his home.

The dog's ears were pinned back in terror. His eyes rolled in his head. This was a new experience. People did not normally shout at him when he was in the park with Oliver.

The large gates of the park were closed. Bandage trotted towards the small side one. As he reached it, two youths appeared, walking through the narrow gateway. One of them lunged at Bandage, grabbing him by his collar.

'Here, Guy, look at this. It's a pit bull.'

'Nah, it's not. Pit bulls are squatter than that and they're brown. He's black and white. And in any case, he hasn't got no muzzle on.'

'Maybe he took it off.'

'Don't be bloody silly. That's the whole point of a muzzle, a dog can't get it off, can it? Has he got an address there? Maybe he's valuable, maybe there's a reward for him.' Guy fumbled with Bandage's name tag. 'Cor, there's posh, those houses are very big and rich.'

'How about it, then? How about we take him back and get a reward?' asked Terry.

'There wouldn't be much point in that now, would there? I mean, he doesn't look as though he's been on the run long, maybe he just slipped out this morning. Better we take him with us, leave it a couple of days, then we'll go round and they'll be bloody desperate to get the dog back, won't they? Then they'll give us more money,' Guy said, proud of his own logic.

'Right then, mate. Come on then, let's get it home.'

Guy had to pull hard on the belt, since Bandage was reluctant to go with them, especially as it was in the opposite direction to home. He dug in his four paws firmly, and they slid across the paving stones as the two boys yanked and pulled at him. Terry, tiring of this, walked round to Bandage's rear and gave him a hard kick. He yelped.

'Serves you bloody right, get a move on,' Terry snarled.

They finally reached their objective, which was a Ford that had seen better days and was now held together by prayer and Superglue. They manhandled a reluctant Bandage onto the back seat, got in the front, and were soon hurtling off into the traffic. Bandage leant his nose against the window, sniffing desperately at the edge of the glass. The car was moving down a wide, busy road and was soon across the Chiswick flyover.

18

The sale of Alan's house in Morristown was seriously delayed. It was, it transpired, the last in a chain, and until the owners of the house two properties back sorted out their negative equity with the building society, no one else could budge.

In some ways, he decided, it was as well, since he'd not been exactly bursting with energy way back in April when he'd begun to pack up. Now he felt full of vim, so he'd taken a couple of days' leave to finalise the packing. He was surprised when the telephone rang.

'Alan? Sorry to bother you, but something's come up.' He heard the familiar voice of Dan, his Chief Superintendent in the Special Operations Unit.

'No problem. What's to do?'

'It's probably nothing, but since you're in the area, it won't do any harm to check it out. The girlfriend of one of the uniformed inspectors was in a pub in Morristown, and she overheard somebody saying that if you wanted a good fight, you should go to The Locomotive. Now that could mean a punch-up fight, it could mean a bare-knuckle fight, or it could mean a dog fight. It's as vague as that. I wouldn't normally bother, but –'

'No, while I'm here. Mind you, I've been to The

Locomotive and all I saw was a Siamese cat – not a pit bull in sight.'

'Another strange thing has happened. We've had a vet call from a good fifty miles from Morristown. He'd had to put a badly wounded dog to sleep. The owner said the dog had been in a fight with an Alsatian in the park. The thing is, the dog was a pit bull.'

'But these fighting types don't normally take their dogs to the vet. They treat them themselves.'

'I know. It's most unusual, and maybe the owner was being honest. He did say that since the dog was muzzled it didn't stand a chance against the other dog. Or maybe he was inordinately fond of the dog, or new to the game. Whichever, the vet didn't like the set-up. The man paid in cash – no name, no address. The vet says he doesn't know why, but he watched the bloke leave.'

'He got his car number?'

'No, not as good as that, but he did see a garage sticker in the back window. A Morristown garage, no less. It's a strange coincidence, isn't it? I suggest you link up with Andy and stake it out together.'

'Great.' Alan was pleased now he didn't have to rush back to Horsham. Maybe he'd even meet up with Kimberley again.

'I always feel safe with you,' Andy said to him as, a couple of days later, they walked through Morristown together. 'Big bloke like you, who's going to duff us up?'

'Famous last words.' Alan grinned and looked down at Andy, a good four inches shorter and three stone lighter. 'Just because I'm big doesn't mean I like to fight.'

The Locomotive had once been a seedy, run-down public house. A couple of years ago it had had a brewery face-lift, and was now awash with maroon buttoned plush, artful lighting, reproduction mirrors and extravagantly decorated frosted glass. No Victorian habitué in a time warp would ever have recognised his old hostelry.

He might recognise the smell though, sour beer mixed with sour sweat, overlaid by stale nicotine.

The bar was heaving, which was good, for they could melt in with the crowd far better. They bought beers and, trying not to look conspicuous, moved amongst the customers and did what they were here for – they listened. It was at times like this Alan realised how boring most conversations were. He felt he could almost predict what people would say, whether it was football, the lottery, sex or the Government. And he was sure he'd heard every combination of every dirty joke there was to tell.

An hour and two pints later Andy was deep in conversation with an old man and Alan, his feet killing him, looked about for somewhere to sit and spied a space at one of the tables over in the corner.

'If you don't mind, Andy, I'm going to take the weight off my feet for a minute, okay?' He did not even wait for Andy's reply, but inched his way, carefully nursing his pint, to the table in the corner, asked the occupant if the seat was taken, and sat down, unaware that he sighed with relief.

'I know how you feel,' said the young, blonde woman with a startlingly red mouth, who was sitting on the plush banquette. 'I've been on my feet all day too.' The bright yellow curls bounced on her head as she spoke to him.

'Really?' said Alan. 'It's the standing still, I'm not used to it.' He rubbed the small of his back.

'Walk a lot, do you?' she asked.

'Quite a bit.'

'What, you a copper?' she asked suspiciously.

'No thanks,' he laughed.

'What do you do then?'

'I've been on sick leave,' he was able to answer truthfully. 'And you, what do you do?'

'I work in that big new Tesco the other side of town. I'm a supervisor,' she replied proudly.

'I haven't been there yet. I've been away.'

'Really? You staying for keeps now?'

'I haven't made my mind up yet.'

'I hope you stay.' She smiled at him in such a suggestive way he wished he hadn't chosen this table, she wasn't his type at all. 'Lots of people don't like Morristown. Me, I wouldn't live anywhere else. There's a lot to do, nice pubs, cinemas, good clubs. I like it here.'

'I went up the sports centre the other day, I was impressed.'

She looked him up and down with a bold expression. 'Bet you got a wonderful body under that there shirt.'

'Bet you say that to all the boys.'

She threw back her head to laugh and the curls bounced as if they had a life of their own. A man appeared at the table holding two glasses, a pint of beer for himself and a lager and lime for the girl. Alan stood up. 'Sorry, mate, did I take your seat?'

'No, of course you didn't, he's sitting the other side of me, aren't you, Vic? This is Vic.'

'I'm Alan,' he replied, glad that surnames were not necessary, but feeling animosity from Vic.

'And I'm Vicky. Vic and Vicky, funny, isn't it?' she laughed. 'Alan's been poorly.' Vic grunted in reply, and his bored expression showed he wasn't in the least bit interested in Alan's health.

'Vic drives a lorry, don't you, Vic? Delivering fertiliser to farms, that's what he does. It's good money.'

'I'm glad someone's doing all right.' Alan stretched his legs; from beneath the table came a soft growling noise, not an aggressive growl, but more a warning. Alan bent down. There, his lead twined round the table leg, securely muzzled, was a large pit bull terrier. 'Hello, what's your name?' He felt a surge of adrenalin at sight of the dog.

'Tyson,' said Vicky. 'It's a good name for him, isn't it?'

'Oh yes,' said Alan, lying through his teeth; how many poor dogs were called Tyson, he wondered. Whenever he heard that name in relation to a fighting breed of dog warning bells rang.

'You interested in dogs?' Vic asked.

'I like them, yes. I haven't got one at the moment. Had a Rottweiler at home,' he lied, in the hope of making Vic open up.

'Yeah, I had a Rottweiler. Didn't get on with the neighbours though, did it?' Vic laughed, and Vicky laughed with him.

'I don't know if I like the muzzle,' said Alan. 'Looks bloody uncomfortable. Stupid bloody politicians, stupid bloody act! A friend of mine's dog got done – no muzzle. He'd only taken it off for a minute, and they took the dog away and it's got to be destroyed. It's a mess of a law, if you ask me.'

'You only have to read in the papers about them dogs what have been locked up for years while their poor bloody owners try and explain that they're not even pit bulls.' Vicky was quite animated when she spoke. 'So when you've got one, a real one, like Tyson here, then you have to be very careful.'

'Very careful indeed,' Vic said, more friendly now.

'He looks pretty docile to me,' said Alan.

'He is. He's an old softy. Enjoys a bit of a scrap sometimes, though, don't you, Tyson darling?' Vicky patted him under the table and the dog's round rump waggled in appreciation. Alan did not see Vic's reaction, but sensed a tension returning.

'Well, if you'll excuse me, better get some shut-eye, I think. Busy day tomorrow.' Alan stood up. 'See you again, then.'

Because of his height he was able, easily, to look over the heads of the other people and indicate to Andy that he was leaving. They walked up the road and zigzagged through various back streets until they reached Andy's dark blue Ford saloon. Andy switched on the engine and they sped away from the area of The Locomotive.

'So?' said Andy.

'I'm not sure. It's pretty obvious, but I wonder if it isn't all *too* obvious. The bloke I was talking to had a pit bull with him, correctly muzzled, called Tyson, of course, what else?'

'Rambo,' laughed Andy.

'It was something the girl said. We were agreeing how docile the dog was and what a mess the Dangerous Dog Act is, and she said something about he liked to scrap occasionally, that's all. The mood changed. I don't know, I may have over-reacted or something.'

'Doesn't sound so to me. I got bogged down with that old boy, and all he wanted to talk about was flaming D-Day. I'd have been interested at any other time. Still, all in the line of duty – as he kept saying ad nauseam. Did they say anything to make you think they're regulars there?'

'No, but I think they are. They sat there as if they knew the pub well and every one in it.'

'Let's pray we're onto something. You coming back to Horsham?'

'No. I've got a few days off still. I thought I'd suss out fertiliser supply companies – our Vic back there works for one. You never know. But I'd better leave The Locomotive for a night or two.' Andy dropped Alan in front of his house with the sold sign. 'See you on Monday.' He banged the roof of the car in farewell.

Once he was in, he put the kettle on for a cuppa and had a pee. He plugged in the television set but, finding nothing of interest, flicked it off again. He went through the mail that had arrived that morning, but it was all boring circulars. He'd dismantled his bed and so made one up on his mother's old sofa, turned the light off and waited for sleep.

Sleep, however, was a long time coming. He had to calm down from the excitement of meeting the pit bull. Over and over again he re-ran the evening's conversation, trying to find a clue he might have overlooked.

Then he began to think of Kimberley. He couldn't get her out of his mind. There was something about her, a sadness he wanted to take away; a loneliness, a bit like his own; a wariness he recognised in himself. The caution of one who has been hurt in the past and is afraid of the future.

19

'Who says the countryside's quiet?' Wimpole was noisily dusting the bookcases in Oliver's study.

'You're certainly adding to the sum of things.' Oliver frowned with concentration as he pushed another button on his computer, and what he expected to see did not turn up on the screen. 'Oh come on, don't bugger about,' he said sternly to the inanimate object.

'What does that mean?' Wimpole stood, hands on hips, her usual stance when spoiling for a fight.

'The computer won't do what I want it to,' he replied obtusely, knowing full well what Wimpole was about.

'You know what I mean – *the sum of things*.' She waved her bright yellow duster in the air.

'I was just commenting that if it wasn't quiet in here it was mainly because of you.' He said this with a broad grin.

'I'll have you know I was woken at flaming six this morning, with all those bloody birds yammering away.'

'Most people enjoy the dawn chorus.'

'I'm not most people.'

'Evidently,' he said under his breath.

'What was that?'

'Nothing.' His grin was not working this morning, that was for sure. 'You a bit grumpy, Wimpole? Something not to your liking?'

'I said. It's bloody noisy here. I hate birds.'

'You wanted to get me a budgie once, don't you remember?'

'That's different. I don't mind them in cages. No, it's those damn crows, and why do the planes fly so low? You don't get that in London, do you?'

'They fly low here because if they crash they kill fewer people. Logical, isn't it? We don't count.'

'Then why don't they fly higher?'

'They're practising, Wimpole, in case we have a war,' he said patiently.

'You needn't talk to me as if I was a five-year-old.'

He longed to tell her not to behave like one then, but he didn't. He might be trying to make a joke of this, but Wimpole was obviously bored and restless. He feared she was not adjusting as well as he had first hoped.

'What about doing some gardening?' he suggested.

'It's raining, but you haven't even noticed, stuck in here with that machine.'

'I thought I might go to London later today.'

'Where you going?' Curiosity, as usual, had got the better of her.

'I'm fed up getting Sophia's answerphone all the time – I'm going up to collect Bandage.'

'And the best of British!' She attacked the bookshelves with vigour. 'And don't forget you've got to interview that cook woman in an hour.'

'Can't you?'

'No, I can't. It's your house, you're paying the wages.'

'Well, sit in on it then.'

201

'I might.'

He smiled to himself – Wimpole would not miss the interview for worlds – and looked about the room with satisfaction. The house was coming together nicely. The builders and decorators had been beavering away under his supervision for over a month now. He'd been to Morristown, London and even Shillingham choosing wallpapers and paints, something he'd never imagined himself doing – Sophia had always attended to such matters – but had found immeasurably enjoyable. And doing so made him feel he was becoming a deeply domesticated animal.

The book, despite the many interruptions caused by his new-found domesticity, was coming along far better than he had dared hope. He worked on the long refectory table which Aunt Phoebe had used. He remembered how it had looked then. On one end of the table would be any reference books required for the particular novel she was working on. In the middle was work that had already been typed up by her secretary, and at the other end was Phoebe's large, black oak chair, intricately carved with reclining lions for arm rests, and the yellow legal pad and proper fountain pen that she always used in front of her. He sat on the chair, but the yellow pad was replaced by his Apple-Mac, and there were no reference books since everything was in his head. He felt enormous contentment at the end of each day as he switched off the machine. Wimpole was going to have to adjust, for Oliver had begun to think he could never live in the city again.

An hour later Grace knocked on the door to announce that her friend, Hazel Anderson, was waiting to be interviewed. Ten minutes after that, Oliver was aware that not only was it he who had been interviewed, not Hazel, but that somehow he'd failed to come up to scratch. It seemed that Hazel had not approved of his modern kitchen, artfully masquerading as rustic, and in keeping with the house. Nor had she liked his Aga, when he'd thought everyone loved them. And finally, he had to presume she hadn't liked him much either.

'Call that an interview?' Wimpole laughed when Hazel had swept grandly from the kitchen saying that she'd let him know.

'You weren't much help.'

'I didn't like her when she walked in. That hair's not natural – bottle blonde. She wouldn't have fitted in.'

'Problem is, Wimpole, what do we do? Cooks aren't exactly thick on the ground round here.'

'You'll think of something.'

'I'll go to Marks in Morristown and get some ready prepared meals.'

'There, solved already,' Wimpole grinned, which was an improvement on her sullen face so far today.

One of the painters stuck his head around the door to let him know the drawing room was finished. Oliver went happily to the task he loved – hanging his paintings.

The hanging completed, he changed and prepared to drive to London. He'd been too patient over his dog. Something had to be resolved. What had galvanised him today was a letter from his lawyer, back from his holidays, saying that Sophia's lawyer had said he didn't know what Oliver was talking about, his client had not consulted him about any dog.

The closer he drove to London, the more excited he became at the thought of seeing Bandage, and the more angry he became at the thought that they had been apart for so long. Her attitude over Bandage had been the pettiest thing of all. If she begged him on bended knee to take her back, he never would. Not now.

Sophia answered his knock on the door of her smart Kensington house in its equally smart square, which had cost him a king's ransom. The price would have bought her a mansion in the countryside.

'Oh, Oliver!' she said, almost as if she was informing him that that was his name.

'Yes, that's me,' he said cheerily.

'You needn't be so facetious,' she replied, and Oliver thought, Oh dear, here we go again. 'Why are you here?'

'Do I have to have a reason? Can't I just pop in like anybody else?' He smiled at her and hoped it looked halfway genuine.

'Hardly! Not you. Have you got the Hockney back yet?'

'I'm sorry?' he said as he followed her along the narrow hallway.

'The Hockney that used to hang on the stairwell, have you got it back yet?'

'I presumed you'd taken it.'

'Don't be silly, we'd agreed on the paintings. I sent it to be reframed for you as a birthday present.'

'Good Lor'.' The words were out too quickly and he couldn't retrieve them. By the stiffness of her back he realised that she had heard them too.

'You know something, Oliver?' she turned and stared at him. 'You know one of the things that irritated me more than anything else about you was your pathetic little attempts at sarcasm.'

'Sorry,' he said, and wondered whether she was going to add 'the lowest form of wit'. She didn't. Instead she opened the door of the small, elegantly furnished drawing room.

'Very nice, like a little doll's house.' He meant it as a compliment, and for once she smiled back, accepting it as such. He crossed the room to the doors which led to the garden. 'Shame they have to have these grilles on, isn't it,' he said. 'Still, no one would try to come in with Bandage here.' He half turned. 'I've been thinking about Bandage, Sophia.'

204

As he spoke, she sat down, not gracefully, but rapidly, all of a heap, not at all like Sophia. What was more, he couldn't quite analyse the expression on her face. Had it been anybody else, he would have said it was fear, but he knew that Sophia wasn't afraid of anything.

'Yes,' she said, in a small voice.

'I mean, everything else went so well. We agreed on virtually everything – that is, that you could have it.' He tried to laugh, found it didn't work, and stopped. For once, she didn't react. 'The truth is, Sophia, I don't want to fall out with you over anything, and that includes Bandage. But you know how I feel about the dog, and I wondered whether it wouldn't be fairer all around, if you need a dog here, and I understand you would feel happier with one, if I bought you another one and I had Bandage back.'

She did not reply. He had expected an instant no so, emboldened, he continued. 'Let's face it, you never were the best of friends, were you? And I've moved to Phoebe's house now, and Bandage would love to live in the country.'

From Sophia emerged a sob. Since Sophia was the last woman on earth one expected to cry, Oliver looked at her in amazement. 'Sophia? What's the matter?' She fumbled in her skirt pocket, produced a rather inadequate handkerchief and blew her nose, but tears continued to tumble down her perfectly made-up features.

He felt a rush of unease, a tightening in his own stomach. He sat down beside her and patted her hand. 'Come on, Sophia, what is it? You can tell me.'

She turned and looked at him with anguished eyes. 'You'll never forgive me,' she said.

'Try me.' He tried to sound encouraging, but was beginning to feel fear himself.

'It's Bandage. He's gone.'

'Bandage? Gone?' Oliver repeated inanely. 'What do you mean? Gone where?' But as he asked, instinct told him worse was to come.

'He ran away. The morning after I brought him back from my father's. I put him in the garage to sleep.'

'You did what?' said Oliver indignantly. 'You know Bandage feels the cold.'

'I know, I know.' She patted her eyes with the now sodden handkerchief. 'I had a new cleaning woman, I told her not to go in there, to leave him alone. But she didn't. He was crying, apparently, and she let him out, then a delivery came and he escaped.'

Even in a sitting position Oliver felt his legs weaken. 'What did you do?' he said, trying to sound reasonable, sympathetic and hopeful, all at the same time. Instead he was seething with fury, anger and distress, and more than anything, wanted to slap this careless, selfish woman's face.

'I went to the police, of course I did. I posted a reward notice in the local newsagents. I spoke to all the shopkeepers and I put an advertisement for one whole week in the local newspaper offering a reward. And, Oliver, I can't tell you how desperately sorry I am, but there hasn't been a word about him.'

Oliver stood, surprised to find that his legs did, after all, support him. 'I see.' He felt cold around his heart. 'I see,' he repeated. 'I suppose there's no point in my looking then.'

'No, not really. It's been several weeks now. That's why I've been avoiding you and not answering your phone calls. I didn't know how to tell you, Oliver. I'll buy you another one.'

At that Oliver swung round. 'Don't be so bloody stupid. You never understood, did you? You can't just buy another one. That was Bandage, he was unique, you can't suddenly go out to the pet shop and buy another Bandage. But you never grasped it, did you? Never realised how I felt about that dog. That misunderstanding sums up our relationship, our marriage, doesn't it? Bloody waste it's all been.' And for the first time, Oliver allowed her to see the bitterness he felt. He turned, walked out of the door and, as he slammed it shut, hoped he would never have to set eyes on her again.

20

Thomasine put down her pencil and gazed out of the window. She could not work today, she was too angry. She'd hoped that by working on her dog illustrations she would calm herself, but it hadn't worked. She wished Robert was here, for she wanted to hit him.

He had not even had the courtesy to phone or write himself, but had arranged for his lawyer to write to her. The letter, which had arrived yesterday, asked for the return of a ring she owned.

'What do you mean, you want it?' she asked over the telephone.

'For Chantal – it's a family heirloom.'

'But your mother gave it to me on my twenty-first birthday.'

'Only because she presumed you'd always be my wife.'

'I'm keeping it.'

'You can't do that.'

'Try me. I love that ring.' It was a pretty Georgian ring of opals and pearls and she did love it, despite her mother saying it would be unlucky.

'It's not the value of the ring. It's the fact that it's always been in my family.'

'I'll leave it to Nadine, then it will stay in your beloved family.' She could not keep the bitterness out of her voice.

'I'll pay you for it.'

'You creep!'

'You must need the money.'

'I'm fine, as a matter of fact. Don't bother.' And she slammed the telephone down, which was so unlike her that she could easily imagine the look of shock and surprise on Robert's face. Serves him right, she thought. She'd always done what he wanted. So often she had acquiesced. How many times, how many things?

She had started to feel angry with him back in April; now it was nearly June and she was furious. Not only had he humiliated her by choosing, over her, a woman young enough to be his daughter, but he'd insidiously worked on Nadine, alienating her too. She learnt in her weekly phone calls to Nadine what presents she was getting, the clothes, the holidays, the treats – none of which she could compete with. Was this the real reason he had not pointed out to her that she could not possibly manage? That he wanted Nadine all to himself?'

She *would* manage, and what was more, she'd insist Nadine come here more often. She was not going to just sit back, the dutiful little ex-wife, and let him have it all his own way. That role had got her nowhere, and she shuddered with anger that she'd ever allowed herself to be such a malleable wimp.

She looked down at her drawing and thought how bad it was. He was even affecting how she worked! She must pull herself together.

Luna going had been a blow she had not recovered from, and yet, today, she found herself wondering if she had used the loss of the dog to hide the misery over Robert. It would explain why she was still so dispropor-tionately unhappy. Not that she intended to replace her; she had no intention of exposing herself to such misery ever again.

From behind the small bookcase she took a chart she had begun to compile earlier in the spring, when the garden had first began to sprout, but since Luna had gone she had not bothered with. Now she pencilled in where the primulas had flowered, shaded in the large bunch of Michaelmas daisies, and where she was almost sure there was to be a fine display of lilies later.

That done, she looked about for other tasks. She studied the illustrations again. She had to finish them, she only had one more week to present them. What she needed was to draw from life.

She pulled the directory towards her and looked up Eveleigh Brenton's number.

Eveleigh's Brenton's sitting room was a cluttered, cosy mess. Aromatherapy oils burned in two small earthenware pots, but the scent from half a dozen of them could not have competed with the all-pervading smell of dog. All the sofas were misshapen, squashed and covered in hairs. Thomasine was glad that she had worn jeans and a fawnish sweater so that Eveleigh need not be fussed about her clothes.

Eveleigh was shouting at her from the kitchen as she made them tea. A large St Bernard was draped over one sofa, and a small King Charles spaniel watched her balefully from a wing chair the opposite side of the fireplace. On the floor, a blanket covering it, was another St Bernard who appeared to be sleeping, though breathing in a rather laboured way.

Eveleigh appeared with the tray of tea.

'Do King Charleses always look as baleful as that one? She's looking at me really resentfully, as if I've no right to be here.' Thomasine laughed at the little dog's expression.

Eveleigh handed her a cup of tea. 'Ah, that's Coco. I'm afraid she was born middle-aged and depressed. I often think that she feels life has let her down, that really she should be living in a great mansion on a silk cushion with strawberries and cream for tea instead of landing up in my cottage with me!' Eveleigh chucked the little dog under the chin. The dog was apparently happy, since its tail was wagging, but it only managed to look more soulful. 'So, how can I help? A book, you say?'

'It's not definite. I have to submit two paintings. It's exciting. There aren't many illustrated novels these days, mainly picture books. But this is to be a novel for eight- to ten-year-olds with colour plates, so it's a big opportunity for me. I probably won't get it, but, of course, I've got to try.'

'Of course.' Eveleigh handed her a plate of sandwiches. 'How exciting, a novel about St Bernards, I shall certainly buy it. What's it about, or is it a secret?'

'I don't think so. Fee Walters wrote it. It's about a group of St Bernards in a monastery in Switzerland who have been made redundant as rescue dogs; replaced by helicopters and Alsatians. They run away and search for their own Shangri-la; of course they have lots of adventures on the way before finding a new home in Scotland, where they become rescue dogs again.'

'How delightful! Oh my darling Issy, maybe you're going to be a star.' Isolde, the St Bernard draped over the large sofa on the other side of the room, managed to lift her magnificent head in acknowledgement for a moment before it crashed back on the cushions. She then stretched her long white legs, ending in huge paws, before relaxing back into a deep sleep. 'The problem, as you see, might be finding them awake long enough to draw them,' Eveleigh laughed.

'Have you always had St Bernards?'

'Oh, yes. When I was a child we had one, Heidi. And when I married, my husband gave me one as a birthday present. Then my interest just grew – that's how most people get involved with the dog world, by stages. I loved the dog, and first I thought how lovely it would be if she had puppies. We mated her, Lorelei she was called, bless her. We had a very successful litter, and what started as a hobby grew. We went to the odd show, but as we became more successful the excitement got hold of us – you know, it gets into the blood. And my husband, he was interested in the King Charleses, and he bred those, and this little one's the last one of the last litter he bred.' She looked away, and Thomasine wondered if it was because she was close to tears.

'And this dog, why is it covered in a blanket?'

'Because he's dying,' said Eveleigh simply.

'I am sorry.' Thomasine was not sure what else to say in the circumstances.

'There's no need to be. He's had a good life. He's fourteen, which is a fine age for a St Bernard to reach. Jim said that my dogs live to such great ages because I love them so much and they want to live for me.' She delved into her pocket for a handkerchief, into which she blew loudly. 'That was a lovely thing for him to say, wasn't it?'

'Yes, but I'm sure he said it because it's the truth.'

'Siegfried is really a kennel dog, but when they're ill or poorly or depressed, or when the end is near, I like to bring them indoors. Fuss them that little bit more.'

'It must be awful. I mean –' Thomasine's hand stroked her thigh. She hadn't thought of this aspect of dog owning. '– fourteen years is a long time. I mean, to know a person and have them leave,' she said, clumsily, she felt.

'It is. And you're right to use the word "person"; they are to me. I tell myself constantly that I'm only to be privileged to have their friendship for a short time. I like to think it helps me when we reach this point. Though it rarely does, it always hurts.'

'How long . . . ?' Thomasine did not like to ask the rest of the question, for in a strange way it seemed not very tactful to ask in front of the dog itself, even though he appeared to be deeply asleep.

'Tomorrow. I've already phoned Jim and asked him to come. I owe it to the dog, he can't go on much longer like this, it would be cruel.'

'The vet comes here?'

'Yes. I like them to die here, at home. All dogs are

frightened of the vet's. And they know, you know, they always know.'

Thomasine felt a tear roll down her cheek. She brushed it away, feeling embarrassed.

'I'm sorry, my dear. I didn't mean to upset you. I'm so sorry. Siegfried here has had a wonderful life.'

'It just suddenly hit me that – I don't wish to intrude or anything – but you were saying your husband had died and you were alone, then the dogs must mean so much more to you. It's like me. The little bulldog I found, she rapidly became so important to me – helped me through a difficult time. I never intended to keep her, but when her owners claimed her – well, I thought my heart would break. But now seeing you like this, perhaps I'm lucky. She's gone, but she's alive. I couldn't have faced her dying.'

'You would have, you know. What I keep in mind is all the joy and all the happiness that my dogs give me in their short lives. That is what makes it all worthwhile. Shall you get another?'

'I don't think so. But, oh how I miss her, it's as if there's a big hole in my life.'

Eveleigh nodded wisely. 'That's what dogs do to you, my dear. They take over your entire life if you're not careful. Still, listen to me prattling on. But if you want to try and sketch my dogs, you're very welcome. Do come any time you want. I'm thrilled to think one of *my* St Bernards might be in a book.'

21

Jim Varley was walking down the lane, Castille padding along beside him. Back in March he'd almost given her up, had thought about putting her down, yet here she was, three months later, with a new lease of life. Trotting along behind him was the reason – the King Charles, totally recovered from her hysterectomy. Jim was pleased with the dog, now called Amtie, thanks to Harry, to which she responded.

He arrived at The Duck and Thistle and pushed open the door, smelled the comforting mix of cigarettes and beer and enjoyed the welcome he received as he ordered his whisky and leant against the bar, the dogs sitting patiently at his feet.

'How are you going to deal with the competition then, Jim?' the landlord asked him.

'What competition?'

'Haven't you heard? A new vet's opening up in Shillingham.'

'You're joking!' said Jim. 'When did you hear that?'

'Our Stephanie works in the estate agent's, she helped do the deal on the premises. They're taking over what used to be that old mill. Going to be a big health centre for animals.'

Jim laughed. 'Well, there's a relief.'

'You're not worried?'

'No. I'd like to think most of my clients will stay loyal to me. But there's a few I'd like to get rid of, I can push them in that direction.' He laughed again as he realised he'd been let off the hook, he needn't make any decisions after all, he thought happily. 'There's been a need for another practice around here for some time. Beth's been nagging me to take on an assistant, but, I don't know, I didn't really want to.'

'You ought to marry another vet, Jim,' the landlord said, not unkindly.

'I doubt whether I'd find another Ann, do you?'

'Well, you won't know if you don't look,' the landlord's wife interrupted, and Jim laughed good-humouredly.

The door opened and Oliver, dressed in jeans, sneakers and a large, shapeless sweater approached the bar.

'Hello, Jim,' he said.

'Oliver!' said Jim, unable to keep the surprise out of his voice.

'Surprised at seeing me still here?'

'Sorry. It sounds rude, but yes. I knew you said you were moving here permanently, but I didn't know if you'd stick it out – not with the lousy weather we've been having. Some summer!'

'I'll have you know I lived in the country all my childhood. I haven't always been a townie.' Oliver had had this conversation several times since he had moved. There was something about country folk that made them think they had a monopoly on living in and understanding the countryside; it always piqued him. 'Still, I know what you mean. I read an article in the paper the other day, written by some anti-dog cove saying he was moving to get away from the dog crap in the London parks. I had to laugh. As far as I can see, the whole countryside's awash with turds.'

'Guess he's in for a bit of a shock.' Jim smiled, warming to Oliver.

His country credentials out of the way, Oliver sipped at his pint.

'I was up at your father-in-law's a few weeks back and your wife was there. I'm sorry to hear about the . . .' Jim stopped, for he wasn't quite sure what to say. 'Problem' sounded rather tame in the circumstances.

'Oh, that. Well, probably for the best.' Oliver shrugged his shoulders good-naturedly. 'Only trouble is, I lost my dog over it.'

'Not the bull terrier?'

'Yeah,' said Oliver, biting his bottom lip; to talk of Bandage still hurt. 'He ran away. I scoured London. I went to every police station I could think of. He's a very distinctive dog, jet black with white markings on his feet, like bandages. No one had seen hide or hair of him, no traffic accidents reported at all. I'm beginning to wonder if he wasn't stolen.'

'Dog fighting, you mean?'

'Yes. Not that they'd get much change out of Bandage. He's the softest creature on two legs. He'd tiptoe round an ant rather than hurt it.' He smiled at the memory of his sloppy dog.

'Sometimes I get odd whiffs of a rumour of something like that going on – it's usually if a dog has been badly damaged. Oddly, these people are sometimes very fond of their dogs, even if they let them fight, and they'll bring a dog in to be patched up, but they lie and say it got into a scrap with a Rottweiler out on a Sunday walk, or something like that.'

'What do you do in a situation like that?'

'What can I do? Patch the dog up. I've no proof. Invariably they'll give me false addresses.'

'You've heard of nothing like that around here?'

'No, not for some time. Drink?' he asked, to change the subject. Just recently the local RSPCA inspector had asked him if he'd had any fighting breeds in. That meant something was afoot. He also knew that these days dog fights didn't just occur on isolated farms, but on run-down council estates in big towns – towns like Morristown. He was not prepared to tell Oliver, not yet, not unless he had some more concrete information. He didn't want Oliver crashing in and ruining some careful investigation which might have taken months to set up.

The door of the bar flew open, and Jim's heart lifted as he saw Thomasine come in. He waved across the bar. 'Mrs Lambert, care to join us for a drink?'

Thomasine's face was pink from the long walk she had just taken, and her hair glistened from the very faint mist of drizzle that had begun to fall. 'That would be so nice.'

'Of course, you know Oliver Hawksmoor,' he said, regretting that Oliver should happen to be with him at this precise moment. Thomasine smiled at Oliver and Jim felt a small frisson of jealousy at the warmth of the smile.

'I nearly knocked the poor man over some time back in Shillingham.'

'We don't often see you in here,' said Jim, keen to get her attention back.

'No, but I suddenly felt all four walls pressing in on me. I thought I needed some fresh air and to talk to fellow human beings.'

'Still missing –' He began, and then stopped, cursing himself for being such a fool.

'The bulldog? Very much, but it's getting better.'

'There's a refuge about ten miles from here, she's always looking for good homes – especially for the greyhounds. They're no trouble – twenty minutes walking a day is all they need.' He had just returned from there and was always conscious, after a visit, of the need to find responsible homes for them.

'I don't think so. I'm better off without. I had tea with Eveleigh the other day. I wondered – her dog?' Thomasine asked.

'Siegfried? Gone, I'm afraid.' He looked at his feet, still distressed at having had to put the dog to sleep. 'Maybe you two can throw some light on this. Eveleigh had an offer for her kennels a while back which she turned down. They've since offered again, twice – each time more money than the last. What can be going on?'

'That land over at Cooper's Bottom's been sold, you know,' Oliver volunteered.

'Eveleigh said she thought it had.'

'It was all very hush-hush. I bet it's for building.'

'They'd never get planning permission there, surely?'

'My dear Jim. Have you not learnt anything's possible if you've got the right clout?'

'But it would be too close –'

'Exactly, to Eveleigh's kennels. She'd object most strongly. Hence buy her out at an offer she cannot refuse and wipe out the opposition.'

'Bit high-handed, isn't it? Those kennels have been there ever since I can remember. If they build it could

216

become a real problem. These days it's not that uncommon. Kennels which were once way out in the sticks get caught up with urban sprawl. She'll never sell up though. Not Eveleigh.'

'Maybe she'll have to,' said Oliver.

'Why, if she doesn't want to?' asked Thomasine.

'Those interested might make her life too difficult. Do you think we should mention it to her?'

'She'd only worry unduly, Oliver. I'll keep an eye on the situation for her.'

Oliver suggested another round.

'Not for me, thanks. I must be going.' Thomasine smiled at Oliver, and he wished he'd seen that smile first, then he might have got there before Jim, who seemed to be lurking around in a very proprietorial manner.

That was odd, thought Jim, they didn't seem to be much of a couple to him.

Kimberley came out of the school grounds, her school bag laden with books, to find Greaser waiting for her.

'Where've you been? You haven't been to the market for weeks.'

'I had bronchitis. I've been home in bed, then the doc wouldn't let me go back to school for ages.'

'We missed you.'

Kimberley smiled, thinking she hadn't missed them. But being ill couldn't have come at a worse time, for she had had to resign herself to never seeing Alan again – he'd have long ago given up on her.

'I'll take that, it's heavy,' Greaser volunteered.

'What are you doing here?' she asked, more surprised by his unaccustomed courtesy than his presence.

Greaser fell into step beside her as she walked towards the large, noisy queue at the bus stop. 'I wondered if you'd like to come and see my new dog?' he said.

'Me? Why should you want me to do that?'

'Butch says you know about dogs.'

'Not a lot.'

'Well, you know more than I do, and more than Butch does probably. He says your dad breeds them, so you must know something.'

'Now?' she asked.

'Yeah, it's important.'

'But I'll miss my bus.'

'That's all right, Butch says he'll run you back on his bike.'

At that, Kimberley was torn. Butch rarely offered a female a lift, and she loved riding on the back of the motorbike, far more than she would ever admit to a living soul. When Butch went fast, and the wind stung at her face, she felt a freedom that was denied her at any other time.

'You sure he promised? Otherwise I can't get back this evening. And I've masses of revision to do, I'm in the middle of my A levels.'

'Sure I'm sure. We're going into partnership.'

She laughed. 'That sounds grand and official, not at all like you and Butch.'

They crossed the road, walked through a small labyrinth of the original artisans' cottages, passed the Locomotive Inn and through a concrete archway into the hell that was the Forest Glade.

'Makes me feel like Theseus in the maze, this place,' she said.

'Who?'

'Oh, never mind.'

But as Greaser led her along one concrete walkway and down another, up one set of steps and down yet more into subterranean passages that interlinked with others, she decided she was right, she would have needed a ball of twine to find her way back to the entrance again. They entered a tower block. Greaser, more out of habit than expectation, kicked the lift, banged the button, and since nothing happened, said they had to leg it.

They climbed to the seventh storey. 'Keeps you fit,' Kimberley said.

'You can say that again.' He dug his hand into the letterbox and pulled out a string to which was attached a key. He popped it in the lock, and let Kimberley in.

Kimberley and her parents did not possess much, but what they did have was clean and well cared for by her mother. Nothing could have prepared her for the shambles which was Greaser's home. The swirling patterned carpet was littered with empty milk bottles, beer cans and piles of dirty washing. The air was full of the pervasive smell of fried food and stale cigarettes. Kimberley was not quick enough to remove the look of distaste on her face.

'It's a bit of a mess, but my mum's not well,' said Greaser defensively.

'I didn't mean . . .'

'No, no one does.'

A voice called out. 'Is that you, Graham?'

'Graham?' Kimberley giggled.

'Shut up,' said Greaser.

'Who you talking to?' the voice asked.

'Friend. Come on, you better meet her.' He pushed open the thin plywood door which led into the small, equally untidy sitting room. In a greasy-looking arm-chair, sat a scrawny-faced woman with lank hair hanging limply around her grey, defeated face. 'This is Kimberley, Mum, what I told you about.'

'The one that knows all about dogs?'

'That's right.'

Kimberley began to open her mouth to say that she didn't, but a glare from Greaser stopped her.

'Well, you'd best tell her to go and look at it. My *Neighbours* repeat's about to begin.'

'Okay, Mum.' He hustled Kimberley out of the room, they walked along the narrow corridor. Greaser stopped at a door, his hand on the handle. He turned and faced Kimberley. 'You needn't be scared, he's not vicious nor nothing.' He went in, and as he did so he switched on the light. Standing in the corner of the room, its back to them, its snout leaning on the wall, was a black, well-muscled dog with white markings on his legs, which looked as if he was wearing bandages.

'What's he doing?' Kimberley asked.

'I dunno, he does that all the time. He'll be friendly for a minute or two, you know. When I feed him he eats, then I say come on boy, come here, and he just looks at me and he goes in the corner of the room, puts his head on the wall like that and he'll stand there for hours, as if he's sulking.'

'Poor thing.'

'Why poor thing? I feed it.'

'It's hardly a nice way to spend your day, is it, in the corner of a room with nothing to look at?'

'I hadn't thought of that. I've taken it for walks, not that it wants to go, but it'll come if you pull hard enough.' He went over to the corner of the room. 'Sly,' he said, and kicked the dog in the rear. Warily, the dog turned round and looked at him.

'He's lovely, isn't he?' said Kimberley.

'Do you think so? I think he's an ugly bugger meself. What is it, that's what we want to know. Is it a pit bull?'

'No, don't be silly, they've got more squashed up faces than this. I think it's a bull terrier or something like that.'

'Bull?' Greaser jumped on the word. 'Like, they're related?'

'Yes, I suppose so.'

'Like it likes to fight, like a pit bull,' Greaser said, his head twitching almost in a nervous tic as he spoke.

Kimberley, who had been patting the dog, paused. 'Hang on a minute, you're not getting involved in that, are you? It's cruel and it's illegal.'

Greaser laughed, took a cigarette out of a packet, twirled it in the air and caught it in his mouth, a trick that had taken him many a week and many a ruined cigarette to perfect. 'Lots of things are, but it doesn't stop you doing them, does it?' He tapped his foot, stood straight and tall and looked cocky.

'But it's such a lovely dog. It would be a shame for it to get hurt.'

'But that's the whole point, isn't it? If you get a dog and you have the best dog, it won't get hurt. It'll hurt the other bugger.'

'I just don't like it, that's all.' Kimberley patted the dog. 'Are there dog fights round here? I'd have thought they were more likely to take place out in the country?' she asked with practised ease, as if she knew nothing about the filthy trade.

'Nah, here. There's one bloke, uses a room in his flat for it, covered in blood it is. People bet on them. It's good, you can make good money from a dog fight.'

'Where did you get him?' she asked, not wanting to think about the blood-stained walls nor the pain they indicated.

'I bought him from a geezer on the other side of the estate. He'd bought it from another geezer who came from London. Don't know how it landed up out here, but this kid I bought it from, his mum said he couldn't keep it, so I got it.'

'And your mum doesn't mind?'

'Nah, if she thinks we're going to make some money she won't bloody mind. What you think then?' And he kicked the dog.

'Stop it! Don't do that.'

'Got to toughen him up. I've been talking to a mate, he says that if you lock him up with another fighting dog, that'll toughen him up faster than anything – he'd have to defend himself to survive. And there's a bloke, what knows another bloke, what's got one of these treadmills, you put them on that, you know, they walk for hours and hours, all day long, going nowhere. Funny, isn't it? Then you got collar things you put on them and they drag these bricks around with them. It's to build the muscles up. This bloke's got a gym down there. You know, pit bull gym. Funny, isn't it?' Greaser laughed.

Kimberley was silent. She knew who he was talking about – her father, and the shed she never went into. The dog looked at her and she looked at it. It wagged its tail, almost imperceptibly, almost as if it was afraid to. It did it again, then the door swung open and Butch walked in.

'Right, then, what is it?' he asked, without preamble.

'She reckons it's a bull something or other, good for fighting anyway.'

'Great. Right, Kimberley, I said I'd run you home, and run you home I will. I'm in a bit of a rush, I've got to meet a man about this bloody dog. The sooner we get it bloodied the better.'

Kimberley patted the dog – she'd have liked to kiss it, she didn't know why, but she would. 'Good luck, boy,' she said instead, and followed Butch out of the door. They clattered down the stairs in silence. He gave her his spare crash helmet, stowed her book bag into a plastic pannier. She swung her leg over and sat on the pillion seat of the bike. He revved the engine, and they were soon skimming through the labyrinth of the Forest Glade estate, out of the centre of Morristown and on to the by-pass towards her home. Kimberley clung to Butch and felt the wind and felt clean and free and put the thought of the dog behind her.

The chain of house sales in which Alan had been stuck began to resolve, and he was back in his mother's house for the last time – the house-clearing people were coming tomorrow, the meters were to be read, he'd finally be shot of it. He cooked himself a couple of poached eggs on toast, ate a tin of baked beans from the tin, a can of peaches with evaporated milk, which was the last of his mother's supplies, and got ready for the night ahead. He'd been to The Locomotive several times on abortive trips – no dogs, no Vic. With nothing else to do, he'd decided to try one last time.

He could have wished for a better night to be out. Flaming June, he thought, as he pulled his anorak tight. It was cold and wet. He put his head down and trudged along the street to where his car was parked. He'd be glad to be shot of Morristown; the people had to be the unfriendliest he'd ever met, and at every turn were memories of his mother and his far from happy childhood. He'd yet to search out the one person he'd met and liked and who had shown a spark of interest in him.

He parked several streets away and it was eight by the time he got to The Locomotive, which was not as crowded as it had been on previous nights. He ordered his pint of beer and chatted with the barman. He glanced about the bar, and his heart leapt with excitement when he saw Vicky sitting in the same alcove as before, but alone. He nodded, and she nodded back.

Two lads walked in. One, he was convinced, was well under age; the other looked familiar, but then so many of these bikers did. He turned slightly so they wouldn't see him full face. They had a dog with them, a dog that apparently didn't want to be with them, for they had to drag it in. It was a beautiful bull terrier, black with white markings, and while he could admire the dog, he felt a wave of excitement. First a pit bull, now a bull terrier.

'Hello, come to see Vicky then?' She was at his elbow. He got a waft of very sweet perfume.

'Wasn't sure if you recognised me.'

'Big hulk like you, course I did,' she giggled, and he knew it was a come-on. He knew he shouldn't react, not when he was working, and not when he'd met her boyfriend.

'Where you been?'

'Oh, around.' He tried to sound nonchalant as the two boys approached them – then felt his heart lurch.

'Hello, Vicky,' said Butch, not even glancing at Alan. 'Where's Vic?'

'He's gone to see a man about a dog. Honest.'

223

'Only, I want to talk to him about this dog,' said Butch, tapping the bull terrier with his toe.

'Ugly looking thing.'

'We didn't buy it for its looks,' said Butch.

'He'll be here soon. Isn't one of you gentlemen going to buy a lady a drink?' she said, smiling coquettishly at Butch first and then Alan. Alan thought it best if he moved away, as if he wasn't interested in the talk of dogs. He began to throw darts at the board. Rather a futile occupation because he kept missing, he was too hyped up to aim properly.

'Don't play stupid old darts. Come and talk to me – I'm bored.' Vicky patted the banquette beside her.

'Where are your mates?' he asked, sliding in beside her.

'Taking that horrid dog round the block. Toughening it up, they said. They'll be back.'

Alan ordered them both more drinks and dug up some small talk to amuse Vicky while his mind reeled in anticipation. If the talk got round to dog fights, as he was sure it would, how could he get himself included? Two pints later Vic arrived, his pit bull, muzzled, in tow. He nodded at Alan, who smiled and said, 'Hello, Vic. Can I buy you a drink?'

'Well, thanks. A pint would be fine – the export special,' said Vic. Alan bought the round of drinks and carried them to the table where Vic had sat himself down beside Vicky. The pit bull had crept under the table and was curled up and already asleep. Alan put the drinks down.

'There were two kids looking for you. They got this horrible black thing with them, wanted to talk about you-know-what, I reckon,' said Vicky. 'Do you have to?' she snapped, bending down and rubbing her shin.

Vic said nothing, but started to sup his pint. Alan was racking his brains for something to say, but neither Vic nor Vicky seemed bothered to be drinking in silence. He tried mentioning football, but all Vic said was 'bloody football.' Talk of fertiliser didn't get much response either. He was rescued by the two youths reappearing, still with the bull terrier.

'You should get that bloody thing muzzled otherwise the fuzz will be on to you. They'll have arrested it before you know where the fuck you are, and then the thing will be put down,' said Vic, the longest speech Alan had heard him make.

'That's not necessary,' Alan said, without thinking.

'How would you know?'

'Because I know that that's a bull terrier and they're not included in the Dangerous Dog Act.' He felt his heart thudding, felt he was being far too knowledgeable for comfort, felt a tenseness about him that hadn't been there before.

'And how would you be such an expert?' Vic looked at him coldly.

'Because my dad's got a bull terrier,' Alan lied, and hoped that it was a successful lie.

'What? *And* a Rottweiler?'

'No, the Rottie was mine, it's dead now.' He picked up his beer and quickly sipped at it for something to do. He felt himself sweat at the stupid mistake he'd inadvertently made.

'Ah, I see,' said Vic.

'That's what Kim said, she's our friend,' said Greaser. 'She knows about dogs, her dad breeds them, said she reckoned that that's what it was. And I ain't got to muzzle it, mate?' He looked at Alan.

'No, you don't have to, but it's probably less hassle if you do. My dad's always getting into trouble with ours, people accusing him unnecessarily.' Alan rattled on now, wishing he hadn't set this conversation in motion. 'Do you live around here?' he asked.

'Forest Glade. You?' Greaser, who seemed more outgoing than Butch, asked.

'Wembley Way,' he answered.

'Nice,' said Vicky.

'You want to know a lot,' Vic added.

'Just curious.'

'That killed the cat.'

'Just asking.' Alan shrugged his shoulders as if he didn't give a damn. They drank without talking.

As the silence lengthened, it was evident he was not going to learn any more. Vic had obviously clammed up, whether out of discretion or suspicion of him, he could not tell. He felt he had lied himself out of the situation successfully, but it had been close – too close. It was so frustrating when he was sure they were getting that bit nearer the dog-fighting ring.

'If you'll excuse me. Busy day tomorrow.' Alan stood, buttoning up his coat ready to leave.

'Nice to see you, Alan. See you again next week? We're not here at the weekend.' She winced. Had Vic kicked her under the table?

'Right,' said Alan. 'See you.' Outside the pub, the rain slashed painfully at his face, which was warm from the bar and the beer. He pulled up the collar of his coat, dug his hands deep into his pockets, put his head down as he moved through the deserted streets of Morristown to his car.

As he walked, he went over the conversation, what there was of it. It wasn't so much what was said, but more the tense atmosphere. He paused in his step. He thought he heard a sound behind him. He swung round abruptly, but there was nothing there.

'Getting neuro,' he told himself, and strode on. He whistled between his teeth, trying to give himself courage, wishing Andy were with him and wishing he'd parked his car nearer.

Suddenly a fist was slammed into the back of his head and a strong arm grabbed him. He was swung round and, too quickly to be identified, a figure lunged, snarling at him, and smashed him with his clenched fist full in the face. He swayed, his knees buckled, he stumbled against the wall and then sank to the pavement. Alan had a split second of thought, wondering whether it was Vic hitting him and if so why – was it over the dogs or Vicky?

As he lay slumped on the pavement he was aware that someone else was kicking him viciously. He writhed, trying to get away from the boots, away from the pain, realising now that it was three men attacking him. Vic and the boys? Possible. He marvelled that he could still think.

A car appeared on the street, moving towards them, and only then did the beating stop and Alan heard his assailants running away into the dark, but not before one of them had slammed something into the side of Alan's head. Before unconsciousness swept over him, Alan's last thought was that he was glad that his mum couldn't see him now.

22

Kimberley sat on the bus, her shopping bags between her feet, and felt miserable. It had been stupid to expect Alan to be there. She had missed too many Saturdays at the fountain since she'd met him. First she'd been ashamed to turn up because of the bruises her father had inflicted upon her face, and then the wretched bronchitis. She'd met him in April, now it was June.

Of course that was presuming he'd meant it when he'd said 'see you'. Maybe he was just being polite, not wanting to hurt her feelings.

It was a shame too, for she'd made a real effort with herself. She'd persuaded her mother to buy her new jeans and a black T-shirt. She'd turned the cuffs of one of her father's old shirts, on which she had stuck a brooch of a panda, and over that she wore an old suit waistcoat of his. She'd washed her hair and wore it loose instead of in a ponytail, and had even bothered to put some mascara on, but nothing else, not liking the feel of make-up on her skin. She looked different from the last time he'd seen her bundled up in her old duffel coat. But now she was having to acknowledge that it had all been a waste of time.

She'd hung around for most of the afternoon on the off chance he might turn up, or that Nadine might be around. Even the gang weren't there.

From the floor of the bus she picked up the carrier bag and checked that the present she'd bought her mother for her birthday was still there. It was a basket of toilet water and soap, lying on blue satin, which was pretty and which she knew her mother would like. She wondered if her father had even remembered. She hoped so, for if not, Sue's feelings would be sorely hurt.

The bus lurched to a stop at a crossroads. Kimberley looked idly out of the window to see her father standing beside his van in deep conversation with a large man she did not know and, of all people, Butch. How odd, she thought as the bus started up and trundled on. The only time Butch had met her father that she knew of, Tom had been rude to him and it had caused a row. Now, to the casual eye, they looked like old friends.

If Butch and her father were in cahoots, then there was even more reason to see less of him. It had not bothered her that none of the gang had been in Shillingham. They bored her, and no doubt she bored them in return, for she said very little. She had never been comfortable with knowing that she was the most intelligent amongst them. She'd never wanted to be superior in that way. It was loneliness which had made her join up with them, and she had gained nothing from the association.

The bus pulled up at the stop by her lane. The driver helped her with the heavy bags as she alighted. She set off along the lane, turned in the gate and began the long hike up to the ugly little cottage, and wished she lived anywhere else but here.

Alan was still in hospital – unnecessarily, he thought, but the doctors had insisted he stay another forty-eight hours, since, at the end of the beating up, he'd been unconscious. There was concussion and, two days later, he still had a headache – not much, but enough to worry the doctor. He'd also suffered two cracked ribs, which bothered him far more than the head; he had twisted his ankle, presumably when he fell, and to top it all, was black and blue from where he had been kicked with heavy boots.

'Apart from that, I'm fine,' he joked to Andy, who was sitting on the end of the bed, leafing through the *Playboy* magazine he'd brought him.

'Do you mind if I nosh these?' Andy asked, opening the bag of grapes he'd brought in with him.

'Be my guest,' said Alan, and winced as he moved.

'You're a right bloody mess, aren't you?'

'Give me a day or two, I'll be back.' He managed to smile.

'Still, it's a pointer that we're looking in the right place. Was something said?'

'Not really. A couple of yobs came in with a bull terrier and the atmosphere changed. I'm worrying, if it was Vic who duffed me up, maybe it was because he was just jealous over the girl.'

'You didn't see who did it, then?'

'No, it was too quick – but there were three of them in the pub, and three set into me.'

'Just looking at him, Vic doesn't strike me as the sort of bloke who'd give up drinking at his local over a girl. Beat you up, yes, kill you even because of her, but give up his boozer – never.'

'Perhaps he's scared I'll be back wanting to give him a taste of the same?'

'Nah, I shouldn't think much frightens him.'

'What if he's worried I'll go to the police? He doesn't know I didn't see him.'

'It would boil down to his word against yours, and you can bet the whole clientele and the landlord would swear he never left the pub – not for a minute.'

'If it wasn't the girl then it's the dogs. I've been thinking, and I could have tipped him off inadvertently. The first time we met I said I had a Rottweiler at home. Then this last time I explained away being so bloody knowledgeable about the Dangerous Dogs Act by saying my father had a bull terrier. Stupid of me, I just wasn't thinking. But it would be enough to warn him.'

'If he remembered. I shouldn't let it worry you. It's done now.'

'I could kick myself. We were really on to something there. There is something else. The yobs who brought in the bull terrier have been bothering me. I'm sure I've seen them somewhere before, but I can't remember where.'

'What did they look like?'

'Short. Spotty. Cocky. One's about nineteen, the other's younger. Trouble is, they just look like any yobs you see lurking about the Forest Glade estate.'

'It's there, isn't it – in that bloody estate. It's so bloody big and every other bugger seems to have a Rottweiler, pit bull or breeds that look as though they could fight – and you can't arrest them all.'

'What's the boss say? Bet he's pissed off with me.'

'He's fairly philosophical. These things happen. He thinks we're on a hiding to nothing. That we don't have enough info to justify continuing – even on a semi-official basis. And he reckons if there's anything there then they've got the wind up and will lie low until they think we're off the scent.'

'I know what you're going to say,' Alan groaned. 'He's pulling the plug.'

'Don't upset yourself. It's not your fault.'

'It's not that so much, but I met this girl. I really liked her, then one thing and another, I've lost touch. I hoped

I'd see her again. Now I've sold the house I've no reason to be here and if this case re-ignites he'll probably send two of the others – someone they haven't seen.'

'Not necessarily. I know I'm off to Yorkshire – same thing up there. And they're so busy with the live exporting hoo-ha – you never know, he's just as likely to send you because you know the area. After all, they're hardly likely to use The Locomotive again, are they?'

'That won't alter the fact that that Vic bastard will recognise me.'

'Cross that bridge when you reach it.'

'Thanks a bunch.'

'Right then. Anything you need? Smokes? Do they let you smoke in here?'

'You must be joking.'

'Well, that's your grapes gone, I'll be buzzing off then. Going out tonight with the missus to a particularly nice little restaurant we've just found.'

'Bastard!' said Alan as he sank back on the pillows, surprised to find that he felt completely drained.

Alan was not discharged until the following Wednesday. A taxi drove him back to his house. His car was safely parked in the street, no doubt arranged by Andy. He was still weak; just a few days in bed and he was quite wobbly on his pins. And when he bent to light the gas fire, shards of light floated in front of his eyes as he stood up.

What to do now? He had to contact the house-clearing people again and apologise for not being here last week. He wasn't up to work yet, that was obvious, but he didn't want to stay here a day more than necessary. He couldn't be rid of Morristown fast enough. Still, he felt quite sad at leaving the district; it was the town he hated. He began to sort through the mail that had accumulated. Amongst it was a couple of house details from the estate agent he'd been to last week.

Was it the prettiness of the local countryside that had made him decide to look for a place, or Kimberley? If he was honest, it was probably a combination of the two.

Yet if he found someone, would it be fair on her? His job, dangerous in some ways – as his bruises showed – was equally dangerous in other ways. It was like a drug, one could become enmeshed in it to the exclusion of everything else. He wasn't alone in going from one case to another longing for the adrenalin high that accompanied it. There was so much to do, so much cruelty to be dealt with, that one could become obsessed with it. He'd seen blokes in the society who cared only about the animals, and had shut people, and any concern for them, right out of their minds. He didn't want to be like that – there had to be a balance.

But since he'd met Kimberley at the fountain, he hadn't noticed any other girls. He didn't know her or anything about her. But for all that, she had hit him hard – a bit like Vic's boot, but nicer.

These thoughts galvanised him. He no longer felt tired and jaded. He stood up, reaching for his shoes with his feet, and slipped them on. He looked in the spotted mirror over the mantelpiece and studied his face. He couldn't go and find her if he looked like something that had crawled out of the swamp – he didn't want to frighten her away. The bruise on the left side of his face was fading and had turned a greeny-yellow colour that wasn't too bad. His split lip looked on the fat side, and kissing might prove difficult. He smiled at that thought, but quit when it hurt.

Abruptly he stopped studying his face. Of course, why hadn't he thought of it before? He could put an ad in the personal column of the local paper. He knew her Christian name, he didn't need her surname. 'Kimberley, meet you at the fountain Saturday noon. Alan.'

'Yes!' he shouted, punching the air with excitement and, grabbing his coat, forgot his aches and pains as he rushed out to drive into the centre of Morristown. God knows if she'd see it, but he'd give it a try. Maybe he'd be in time to get an ad in the Friday edition.

It was just Kimberley's luck that as she was about to finish her schooling the job market should be so difficult to break into. Although she was expected to do well in her A levels, half of which she had now sat, her interview with the careers teacher this afternoon had not been encouraging.

'The banks are cutting back on staff, Kimberley, that's part of the problem,' Miss Mitchell had said. 'Is there no chance of you going to university? It's not too late, you know.'

'No chance at all, Miss Mitchell.'

Miss Mitchell sighed. In Morristown she'd found that her most able pupils too often had the most unco-operative parents. 'Have you thought of any other possibilities? Insurance? Nursing? The police?'

'I'd always set my heart on a bank. I could still try,' she said, though smiling inwardly at the thought of her father's reaction if she even said the word 'police' to him.

'Of course, my dear. Don't worry too much, will you?'

That was a stupid thing for the teacher to have said, Kimberley thought as she later laid the table for supper. Miss Mitchell was safe in her job, she wasn't having to escape. She put the freesias she'd bought on the way home from school in a vase in the middle of the table. They were her mother's favourite flowers, though she never understood why since she couldn't smell them – the result of Tom's fist landing smack on her nose one winter night.

'What's the cloth for?' Her father eyed the table suspiciously as he clumped noisily into the room.

'It's Mum's birthday. I'm cooking supper for her.'

'You could have reminded me.'

'I'm sorry. I didn't think,' she replied, as she went into the kitchen to check the casserole. She could have reminded him, she was not sure what perversity had prevented her.

'You look nice. Happy birthday, Sue. Bet you thought I forgot.' She heard her father kiss her mother on the cheek – hypocrite, she thought. 'I know it's today, but I've planned a little surprise for tomorrow.'

'Tomorrow?' Her mother sounded uncertain.

'Yes, I thought I'd take you to that Chinese restaurant in Shillingham you said you liked the look of.'

'Oh, Tom. How lovely, but I thought –' Her voice trailed off.

'No. Not tomorrow. Not around here for a bit. Vic reckons someone's been snitching. He had to put the frighteners on a copper who'd been snooping.'

'Oh, Tom, be careful.'

'Don't you worry about me. Next weekend we'll be off up north. Lie low for a bit. Only for a bit, though.'

And what did all that mean? Kimberley asked herself as she lit the gas under the potatoes.

'You seen my paper, Sue?'

'No. They sold out.'

'What you mean, sold out?' His voice was raised; her mother's had become fearful. That didn't last long, thought Kimberley as she collected three cans of beer from the old and dilapidated fridge in the pantry.

Once the meal was over Kimberley excused herself and went to her room. She spent a lot of time in this room, using school work as an excuse even when she'd done it all. From there she heard her father clatter into the yard, and a few minutes later her mother tapping at her door.

'Kim. You awake? Look at this.'

'What's that? But you said –'

'I know. But I didn't want your father to see this. Look.'

Kimberley followed her mother's pointing finger down the personal column. 'See.'

Kimberley, meet you at the fountain Saturday, Alan.
She read and then re-read, in case she was hallucinating.

'Is it meant for you?'

'I think so,' she said, her voice sounding as strained and unsure as she was herself.

Kimberley could not sleep. She was frozen with fear that her father would somehow see the advert. And she couldn't sleep from the sheer excitement at the thought that tomorrow she would see Alan again.

When Kimberley looked into the yard the following morning, the yellow van stood with its back door open and her father was loading his two pit bull dogs into the back.

'Where's he taking them this early?' she asked her mother.

'He's going up north with them. Don't ask me, I don't want to know.' She flapped her hands as if brushing all knowledge away.

'But I thought he was taking you out?'

'Something came up.' She shrugged resignedly as if she'd half expected it.

'Would he give me a lift into Shillingham?' she asked. 'It'll save on the bus.'

'Probably, he's in a good mood.'

So Kimberley rode in silence beside her father into Shillingham, the two pit bulls slithering around in the back of the van behind a metal grid.

She saw him sitting on the wall of the fountain as she alighted from the van. She hoped he didn't see her, not with the dogs in the back. Carrying her shopping bag, she walked, heart racing uncomfortably, the palms of her hands damp with sweat, towards him. He was looking in the opposite direction.

'Hullo, Alan.'

'Kimberley! At last!' He jumped to his feet. 'Oh, am I glad to see you.' He put out his hand to touch her and then drew it back, embarrassed. She longed for him to do

235

it again, but he didn't and she stood looking at the cobbles feeling awkward and wondering what was wrong with his face, but not liking to ask.

'Sorry about my mush,' he said, fingering his bruises. 'I walked into a door.'

'I see.' She sounded non-committal. She'd heard her mother use that line once too often to believe him.

'How long have you got?' he asked.

'I must do my mum's shopping, then I'm free,' she said, blushing to the roots of her hair.

'Great. Let's do that, and then what? Shall we go for a drive?'

'It's a lovely day for a drive,' she replied, for want of anything else to say, and she felt weirdly old as she said it.

The shopping finished in a trice, the bags loaded in Alan's car, she sat beside him feeling suddenly very grown up as, knowing the area, she directed him to her favourite beauty spots. He looked so smart in his blazer and jeans, she could hardly believe he wanted to be seen with her.

'I was worried you wouldn't see the advert.'

'My mum did.'

They had lunch at a pub called The Duck and Thistle. 'This village would be the place to buy a cottage.'

'No one can afford it – it's too expensive now. But I've an aunt lives here.'

'Want to pop in?'

'No thanks. I haven't seen her in years.'

In the afternoon they went to the cinema. Kimberley would have preferred to sit in his car and talk, but she hadn't liked to say. She hoped in the cinema he'd put his arm about her, kiss her even. But he didn't. So she sat through *Four Weddings and a Funeral* and must have been the only person in the whole audience who didn't laugh, since her mind was on other things. How to get him to kiss her being paramount.

'Fancy a Chinese?' he asked as they emerged from the cinema.

Over the dim sum he told her he was leaving. She felt as if the world was crowding in on her, as if the walls of the restaurant had suddenly shifted.

'Oh no,' she said, and immediately realised how obvious she sounded. 'Where to?'

'Horsham. I've a flat there.'

'Oh, I see. Why?'

'My job.'

'Oh, I see.'

'I'll be back. I promise.' He put his hand over hers and she felt a jolt and had to look away so he could not see the longing in her eyes.

'When?' She sounded desolate.

'I'm not sure. I'll let you know, though, if you give me your number.'

'We don't have a phone,' she lied, as she'd done so often in the past.

'Then give me your address. I'll drop you a line.'

'I can't.'

'What do you mean, you can't?'

'Just that.'

'Then how am I supposed to get in touch with you?'

'I don't know,' she said, feeling hopeless.

He looked at her long and hard. 'I'm sorry,' he suddenly said and waved to the waiter for the bill.

'You don't understand –'

'You can say that again.' His mouth was set in a hard line.

She walked in front of him out of the restaurant, misery clouding her mind, making her feel she could not think straight. 'It's my dad,' she eventually said as they drove along. 'He doesn't like me to have friends.'

'Then why didn't you say that back there?'

'I don't know.'

'If you want to see me again, then I suggest you come up with some idea of how we get in touch.'

'I don't know . . . I . . . Could you stop here?'

'But it's nowhere.' He looked about him at the emptiness.

'No, here's fine.' She already had the car door open.

'Suit yourself, then.' He leant over and slammed the door shut.

'I'll be by the fountain –' she called, but she doubted if he'd heard as the car, sounding as angry as him, roared away from her.

She watched the rear lights disappearing into the distance, covered her face with her hands and ran crying along the lane towards her home.

July

23

Bandage, still known as Sly, had been in the hands of Butch and Greaser for well over a month. In that time they had not, oddly for them, been idle. To the relief of the inhabitants they had not once been to the Market Square in Shillingham, and without Butch the group had rapidly disintegrated. Butch had traded his motorbike for a van. The selling was not as traumatic as it might have been, for in Sly he was convinced he had the makings of a lot of money, and it would only be a matter of time until he could buy an even bigger and better motorbike.

The van was needed to transport Sly to his 'gymnasium', as they liked to call it, which always made them roll about laughing, and back to Greaser's mum's flat on the Forest Glade estate.

The gymnasium was a lock-up garage they'd rented down by the old railway station and Butch, quite a good mechanic when he put his mind to it, rigged up a treadmill using a small conveyor belt which had once been used in a mini-market, powered by an old motor mower. He'd seen a shot on TV of a pit bull on one, and had determined to make one for Sly. It only had one speed, but Butch was working on how to incorporate a three-speed drive. On this Bandage was placed in a harness so that he could not escape. At first he had trouble keeping his balance and often fell over, which they found funny, but he quickly got the hang of it and made no fuss when the harness was strapped on.

'You'd think the silly bugger would realise he wasn't going anywhere, wouldn't you?' said Butch as they watched him one day, tongue lolling, saliva dripping from the exertion.

'Perhaps he's trying to please us.'

'Don't be such a silly sod.' Butch pushed Greaser. But all the same, despite Butch's sneering at him for being a soft bugger, Greaser always patted the dog and said 'good boy' to him.

The garage was isolated, so they were not watched when they clipped cement blocks onto another harness they'd fashioned, and forced the dog to drag them, to make his shoulder muscles grow.

They'd hoped Vic would help them, but he did not want to know. 'It's like he don't trust us,' said Butch, affronted when Vic had been cagey with them one evening. 'Dog fights? What dog fights?' Vic had said. 'I don't know nothing about no dog fights.'

'Bloody liar,' Greaser complained. 'And I didn't like the way he laughed at old Sly here – said he'd never make a fighter. If he don't know nothing about any dog fights, then how's he know if our dog can fight or not? Tell me that.'

'Exactly. Bloody creep. Still, all's not lost. Do you know Tom White, Kim's dad?'

'Not likely!' Greaser laughed. 'He's an aggressive bastard. Didn't he tell you to fuck off one day when you took Kim home?'

'He did too. I've met him since though. He's a friend of my uncle – the one what does the MOTs . . . you know.' He winked exaggeratedly. 'I could tell you a thing or two about him, know what I mean?'

The opportunity arose when Butch's uncle Sid needed a package delivered to Tom White and Butch, who happened to be lurking about, much to his uncle's surprise volunteered to take it and raced around to collect Greaser and Bandage.

'What's in the package?' Greaser asked.

'Where my uncle's concerned it's best not to ask.'

Greaser had always fondly thought that there was nothing in the world that could frighten him; that was until he met Tom that first time. He hoped to God that Tom never found out that he and Butch knew Kimberley. He glanced nervously about the yard, hoping she would not suddenly appear. The package delivered, they stood smoking and talking about motors and horses, until Butch plucked up the courage to mention Sly and how they wanted to find out about dog fighting.

'Easier said than done, Butch. The pit bull fraternity is a closed shop, has to be.'

'Of necessity, Tom. They don't know who people are, do they? But you know my uncle Sid, so you know me – would I grass?' Butch looked stricken to his soul at the very idea.

'There's some as would grass on their grannies if there was a quid in it.' Tom stood, hands thrust into his trouser pockets, and looked at Butch with an amused expression.

'If you'd just look at our dog. You know about dogs.' Butch put on a wide-eyed, expectant look.

'No harm in that, to be sure,' said Tom, and turned to the van and watched while Greaser opened the back door and yanked Sly out onto the yard. Tom stood back, eyeing the dog, like a show judge. But as he stepped forward and began to run his hands down his sides, Sly began to tremble.

'Nice dog,' he said as he stood up. 'Bit of a wimp though, isn't he?'

'He's not used to being outside,' Butch explained.

'Agoraphobic, like my mum,' Greaser volunteered, but stopped when Butch glared at him.

'The thing about dogs is they don't naturally want to fight each other, they have to be "persuaded",' Tom said with a sinister laugh. 'If – and it's a big if – if I just happened to meet someone who might invite you along, that dog won't fight.' As if to demonstrate, he kicked at Sly, who whimpered and cowered on to the yard. 'See. You've got to strengthen the dog and build up its muscles before you could put him up against a good fighter and make any serious money.'

'We've begun to do that.' And Butch explained about the treadmill and the cement blocks.

'You mean business, then?'

'Too right, Tom.'

'Well, if I hear of anything.' He tapped the side of his nose.

'Right on, Tom,' said Butch.

'I hear you breed dogs,' Greaser said, while Butch glared even more angrily at him.

'And who told you that?' Tom asked.

'I can't remember . . .' Greaser said lamely. 'It's just, I like dogs . . .' His voice petered out.

'Oh what the hell. This way.'

Tom led the way to his breeding shed. At the door he paused. 'If you want to get anywhere with that dog you're going to have to make him nastier, you realise? Still, no doubt you'll manage that.' He laughed and unlocked the padlock on the wooden door.

At the sight of the dogs in their pens Greaser went all soft, and Butch had to kick him, but even then he bought a puppy – a German Shepherd – for his mum, and they took it home with them to Forest Glade.

To make Sly nastier, as Tom had told him, they devised various exercises of their own. They might be amateurs at this game, but their methods began to show results. The docile dog that they'd acquired was not as docile any more.

When they weren't training, the dog stood in the corner of the room in the small flat, resting his chin on the wall, his back to them.

'He's a moody bugger, isn't he?' said Butch, eyeing his rump, twirling the billiard cue he used to prod it.

'Not what you'd call a friendly dog,' said Ginger, who had recently been allowed in on the secret and had just turned up.

'I hate it when he does that, it's like he's sulking, like he's not going to talk to us,' Greaser said.

Butch whooped with laughter. 'Greaser, don't be so bloody daft, dogs can't talk.' He whacked the dog on the rump with the cue. 'Come on, boy, play.' The dog turned, grabbed at the stick, snarling. 'Cor, that's better. That's what we want to hear, my boy, nice bit of aggressive growling, bit of salivating, bit of slashing teeth. That's my boy.'

The telephone rang, and Greaser answered it. 'It's for you.' He handed the instrument to Butch.

There was nothing for Greaser or Ginger to listen to, since Butch's responses to the conversation were a few 'yeses' interspersed with the odd grunt and one 'right on, man'. They looked up expectantly as he replaced the receiver.

'Tonight. It's on!' he exclaimed, his eyes shining with a strange excitement.

'What's on?'

'The fight, Ginger, you dork.'

'No! When? Where?' asked Greaser.

'An hour, out at the old Berry factory.'

'Do you think he's going to be strong enough against Vic's pit bull?' asked Ginger.

'He's not fighting that. Not yet. Vic said we should regard tonight as Sly being blooded, letting him know what's what. Vic's arranged for an old has-been of a dog. Sly should soon make mincemeat of him, Vic said.'

They piled into the van, stopped for fish and chips, which they ate as they drove out of town along the by-pass until they turned off into a disused factory site. Half the roof had gone and there wasn't one unbroken window, but three parked cars and Tom's van told them they'd come to the right place.

'There's not many here,' Greaser said, surprised.

'This isn't a proper dog fight, stupid,' Butch said.

'Then what is it?' asked Ginger.

'A proper fight you'd only have a couple of dogs. This is as a favour to us – to test Sly out.'

'Why they doing us a favour?' Greaser asked.

'My uncle Sid had a talk with Tom and persuaded him, like. That's why –'

'What? Made him an offer he couldn't refuse?' Ginger laughed.

'Something like.'

Inside the building there were about ten men, none of whom acknowledged the friends, but there was a rustle of interest in Sly.

'Who's he?' Tom, who had sauntered up, asked.

'My mate Ginger.'

'You didn't say he was coming.'

'Didn't know I had to ask permission,' Butch said, trying to sound sarcastic, but only managing to sound scared.

'You always ask, Butch. It's healthy to remember that,' Tom said.

A pit bull was already being held in position in the ring. He was growling, snarling, snapping at anything or anyone, and ready to go. He was called Samson, and he was a veteran of a hundred fights, as witnessed by his ragged ears, many scars and the permanent limp in one back leg. Butch dragged Sly and held him, as he saw Samson's owner was holding him, on one side of a painted red line which showed which half of the ring was Sly's.

'He doesn't look as though he's going to fight,' shouted one bloke.

'You wait and see,' replied Butch, with a confident jerk of his head.

'When Samson attacks, he'll fight then,' said Vic.

'Right, seconds out,' the organiser shouted.

Butch took Sly's collar and lead off and gave him a shove towards the pit bull. At the same time the pit bull's owner let him loose; he ran silently towards Sly who, looking up with alarm, backed off. The pit bull raced round him in circles, every so often making a lunge at him with bared teeth. Sly stood in the middle of the ring shivering and with eyes lowered so that he made no eye contact with his adversary.

'What a waste of time this is going to be. Prod him up the arse,' someone shouted.

Butch leant forward and shoved Sly in the rump with the billiard cue. Sly shot to his feet as if stung. The pit bull, taking this as an aggressive action, jumped onto Sly's back and sank his teeth into his shoulder. Blood spurted in all directions. Sly tried to roll on his back in submission, but the pit bull was too big and heavy, and his teeth were still embedded in Sly's neck. Sly shook his powerful shoulders, then again, and again, until, with an almighty heave, the pit bull fell backwards.

Sly tried to reverse out of the ring, but the breeze blocks were in the way, and beyond them the men, who were all shouting and yelling at him. Shaking with fear he ran in circles, desperately looking for a way of escape. The pit bull, his teeth bared, stalked him. Suddenly it lunged at his throat. With a mighty heave Sly shook his head until the pit bull lost its grip and slid to the floor. Quickly Sly sank down and rolled over on his back, his paws in the air, in the time-honoured gesture of submission. The pit bull stood still, looked at the dog on its back, then up at his master expectantly.

'Kill the fucker!' A man screamed from the back.

'Nah. Mismatched. Shouldn't be allowed. This isn't sport,' his owner said, leaning forward. Grabbing his dog by the scruff of the neck, he yanked him away from the cowering Sly. Sly inadvertently and innocently had ended the fight. The pit bull had won on a submission. There was a muttering of discontent from the men around the ring, disgruntled and disgusted at such a short, one-sided fight. Greaser, on the other hand, had run outside and was being sick.

Butch jumped into the ring and pulled at Sly. 'Come on, you silly old bugger, you're not that hurt,' he said, feeling somewhat queasy himself. He'd thought he'd like the blood, but he wasn't so sure now.

Tom White approached Butch. 'Just as well we set up this trial run for you. A cock-up like that with real money on it, and things could get very nasty for you.'

'I can handle myself,' Butch said cockily, but his palms were wet with sweat.

'What made you think this brute was ready? It's got no bloody spunk at all. You've been stupid, putting it in the ring when it doesn't know how to fight. It's got to want to fight. They don't just naturally fight, you know, dogs. They're not like men, they quite like each other, you've got to make the things aggressive.'

'Lecture over?' Butch tapped his toe with simulated impatience. Sly, exhausted, sat at his feet panting and bleeding.

'How much did you pay for it?' Tom asked.

'Two hundred quid,' Butch said, his eyes flickering as he lied.

'Oh yeah?' Tom laughed. 'I'll give you twenty for him.'

'You've got to be joking! Twenty, twenty quid! That's a pedigree dog, that is.'

'How much do you want then?'

'A hundred.'

'When you paid two hundred for it?' Tom smiled sardonically.

Butch shrugged. 'I can stand the loss. In any case, it's a pain in the arse, that dog. The flat's too small for it.'

'Tell you what, I'll give you fifty, that's fair and square, I'll take it off your hands.'

'All right, then. You're on.' The money changed hands and Butch handed the lead over to Tom, who patted Sly, and the dog, oddly, trotted quite happily behind the man to his yellow van which was parked outside. He opened the door and hurled Sly in. There was a snarling and a growling from inside. 'That's my pit bull, Hannibal, he'll sort him out,' Tom laughed. 'Staying for the real fight?'

'Nah, I've got to get back – business, you know,' Butch said, trying to sound nonchalant, but still feeling sick. He swung round and sauntered off to look for Greaser, who was leaning wanly against the wall. Ginger, looking none too happy himself, was smoking.

'What's wrong with you two?' asked Butch.

'It was horrible,' Ginger stated.

'I like dogs,' said Greaser, tears running down his face. 'I didn't like that.'

'Go on, dog's all right.'

'He wasn't all right, he was hurt, and all that blood, I didn't know it was going to be like that,' said Greaser.

'What the fuck did you expect then?' Butch said belligerently. 'Come on, let's go and get a curry, I've sold him. Here you are.' And he gave twenty-five quid to Greaser.

'My mum won't like that, she liked that dog, she said she felt safe with it there.'

'You've got her the other one. The flat was too small for two,' said Butch logically.

24

Thomasine, like most people, accepted that there were times in life when everything appeared to go wrong, but she felt she'd had her quota without this.

Distilling its contents, she re-read the letter in her hand. It was from the publishing company thanking her for her *lovely* work, but *no thanks*. In the accompanying envelope were the three sample paintings she had sent them with such confidence.

She regretted how confident she'd been, so foolhardy of her, but then she'd had reason to hope. The sketches she'd done at Eveleigh's kennels had helped her enormously. Once she was able to use sketches from life rather than photographs, then the illustrations for the book came to life. It was the best work she had ever done. And it wasn't good enough.

She looked down at the work on her desk. She'd begun to paint watercolours of the locality in the hope she could sell them. The painting of the river Shill, which she'd been pleased with before the post came, now looked like rubbish. She stretched. Her shoulders were stiff, she'd been working since five this morning. It always amazed her how quickly time went when she was painting. Still, she wouldn't be doing much more of that, not now, not when it was such a waste of time and effort. She began to clean her brushes. She had grown to love this little room which she fondly thought looked more like a studio. Off the kitchen, it was warm from the heat of the wood burner which filtered through the door. It had a north-facing window, which gave good light when she was working at her drawing board, her paints neatly set on the table beside her. She resisted looking at the corner where Luna's basket used to be. She still missed the dog far more than she would have thought possible.

At least the publisher's rejection had solved one problem for her, whether she could afford to get her hair done – she couldn't, so, therefore, she would. She needed something to cheer her up. She phoned for an appointment later in the day and, deciding to do the other things she invariably did when fed up, ran herself a bath.

What on earth had she done for the gods to be so cross with her, she thought as she soaked in the oil-scented water – expense again, but hang it, she said to herself as she dripped the Hermès bath oil in.

The day stretched ahead. What should she do with it? She wanted to ease the disappointment by indulging herself. After her hair-do she could have lunch in Shillingham, then she'd browse in the shops, go to the library, buy herself some flowers. But what should she do with herself in the evening?

It had been over four months since she'd arrived here. She still liked it, was fond of this house. Why, she'd even adjusted to being alone, and there were advantages. She could watch shows like *Blind Date* if she wanted to. Robert would never watch such a programme, and neither had she, simply because he'd have made such a fuss. Now she could watch all night if she wished.

Socially, things hadn't worked out quite as well as she had first hoped. Available men seemed to be thin on the ground. She liked the vet, but he was obviously claimed, if not by that brittle Sophia Hawksmoor, by the very attractive housekeeper he employed. There was, of course, Oliver Hawksmoor, but she'd never really got over her initial dislike of him. He was too charming, too smooth – such types, she was sure, led only to disaster.

Still – she topped up the hot water – it would be nice if an unattached man moseyed into her life. Not for any great romance, she wasn't ready for that yet, not until all the bruises had faded. Just for company, that would be nice. But Nadine would not countenance another man in her life – even if it was only for friendship, she amended quickly.

Every time she thought about her daughter she felt uncomfortable and guilty. Nadine was hurting, it was obvious. Her much flaunted vegetarianism was a gesture to make people more conscious of her, an attention-seeking device. Still, what was understandable in a nine- or ten-year-old was intensely irritating in a sixteen-year-old.

'And I thought you'd done a bunk. I said to Justin, where's that nice Mrs Lambert?'

'Holed up and feeling sorry for myself,' Thomasine replied, and wondered, not for the first time, why it was so easy to tell one's hairdresser what ailed one.

'Got a new dog yet?'

251

'No. I thought about it, but I don't think I'd want to be that miserable again if something happened to it.'

'What a doom you're in. We'll have to see about this. You're too young and attractive to hide away.'

'Well, hardly. I do go out sometimes.'

'Tell you what.' Gill stood, scissors poised like a weapon. 'Come to a dog show with us? Justin, what do you think?'

'You'd love it, Mrs Lambert. We have such fun! Gill's right, do you a treat.'

'Oh, I don't know . . .'

'I'm not going to listen. So there. We'll come and pick you up. No argument.'

'But what about the salon?'

'Oh, we shut it up. Haven't you seen all the dates we're shut in the window? Dogs come first. No doubt about it.'

'Well . . .'

'Then that's settled.' He clicked away with his scissors. 'Isn't it a joy? Those rough creatures have gone from the market square. One can walk about safe now, can't one? Right, that's you done. Out with the dryer.'

That night, alone with the TV and her bread and cheese, Thomasine decided she would, after all, go to the dog show. It would be something to do.

Oliver stood dejectedly looking out of the arched window of his great hall and wished it were raining – glorious sunshine and blue sky seemed an affront in his present mood. He turned away, a good measure of whisky in the tumbler in his hand and, thinking food might work, made for the kitchen. He opened the fridge, looked gloomily at the empty interior, and sighed at the prospect of yet another trip to the supermarket. He had to hand it to Sophia, when they lived together he could not remember ever finding an empty fridge. He wished Wimpole were here; she'd tell him what to buy.

Wimpole had gone to Whitstable, where she had a

large extended family. She'd said she was going on holiday, but it wasn't really a holiday; she'd gone in a fit of pique. He hadn't meant to upset her, but in the way of rows, one thing had led to another.

It had started by him innocently asking her if she was bored. He thought he'd asked kindly enough, but she'd taken it as an accusation and had cloaked herself in umbrage and said he thought her shallow, which had reminded him of an argument with Sophia, so he'd told her to shut up and from there all hell had broken loose.

The problem was, row or not, he knew he was right – Wimpole was bored and, he believed, longed to go back to London. Whereas life for him had settled into a pleasant routine. He'd never been an early riser, but here he found an early start painless. Mind, Wimpole had said, wait until winter and he wouldn't be so keen to leap about early then. She might be right.

He'd given himself the task of alleviating Wimpole's boredom. She needed friends, he decided, but who? Whilst Grace White and she got on, he doubted if they'd ever make best friends.

It was when he was in Shillingham picking up some two-stroke for the mower that the solution drove onto the garage forecourt – Rudie Adams, Ben Luckett's chauffeur-handyman. Perhaps Wimpole needed a gentleman friend, he thought, grinning at the idea as he ambled over to the Range Rover.

'Rudie, just the fellow. I'm thinking of making a large pond in my meadow. Maybe attract some geese and ducks for the odd pot shot. I was wondering if you could advise me?' Oliver beamed as he lied through his teeth. He might enjoy eating duck; he couldn't abide shooting them.

'Sure thing, Mr Hawksmoor, when would be convenient?'

It had been so easy to arrange, and Rudie was nigh on perfect for Wimpole. Just sixty, a widower and, Oliver was pretty certain, attractive to women. With his thick mop of silver hair, rugged face and blue eyes, he'd always reminded Oliver of a Marlboro cigarette advert come to life.

The following day they had trudged over the meadow planning Oliver's pond, and what was more natural than for Oliver to invite him into the house for a drink?

After he'd made the introduction he sat back to watch developments. He was disappointed, for Wimpole showed no interest in Rudie and instead was quite brusque with him.

'If you don't mind taking your boots off, Mr Adams,' she'd said sharply. 'But some of us folks are partial to a clean floor.'

'I'm sorry, Wimpole, I didn't think,' he said, and despite his years looked flustered.

'Miss Wimpole, to you, if you don't mind.' Her voice, to Oliver, sounded full of steel. 'Tea or coffee, Mr Adams?'

'Tea would be nice.'

'I'm sure a whisky would be more appreciated,' Oliver interrupted.

'No thank you, tea would go down a treat.' Rudie attempted a smile and Wimpole looked insufferably smug. His attempts at matchmaking failing so completely Oliver excused himself, saying something about his book, and escaped to his writing. If there was one thing he couldn't stand it was Wimpole all starched and formal.

An old school friend who was a literary agent had shown interest in what he'd written so far, and only yesterday had phoned to ask when would it be finished? In a fit of enthusiasm he'd said four weeks, which, if he continued to row with Wimpole and fret about her being bored, was unlikely. He supposed he would always worry about her. 'You're too nice for your own good,' he said out loud. 'Bloody saint, that's what you are.' He drank a toast to himself in the whisky that Rudie had refused.

After this abortive attempt to help Wimpole he wondered if he might have been somewhat heavy-handed, for she began behaving oddly, almost secretively. She borrowed the car several times and then refused to say where she'd been. And that, of course, was the second reason for the row which was now upsetting him.

'At this rate I'll think you've got a fella,' he'd said, meaning it as a joke.

'And what if I have?' she replied, in a grotesquely arch manner.

'Wimpole, you don't mean – ? You do! Who?' Such news had quite killed their row and he was jumping about with excitement.

'Rudolph, of course,' she replied, with a proud lift of her head.

'What, after the reindeer?' He chuckled at his own joke.

'No! As a matter of fact his mother was a romantic.'

'Sorry?'

'Valentino, clot,' Wimpole snapped back.

'Well, it's a very grand name,' he said, trying to make amends, but succeeding only in making matters worse.

She spun round on one heel to face him. 'What, too grand for the likes of me?'

'I didn't mean that,' he blustered.

'Then you should be more careful what you say to a body. Bloody insulting, if you ask me. I bet you thought I'd marry a Bert or a Fred; that such names suited me better. You're a nasty little snob, that's what you are, Oliver. I've always suspected it.'

'Wimpole, I'm sorry. Don't let's argue. It's just it's a bit of a surprise, that's all. Forgive?' He put his hand out to grab her because she looked as if she was about to rush out of the room.

'Well, if you're really sorry,' she said grudgingly.

'Oh, I am. I am. But when did you meet him?

'You had a stroke or something? Here of course.'

'Here? Rudolph? I don't know . . .' His voice wavered as the truth dawned. 'You don't mean *Rudie*? I didn't think. Of course his name must be Rudolph. Did you say marry? I'm going to have to sit down.'

'So? What's wrong with me getting married, or have you got something against him, then?' She stood, hands on hips, leaning towards him, her whole body aquiver with indignation.

'Nothing, it's just –' he started, and then stopped, not knowing quite how to go on.

'You can't start a sentence and then stop and leave a body hanging in the air.'

'I wasn't accusing him or anything, it's just . . .'

'If you say "*just*" one more time, so help me I'll clock you one.'

'I didn't expect you to talk about getting married, that's all.' He felt quite stupid as he spoke, but it had been a shock, he hadn't had time to adjust. 'I mean, isn't this all happening too quickly. Aren't you rushing things a bit? You never ever said you wanted to get married, why now?'

'Maybe I never met the right bloke before. I'm getting on, there's no point in hanging about, is there?'

'No, but – hell, I never even knew you had any "*friends*" – you know what I mean?' He looked as confused as he felt.

'Crikey, you'll be calling them *gentleman callers* next.' At this she did manage to laugh, but it was not prolonged and she was serious again. 'You never asked, did you, Oliver? Too wrapped up in yourself – self, self, self – that's all you're any good for. Well, for your information, I do have a life of my own, even if you have never shown any interest in it,' she said sharply. 'Don't you want me to be happy? Frightened of having to cope by yourself?'

'That's not fair. How the hell was I to know if you never let on. I thought you were content as we were. I didn't think.'

'Then it's about time you started. When you suggested we moved out of London and into the sticks it came as one hell of a shock. Oh, you made your pretty speeches about not doing it if I wasn't happy with the idea. I wasn't born yesterday, Oliver, I know you better than you know yourself. You've always done what you want. I could vacillate until the cows came home – I knew what it was you wanted. What's next, that's what worries me? How long before you marry again, tell me that?'

'It's hardly likely –'

'Isn't it? What if your new wife doesn't like me, how long will I be welcome here then? I've got to look after meself. And getting married will ensure I'm all right.'

'Wimpole, please. I wouldn't desert you ever, I can't believe what I'm hearing. This is no reason to rush into marriage.'

'Isn't it? And I'm not *rushing* – I've thought about it, and I've made my mind up and that's that. It's time I had some security in my life.'

Despite that remark hurting him, he managed to stay silent even when Wimpole flounced from the room. The door reopened. 'I've got holiday due, I'm taking it now. All right?'

That had been two weeks ago, and she hadn't even sent him a postcard.

No food, no Wimpole, no Bandage. 'What doom!' he said aloud, and wondered how often these days he talked to himself, more than before, he was sure. He looked at the glass in his hand. Whisky at this time was not a good idea either. What the hell was happening to him, what was he *allowing* to happen? He poured the remains of the whisky down the sink and made himself a pot of coffee.

Wimpole had been wrong. It wasn't that he couldn't manage without her, that was too simplistic, of course he could. No, because of this row he faced losing the one person he knew, without doubt, had always loved him, despite all his faults. His parents had barely been aware of his existence, let alone loved him. Aunt Phoebe had, in her detached and mildly eccentric way, but she was dead and who was there now? Had Sophia ever loved him, or had he imagined she had because he'd wanted her to? If he was totally honest, the only creatures who'd ever loved him unconditionally had been his dogs. All his life there had been a dog trotting behind him, adoring him. Now he didn't even have Bandage.

He sighed deeply. Maybe he should buy another one. It was three months since he'd disappeared. Yet to get another dog would seem so disloyal – and how would Bandage feel if he came home and found another dog in his basket? He shook his head at that thought – it was stupid of him to cling onto such hopes. He had to mourn for Bandage as he had for other dogs in the past when they had died. His hoping that Bandage would return had been preventing the grieving process from beginning. And until it was over, another dog was out of the question.

He stood up. Sitting here wallowing in self-pity was not going to solve anything. He'd do some gardening, take over where Wimpole had got bored.

As he changed his shoes the telephone rang.

'Oliver duck, it's me, Cora.'

'Hullo there.' He forced a measure of cheerfulness into his voice.

'Ben's birthday lunch – next week. Of course you'll come?'

'But Cora . . .'

'I don't want to hear any buts. I know you're on your own, that Wimpole's gone off on holiday.'

'How do you know that?'

'I know everything.'

'I don't think I can face Sophia.'

'Don't be silly, just ignore her. You can't spend your life avoiding her. We'll be twenty for lunch.'

'Twenty? Who?' he asked, his curiosity getting the better of him.

'Odds and sods. Waifs and strays, you know me,' Cora laughed her attractive throaty chuckle.

'I don't know . . .'

'You don't have the number of that nice Thomasine Lambert, do you? I liked her, so did Ben. I thought I'd call her,' Cora said, with low cunning.

'Sorry, no. You'll have to try directory enquiries.' He tried to sound as nonchalant as possible.

'So, what about you, Oliver? We've got some Beluga – does that tempt you?'

'You know, Cora, it might just do that.' He couldn't care less about Beluga!

25

Kimberley had finished attending to the dogs and was returning to the house when she heard a whimpering noise coming from the shed where her father kept his pit bulls, Hannibal and Hector. She preferred not to enter: she'd only seen them once, and they looked so unpleasant they frightened her. Ignoring the noise she walked on, but the whimper seemed to follow her and grow louder, and compassion defeated fear.

She pushed the heavy door open and peered in. Compared to the puppy shed, this was a palace. It was clean, and filled with the comforting smell of good fresh straw; in the corner she saw a large gas heater, presumably for winter. The water bowls held clear water, and the two dogs looked up with interest and lolloped over to the fencing to welcome her.

Her father had acquired a third dog, and it was this one who must have been whimpering. He lay in a disconsolate black heap, and two eyes set almost on the sides of his head watched Kimberley's approach warily.

Kimberley leant on the gate to the pen. The dog sidled

on its belly away from her, and she saw it was shaking.
'Is it you, Sly?' she asked, recognising the white fur on
one of its front paws. 'Sly?' The dog did not respond.
Kimberley wondered whether to approach further or
not. But the pathetic way the dog held its head, the
obvious fear, made her mind up for her.

Gingerly she opened the gate, talking to the dog all the
time. She stepped nearer, holding out her hand, speaking
encouragingly. She bent down and balanced herself with
one hand in the straw and felt something wet and sticky.
She looked at the palm of her hand and saw it was
covered with blood.

'You poor old boy. Let me see.' She was on her knees
now as she moved towards him. 'You're that dog that
Butch had, aren't you? Not having much luck, are you,
ending up with my dad.'

The dog lay still, his eyes watching her, but always
looking away whenever her glance met his. Her hand
was close to his face now. She let him sniff her, saw him
relax. 'You know, I think you should really be called
Bandage.' She enunciated the word clearly. He
responded with a twitch of his rump, but this movement
obviously hurt him, for he whined and then flopped
back on the straw and stretched his neck. She saw
the blood glistening on his fur. 'Bloody hell, what happened?' She knew it was a stupid question, she knew
very well what had happened to the dog – he'd been
fighting, or rather been made to.

She stood up and the dog looked at her appealingly, as
if afraid she was leaving him. He started to whimper
again. She crossed to a tap. She found a cloth which she
wished could have been cleaner and rinsed it out.
Bandage lay almost contentedly as, gently, she bathed
his wound, yelping once when she pressed a little too
hard. 'Sorry,' she said, and kissed the top of his head.
The dog then turned, as if to show her the wound on the
back of its neck. That was wider, as if the skin had been

ripped. She needed several trips to the sink to rinse the blood from the cloth.

'You poor love,' she was saying when the door burst open and her father entered. At the sight of him, the dog began to shake.

'What're you up to?' he shouted.

'Dad, this dog's badly hurt.'

'So? It's its own bloody fault.'

'Can't we call the vet? It needs stitches, antibiotics.'

'Don't talk bloody stupid. A vet here – are you mad?'

'No, just fed up with what goes on here. It's not right.'

'Well, you know what you can do, don't you?' He glowered belligerently. 'You can piss off and leave your mother and me alone. Understand? Mind your own fucking business.'

'Right, if that's what you want, then I'll do just that,' she said with false confidence.

'Good. I've had enough of you. All this grand education and where's it going to get you? You're nothing but a bloody parasite. But I warn you.' He stepped menacingly towards her. 'You listen. You breathe a word about this to a living soul and, I warn you, I'll get you. Understood?'

'I won't say a word.' The look of fear and horror on her face was sufficient to reassure him that she meant what she said. She stepped back from her father, the dog cowering behind her.

Kimberley had been tired before she started. Now, trudging along, a case in one hand, a half-filled canvas holdall over her shoulder, Middle Shilling felt as if it was forty miles away. She had hoped to be able to hitch-hike, but she'd been walking for over an hour and had not seen one car.

She felt completely alone in the world, which in a way she was. But that was a thought she had no intention of lingering over. It was done now; she'd finally left.

It had been hard leaving, and she'd dallied too long

and as a result had nearly bumped into her father – the last thing she needed. Last night, after the row and his ultimatum, she had gone to her room and packed her bags – everything she possessed in a case and the holdall. She had made two trips down the stairs, banging the case and bag, making what she was doing obvious. She wasn't sure why, almost certainly to make her mother come to see what all the noise was about – but she hadn't. Instead, this morning, when Kimberley had stood in the kitchen doorway, her mother was at the table making an apple pie.

'I'm going, Mum. Dad said I was to.'

'I know.' Her mother did not look up.

'Well, I'll be off then . . .' She lingered.

'Goodbye.'

Kimberley swung round and took a step into the warm, shabby room. 'Is that really all you've got to say?'

'What is there to say? What can I say?' Her mother paused in her task and looked up, and Kimberley saw how afraid she was, how sad.

'Oh, Mum!'

'It's probably for the best. You know what he's like.'

'Yes. I suppose so. But what about you?'

'I'll be fine. It might be better – less arguing, if you know what I mean.'

'No, Mum, I don't know. Are you blaming me for all the upsets? Is his filthy temper my fault?'

Her mother passed a weary hand over her eyes. 'Sometimes, yes. You answer back when it's best not to. You question what he does – no man likes that. You make him feel he's not master in his own house any more.'

Kimberley shook her head in disbelief. 'He's a bastard, Mum, rotten to the core. You know that.'

'He's my husband.'

'So? Does that excuse him? Does that make what he does right?'

Kimberley stood, her arms hanging awkwardly at her sides, not sure how to continue, how to end their conversation. Wanting her mother to fling her arms about her and beg her to stay, and knowing how unlikely that was.

'Here, take this.' From the pocket of her pinny, Sue took a small roll of folded notes. 'See you on your way.'

'You can't afford to give me that.'

'Yes I can. I've always got a little put by – just in case. He won't know about this.'

Kimberley wanted not to accept, but she had ten pounds in the world and since she had no clear idea what she was to do, she took it. She zipped it into her shoulder-bag, said thanks and, not sure if her voice would allow her to say more, put her head down so that her mother would not see the distress on her face as she ducked out of the back door.

She crossed to the barn where the fighting dogs were kennelled. She had planned to take the bull terrier with her. There was something about the dog, a lost look, a longing to be loved that found an echo in herself. But Sly, though she called him Bandage, was stiff and could barely move, let alone walk the distance she must travel. The cuts were congealed with blood. She wondered whether to bathe them again and decided against it, fearing further water on the wounds might open them again. Instead, she lay down on the straw beside the dog, scooped him into her arms and allowed her sense of isolation and betrayal to take over from the brave front which was so difficult to maintain. The dog whimpered and nuzzled her neck as if he understood her problem.

'I'm sorry, Bandage,' she whispered in the dog's ear. 'I've got to leave. I'll try and come back for you – that's a promise. One day when I'm settled.' She had to look away from the pleading expression in the dog's eyes, quickly left the barn and struck off across the field towards the road which would eventually take her to Middle Shilling and the house of her Aunt Grace.

Grace White was an aunt by marriage. Her husband had been Tom White's older brother who had died five years ago. Kimberley had met her aunt but did not know her. It was not in Tom's interests to be friendly with anyone, and that included family. But then the brothers had never got on, her mother had told her that. Kimberley had last seen this aunt three years ago when, on a rare shopping trip with her mother, they had bumped into her in Morristown. They'd gone to Mac-Donalds for a hamburger and coffee. Kimberley had been fascinated to meet her, and decided she liked her. Now all she could hope was that the woman had liked her too.

Her bags slowed her progress dramatically. It was already afternoon, and her arms felt as if they had been stretched like elastic, when she finally found her aunt's house on the small council estate and knocked on the door.

Grace took one look at her weary niece and swept her into her arms. Kimberley felt she'd never known such a strong sense of comfort and security as she felt now, clasped to Grace's ample breasts.

'My Terry, your uncle, he often said "One day it'll get too much for that little one".'

'He knew?' she asked, as they sat at the small table in the tiny, cluttered kitchen. They were alone. Her cousins, after their initial curiosity had waned, were in the next room watching television.

'Chalk and cheese Tom and Terry were.'

Later, after Kimberley had told Grace what had happened, she said, 'And she let you go, don't forget that. They don't deserve you, that's for sure. So, what are your plans, or haven't you had time to make any?'

'I'd started to look for a job, but it's proving more

difficult than I'd realised. I thought I wanted to work in a bank, but I'm not sure if I could stand being cooped up in an office.'

'What about school? I always heard you were the clever one.'

'That's finished. I've just got to wait for my results. I did wonder about getting a job as a nanny or something like that. I think I'd be good with kids, and I'll need a job where I can live in.'

'Do you like dogs?'

'Dogs?' Kimberley looked up sharply. 'What about dogs?' she asked cautiously, the years of training by her father still paramount. What did Grace know?

'Would you like to work with them?'

'I'd love that – provided it was proper . . . you know.' Her voice trailed off, not able to explain further, frightened she might let slip about the puppy farm and compromise her father.

'I sometimes help out a lady near here who's got a big kennels. When she goes away, I pop up and give the dogs their food. Her last kennel maid left and she's not found anyone suitable – very fussy she is. But she's rushed off her feet.'

'I'd like that.'

'I can't promise, you understand. You might not suit. But I can mention you to her next time I see her.'

Thomasine wondered if she was becoming a recluse. She's always liked driving and normally enjoyed going to pick her daughter up from school, stopping for lunch on the way there and tea on the way back. However, this time was different. No sooner had she set off than she longed to be back home. It was as if the house had become her safe haven. To speed the process she did not bother to stop for lunch and chivvied Nadine into hurrying her goodbyes.

'We usually stop there,' Nadine said as they shot past the old coaching inn.

'I'd rather press on.'

'Why? What for?'

'I don't know. I just want to get home. Getting middle-aged, I suppose.'

'Getting!' Nadine snorted, but Thomasine decided not to rise to the bait. 'Have you changed my room?'

'Yes.'

'What's it like?'

'It's a secret.' Thomasine smiled, confident she would like this one. 'I expect you're excited about Tuscany. Quite the jet-setter, aren't you? France at Easter and Italy this summer,' she said lightly, which was quite an achievement since she was still upset that, yet again, she was to lose her daughter for the holidays. Nadine, reasonably enough, was seduced by the idea of a month in a villa with a swimming pool. She did not blame her, but rather Robert; chequebook power, which, in the circumstances, was a long way from fair.

'You don't mind me going, do you?' Nadine asked anxiously, to Thomasine's surprise. 'I mean, it does seem grossly unfair on you. That's presuming, of course, that you'd want me home with you.' She said this almost shyly.

Thomasine, while keeping her eyes on the road, felt for Nadine's hand and squeezed it. 'That goes without saying.'

'Then I'll stay if you want.' Thomasine smiled, for her daughter's voice was such a mixture of duty and disappointment, making her voice slip down only for hope to raise it again.

'Nadine, darling, I'm fine, really. I do understand, you know.'

'What?' she asked suspiciously.

'How difficult it is for you being pulled all ways. And

of course you must go to Tuscany, it all sounds delicious. I'd go if it was offered to me.'

'I know Dad's trying to buy me. I'm not thick.'

'That's not fair. He loves you. Everything he does is because of that. Don't be hard on him,' she said, regretting that she had to be so reasonable, but with her heart singing that Nadine wasn't fooled.

'It is gross, though, isn't it? You're strapped for cash and can't bribe me in the same way. I wouldn't put it past him to have made sure you were short of money.'

'No, that's my stupidity. I'd never had to manage before, and I miscalculated.'

'What about the book illustrations?'

'They didn't like them – well, not enough.'

'What dorks.'

'Bless you for that.'

'The problem with Dad is he's not an objective person. He only sees things from his viewpoint. Not like me, I always take a balanced view of things. He hasn't got my tolerance,' Nadine said gravely, and Thomasine had to pop a Polo in her mouth to stop herself from shrieking with amusement. How wrong could one be? She smiled inwardly instead.

'I sometimes think I've been intolerant of you, though,' Nadine continued, and Thomasine received one of those shudders that one does when one's mind appears to have been read.

'In what way?' she asked innocently.

'I suppose I was angry with the split up, so I took it out on you. I just wanted to lash out. But I've changed all that. Tell you what, I'll make sure I spend Christmas with you – no matter what he offers?'

'What did he offer this time?'

'Driving lessons when I'm seventeen.'

'Did he now?' The creep, she thought, but said nothing and concentrated on her driving and relished the fact that her complicated daughter appeared to be less complex this time – or at least she hoped so.

At the school house, she was pleased to note Nadine prowling around the kitchen and sitting room as if checking if anything had changed, as she had invariably done at their home in London. 'Isn't it odd here without Luna?' she suddenly said, her tour of the sitting room complete.

'Horrible. I miss her dreadfully.'

'Get another like her, I say.' Nadine grinned at her broadly.

'Who could replace Luna?' she said as the telephone rang. Nadine wandered off as she answered it.

'Cora? How nice.' She listened as Cora explained about her lunch party for Ben's birthday. 'I would have loved to come, but unfortunately I can't. I have to drive my daughter to Heathrow that day – she's off to Italy.' And damn, she thought, the one day she'd received an invitation! 'Never mind, another time,' Cora said vaguely, and as the call was disconnected the door burst open and Nadine shot into the room.

'Mum! How could you! My room!'

'You don't like it?' Thomasine's heart sank.

'Like it? It's gross! Red! It's grim! I wanted black – I told you.'

'Wouldn't black be even grimmer?'

'You never listen to me do you? What I want never matters.'

Thomasine looked at her fuming daughter and marvelled that anyone could change mood so quickly. Still, the car ride home had been pleasant. 'Well, I'm not changing it again, and that's flat.'

Nadine opened her mouth, about, no doubt, to give a sharp reply, but was foiled by the front doorbell ringing. Even as she wondered who it could possibly be, Thomasine was grateful to them for interrupting what appeared to be a full-scale row in the making.

She opened the door to find the Tregidgas standing on the step. 'Mrs Tregidga!' She smiled politely, and then she saw Mrs Tregidga was cuddling a puppy to her. 'Oh, how sweet.' She patted the small head. 'Come in, do. How kind of you to call.'

She ushered them both through to the sitting room, where Mrs Tregidga gently placed the puppy on the rug. Thomasine was quickly on her knees. 'Oh, you sweet little thing.' The puppy, whose stomach appeared to be larger than its head, waddled over to her, clambering up onto her lap. Thomasine looked at Mrs Tregidga. 'One of Luna's?'

'Yes. It's a bit early to see, but the colouring will be exactly the same, and she's as stubborn as her mother.'

'You are *adorable*.' Thomasine nuzzled the small dog, who by now was removing her earrings with teeth as sharp as razors. 'Ouch,' she cried. The puppy stopped and, her head on one side, looked quizzically up at her. 'Look at that, just like Luna. It's so kind of you to bring her to show me. I did sometimes think of taking you up on your invitation to visit, but I didn't think I could cope with seeing Luna. Silly of me.'

'No, we understand, really. We're selling the pups now and, well, we didn't want them all to go without you being given a second chance to decide if you want one.'

'As a present, you understand, Mrs Lambert, for all you did for Luna,' Major Tregidga added.

'How kind of you. I don't know.' Thomasine shook her head. 'Only a moment ago I said to Nadine there wasn't a dog that could take Luna's place. But, she is sweet, isn't she?' The puppy licked her face excitedly. 'I'd love to keep her. I didn't know I'd want one – I thought I didn't – but now I know I do,' Thomasine said suddenly and laughed at her jumbled sentence. 'What's she called?'

'We left that to you. But let me know as soon as possible, I must know for the Kennel Club registration.'

'Nova. That's it. She's called Nova.'

In all the excitement she had not seen the major was awkwardly holding a box of puppy food and mineral supplements. 'Have you still got the baskets? If not, I've one in the car.'

'I've still got everything in the garage. Maybe deep down I always knew I'd succumb again.'

Drinks offered and drunk, the Tregidgas departed. 'Who was that?' Nadine asked sulkily, appearing in the doorway. 'Not another one! You said you didn't want one.'

'I changed my mind. Just look at her, isn't she sweet?' Thomasine fondly watched the puppy trying to chase her stubby tail and not succeeding. 'In any case, you just said I should get another.'

'That was then –'

'Before you saw your room?'

'Exactly.'

Thomasine sat back on her feet, the puppy playing with the folds of her skirt. 'Nadine, we can't go on like this,' she sighed. 'You must try to control your temper and learn to be a bit more reasonable.'

'I don't have to do anything I don't want!'

'Then you'll have a miserable life.'

'I realise that. Especially now you've got that mutt to love more than me.'

'Oh, Nadine!' she began, feeling sorrow and exasperation in equal doses, but Nadine had already slammed out of the room.

Nova suddenly collapsed on the rug. One moment she'd been playing, the next her legs gave way and she was asleep. 'I reckon you were asleep before you hit the rug, Nova.' Thomasine gently stroked the soft fur of the puppy, who was contentedly wiffling. Perhaps this was

270

the wisest thing she could have done; she needed someone to love, and loving Nadine was becoming more difficult. She sighed, but then found herself thinking there was another plus factor – the puppy would give her an excuse to see that nice vet again. And then she resolved, no matter how hard it was, to ignore her daughter's tantrums and not let her pull her down.

26

Eveleigh felt happier than she had in weeks, ever since the letters from the solicitors had started to arrive. With a panache learnt from long experience of driving her battered Bentley, she negotiated the narrow lanes. Her style at the wheel of the enormous car frequently put fear into the stoutest heart. Many men who had faced the enemy in battle, bent the will of the wildest horses to theirs, and in one case stood firm in the face of a charging bull elephant, had emerged from Eveleigh's car white about the gills and in desperate need of a restorative.

Even the sun, which this summer had been a marked failure, had chosen to shine. The fields and hedgerows, because of the endless days of rain, were a healthy green, which, with the clear blue sky, seemed to lift Eveleigh's spirits even higher.

If she could sing, she would, she thought, for she was about to do what she loved most of all – to judge a dog show. When Reggie had been alive she had judged far more than she did these days. It had been easier then, with the two of them able to share their duties. She could travel to Edinburgh, one heady time even to Lyon, knowing that all was well at home in Reggie's capable hands. They'd had reliable kennel maids then – whether because standards were different or because Reggie was a better judge of character than she, she did not know.

She'd certainly had more time then, with everything shared, than she did now that she ran the kennels alone.

She had been up since five this morning seeing to her dogs. She had typed out a long list of instructions for Grace White, who would only look after the dogs provided a list was left for her detailing their routines and needs. Rather unnecessary, Eveleigh thought, for she had every confidence in Grace – she would never leave her dogs with anyone she did not trust totally. So each dog's next feed had been measured out in bowls, and each bowl was labelled with the dog's name. For all her preparations, she knew Grace was afraid that she would do something wrong and harm the dogs, even though Eveleigh had pointed out to her that it was very difficult to hurt a St Bernard. Far more likely that Grace could be hurt by a friendly tap from one of their enormous paws.

Better still, this time Grace had an assistant, her niece Kimberley. Eveleigh had had a long talk with the girl and had liked her from the start. She appeared to have a genuine interest in dogs. However, from past experience, Eveleigh was wary of such claims. She had learnt that the inducement of the flat which went with the job had, on three previous occasions, made applicants declare a love for dogs which was painfully lacking when the hard work of helping to run a large kennels was faced. Kimberley presented another worry in that Eveleigh wondered if the job would be enough for her; she seemed very intelligent and an ideal candidate for university rather than a job as a kennel maid. Still, she'd agreed to take her on for a trial period and today would be her first day at work. But she was to stay at her aunt's until Eveleigh decided the post was permanent.

Yes, she thought as she tanked along, everything was most satisfactory, if only the persistent letters from the solicitors wanting to buy her out would cease.

It was all such a mystery. As Jim had said, normally

their patience would have run out by now, but as far as she knew no application for planning had been made and nothing untoward had happened. It bothered her so that she could not sleep. Eveleigh felt as if she were waiting for something – what, she did not know, only that it was likely to be unpleasant when it came.

'It's probably someone you know who doesn't want to upset you,' Oliver had volunteered, and she had begun to wonder if this was so. It wasn't Oliver, that was for sure, and although she had several wealthy acquaintances, none among them were rich enough to buy the land and then let nothing happen for such a long time. She had thought of Ben, but when she'd asked him, he'd said it was never his practice to risk buying land with no planning permission – people lost money that way, he told her sagely.

The problem of the letters occupying her mind, the miles scudded by, and she was rather surprised to find she had arrived at the town two hours from Shillingham with no memory of getting there. Not the best way to drive, she lectured herself sternly, as she swung the heavy car round the streets in the direction of the large park where the show was to be held, in the open, provided this good weather continued.

She showed her judge's ticket to the man on the gate, which allowed her to park free. She placed the car neatly, despite its size, and rummaged around in her capacious handbag searching for both pairs of spectacles. She always carried two pairs for fear of losing one. She was, she realised, a strange mixture – anything to do with her dogs was ordered and meticulous; anything to do with herself was chaotic and muddled. She wondered if it was because she had been born a Gemini.

She sat for a while, as she always did, composing herself. But also she liked to spend these few minutes watching the people unloading their dogs. It was the first

273

sight she would have of many of them, and in that first glance she could learn a lot. Several times she had sat in her car watching them and thought *that one will win*, and later, in the show ring, these dogs had proved her right. It gave her pleasure to see the affection and care most owners showered upon their charges: watching people as besotted with their particular breed as she was with her St Bernards always made her feel less alone.

She watched as dogs from the size of Yorkshire Terriers up to English Mastiffs were fussed towards the show ground. Poodles, terriers, spaniels, boxers, Great Danes, Chihuahuas, German Shepherds and Labradors – they were all there. This particular show was an important one in the calendar of shows; it was a county show, recognised by the Kennel Club, and there would be other judges here. Eveleigh's job today was to judge the St Bernard, Great Dane and Labrador entry.

She looked up with surprise as she saw Gill and Justin unloading Sadie and her new puppy, Sukie. She'd quite forgotten Gill had told her he'd be here. She was glad she hadn't been asked to judge the poodles. Judging a friend's dog was not easy, since she always dreaded offending a friend. Not that she could ever be accused of favouring a friend's dog over the rightful winner. It made things awkward, that was all.

'Thomasine too, this is a surprise,' she said, as she reached their car to find her new friend standing beside it.

'This is my daughter, Nadine.' Thomasine smiled broadly, but Eveleigh's sharp eyes saw her nudge the girl in the back and her equally sharp ears picked up the urgently whispered 'shake hands'.

'Hullo, Nadine. Do you like dogs?' Eveleigh asked.

'Some dogs,' the teenager answered sulkily. Not for the first time, Eveleigh wondered why was it that the pleasantest people always produced scowling children.

Such encounters often reinforced Eveleigh's sense of relief that she had not been 'blessed' with any.

'Jim tells me you've another bulldog?' Eveleigh decided the safest course was to ignore the daughter and concentrate on the mother.

'Yes. Nova – Luna's pup. That's why we came in two cars – I don't want to leave her alone too long, or I won't have a home to go back to.'

'She's a chewer?'

'You can say that again. Any advice?'

'Well, don't give her an old shoe. So often people do, and then they wonder why, later on, the dog still chews their shoes when, of course, to the dog, it's the most reasonable thing to do. And avoid throwing sticks. It's so dangerous. Not only can they get splinters in their mouths, they can impale themselves and often it's fatal.' Out of the corner of her eye Eveleigh was aware that Nadine was yawning. 'Toys made specifically for dogs are best,' she finished in a rush, but Nadine had already wandered away. How rude, thought Eveleigh.

'Thanks for the warning, I wouldn't have thought of all that. She didn't really want to come.' Thomasine looked towards the humped figure of her daughter. 'But then she didn't want to be left behind. Confusing!' Thomasine said, laughing nervously in apology. She had an extra bundle of guilt this morning – she'd woken and found she was looking forward to next week, and Nadine's departure.

'Well, if you'll excuse me, I must be going,' Eveleigh said.

At the entrance to the marquee she was met by May Westmacott, an old friend of long standing, a breeder of whippets whose home town this was.

'You're looking in the pink,' said May.

'And you too. Good entry?'

'Very good, but I've a massive problem. Tom Grant was to judge the final line-up, but he's telephoned he's broken down and won't get here in time. Would you do it for us? You're the most experienced here.'

'I'd be honoured.'

They crossed the marquee, the heels of their sensible shoes sinking into the uneven surface. Eveleigh sniffed appreciatively: she loved that special warm smell of trapped heat and flowers so peculiar to an English marquee in the summer.

Eveleigh knew the other judges from countless shows. Some she liked enormously, others she was not so sure of, but they were all united on the one subject of dogs. Teacups were handed around and Eveleigh was soon enjoying a good old gossip. A heated discussion was soon under way about the merits, or not, of tail docking, on which as some thought, the Kennel Club was not making a strong enough stand for either case. For Eveleigh, there was no choice. A tail should not be docked; it was such an important means of expression for a dog, she argued. She was almost sorry that the discussion had to end but May said it was time, and ushered them through into the open where several rings, marked out with ropes, were laid out.

Open air shows were a joy, thought Eveleigh, as she walked towards her ring. There was a carefree, almost holiday-like atmosphere. She always thought the dogs enjoyed them especially too.

The day sped by happily. When not judging she watched the elimination process in other breeds, noting there was nothing she would not have done or chosen herself – it was always a comfort to know her judgment was shared by the others.

Today there was a particularly fine St Bernard – not bred from any of her own kennel's progeny, she was glad to see. That always made judging more difficult, even if it was several generations on. 'How on earth do you know, Eveleigh?' friends would ask her in amazement when, having eyed up a St Bernard she would say, 'I see

Wotan in her.' Or Isolde, or Kundry or whoever the ancestor might be. She always gave the same answer, which in a way was no answer – 'I just know,' she would say, and smile modestly. But this St Bernard she recognised immediately. From the massive set of its shoulders she knew it must be one of Connie Cunningham's, and a prime candidate for success at Crufts next year.

She had taught herself to be totally scrupulous when judging the working dogs, which included St Bernards, but she always had to fight herself a little when St Bernards and King Charleses were in the final line-up, as today. It was hard to steel her heart and not automatically award first place to the St Bernard and second to the King Charles, which was the order in which they stood in her heart. But of course her integrity would not allow any such thing and she did question if, sometimes, she was not a little too hard on those two breeds in over-compensation.

There was little anyone could do to pull the wool over Eveleigh's eyes. She had learnt to recognise the silver shoes which were always worn by one particular breeder of Salukis. Most judges only looked at the dogs, so shoes were a good ploy to let a judge know who was at the other end of the dog's lead. Pink suede, silver, gold, tartan – she'd seen them all. She had seen women virtually throw themselves at male judges, and had heard that some gay breeders would only show to equally gay judges. One woman who bred Rottweilers drenched herself in Poison perfume to let whoever was judging know it was her. Eveleigh would never have anything to do with such subterfuge. It was the dog that mattered, not who bred them, or from where.

The tea break came prior to the final judging and Eveleigh, having downed her tea and nibbled at a sandwich, excused herself and went to the judges' loo.

She went straight into one of the cabins, came out, crossed to the basin to wash her hands, and as she did so idly looked at the mirror above her. Then she stood stock still, water cascading over her hands, the basin filling dangerously full. She felt as if she were frozen. Finally she spoke. 'Oh no,' she said. 'Oh dear God, no.'

Above her on the mirror, written in scarlet lipstick was the message: 'E. Brenton is a cheat! Only her favourites win. Bitch!'

Slowly, Eveleigh removed her hands from the basin and began to dry them on a paper towel. What did it mean? She'd never cheated. Her honour as a judge was impeccable. There had never been a whisper against her.

She felt sick, and had to lean against the basin for a moment, taking deep breaths. There was a tap on the door. 'Are you ready, Eveleigh?' she heard May call.

'Just a moment, May, if you don't mind.' Her voice sounded weak. What should she do? 'No, come in,' she decided.

'Eveleigh, my dear, are you all right, you look as though you've seen a ghost?' May asked, her voice full of concern. Eveleigh did not reply, merely pointed at the mirror.

'Who the hell did that? My dear Eveleigh, I do apologise.'

'But what does it mean, May? I've never cheated in my life.'

'Of course you haven't. Somebody's disgruntled. Perhaps you didn't let their dog win in their class, so they're just being spiteful.'

'But it's true, I have almost made up my mind, the final selection will be the St Bernard.'

'And rightly so. It's obvious to anybody who knows anything about dogs that that one is a champion in the making – and I don't even like the breed,' said May comfortingly, and then, realising what she had said and

278

to whom, clapped her hand over her mouth. But Eveleigh had not, apparently, even noticed.

'I can't now *not* award to that dog just because of this message,' said Eveleigh.

'But of course you can't, my dear. You've just got to put it out of your mind and ignore it.'

This was easier said than done as Eveleigh stood in the middle of the large ring and the final six dogs, one chosen from each class, circled her. The excitement of their owners transmitted itself to the dogs, as one by one they ran round the circle showing off their shape, their paces, showing her how pretty they were, how perfect. But Eveleigh was finding it very hard to concentrate – all she could think of was the bright scarlet slash across the mirror in the toilets. Was the person who had done it here, watching her? Although the afternoon was hot, Eveleigh felt cold, and in the middle of the ring hugged her woollen jacketed arms around her. One by one she inspected the line of dogs. She liked the American cocker spaniel, she had a special word for the basset, she enjoyed feeling, once again, down the massive flanks of the St Bernard. She was fair with the King Charles. She paused long and hard in front of a fine West Highland terrier, and admired, particularly, a very fine white poodle – she didn't look·up, she knew it was Sadie. Down the line she walked again. The tension in the hall mounted as she stood back, deep in thought, looking at all the dogs.

She abruptly pointed at the St Bernard, unaware how dramatic the action appeared. Judging by the applause, her choice of the poodle as Reserve was popular. Next she chose the Westie, and finally the King Charles in Fourth. The St Bernard's owner was jumping up and down hysterically; the dog knew immediately that it had won and it too ran round in circles, twining its lead around the owner's legs until she was tied up, as if to a maypole, and everyone was laughing – except poor

Eveleigh. She did not talk as long as the owner had expected her to, nor the audience, just long enough to check that she had been right and that it was from one of Connie Cunningham's litters.

'You've a future champion there,' she said to the excited young woman. 'Guard her well,' she smiled, nodded to May and said, 'I really have to be going.'

'Yes, of course, of course.'

She could not look at the faces of the people smiling and nodding at her as she made her way towards the car park, because she was so afraid that one of them was the person who had left the message for her. She virtually ran to her car and started the long drive home.

She felt a depression so intense it was a physical thing, as if it were sitting on her. Yet she had set out this morning in such good spirits, full of joy and lightness. That anyone could attack her integrity was alarming.

'Didn't you think that Eveleigh was a bit shaken up?' asked Gill of Justin as they loaded the dogs, Sadie sporting her rosette, and their equipment into the car.

'Well, she never does talk to us if she's judging.'

'No, it wasn't that. She seemed flustered.'

'Haven't you heard?' a big-breasted woman, who was helping her husband load their bassets into a Range Rover, said. 'Plastered all over the mirror in the ladies loo – accusations of cheating. Favouring the St Bernards. Probably did too.' She patted her basset as if to confirm her suspicions.

'Eveleigh Brenton would do no such thing,' Gill said staunchly.

'You want to watch who you're mouthing off,' Justin added for good measure.

'Oh, yeah, and what? You going to tell her? Who'd believe a couple of poofters?' the husband sneered. Justin put a restraining hand on Gill as he stepped forward.

'Leave it, Gill. Moth-eaten old bassets like that wouldn't win anyway.'

'You're right, Justin.' Gill climbed into his car, but wound down the window. 'Tell me,' he said to the woman. 'You know the theory that we all begin to look like our dogs? Are you as low slung as that basset of yours? Must be agony. Ta ra.' And in a triumphant flurry they were away.

27

Bolstered by alcohol, and the determination of everyone present to enjoy themselves, Ben's birthday lunch was beginning well. Cora had been over-optimistic that they would be twenty at table – or rather, Oliver thought as he looked around, she'd been exaggerating as usual.

As it was, they were ten in number – the family, Toby Watkins, a friend of Cora's, and Eveleigh, and four who were strangers to him. Two were women of a 'certain age' who, he quickly discovered, were both reeling from the traumatic effect of errant husbands making off with younger women. One was bitter and brittle, the other damaged and demoralised; both were trying too hard in Oliver's direction, which made him shy away with alarm. He'd have to have a quiet word with Cora about matchmaking for him. The other two were men: a totally humourless business associate of Ben's who, after a mere two minutes' conversation, obviously decided that Oliver was not worthy of his attention, and an Italian who, from the way he was paying court to Sophia, convinced Oliver that he must be a plant to make him jealous. He was too slick by far, and his suit matched. Oliver watched the play with amusement, since he couldn't for one moment imagine Sophia running her fingers through that pomaded hair.

He couldn't understand why Sophia wanted to make him jealous. Very odd. But had he ever understood her or what made her tick? Sophia could flirt away, he was not interested. Whatever affection might have remained from the marriage, she'd destroyed by so carelessly losing Bandage. Why, when he arrived this morning, he'd had the greatest difficulty being polite to her.

'Do you live here?' he asked, the minute he saw her.

'Of course I don't.'

'Then why do you spend more time here than in the house I bought you? I might as well have saved myself the moolah.'

'Where I live is nothing to do with you, Oliver,' Sophia replied, all dignity and ice.

'Thanks be to God!' Oliver enjoyed watching the dignified demeanour crumble into indignation.

Eveleigh, sitting opposite him, was, he registered, quite flushed, and in rather an attractive way. He could not recall ever thinking of Eveleigh in terms of attractiveness. In fact, she was one of those women whose gender was immaterial; a good sort, a friend, not a *woman*, not a feminine person. Suddenly he found he was seeing her as if for the first time. She had rather a fine face and exceptional eyes, and a good figure, he'd not noticed before. She was talking and laughing with Toby, who was sitting beside her, and then looking almost demurely down at her place setting. And then he suddenly realised she was drunk!

Oliver had never seen Eveleigh drunk, or so animated, before. Good God, he said to himself, she's flirting too! He looked at Toby Watkins with renewed interest; he did not know him well, he was one of Cora's friends, a widower in his fifties, ex-army by the look of him. From the end of the table he was aware of Cora grinning at him, and winking so obviously that her face was lopsided from the effort.

'Matchmaker,' he mouthed at her.

'And why not?' she replied.

'Why not what?' asked Ben.

'Nothing,' said Cora, smiling secretly at Oliver, and Ben looked at him sharply. Oliver hoped his father-in-law wasn't getting the wrong end of the stick. Although he quite liked Ben, he was never too sure about him – he'd seen him lose his temper once too often. He was an odd mixture, full of bonhomie one minute, a tyrant the next.

'Did you make Wimpole's match then, Cora?' he said, to distract Ben.

'With Rudie? It's good news, isn't it?' Ben beamed.

'I don't think Oliver's too sure,' Sophia piped up. 'He's probably jealous,' she added spitefully.

'No such thing.' Oliver glared at his wife; what a bitch she was. Still, she knew him so well that sometimes it was frightening. In this case he wouldn't go so far as to say he was jealous, that was a word which could too easily be misunderstood, but he was still adjusting to the idea of her leaving him, there was no doubt about that. 'I shall miss her, but I reckon she's found a good 'un in Rudie,' he said.

'It's nice for Wimpole, and she'll be less of a liability to you, Oliver.' Cora smiled benignly.

'Wimpole was never that.'

'You can say that again!' Sophia drawled.

The first-course plates were cleared away by, Oliver saw, his, or rather Sophia's, Filipino servants.

'I do hope they'll adjust,' said Cora, when the man and woman had left the room. 'They're absolute dears.' Sophia glared with such malevolence at Cora that a more sensitive soul would have wilted.

'Adjust to what?' the brittle woman asked.

'Life in the countryside. They're used to living and working in London.'

'I thought they still did,' Oliver said quietly. He saw that at least Sophia had the decency to look slightly embarrassed, and wondered whether to make some smart-arsed remark about his paying Ben's bills, but decided against it.

How tacky, he thought. How could Sophia be so petty as to lie over such sums, why hadn't she just asked for more maintenance? Still, in a rather comforting way he found her subterfuge gave him the moral high ground – that was, until she thought up some scheme to take it away from him again.

He'd stop thinking about her and concentrate on the pleasure of watching Eveleigh, of all people, being courted.

'Any news of dear Bandage?' Eveleigh asked, aware of his gaze upon her.

'Sadly, no. I've stopped putting adverts in the local papers and free sheets.'

'How sad for you.'

'Yes, it is rather.' Oliver noticed it made his throat ache when he talked of his dog. 'I still sometimes go up to London and drive around the streets, hoping –'

'One must never give up hope. A friend of mine moved to Scotland and her cat which, thinking it was kinder to leave it in its familiar environment, she'd left behind, followed her – it took three months, but it got there,' Eveleigh said kindly.

'That was a cat, not a stupid dog,' Sophia said sharply, with her customary insensitivity.

'Bandage is not stupid.'

'Then where is he?'

'Being held against his will,' Oliver said, feeling murderous towards Sophia.

'Dead, more like.'

'Do you have to be so bloody unfeeling?'

There was a perceptible rustling at the table as everyone changed position in their chairs and re-arranged their knives and forks to cover their own discomfort at seeing others' battles being publicly aired, and everyone concentrated on the next course.

'I thought you said Thomasine Lambert was coming?' Sophia said to Cora some minutes later. She did not look at Oliver as she spoke. He was grateful to her, even if he didn't want to be, for asking the question uppermost in his mind.

'I phoned her, she said she couldn't. She sounded a bit odd to me, agitated, only half interested in what I was saying.'

'Maybe you interrupted her,' Sophia laughed, not a noticeably happy laugh.

'Doing what?' Cora asked.

'Oh, you know . . . don't press me too far,' Sophia fluttered her lashes at the Italian who leered back.

'You don't mean?'

'What else?'

'But who with? I haven't heard a dicky-bird.'

'And you're usually the first,' Ben interjected.

'Why, Jim Varley of course. Who else?' said Sophia.

'Jim and Thomasine? Well, I never.' Cora flopped back in her chair. For some peculiar reason Oliver felt his stomach flip, his heart patter, and knew this was something he did not want to know.

'I think you've made a mistake there, Sophia. Jim has that nice Beth,' Eveleigh said innocently, unaware of the undertones of emotion swirling around the table between Sophia and Oliver.

At this Sophia threw her head back and really laughed. 'What, the dreary tragedy queen, Beth? You must be joking. He *employs* her.'

Oliver opened his mouth to speak, and then snapped it shut. Sophia was bored, she was stirring things up on purpose. He wasn't about to pander to her whim. 'Any further news from those solicitors, Eveleigh?' he asked, changing the subject.

'I write letters. They write letters. It's all so stupid.' She fluttered her hand across her face as if to remove the cobwebs of concern that were always with her, now augmented since the show.

'What's the problem?' Toby Watkins asked.

'I don't think we want to bother Toby with this if it's legal, Eveleigh, there's a good girl,' Ben said in an avuncular tone.

'Well, really!' If she had had hackles, they would have risen, for Eveleigh looked extremely indignant.

'Why not?' asked Oliver.

Ben slowly turned and looked at Oliver with a cold expression. 'Because I said not.'

'May I be the judge?' Toby asked.

'I'd rather not, if you don't mind, Toby. Some other time.'

'Toby's just retired from his law practice, haven't you, Toby? He's one of the best minds in the profession.' Cora smiled benevolently at her guest.

'Oh, I don't know about that.'

'So we don't want to bother him, do we, Eveleigh? Not at a social function.'

Ben, whose colour was normally high, now looked almost magenta, and his eyes were bulging dangerously. Suspicion flooded Oliver's mind like a flock of ravens. He wondered how he could ever have been so dumb.

'Unless, of course, you don't want Eveleigh to have Toby's advice?' Oliver said quietly.

'And what do you mean by that?'

'I mean I think you're behind the person offering to buy Eveleigh's kennels. I think you've been a bit hypocritical with our friend.'

'Watch what you say, Oliver.' Ben waved a forefinger at him.

'Do you mean that when I asked you, Ben, if you had bought that land, you lied to me?' Eveleigh asked.

'He did, Eveleigh. And why? Because if he put in for planning permission, you, of course, would object and, if he doesn't get rid of the kennels, who will buy the

286

ticky-tacky boxes he intends to put up, pretending they are houses?'

'Oh no!' Eveleigh looked dejected.

'Ben, say it isn't true. Tell him.' Cora was standing, leaning forward on the table.

'You can't, can you, Ben? It doesn't matter, Cora. Eveleigh would have found out eventually.' Oliver got to his feet.

'You think so?' Ben sneered. Everyone turned to stare at him.

'Hidden, is it? One company inside another so she'd never find out who bought her? Is that what you mean?'

Ben sat silent. 'Oh, Ben! No!' Cora wailed. Eveleigh was standing now, and the rest of the guests looked confused and uncertain.

'For God's sake, it's all a storm in a teacup. Dad will compensate Eveleigh handsomely and she can open up somewhere else – no problem.'

'Sophia, you don't understand anything about human nature, do you?' Eveleigh bent to pick up her handbag. 'I'm sorry, Cora, but in the circumstances . . .' She pushed her chair back.

'Eveleigh, don't go, we can sort something out,' Cora wailed.

'I don't think so. I feel betrayed.' She turned and faced Ben. 'I thought you were my friend. I can't believe you'd act behind my back in this way. How could you?'

Ben looked up at her, his eyes darting from right to left as if looking for a way of escape. 'I sold my interest,' he finally said.

'Thank God for that,' Cora sighed.

'You did what?' Oliver shouted.

'But if he's sold it, it's nothing to do with us. The problem's solved.'

'Oh, Cora, don't be so dim. He could have kept the land and dropped the plans – he's rich enough. But no, he sells it. Now Eveleigh will have to fight God knows who. What a family!' Oliver now pushed his chair back. 'Sorry, Cora, I couldn't eat another morsel, not knowing this.' He began to follow Eveleigh out of the room.

'Creep!' Sophia shouted.

At the door Oliver paused and turned back to face her. 'Do me a favour, Sophia. Why don't you try, one of these days, to join the human race?'

28

Seeing Thomasine again, with her new puppy, had cheered Jim. Now she had a dog he'd be seeing her on a regular basis, and that pleased him greatly. He did not know what it was about her that attracted him – she was physically attractive, but then so were lots of other women and he didn't automatically fancy them. He thought about it a lot and reached the conclusion that it was something he'd never be able to explain – he wanted to look after her, pure and simple.

He was working in his surgery. A cat brought in by its distraught owners had been caught in a trap, and the skin on its leg was wrinkled up just like a sleeve pushed back up an arm. It must have fought for hours, if not days, to free itself; it was dehydrated and shocked. The owners had been convinced it would have to be put to sleep, but Jim had decided to operate and see if he could save the leg. He worked slowly, methodically repairing that which at first sight had looked irreparable.

Life was getting better, there was no doubt about that. Now the new veterinary practice had opened in Shillingham he had the time to devote to a cat like this: before, he might have been too rushed and busy. He swilled out the wound with sterile water and prepared to suture it up.

It was easier with Beth too. In an odd way his being

annoyed with her had done her good. She was not quite so organising now, didn't witter at him, was less wife-like. Just as he wanted their relationship to be. Taking Harry out had helped too, he was sure. It had made her more relaxed, and he really enjoyed the child's company. He'd even taken him out on his rounds occasionally, and now Harry wanted to be a vet.

'Did it survive?' Beth looked up from her sewing, Harry from the radio-controlled car Jim had bought him for his birthday.

'Keep your fingers crossed, I think it's in with a chance.'

'Only you could do that, Jim,' Beth smiled at him with admiration.

'Thanks, but any vet would have done the same.'

'No. Only you.' And she looked at him intently, but not smiling this time, and there was a moment which he felt they were enjoying alone, and then Harry spoke. It was an odd thing, but just then, when they looked at each other, he felt a strong attraction towards her. He found himself looking at her properly, thinking what a pretty woman she was and how blind he'd been. But there was no future thinking along these lines, she'd never shown him she fancied him. But that look – he didn't think he'd imagined it – said she'd felt the same.

'Uncle Jim, can we go to the fair next week?' Harry asked.

'Don't bother Jim now, Harry.'

'If you want.' He ruffled the child's hair, glad he'd interrupted his chain of thought. He shouldn't be feeling like this: it was wrong, there was the child to consider . . . 'Fancy a coffee?' he asked. 'I'll bring it through to the sitting room.' He put the kettle on as she left. He laid a brandy and a liqueur glass on the tray with the cups. 'Are you coming?' he asked Harry from the doorway.

'No, the car works better on the tiles.'

Jim shut the door.

Beth was sitting in the half-light, only the fading

daylight illuminating the room. She sat, her legs tucked up under her, on the old, squishy sofa. A CD of Chris de Burgh was playing.

'That's not mine,' he said, as he placed the tray on the coffee table.

'No, it's mine, my favourite,' she smiled up at him, and there was the look again.

'I didn't think you'd want a brandy, so I brought a liqueur glass.'

'Drambuie's the best,' she said.

As he poured the drinks, he realised that despite having lived in close proximity to her for well over a year, there was so little he knew about her – what her favourite things were, what her opinions were. She'd always been just Beth. And yet something had happened. Was it her owning up, telling him of her past? Whatever had happened, he realised with a jolt, he was rather enjoying it.

He handed her her drink. 'Beth?'

'Yes?' she looked up at him and patted the cushion beside her, he sank down on it.

'It's really odd,' he began, and as he did so, the telephone rang. 'Damn it,' he said, as he crossed the room to answer it. He listened for a minute to the apologetic voice at the other end. 'No problem, I've eaten. I'll be with you in ten minutes.'

'What's up?'

'Bill Lyley from Merrybank Farm, he's got a cow in trouble calving.'

'Oh no,' she said, not bothering to hide the disappointment in her voice. 'But what about the Shillingham vets?'

'Both out on call,' he said, rather regretting having to go. 'I shouldn't be long.'

The house was in darkness when Jim returned. It had been a nightmare calving. Everything which could have gone wrong had. His body, but especially his shoulders, ached from the pulling on ropes – and all for nothing, both calf and cow had died. He hated such failures, and on the drive back had tortured himself over whether, had he done things differently, he could have saved them.

The one consolation, he had decided once he was away from the house, was that the call had got him away from Beth and the sudden temptation he had felt, after all this time. He'd have to watch himself with her in future; getting involved with Beth would solve nothing, only make for further complications, in her life as well as his own.

One thought cheered him. Since his wife had died, he could honestly say he had never felt anything quite like that for another woman. But things seemed to be changing. First he had reacted to Thomasine as a woman, and now this reaction towards Beth. Perhaps it meant he was emerging from the desert of mourning he'd been living in.

On the kitchen table was a plate of sandwiches left him by Beth which he pushed aside – he was too weary to eat. Instead he poured himself a large whisky and climbed the stairs with aching limbs. He would have preferred to collapse on his bed, but forced himself to take a shower and wash the sweat and the stench of death away. At long last he was in bed, and was asleep almost as his head touched the pillow, the glass of whisky untouched on his bedside table.

Thomasine came to Jim in his dreams. He felt as if he were lying on billowing clouds. Her thick, lustrous hair brushed his face and he could smell it. Her full breasts gently touched his body, exciting him, making him search for them to caress them. He felt in his dream her mouth kissing his body, moving further and further down him. And then he awoke, but the dream continued. He heard himself groaning from sheer pleasure as his penis stood erect, and he felt lips sucking at it, tugging gently, thrillingly. He lifted himself up on his elbows.

'Beth, no!' he cried out, seeing her and not Thomasine.

'Yes, my darling. Oh yes.' And Beth hauled herself onto him, her thighs clasping tight on either side as she lowered herself, and cried out with pleasure as she impaled herself upon him.

He bellowed 'No', but then abandoned himself to the joy of Beth riding him, her hands behind her head, thrusting her breasts at him. He was lost on a sea of lust and pleasure.

August

29

The summer arrived late and settled in. The Shillings shimmered in a heat haze to which there seemed no end. From morning to night mowers clattered over pampered lawns; weeds were annihilated; under cover of darkness hosepipe bans were broken; the pungent smells of barbecues were everywhere; the noise of radios, CD players, domestic racket and family rows filtered from ever-open windows. There was a loosening of reserve, a new friendliness in the air, as the inhabitants marvelled at this very un-English weather. And Thomasine, sunbathing on her lounger, a jug of freshly-squeezed lemonade beside her, with a good book and a new-found indolence, knew she should be ashamed of herself, but could not help relishing the weather reports that Italy was deluged by rain.

At Oakleigh kennels, the St Bernards suffered in the unusual heat. Eveleigh, every day, offered up a silent prayer of thanks that Kimberley had come to work for her; she would never have managed on her own. Each day they worked constantly to ease the dogs' distress, checking regularly that they were not dehydrating as they lay, tongues lolling, their great chests rising and falling rapidly as they panted for relief. They sponged them at intervals, changed water bowls endlessly, and in the background was the constant whirring of the electric fans Eveleigh had set up in the kennels. She was determined she would not lose one dog to the heat, as some had done in previous heatwaves.

Kimberley was almost happy, installed in her small flat over the stables which had once been full of horses, but were now an overflow for dogs and storage. She delighted in having her own home, a place to retreat to, where even Eveleigh knocked, respecting her privacy.

She had volunteered to decorate it rather than wait for the painter to come, and so she had the blue, yellow and white decor she'd always planned. Her wage was more than adequate, with no rent or electricity to pay for, and already she was beginning to save money. The list of things she wanted to buy was long, but not impossible – she longed for a duvet set she had seen in Morristown, a blue-and-white vase in a shop in Shillingham, china she'd seen in Tesco, a wok, and new clothes.

If only the miracle would happen, then she would be totally happy. If only Alan would come back into her life, somehow contact her, find her. She'd several times gone to the Market Square and sat on the fountain and prayed he would turn up, but she did not bother any more. She tried to forget him. During the day when hard at work with the dogs this was fairly easy, but at night, in bed, treacherous dreams slipped unbidden into her mind.

Eveleigh tried to persuade her to go to a disco, join the Youth Club, but for the time being Kimberley could not see the point.

The dogs made her happy. She drew great comfort from their uncomplicated love and devotion. She had her favourites, Isolde and Brünnhilde, but she tried to hide from the others that this was the case. Surrounded by happy, indulged dogs, she often thought of the dogs in the hell she'd left behind, and of Bandage in particular.

During these weeks Eveleigh felt that if she had not had the support of this young girl she would have given up, for there was no one else. She rarely saw Jim these days, the one person she found it easy to talk to – whether he was busy or avoiding her, she did not know. It was silly of her to think she had offended him in some way, but reasoning did not stop her constantly worrying that, inadvertently, she had. So the strange things happening in her life she faced alone, with only Kimberley to turn to.

After the scrawled message on the mirror, Eveleigh had felt like cancelling all other appearances as a judge. 'But then the person who wrote on the mirror will have won!' Kimberley sensibly told her. When the heavy-breathing telephone calls started, it was Kimberley who suggested she buy a high-pitched whistle to deafen the caller, and she quite enjoyed that.

She began to think there were two campaigns against her. The company who had bought the land from Ben Luckett, whose identity she was no nearer discovering, were most likely behind the phone calls and the increase in junk mail which daily poured through her letter-box. And then there was the vicious campaign from some disgruntled dog owner. Both were frightening, both led to sleepless nights.

One night, soon after the show where the spite had started, with her increasing difficulty in sleeping she had tried everything – a whisky nightcap, hot chocolate, some Alka-Seltzer – and all that had happened was that she felt sick. She moved in the bed, searching for a more comfortable position. From next to her feet came a disgruntled sigh, to the left of her a deep uninterrupted snoring. Eveleigh leaned over and put on her light. In the debris on her bedside table she found her reading spectacles, from the floor picked up this month's copy of *The World of Dogs*, and she settled back to read, hoping to tire herself out.

'No, Coco, you do not want to pee now. Go to sleep,' she ordered the Blenheim King Charles Cavalier on the end of her bed. The dog, sensing the finality in her voice, stood up, did three circles and plopped back down in exactly the same position. Isolde, one of her favourite long-haired St Bernards, wearily lifted her head from the pillow beside her to see what was going on. Finding it was nothing, she crashed her huge head down again, muttering her displeasure at being woken.

Eveleigh read for ten minutes, slumped back on her

pillows, idly patting Isolde, but suddenly she sat up with a start. Smiling at her from the pages of the magazine was the face of Penelope Troughton. It was the accompanying caption which had startled Eveleigh, for Penelope had been billed as the country's leading expert on St Bernards! 'Who says?' she muttered, but she already knew – Liz Cooper, the editor of the magazine. It was slotting into place now – the smug smirk on Penelope's face when she'd last seen her at a show, huddled over a drink with Liz. She'd expected to be invited to join them; instead she'd felt distinctly in the way. No doubt they'd been planning this coverage. What really annoyed Eveleigh was that Liz was editor of that magazine largely because Eveleigh had recommended her so strongly for the job to the publisher, a personal friend of long standing.

She had weathered that slight, reasoning that Penelope had won a commendable number of Challenge Certificates and her pups, sold on, were doing well too. She must not regard her position as unassailable, think she was impregnable. If she was slipping, then it was her fault and she must not be paranoid.

Then a fortnight ago Pippa Cunning, one of her oldest friends in the dog world, had taken her on one side and told her that a rumour was going the rounds that at a West Country show she had favoured a dog which was from a litter sired by her Champion Siegfried Neibelung, and that the dog was well below par. Eveleigh could barely believe what Pippa was saying.

'But, Pippa, that was a fine pup – good colour, fine head, deep broad chest. It was the best there. I care too much about my reputation, let alone the dogs, to award to an inferior dog.'

'I know that, Eveleigh. It's jealousy, pure and simple. Try to forget it.'

But Eveleigh hadn't forgotten, and had returned to

her home and her dogs and, too ashamed this time to confide even in her new kennel maid, she had fretted the problem until it had grown enormous. She knew it was not her imagination that people she had known for years had begun to avoid her. At the end of the last show she had found herself isolated instead of the centre of a crowd clustering around, discussing the whole show and the finer points – for Eveleigh, always the best time of all. She was convinced that nothing could get worse, but it had. Last week Pippa had called her.

'Eveleigh, there's only one way to tell you and that's straight out. The rumour is you're taking bribes.'

Eveleigh's legs felt as if they were made of rubber and she sat down with a bump on the stool by the telephone. 'You're not joking, are you?'

'I'm afraid not. I think you have to do something about this, it's so patently a lie.'

'But who would start such a lie?'

'Probably someone whose dog you overlooked in a show.'

'I find that so hard to believe. We've all had dogs we were convinced would win only to come nowhere – it happens. Maybe someone wants me banned as a judge.'

She had replaced the receiver and, unusual for her in the middle of the day, poured herself a large whisky.

'Anything wrong?' Kimberley asked as she passed through the kitchen.

'Nothing,' Eveleigh answered vaguely. This was far too serious a problem to confide in anyone. How she wished her husband was alive. Reggie would have known what to do.

Without even consulting Pippa she had taken out an advert in a magazine, which was read by most breeders, which declared her innocence. What a storm! The advert had been seen by the mainstream press and the story unfolded first in the tabloids and then, shame of shames, in the *Daily Telegraph* itself. The dog world erupted, some siding with Eveleigh but – and this hurt – many criticising her for her action. This morning she had received a letter from the Kennel Club which politely but firmly pointed out that such *little* problems were best sorted out within the structure of the Club and not in the national press. It was the use of the word *little* in relation to what was to her a catastrophe that had stung. She had replied immediately, in a letter which, she was now aware, had not been a model of tact and diplomacy, and had posted it this afternoon. She should have waited and calmed down. What if, by reacting so swiftly, she had fallen into her enemy's hands and blown her credentials as a judge?

She had stood on the scales in her bathroom before going to bed and had seen she'd lost more weight. She couldn't eat, that was the problem. She felt as if her life was imploding, and she did not know what to do to rescue it.

When Wimpole returned, to Oliver's relief she appeared to be devoid of rancour. In fact, he even wondered if he'd dreamed the row. He realised he hadn't when, with the slightest defiant lift of her chin, Wimpole announced the wedding would be in October.

'That's great. What do you want for a present?' he said. One good thing to come out of Wimpole's trip was that he'd adjusted to the idea of her leaving.

'Signed copy of your book when it's published.'

'Is that all? That'll be cheap.'

'Rudolph's got a lovely cottage at Ben Luckett's. Tucked away in the woods with a pretty garden,' she said as if boasting.

'That's nice. Is it furnished?'

'Oh yes. Rudolph's got everything we need. He's a widower, you know.'

'Yes. I know. So you're not going to call him Rudie?'

'Why should I? Everyone else calls him that,' said Wimpole, unable to keep the satisfaction of her new status out of her voice. 'It'll be nice to have dogs around again. I miss old Bandage more than I ever thought I would. Rudie looks after the kennels, you know.'

'Kennels? Ben's only got the labs and the Jack Russell.'

'No, he breeds dogs too. How odd you didn't know.'

'Ben's always been a bit of a mystery man. What sort of dogs?'

'You know me – all mutts are the same, except dear old Bandage. Terriers, hounds, that sort of thing. Not pets.'

Oliver, his relationship with Wimpole re-established, gave her a cheque to buy her wedding clothes and promised to pay for their honeymoon. Wimpole chose the Canaries. She spent half her time at Rudie's cottage, scouring it out – nothing would ever be clean enough for her – and redecorating the main bedroom, no doubt to expunge the presence of the first Mrs Rudolph Adams.

Oliver couldn't fault Rudie. He courted Wimpole in the manner of another age. He sent her flowers, brought her chocolates, arrived for their dates impeccably suited.

'Right gent, isn't he?' Wimpole glowed with pride. 'The tops.'

With such attention Wimpole blossomed, seemed to shed years and become softer, her tongue less sharp, more amenable. It crossed Oliver's mind that perhaps it was sex making this transformation but, hard as he tried, there was no way he could imagine Wimpole in bed with Rudie.

He was alone, writing, when he heard the sound of an unfamiliar car. He decided to ignore the doorbell in the hope that whoever it was would go away. He paused in his work to pour himself a drink. It was barely noon, but to hell with it.

'Bit early in the day, isn't it?'

The voice made him jump. He swung round to see his wife standing in the doorway to the hall, a picnic basket in her hand.

'How did you get in?' he asked, as icily as he could.

'I've still got a key, sweetheart. Don't you remember? Sweet of you not to change the locks.'

'There wouldn't be any point, would there? You've already nicked more than enough to fill your new house twice over.'

'Oh, Oliver, don't be so grumpy,' she pouted. 'I've a surprise for you. A couple of surprises, actually.' She bent down and pushed back the wooden peg holding the wicker basket closed. 'You didn't think I'd forget, did you?' The wicker creaked as she opened it. 'See. I went to Harrods this morning. All your favourite things – quails' eggs, that wonderful Austrian ham, cut so thin you can read a newspaper through it. Strawberries. Caviar. Chablis.'

'It's overcast, Sophia, the heatwave has passed – not picnic weather at all.' Oliver loved a picnic, but not with Sophia, not any more.

'So? We light a fire and eat on the hearth rug.' She laughed her deep-throated chuckle, and slowly stroked the side of her immaculately pressed jeans with a long-fingered hand on which glistened the large diamond rings he had bought her. Oliver was immediately on his guard. 'What do you say? Here in Aunt Phoebe's great hall, or the drawing room, or in our own rustic kitchen.'

'*My* rustic kitchen.'

'Oh come, Oliver, don't be such a bore, not today of all days.'

'What day?'

'Why, our wedding anniversary, of course. Don't tell me you've forgotten.'

'For Christ's sake, Sophia, we are in the throes of

getting a divorce. We don't celebrate anniversaries like that any more.'

'Who says? Why can't we? We're friends, after all.'

'Are we? We've done nothing but snipe and carp at each other ever since we separated, or haven't you noticed?'

'There you go again, what has got into you, Oliver? You're usually such a sunny person.'

'It depends on the company I keep.'

'Oliver! How quick of you, just like a smart little sixth-former, aren't we?' She spoke and smiled with condescension. It was far safer to ask her to leave, he knew that, but natural good manners prevailed, or so he told himself. Or perhaps he was wary of the scene she might make if he did. 'Drawing room?' he chose. He couldn't explain, but he didn't want Sophia in his work room. It was his alone, safe from her presence, and he wanted it kept that way.

'All right then,' he acquiesced. 'I'll carry the basket, it's too heavy for you.'

'Bless you, darling,' she purred and led the way. 'You know, you really should redecorate Phoebe's hall – it's so grim. I see it in Etruscan red.' She waved a hand expansively at the pitch pine panelled walls, and he was glad he'd decided on another room.

Sophia had even brought a flower-sprigged table-cloth, which she carefully laid on the Persian rug in front of the fireplace, then she daintily set out the food while Oliver laid the fire.

'Woman's work, man's work,' she smiled as she spoke, and alarm bells were clanging even louder in Oliver's head. 'Sit you down,' she said, patting one of the cushions she had placed on the carpet. She produced two crystal glasses from the hamper and, shaking a silver cocktail shaker, poured a drink; from a small, silver box she took two olives, which she added to the alcohol.

'There you are. It's a bit early to eat, but you always said no one made a martini quite like mine.'

It was obvious very early into the meal that Sophia was pulling out all the stops to seduce him. It was an odd experience, for he was able to watch himself as if he were a stranger, knowing he felt no interest in the woman whatsoever. Why? She'd pushed for a divorce, not him. Left to his own devices he'd have muddled along with her. So why? She'd had such plans for herself. And then with a mental jolt he wondered if he'd been the fool of all time. Had she had a lover he knew nothing about, and that was what had prompted her to leave? If so, had life with this new man not lived up to her expectations? Was it over, perhaps? All mysterious, but of only partial interest since he was grateful to her now for showing him the way.

'I wish you'd stop, Sophia. You're not getting anywhere.'

'I don't know what you mean!'

'You're trying to seduce me, and I don't want to be seduced. And I can't help but wonder why you're bothering.'

'What a thing to say, Oliver.'

'It's the truth, isn't it? I thought you wanted to be shot of me. I thought . . .' But he did not finish, for Sophia began to cry.

Normally a total sucker where weeping women were concerned, Oliver sat in silence, aware she wanted him to ask her why she was crying, determined not to, and wishing she'd get it over with.

'You're so hard, Oliver,' she sniffed, patting her eyes with one of the ridiculous scraps of lace she called a handkerchief. He watched her warily, feeling they were playing some complicated game with their emotions, and fully aware he had not been given the rule book. 'I want to come back,' she said.

'Don't be silly,' he said bluntly, without thinking.

That only made her cry again. Oliver lit himself a cigarette, feeling he'd earned this one.

'I can't cope, Oliver.'

'What do you mean?'

'Smoking's so bad for you, Oliver. Please don't do it. I couldn't bear it if anything should happen to you.'

'You didn't think like that six, eight months ago.'

'I was a fool then. I see clearly now. We should never have parted. We had a good life together.'

'You *are* joking, aren't you? We did nothing but row.'

'Because we cared. Because we loved each other,' she cried dramatically, and Oliver quite expected her to beat her breast.

'Come off it, Sophia. You stopped loving me years ago. I was a bit slower, hung on to love a little bit longer. But it died. And then we were just a habit to each other. What is it?'

'I don't get invited anywhere – not like *we* used to be. Our friends have deserted me.'

'I'm glad there's some loyalty left in the world,' he said without a trace of irony. 'But a lack of social life is hardly reason to return to each other.'

She wrung her hands as if in distress, but he knew she wrung them for effect. 'I can't manage. I don't have enough money.' She blinked prettily through her tear-drenched eyes.

'Ask your father for more.'

'He won't give me any. He says he can't afford to.'

'Your father can't afford to? I don't believe it. He's as rich as Croesus.'

'He isn't. Not any more. He says it's the recession and Lloyd's.'

'I never knew he was a name.'

'He didn't tell anyone, said it was too showy.'

'And now?'

'He's paid oodles and still owes and says it's open-ended – whatever that means.'

'It means he's in dead schtuk. Poor old Ben.'

'What about poor old me?'

'Honestly, Sophia, I don't see how you can't manage on what I give you. Other people do – why, whole families get by on a percentage of what I give you.'

'I'm not other people,' she said with her old spirit.

'Then perhaps you'd better make a list of your best talents, and instead of playing at work, get a proper full-time job. How much do you need?'

'Oh, my darling, I knew you would help me out.' Sophia flung her arms about him, rubbing her thigh against his.

'It's all right, Sophia. You don't have to pay for it,' he said coldly.

Once the cheque was in her handbag, Oliver was amused at the speed with which she packed the remains of the picnic back into its basket. But he felt only relief that it had all been a trap just to get money. Everything was as it should be, and Sophia had not, as he feared, changed dramatically. He helped her carry the basket out to her car and loaded it in the boot.

'Oh, silly me. How stupid. Your present, with love, Oliver.' Dramatically she opened the car door and dived into the back, emerging holding a bull terrier puppy in her hands. 'For you, Oliver. My way of saying sorry for losing Bandage. Though it was an accident,' she added hurriedly.

Oliver looked at the all-white dog. His hands itched to hold it, but he controlled himself. 'And how long before you claim this one as your own? Your track record in giving animals as presents isn't that good.'

'Oh, Oliver. What a grumpy old man you're becoming. Of course I don't want it back. I'm not good with dogs, I realise now – they're too messy. Here.'

She thrust the puppy at Oliver, who took it, nestling his nose into its neck, smelling the warm smell of biscuits which puppies always had. Feeling the soft, pliant body trustingly moulding itself to him. 'Hullo, boy,' he said, knowing full well that within seconds he was in danger of falling seriously in love with it.

'It's a girl,' said Sophia. 'I thought a bitch was less likely to run away. What are you going to call her?'

'Slipper,' replied Oliver, not sure why.

30

After the show when Eveleigh had been so humiliated, Justin and Gill worried at the problem, just like Sadie with a bone.

'That dear lady, we've got to do something,' said Justin, wielding the brush on Sadie's elegant rump.

'But what? We don't have time to find out who the scumbag is who planted the message.'

'Whoever it was, they lied.'

'Too right.'

'Still, I'd like to cheer her up.' Justin continued with his grooming and Gill with the salon's books which he was neatly balancing.

'Sadie's birthday!' said Justin.

'Sadie's birthday!' said Gill at exactly the same time. This thrilled them to bits, for they relished these moments when they thought as one.

'A tea party for dogs.' Justin clapped scissors and comb together.

'With a cake.'

'And candles.'

'Bliss!'

Justin spent several evenings designing an invitation. He rejected every one until he was finally satisfied with a cut-out of a poodle with the date, time and RSVP inside in his best italic writing.

In the first flush of enthusiasm they planned to invite every dog they knew, but sense, or rather Justin's concern for the carpet, prevailed. 'But we can't just invite Eveleigh, it wouldn't be festive enough, would it, Justin?'

'On the other hand, would she want to be in a crowd when she's so fed up?'

'There's that nice Mrs Lambert and her bulldog puppy.'

'But how many dogs should Eveleigh bring?'

'You'd better invite just *one* dog! Imagine if she brought the lot!' Gill looked around the immaculate sitting room with a grin as he imagined Eveleigh's St Bernards packed in like sardines – it might be fun to try, he thought. 'No, best just the one,' he said aloud as sense once more came galloping to the rescue.

When Thomasine received the invitation she looked at it in amazement. A birthday tea party for dogs! Justin and Gill must be mad. Was this what happened to dog owners? Did she risk becoming like this? What could she possibly give a poodle who had everything?

Eveleigh smiled when she read her card. Dear men, she thought, how kind. It was not strange to Eveleigh that Sadie's birthday should be marked in this way. She might have a kennel full of dogs, but still she knew each dog's birthday and she always arranged a little treat on such occasions. She resolved to wrap, in pretty paper, a particular brand of canine toothpaste which her own brood liked enormously.

As Thomasine watched the dogs romping about Gill and Justin's sitting room, racing and chasing each other in and out of the patio garden, each dog with a different coloured bow attached to their collars, she found herself being reminded of Nadine's birthdays when she was very small and the youngsters had run wild, just like

these puppies. Nova was almost hysterical with excitement and Thomasine feared she would soon be sick, as
she had often worried over Nadine.

'You look a bit down, Mrs L,' Gill said, propping
himself on the arm of her chair while he topped up her
glass of Chardonnay.

'Thomasine, please. Do I? I don't feel it. This is such a
happy idea.' She indicated the playing dogs. Nova and
Sukie seemed bent on twisting each other's back legs off
whilst their short tails wagged with sheer enjoyment;
Coco and Sadie were chasing each other in ever-dimin-
ishing circles, yapping all the time.

'Heaven, isn't it? Just like kids, aren't they?'

'That was what I was thinking.'

'So was that why you looked sad – remembering the
past?'

'Something like that.' She looked intently into her
wine glass so as not to have to look at Gill.

'Are you lonely, Thomasine?' he asked suddenly.

'Me? Heavens, no. What a silly question. I've too
much to do. My daughter visits, there's Nova – yes, I
am,' she finished abruptly and returned to studying the
swirling vortex of her wine.

'You needn't be, you know. We're always here. You
can give us a bell any time – right little pair of counsellors
we are.' He laughed.

'I'm not sure if it helps – you know, talking about
things. Maybe talking only makes matters worse.' She'd
never had a friend to confide in, had never needed one,
she thought.

'How wrong you are. Talking things out is such a
relief. Like a cleansing. Why, Justin and I couldn't exist
without baring our souls to each other, having a good
old purge.'

'I've never done anything like that, not even with my
husband. In fact . . .' She stopped, wondering if she was
being disloyal, and then took a deep breath as she
concluded she wasn't. 'It's only now I'm realising how

309

little I knew him. We talked about the house, our daughter, friends, but I don't think we ever talked about ourselves. I suppose I'm as much of a stranger to him.'

'I don't think Justin and I could survive on that level. I want to know what he's thinking every minute of the day. I'd feel shut out otherwise.'

'You must love each other very much.'

'Totally. The day we met was the true beginning of our lives.'

'What a lovely thing to say. I'm beginning to believe that although I *thought* I loved my husband it wasn't really love – not love, love.'

'Once you've experienced it, there's no question in your mind. So many people settle for second best because they've never known the real McCoy. Like saying rump steak's your favourite because you've never eaten fillet.' He leant over and kissed her forehead. 'Just remember, we're always here. Oops!' He jumped up and quickly crossed the room to separate Coco and Sadie, who were disputing the ownership of a cushion from which, torn in the tussle, feathers were beginning to burst.

Thomasine smiled to herself. She had thought she was stuck with being Robert's sad ex-wife, still carting the baggage from that marriage with her, still the same old Thomasine. She wasn't. It might be slow, but she was actually moving along a path to becoming her own person, one with a clearer vision of herself. Why, she'd just talked to Gill in a way she had never talked to anyone before. Emotions, thoughts, were to be bottled up inside, never allowed to escape. Robert would be mortified to know who and what her first confidant was. She was having a last laugh after all. She looked up at the sound of a loud sob to see Eveleigh shaking out a large white handkerchief and disappearing behind it.

'Gracious! I must be going down with a cold, or there's something in my eye.'

'No, Eveleigh. You're upset. You must realise you

310

can't shoulder all this alone. You've got to talk.' Justin had put his arm round her.

'There's Jim. I talk to him. He's a great help.' Eveleigh blew into her handkerchief.

'But have you told him about the message on the mirror?'

'No, I can't. I've been too ashamed.'

'What message?' Thomasine asked, and Gill exclaimed.

'Oh don't talk about it, please. I loathe to hear it, it makes it more real.'

'But why should someone do something like that to you? It must be tied up with this land thing.' Thomasine crossed the room and crouched on the carpet beside Eveleigh and patted her hand. Nova and Sukie joined them and snuffled noisily around.

'It's all such a great worry. I love judging – the dog world is my world. There's nothing else.' And she looked on the point of tears again, but bent forward and concentrated on patting the puppies instead.

'Now, Eveleigh, stop talking so silly. You're one of the best, the fairest judge in the whole country. You are not to let this get you down in this way. I won't have it.' Gill stamped his feet in their velvet embroidered slippers, and Eveleigh managed a laugh. 'Why, just think of the old Major and then think who's the best?'

'Who, why and what's the Major?' Thomasine asked.

'He was a menace, nothing in a skirt was safe from him and his marauding hands,' Gill explained.

'The problem was, Thomasine, he never awarded a prize to a dog shown by a man. Never! Too often he chose on the looks, and I'm afraid the age, of the handlers and not the dogs. And he always seemed to think he should be rewarded too.'

'A sort of droit de seigneur,' Gill suggested.

'Exactly. Apart from this little problem he was a dear man and had done much good for dogs generally. So we

311

had to solve the problem somehow. You tell Thomasine, Gill.'

'Well, we had a friend who cross-dressed –'

'You didn't!' Thomasine sat with hand over mouth.

'We did. We popped him in the ring with an Afghan that complimented his blond wig to a tee. The Major gave him best in show. Chased our friend behind the judge's marquee, and we've never had any trouble from him since! Look at that!'

Both men dived across the room as Sukie and Nova appeared dragging Sadie's water bowl between them, water slopping over the lip. They were too late. Nova tugged too hard, the bowl tipped up and water drenched the carpet.

'I've always loved aqua follies!' Gill exclaimed.

Later, the mess cleared up, the dogs asleep, exhausted from all their playing, the four friends shared another bottle of wine and chatted. There was no doubt that Eveleigh looked happier now, and Thomasine felt more relaxed and content than she had in ages. Gill was right, she thought, to talk did help. She looked at the little group. She had friends, true friends, and the thought made her feel as if she were glowing.

Nova had rapidly eased the longing for Luna in Thomasine's heart. Her affection for Luna would never be totally supplanted, but she could think about her now and not be overwhelmed with sadness as before.

Even Nadine, upon her return from Italy, had been quite polite about the dog. As was normal now, Thomasine awaited her arrival with apprehension. She could never be sure how her daughter would be with her. She was, however, tolerable, even though she resented Thomasine's English tan, far deeper than her water-logged Italian one.

Thomasine controlled herself and did not pry into the workings of her ex-husband's new life, but bit by bit she was shamefully pleased to gather that Chantal was a 'pain', Robert was a 'misery', and that they were constantly snarling at each other. She kept a straight face as her daughter told her, but she was singing with joy inside. Not, now, in the hope that these were signs that he might return to her but, rather, she was ashamed to admit, sheer spite that not everything was perfect for him.

Nadine returned to school, and a calm descended on the Old School House, a calm Thomasine was learning to relish. She quickly re-established her routine and, with Nova for company, needed no one.

'You should show that little one, she's precious,' Justin said. Today he, instead of Gill, was doing her hair.

'I enjoyed that show of yours, but I don't know if I could manage it myself.'

'We always make the time – it's like a drug.'

She hadn't meant time, but rather money, but let the remark go uncorrected. 'Nova, here,' she called, for Nova had slipped from under her chair and was padding across the salon in search of attention.

'You know who that dog reminds me of?' Justin asked. 'She walks like Mrs Thatcher – all boss and bustle.'

'But no handbag.'

'If only she had a handbag!' Justin laughed. 'But you know, Thomasine, seriously – I'm no expert on bull-dogs, but she looks like a prizewinner in the making to me.'

'But this showing business seems so complicated. At the one I went to with you I was completely confused.' Nova settled down again under her chair.

'It's simple. There are six groups – gundogs, toy, terrier, hounds, working – Eveleigh's St Bernards are in the working group. Mind you, it's difficult to see her sleepy old giants working at anything. And our Sadie and your Nova would be in the Utility group.'

'Why Utility?'

'Because they're not sure what else to call them, I

reckon.' Justin wielded brush and hair dryer. 'Then each breed is divided into classes within its group. Some are age-related – Puppy, Junior, Yearling, Veteran. Then others are by the previous wins they've had. If it's an Open Class, then any dogs of the breed for which the class is provided can enter. See?'

'Sort of,' she said, even though she didn't.

'Then dogs are judged – always first.'

'Hardly fair.'

'It's sex rearing its ugly head. You have to do the dogs before the bitches' scent is in the arena, otherwise they might be a bit of a bother and not concentrate.'

'But what does CC mean – when you see it written after Sadie's name?'

'That's a Challenge Certificate – best dog or best bitch. When a dog has won three of those, then it's a Champion, and you'll see Ch in front of her name – that'll be the day! Then the best dog and best bitch compete and that one is a BOB – Best of Breed. Then all the BOBs in the group compete and we end up with Best in Group. Then those six all compete and from them is chosen the Best in Show. Simple really.'

'If you know how,' Thomasine laughed.

'Of course no dog can compete unless it's registered at the Kennel Club. Only pedigree dogs. But there is a show called Scruffts now – that's for cross-breeds. Sweet! Still, I digress. It's best to start with an Exemption Show – it's good training for the dog and it's all a bit of fun. Get the feel and then move on to the Sanction Shows – they're all novice dogs there, no champions allowed. Then you move on to the Open Shows – you don't win any CCs at those, but you're competing with dogs who already have them. You really learn then if your dog is going to make it. To get your CCs only Championship Shows count. I know it sounds confusing, but honestly, it's as easy as pie once you start.'

'So to go to Crufts you have to qualify at one of these shows?'

'That's right.'

'It might be fun.'

'We and Eveleigh would help you with ringcraft, that sort of thing.'

'Ringcraft?'

'How to show – it's an art, you know. There, see the back, I've taken a couple of inches off, just as you said.' He held the mirror up for her to see.

'We must stop meeting like this,' Oliver laughed as he bent down to pick up Thomasine's handbag, which she had dropped upon bumping into him outside Snippers.

'Maybe I should get my eyes checked!'

'Since we have met, how about a coffee or something?'

'It'll have to be the something. Dogs are banned in the Copper Kettle.' She tugged at Nova's lead and the dog appeared and began to trot along beside her.

'Another bulldog,' he said, as they walked towards the White Hart.

'Yes, Luna's puppy. Sweet, isn't she?'

'Adorable. I've a new one too – Slipper. But she hasn't had all her injections yet, so I've left her sulking at home with a disapproving Wimpole.'

'I thought Wimpole liked dogs?'

'She does, but not this one apparently.'

'I heard she's getting married?'

'She is. Some time in October.' They settled at a table in the lounge bar, Nova happily sitting on Thomasine's feet. He ordered their drinks. 'This is nice,' he said, sounding satisfied. He looked across the table at her and thought again what an attractive woman she was; not beautiful, but with an alive, intelligent face which he liked more. Still, he told himself, this was the last sort of complication he needed at the moment – getting involved with Jim Varley's woman was not the best way to make friends.

'So, what's new?'

'Not a lot,' she smiled. 'Life in the Shillings is remarkably uneventful, I'm happy to say. Justin, the hairdresser, has been trying to persuade me to show Nova.'

'I thought about doing that with Bandage. Maybe I'll have a go with Slipper. We should do it together.' He smiled broadly.

'That would be fun,' she replied, but immediately registered that he did not mean it, it was just one of those things people said to be friendly. She accepted her gin and tonic.

'It will be strange for you without – Wimpole, I suppose.' She nearly slipped up and said 'Nanny' but stopped herself in time.

'What, how will I get on without my nanny?' He smiled as he spoke, but she knew she blushed, as if he had read her thoughts, how awful! And he thought how pretty she looked when she did. 'My wife was always teasing me about Wimpole. Said I was soft. But she's always been there, you understand. I didn't see an awful lot of my mother, she wasn't that interested in me, but I had Wimpole, so it didn't matter so much. And since she never left once I was an adult it'll be really strange without her.' She had an almost unbelievable longing to take hold of his hand, and felt quite shaken that she did.

'I do worry about her, too. I mean, I'm not sure why she's suddenly getting married.' He looked at her, puzzled, as if she might have the answer.

'Presumably because she's in love. That's most people's reason.' And she realised as she spoke that that had not been the case with her, she'd only *thought* herself in love.

'But I'm not sure she is. She's not behaving as if she is.'

'Maybe that's an age thing. Her generation are far more buttoned up about emotions, aren't they?'

'Do you think so? I hope you're right.'

'Why don't you ask Wimpole how she feels?'

'I'm not sure I could. She might bite my head off.'

She had only meant to have the one drink, but found herself accepting another. And when he invited her to have a bar snack with him, she looked at her watch.

'I don't know why I'm watching the time – I've nothing to go home for. Yes, that would be lovely,' she accepted, taking the menu.

'There are so many adjustments to make when a marriage ends, aren't there? Having time to oneself, for one.'

'Or too much of the stuff.' He wondered if he'd imagined that she sounded wistful, and Jim Varley or not, had a longing to stop her feeling so.

'Do you miss being married?' he asked tentatively, not sure, since he hardly knew her, if he should venture on to such territory.

'Yes and no. I miss having someone to care for, and yet I quite enjoy the freedom to do what I want. Problem is, I'm not sure what it is I want to do.' She laughed, but he was sure she was being brave. She was wishing he would not talk about marriage; it sounded as if he regretted the end of his.

They were both rescued by Nova who, smelling their toasted cheese sandwiches, chose this moment to investigate further and jumped up, trying to peer at the plates.

He smiled at the small dog. 'They cost an arm and a leg, don't they?'

'She was a present from the owners. There's no way I could have afforded to buy one, or any breed come to that. I'm just hoping the vet's bills won't be too horrendous.'

He looked up in surprise. If she was going out with Jim he was surprised she had to pay the bills for her pet – Jim didn't strike him as mean. But also, from her clothes and the expensive handbag on the seat beside her, she looked as if money was the least of her worries. Still, one could never tell. 'What's the problem?' he decided to ask.

'I've been incredibly stupid. I just thought I could make

a career for myself as a book illustrator – no problem.'

'And there is?'

'The world is full of illustrators – proper ones, and the housewives like me who think how nice it would be to paint a bit.' She laughed, but somewhat tentatively as if, he thought, she was covering up a hurt. 'I did some paintings of Eveleigh's St Bernards. I *know* they were the best thing I'd ever done, but the publishers rejected them.'

'Then they're stupid,' he said, not liking to see her distressed and wishing there were something he could do about it.

'That's kind of you. No, they know exactly what they are looking for. My best isn't good enough. And the problem is I can't do better – I'm aware of that. I shouldn't have so blithely counted on making a living from it.'

'Is there nothing else you feel you can do?' He wondered what her ex-husband was about.

'At the moment, no.'

'You know what I'd do if I were you? Make a list – write down all your talents and see where you go from there.'

'What talents?' she laughed.

'You'd be surprised.' He was pleased to see she smiled. He liked her smile, and it flashed across his mind, why did he have to be so honourable where Jim Varley was concerned? He didn't owe him anything, and he already had that Beth woman he was shacked up with.

Thomasine looked at her watch. 'Help! Is that the time? I really must be going,' she said, just as Oliver had opened his mouth to ask her out to dinner.

'Must you?' he said, longing to ask her why time should suddenly have become important.

'I'm afraid so,' she replied, wondering what on earth made her think he sounded as if he didn't want her to go.

*

As she drove home Thomasine began to make a mental list of her talents, just as he had suggested. It was rather a meagre list, since all she had ever done was be a wife and mother. She could arrange flowers, keep a house clean, sew, drive a car and cook. These, and a small painting ability, were all she possessed.

Get a live-in housekeeping job and let out her house was the obvious solution, but out of the question now she had Nova to consider. And she would hate strangers in her house too. And where would Nadine stay when she condescended to visit? She could just imagine her reaction to such a career for her mother – fury, no doubt.

She wished she knew someone close by with a young daughter to talk to about Nadine and the trials and tribulations of living with a teenager. But she knew no one here who fitted the bill, and, as Nadine catapulted from one violent reaction to another, there was no comforting voice to reassure Thomasine that it was 'just a phase.'

Thinking about Nadine just piled on the worry. A letter from the bank this morning had not helped. She was overdrawn and sliding, at an alarming rate, into a debt which would quickly become serious.

She frowned deeply as she drove through the afternoon sunshine. What the hell was she to do? She knew what solution her mind was about to present her with, and saying 'no' out loud and firmly did not stop it. Robert. She would have to ask him for help.

This thought so upset her that she crashed the gears as she changed down to negotiate a tight corner. She could just imagine the smug smile on his face if she asked for financial help. There would be an 'I told you so' lecture, followed, no doubt, by one on the realities of life and the necessity to budget carefully.

She drove into her driveway, parked outside the small garage which had once been the school's latrine block, and sat for a while, her hands on the wheel even though the engine was silent. When had she begun to think of

Robert in such a way – in, if she was honest with herself, a totally realistic way? She had just thought about her husband as if she did not like him, and yet only four months ago she was planning how to get him back; dreaming of what she would say, how she would handle the situation when he asked her back into his life.

More had happened to her than she had at first realised. Despite the many worries there was a contentment in her life, a placidness. If he returned, such equilibrium as she had evolved would, she was now certain, be disrupted.

She did not want that. Nor, she realised suddenly, did she want him.

She opened the car door. She'd come a long way without even realising it.

31

Jim Varley had taken to staying out on calls for as long as possible. If he was offered a cup of tea or a drink he accepted. This surprised his clients who, in the past, had been used to Jim rushing in, dealing with their animals, and rushing out again as quickly as possible. Not any more – he lingered, talking of animals, crops, politics and, occasionally, local gossip. Of an evening he was, more often than not, in The Duck and Thistle, and when not there he'd isolate himself in the surgery and catch up on all the latest veterinary literature.

His explanation for this change in routine was quite simple – he had more time. The opening of the new, modern veterinary practice in Shillingham, called The Animal Hospital, had certainly relieved his workload considerably. He was not worried; he'd quite enough clients to keep the practice busy and profitable. It was pleasant not to have to work too hard and he was learning to enjoy not being tired all the time. The farmers in the main had stuck by him, as had Ben Luckett with his stable of horses, and the local riding school, and local pets were still brought to him. It was the Shillingham dogs, cats and gerbils he'd lost, and that did not bother him unduly.

These were all reasonable explanations for his new-found relaxed attitude and sociability. Except it wasn't the whole truth. He avoided going home because of Beth.

He was ashamed of himself; he was behaving badly, and was only too aware of how badly. Since the night Beth had climbed into his bed when he had thought he was dreaming, she had done the same another six or seven times – and he'd let her. But, worse, there were the nights he'd crept along the corridor and stealthily opened her bedroom door, conscious of the loud clanking noise the iron latches made, afraid of waking Harry, but driven by lust to ignore his conscience. And on these occasions, since he was the instigator, he could not pretend he'd been dreaming: there was no one to blame but himself. He was ashamed of himself, but it didn't stop him.

The only reaction he'd had before now was when he'd met Thomasine and his physical reaction to her had shaken him, since it had not happened for such a long time. Even that had come under control once he'd found out she was seeing Oliver. A pity, but just as well, he'd told himself. He'd no desire to find anyone, he was quite content, and when he needed a female slant on things, there was always Eveleigh to turn to.

And then Beth had crept into his bed. In one night she had awoken the buried desires and needs in him. And now he could not stop them, even though he knew he should. He didn't love her, he never would, he was certain. Therefore, he must stop the sex, get control of himself. He must tell her he did not love her and hope she was not too deeply hurt. He had to sack her, that was the bottom line.

He shuddered and shifted his hands on the steering wheel as he thought of that. It was such a brutal way to treat someone who had never hurt him and whose only fault was that she loved him.

He was relieved when he turned the corner in the lane that approached Oakleigh Kennels to see, in the fast falling dusk, his friend Eveleigh. She was standing with a shovel, one wellington-booted foot resting on a huge pile of gravel which was blocking her driveway. She looked as if she could do with some help; he would offer and then, hopefully, she would invite him to have a bite to eat and he wouldn't be home until late.

'Eveleigh, what on earth?' He was laughing as he got out of his car, safely parked well into the hedge behind Eveleigh's Bentley, in which two St Bernards were resting their heads on the backs of the seats, viewing the goings-on through the windscreen.

'Well may you ask. I'd been to a show and came back to find this – not ordered by me.' She kicked at the gravel with annoyance. 'I can't get the car in. It only needs a lorry to come along and with a car the size of mine the lane will be blocked.' She pushed back her hair from her face with an irritated gesture.

'Were you successful at the show?'

'Yes. Brünnhilde – another Challenge Certificate.'

'Brilliant.' He beamed, but Eveleigh was in no mood to join in. He walked round to the side of the Bentley. The name had such a fine ring to it, redolent of luxury and glamour. Not in this case. Eveleigh's Bentley was dented from her many encounters with gateposts and the like. The interior was wrecked, and Jim knew from experience that rather than the sweet smell of leather and polish, it whiffed potently of dog.

'Do you know who dumped it? Telephone them and insist they send someone round to clear it for you, that they've made a mistake.'

'No idea at all. No delivery note, nothing. Just this obstruction.' Angrily she wielded her shovel, filling it a couple of times and scattering the gravel on her front driveway.

'That's going to take for ever. Look, the main problem is your car. What say you drive it to my place? I'll follow and bring you back – my Land Rover's smaller.'

'Would you? What a dear you are, Jim. The main worry is I haven't fed the dogs their supper.'

Used to Eveleigh's dogs barking, he had not at first been aware of them, but now he realised they must all be calling, their huge black snouts skywards as they demanded their food.

'Where's Kimberley?'

'It's her day off – she's at her aunt's. I only went to this show because it was in Morristown.'

'One thing's for certain, your dogs may be put out, but they're so well fed, no harm is going to come to them if they have to wait an extra hour.'

He drove, glad to be in front of Eveleigh, for he was often reminded of Panzer troops in tanks when seeing Eveleigh behind the wheel.

Beth was puzzled when she heard them arrive and they did not come into the house. She looked out of the window to see Eveleigh getting into Jim's Land Rover. She relaxed – at least he was with the one woman she didn't have to fear. Jim was safe with good old Eveleigh.

From Eveleigh's Jim checked in for any urgent calls. There were none. 'When will you be home?' Beth asked in the wifely way which terrified him.

'I don't know. Don't wait supper for me, I'll grab a bite. Eveleigh's got a bit of a problem here.'

'A bit!' Eveleigh laughed as she passed him by. 'How about a large drink before we start?' she suggested, picking up a bottle of Macallan. Jim needed no second bidding.

'Then I'll start on the gravel and you feed your dogs –

it sounds as if they're about to start chewing their kennels.'

Two hours later Jim was exhausted. The gravel had been moved from the gateway, even if the drive was going to need a good levelling off.

'It looks like a lumpy mattress,' said Eveleigh, surveying her undulating front drive. 'Would you care to stay to supper, Jim? It's the least I can do.'

They ate overcooked lamb chops, frozen chips and peas, which was washed down with a St Emilion so good that it compensated for the rather basic meal. But given Eveleigh's startling news, it was doubtful if Jim would have noticed what he was eating.

'Quite honestly, it's beginning to worry me sick. Whoever's playing games with me, it's beyond a joke. I've had mail-order catalogues a yard high, none ordered by me. I had a load of horse manure delivered – paid for, mind you, but not with my money. I've had I don't know how many insurance agents call, double-glazing salesmen – most of them got really irate when I said I didn't want anything, that I'd not asked them to call. Then there are book clubs I've not joined, and it's cost me a small fortune to send the books back, home study courses – you name it, I've received it. It's so time-consuming sending everything back and having to explain. I just hope whoever's doing this has paid for the gravel. The front drive needed it, but I couldn't afford it, not at the moment.'

'Have you told the police?'

'Told them what? What is there to tell?'

'How long has this been going on?'

'Since about June – I can't really remember.'

'Any more letters offering for the kennels?'

'Yes, but I've been in correspondence with new lawyers – presumably they changed after Ben sold his interest in the land.'

'Have you thought that, because you won't sell, they could be using these devious tactics?'

'Lawyers?'

'They probably don't know. No, the owners of that land. I don't want to depress you but it could get worse, you know.'

'In what way? I couldn't imagine anything worse.'

'I had a friend who wouldn't get out of his flat when the block was sold. He had dog crap posted through his letterbox. Endless nuisance phone calls. Then a wreath came with his name on it, followed by a firm of undertakers come to measure him for a coffin.'

'What lengths to go to!' Eveleigh laughed, but there was little humour in it. 'Thank goodness I've got my dogs or they might try to burgle me, or worse!'

'We cannot be alone in knowing that St Bernards will lick a burglar near to death in welcome.' Even as he joked, he wondered how best to say what was uppermost in his mind – that things could get really nasty 'Have you thought of an alarm system?'

'I can't afford it.'

'Get a couple of geese. The best alarm in the world.'

'I could, couldn't I?' She looked frightened, but also indecisive, as if she hadn't told him everything.

'Eveleigh, is there something else?'

'I don't think I could tell you. I'm so ashamed.'

'Try me.'

It cost her dear to tell him she'd been accused of being unfair in her judging, of taking bribes, and that today at Morristown she'd heard another vicious rumour, that at a show she'd swapped dogs – entering an inferior bitch and then having her Champion Brünnhilde appear in her place.

'Whoever knows you would know that is totally impossible.' He took hold of her hand. 'The land thing can't be the only problem – we're getting paranoid. It must be someone in the dog world doing this to you. Someone jealous of your success, or someone whose dog you passed over.'

'But how do I prove that? How can I carry on?'

'You mustn't give in. This is a form of blackmail.'

'I almost hope it is the owner of the land, that would be easier to deal with than having to acknowledge that my fellow breeders could behave in this way.' Eveleigh never cried, not since her husband died, and even then she'd locked herself in the bathroom so that no one would see. But as Brünnhilde, in the house as a reward, put one enormous paw on her lap as if comforting her, her eyes brimmed with tears.

'Dear Eveleigh. Please don't cry. We'll get to the bottom of this.' He hated to see Eveleigh of all people in this state, she was such a dignified and private person that to see her so demoralised was, somehow, more shocking and painful. He felt useless as he passed her one of the Kleenex she always had handy to mop up her dogs' chins.

October

32

Kimberley never knew what to do with her days off work. With Alan gone, the gang broken up and only a bicycle for transport, her world was limited. She would have been quite happy to work, but Eveleigh refused, insisting she have free time. Mostly she spent it in her little flat, cleaning it spotless and making do, but sometimes she went to her aunt's. Aunt Grace had said she should come each week, but Kimberely did not want to impose – her aunt had enough work as it was, juggling home and job. But also she rationed her visits because she did not want to become too involved. Families, to Kimberley, were dangerous things. Better, she told herself with youthful wisdom, to stay clear of them.

Grace always welcomed her warmly. With two sons and no daughters it was nice to have another female to talk to. And Kimberley was such a help. Often when Grace came home from her charring she was too exhausted to do her own cleaning, for she was a large woman and the extra weight she carried made any task doubly hard for her. If Kimberley let herself in with the spare key, Grace would find her house spotless, food prepared and the kettle on for tea when she'd scarcely had time to put her own key in the lock.

'Do you think you ought to go and see your mum?' said Grace on such a day, over the lunch Kimberley had prepared.

'I can't see the point. I telephoned her again yesterday, she says she wants nothing to do with me. That I've hurt her and Dad too badly.'

'Well, there's a turn up!' Grace snorted with derision. 'Hurt your dad, have you – and a good thing too! Horrible man. Your uncle said to me on the very day they got married that your mother had seen the last happy day of her life, poor bitch.'

Kimberley shudddered. 'I wouldn't stay with a man, not if he made me as unhappy as Dad makes Mum.'

'Nor me.' Grace sipped at her sweet tea. 'It's those poor dogs bother me – after all your mother could walk, like you, but she chooses to stay there. But them poor dogs, what can they do – put up with it, that's what. Something should be done about them, I say.'

Kimberley looked up at her aunt, her heart thumping, her mind longing for her aunt to do that something.

'Still, he's family when all's said and done, and I couldn't welch on me own hubby's flesh and blood, now could I?'

'I suppose not.'

'That was lovely, Kimberley. You make a lovely omelette, but if you'll excuse me, I must be off.' She lumbered to her feet and picked up her coat.

'Haven't you finished for today?'

'No, I've got to give Mr Hawksmoor an extra day. They've got a wedding reception up there in two weeks – there's a lot to sort.'

'Would you like me to help?'

'On your day off?'

'I've got nothing else to do.' And so she'd joined her aunt on the walk to Bishop's End.

'Bless you for coming. I'd never have got it all done myself,' Grace thanked Kimberley as she stacked the last of the silver away, all polished, washed and dried ready for the reception. 'Would you dust the Great Hall for me? I'll hoover, but let's have a cuppa first.'

'Who is this Wimpole? Funny name, isn't it?'

'She's Mr Hawksmoor's old nanny.'

'His what?' Kimberley hooted with laughter. 'His nanny? You're joking, he's an old man himself.'

At this Grace trumpeted with laughter too. 'Don't let him hear you say that, he's only forty-five.'

'Forty-five! That old!' Kimberley said with youth's

horror of age, which only made Grace chortle louder.
'Then how old is she?'

'Lord! That's a state secret. Sixty-something, I
suppose.'

'And she's getting married. It hardly seems worth the
bother, does it?'

'A late flowering, you might say,' Grace said with a
grin. 'But she could go on into her eighties.'

'Who's her husband?'

'Rudie Adams – works out on the Luckett estate. I've
never liked him much myself, but your uncle did. I think
he's more of a man's man. I always find him a bit too
charming, meself. Drat it! I forgot the silver photo
frames in the Great Hall – would you bring them in here
once you've done the dusting, there's a love.' And Grace
collected together the silver-cleaning materials which
she had already put away.

Kimberley stood in the doorway to Phoebe's Great
Hall and looked about her with amazement. She'd never
seen a room quite like this in her life. The sun was
streaming through the high arched windows, dappling
the blood-red Turkey carpet. The walls were covered in
paintings – real ones, not prints – and where there were
not pictures there were books, thousands of them, it
seemed. A long refectory table stretched across the
room, littered with books and papers, and Kimberley
thought it was probably best not to disturb them. At the
centre was a potted plant, and at the far end a collection
of photographs in silver frames – the ones her aunt had
forgotten. Her dusting finished, she began to collect
them. As she reached out for one photograph and saw
the subject she stood rooted to the spot, her stomach
churning with anxiety. She jumped. There was a clicking
noise and she turned, white-faced, to see a pink-eyed
white bundle of a dog skidding across the oak floor
towards her and falling on its snout as its paws tripped
over the Turkey carpet.

'Slipper, if you pee in there I'll have your guts for

garters,' the man in the doorway called out. 'Hullo, who are you? I'm Oliver Hawksmoor.' He held his hand out and smiled warmly at her. She looked at him and wondered why on earth she had presumed him old. He might be, but he didn't look it, not like her father. With a clatter she put down the photo frame she was holding.

'I'm Kimberley White. Grace's niece. I'm helping her out. She couldn't manage.' She spoke in short staccato sentences, from breathlessness and nerves.

'That's kind of you. Slipper, get down. Push her off.'

'No, no. I like dogs,' she said, bending down and letting the puppy lick her face.

'She likes you too. Dogs always know.'

'What is she?' she asked, but was pretty certain what his answer would be.

'A bull terrier. Sloppy old things they are. I get the odd person recoil in terror.'

'I think she's lovely. Who could be afraid of her?'

'You'd be surprised. I was catching a train to Scotland with my previous dog. We were strolling along the platform minding our own business, and this interfering old codger came roaring up to me, "Muzzle that brute!" he was shouting, jumping up and down, waving his fist at me. Quite a little exhibition. "Why?" I asked, knowing full well what was coming. "You're breaking the law. That dog should be muzzled – it's a pit bull." "Don't be such a silly arse," I said. But off he rushed and got a policeman, a fine song and dance I had explaining his antecedents to the majesty of the law. I always carried his pedigree with me after that – stupid act!' He grinned, which, Kimberley thought, only made him look younger. 'Sorry, but I do feel strongly about it, and I loved that dog.'

'What happened to him?'

'He ran away – nearly six months ago, but it's not something you get over.' He crossed to the half-dresser

332

and picked up the photo frame Kimberley had been holding. 'Here he is. Lovely dog, he was.'

'What's his name?' she asked, but knew it was an unnecessary question.

'Bandage,' Oliver replied.

She was scared now, really scared, but when she looked up at him, to her astonishment, she saw his eyes were full of tears.

33

Whichever way she did her figures, Thomasine's problems were getting worse. A situation which was not improved when, unannounced, Nadine arrived home, white-faced and gaunt, carrying a suitcase.

'This is a nice surprise!' Thomasine managed to say upon seeing her forlorn daughter standing on her doorstep. 'You didn't mention you were coming when I phoned two days ago,' she said, more in puzzlement than reproof.

'I'm sorry to inconvenience you,' Nadine flounced, misinterpreting her mother.

'Don't be silly, Nadine. I'm pleased to see you.' Thomasine's mind was already racing over how she could cope with her daughter's diet – preparing vegetarian meals had always worked out more expensive, she'd found, since she was far from expert in doing them.

'I had nowhere else to go.' Nadine dropped her case on the floor with a clatter, turned abruptly and flung herself into Thomasine's arms with such force she nearly knocked her off balance. Thomasine began to laugh, but stopped immediately when she realised Nadine was crying. Patting her shoulder and saying 'There there,' repetitively, she guided her daughter into the sitting room and, easing her limpet-like hold, edged her into an easy chair.

'Darling, what's the matter?' she asked, kneeling down in front of her, having to push an inquisitive Nova away. She was worried for she had not seen Nadine in tears for years. She waited patiently, handing out Kleenex.

'No one likes me!' the girl eventually said, but in saying it she released many more tears and a good few minutes elapsed before they could start to talk again.

'What makes you say that?' Thomasine prodded in a gentle tone.

'It's true.' Nadine looked at her wildly. 'Dad's got no time for me – I just get in the way. He doesn't want me there.'

Thomasine patted her hand comfortingly, but abided by her rule to say nothing against Robert, lest it be construed as criticism.

'And I hate Chantal. She's a conceited, stuck-up bitch. She never stops nagging me. "Nadine, do this, don't do that. Oh, Nadine, Ooh la la." ' Her daughter expertly imitated Chantal's pronounced French accent, making Thomasine smile.

'She's not my favourite person, either,' she said, since her vow of reasonableness did not cover the usurper of her husband and home. 'She's got a mean mouth, I always thought.'

'And she doesn't shave her armpits,' Nadine added, her face twisted with disgust. At this Thomasine could not suppress her laughter. Nadine at first looked with annoyance at her mother, but then, seeing the funny side, joined in.

'It wasn't *that* funny,' Nadine said when they had calmed down.

'No – but funny enough. Fancy a glass of wine?' Thomasine asked as she scrambled to her feet. Nadine followed, and Nova brought up the rear, as they went into the kitchen and settled at Thomasine's favourite place when a talk was in the offing – the pine table.

'Dear old table.' Nadine patted it. 'You've had it longer than you've had me, haven't you?' She accepted the glass of wine her mother had poured her. 'You know it's wrong to have a bulldog,' she continued abruptly as Nova fussed about her.

'I thought of getting her a companion. It must be a lonely business being an only dog. But I can't afford another one.'

'I didn't mean that – you getting more dogs. I meant bulldogs shouldn't be bred. It's cruel, they can't breathe. Man's manipulated them to look like that.'

'Nova doesn't have any breathing problems. Listen to her.'

'Bulldogs have over thirty defects.'

'Possible defects. In a well-bred bulldog it isn't necessarily so. Good breeders are trying to eliminate such problems,' Thomasine said defensively.

'Of course if you do get another dog, you're only perpetuating the wickedness, aren't you?' Nadine neatly moved away from an argument she was not sure she would win.

'What wickedness?'

'Of pet ownership. It's demeaning to dogs, you know. There's no difference between a lion in captivity and keeping a dog in the home. It should have the dignity of running wild.'

'I haven't noticed any dogs complaining.'

'You never take me seriously, do you?' Nadine flared. 'Whatever I have to say, you just grin and make some smart-arse reply.'

'Perhaps if you didn't make such asinine statements I wouldn't need to.' Thomasine could feel the old irritation with her daughter welling up inside her and made herself choke it back. 'Look, Nadine, I'm sorry. You're right. I should listen to you.'

'I should think so.' Nadine moved her shoulders back

and forth, reminding Thomasine of a bird adjusting its feathers.

'Does your father know you're here?' she asked.

'He told me to come. I told him I'd been expelled, that I hated Chantal, and so he said "Well, piss off to your mother if you feel like that". So I came. You got any nuts or Twiglets or anything?'

'No, I haven't. Did you say expelled?' Thomasine shook her head in amazement at the way her daughter could flit from one subject to another.

'That's right, E-X-P-E-L-L-E-D.' She spelt out, as if proud of the fact.

'What on earth for?'

'If they hadn't, I'd have walked out anyway,' Nadine said defiantly.

'Why?'

'I went on a demonstration, and to do that I had to bunk out. It would have been all right, except the creeps saw us on TV.'

'Us? TV?'

'There were four of us. I wasn't alone,' she smiled, proud of the fact. 'We were demonstrating about the export of calves. You must have seen it?'

'Yes, yes, of course.'

'Poor little things. I had to do something. It was great, though. I met some wonderful people and everything. Real animal lovers, real concerned people.'

'I can imagine,' Thomasine said with irony, remembering the pictures she had seen, not just the concerned, ordinary women who had started the campaign, but the animal activists who had appeared to hijack the demonstrations. She supposed it was their view of dog ownership Nadine had been spouting.

'I bet you're going to say it doesn't matter where and how the calves are raised.' Nadine glared at her.

'No, I'm not. I agree with you.'

336

'But you eat meat.'

'Yes. Often I wish I didn't, but I know I couldn't give it up. But that doesn't mean you mustn't respect the animals and ensure they have a good life and a decent, quick death.'

'Oh, great. Sorry, you're only a few months old, but here's the blindfold and I'll aim for the heart. Don't you know what an abattoir is like?'

'No, but no doubt you are about to tell me.'

'Hypocrites like you make me sick,' Nadine shouted angrily at her.

'As do hypocrites like you who lecture people like me and bang the veggie drum and then eat hamburgers when they think no one is looking.' Thomasine watched as Nadine's face went bright red and her mouth hung slackly open with surprise. 'I saw you in Shillingham last time you were here.'

'You never said.'

'I wanted to save you embarrassment. But you've just annoyed me, really annoyed me, and I wonder why I bother.'

'I'm finding it hard to do – be a vegetarian I mean. Sometimes I slip, but then I hate myself so much. I love animals, Mum, I really do.'

'And so do I. You've just got to temper your reactions more, Nadine. You won't win any converts getting up people's noses like that. And if we are to live together again, I think we both have to make some compromises.'

'Like what?'

'Well, I won't nag you about animal activists and vegetarianism if you won't nag me about not agreeing with you one hundred per cent. It's called give and take.'

'I realise *that*.'

'And if you're to live here, I think you should watch your step. You're a town girl, as I am, and we can't crash into the country and shoot our mouths off and try to alter thousands of years' tradition in a matter of months. Things will be changed far faster with reason than with riots.'

Even as she spoke, Thomasine knew this was not what she believed entirely, but in the short time she had been here, she had seen how tempers were fraying, how antagonism to the townies was mounting. She did not want trouble, she did not want her daughter hurt.

'What about school, then? There's no chance of them taking you back?'

'I wouldn't go if they begged me.'

An unlikely scenario, Thomasine thought. 'I gather there's a high school in Morristown, but it's pretty rough.'

'I can handle it,' Nadine said with a brave flick of her hair. 'I might meet up with Kimberley – you remember, the girl with the dad with a gun.'

'What a nice idea,' Thomasine grimaced, but at least Nadine realised this time that she was joking. 'But Kimberley's left school. She's working near here, at a kennels.'

'A kennels!'

'Now come on, Nadine. Give and take. And I can assure you these kennels are run like a dogs' five-star hotel.'

'Breeders!' Nadine's face twisted with disgust, as if she were talking about mass murderers. If her daughter was here full time Thomasine could, she thought, ask her ex-husband to contribute more – teenagers were an expensive pastime, anyone could tell him that.

'They got married,' Nadine announced.

'Who?' Even as she asked, Thomasine knew it was a stupid question.

'Chantal and Dad.'

'When?'

'Last week.'

'They might have told me.' Thomasine realised that that was all that bothered her.

'And me!'

Thomasine looked at Nadine with shock etched on her face. 'They didn't tell *you*? That was unforgivable.'

'Oh, I don't care. Sod them. Why should I bother about them if they don't care about me?'

Thomasine edged her hand across the table and caught hold of Nadine's. 'Darling, I'm so sorry,' she said, everything now explained. Her daughter might be seventeen, but she still hurt as much as if she were ten years younger, probably more.

'How many puppies was it that Luna had?' Nadine asked in her strange, flitting way.

'Five – four bitches, one dog.'

'You'd rather have the puppies than me.' Nadine was laughing as she spoke, but it was a false laugh. And it was the intent way she looked at her as she said this that made Thomasine realise how desperately insecure her daughter was. That her lashing out was only a sign of this insecurity.

'Don't be silly. It'll be lovely, just the two of us.' And she held her arms wide open for Nadine to fall into. 'I love you, you know, even if we do row all the time,' she whispered into Nadine's hair as with one hand she stroked it, and with the other patted Nova, who was scrabbling to be picked up and to join in the hugging.

Thomasine was in Shillingham shopping. She could not remember when she had last felt so nervous. It was no matter that she kept berating herself for being so stupid – heavens above, she thought, if she could calculate how many meals she'd cooked in her married life; how many successful dinner parties she had given; if she kept that in mind, maybe she wouldn't be so scared. It didn't work, her stomach seemed to have acquired a life of its own.

She realised there was an inescapable difference between food she had prepared before and what she was doing now. She was being paid, and that made all the difference in the world.

It was odd, almost as if their minds had been working on the same track. She had taken Oliver's advice and had made her list of talents, and cooking kept surfacing, but how to use it? In a way, she hadn't been surprised when Oliver had called and asked her about cooking.

'It was just an idea I had in the middle of the night. Why don't you set up as a caterer – you know, cooking dinner-party food for others? I know people who have made a fortune doing it in London. It might solve your problems.'

'But that was London. I hardly think one could make a success of it here in the Shillings.'

'Then I think you're wrong, Thomasine. I know quite a few people who can no longer afford to employ a full-time cook who'd jump at the chance of employing you to do their dinner parties for them. I reckon it's worth a try.'

'But what would I charge?'

'I'll find out for you from friends in London. Then knock a bit off because this is the country. I'd reckon on something like a hundred pounds a dinner.'

'You're joking! To do justice to a dinner, say of six to eight people, most of that would go on food and wine.'

'No, you've got it all wrong. They pay for the ingredients, not you. That'd be for you.'

'Oh, I'm not so sure. I'm not a professional, I've no training.'

'I bet you're an ace in the kitchen.'

Modesty prevented Thomasine from commenting.

'I'll book you first. Thursday evening for four.'

Now it was Thursday morning and Thomasine was shopping from a list that had taken her the intervening two days to compile. She'd consulted every cookbook she possessed and had wavered and dithered over menus until she had arrived at one she hoped would do.

She'd already made the vegetable terrine, which was chilling in her refrigerator; she'd still to buy the ingredients for its coulis. She had decided on duck, which she'd do with a honey and lemon sauce, and for pudding she'd opted for a light home-made ice cream to be served with her own crisp almond biscuits. That and a cheese board would be enough, she hoped.

Her problem, as she selected and rejected, was that she'd been alone too long and had not cooked dinner-party food for such a time that she was afraid she would not buy enough. On the other hand she worried that perhaps she was buying too much.

Turning out of the small grocer's in Shillingham, which had the best selection of cheese outside Harrods, she bumped into Gill.

'Thomasine! Long time no see,' he said, looking pointedly at her hair, which she touched with one gloved hand with nervous guilt.

'I know. I'm sorry.'

'It won't do, Thomasine. Hair has to be looked after. I've got a cancellation, why don't you pop in?'

Thomasine looked around wide-eyed, with the expression of one who felt trapped. Her new budget did not include trips to the hairdresser's.

'What's the matter? You look so startled. What on earth have I said?'

'Nothing, Gill. It's me. I'm in a bit of a tizz, you see. I'm just starting a new job and I'm a bit worked up about it.'

'Honest? Doing what? Painting?'

'No, that didn't work out. Cooking actually,' she said with a defiant shake of her head, daring him to comment or, by a flick of an eyelash, show any disapproval. She'd already had enough of that from Nadine who, she had been at pains to point out to her, was *mortified* at the prospect of a cook as a mother.

'Cooking? That sounds interesting. What, catering from home, that sort of thing?'

'No, dinner parties, lunches – I'm hoping people will let me into their kitchens to cook for them.' She laughed nervously.

'Shillingham's been crying out for someone like you for yonks. If I wasn't so successful as a crimper I'd have been doing it myself.'

'Really?' Thomasine, for the first time that day, felt relaxed enough to smile.

'Tell you what – I'll stick your card up in the salon, push customers your way.'

'I haven't got a card.'

'You must get some – essential. Thought of a good name?'

'Not yet. I wasn't sure . . .'

'Name's all important. Come into the salon, I'll do your hair and Justin and I will come up with a name for you.'

Thomasine stood on the pavement clutching her shopping and felt awkward with embarrassment. She took a deep breath.

'The truth is, Gill, I'd love to have my hair done, but I've had a bit of a setback, and well, I can't afford it.'

'Then have one on the house.' Gill grinned, liking her for her honesty; not like many of his customers, who'd rather die than admit they were short of cash.

'But that's no way to run a business, Gill.'

'I owe you one.'

'How come?'

'That bulldog of yours. Didn't I tell you? Stupid me. Those nice people came back to me and insisted on rewarding me for putting them on to you. They said you

342

wouldn't take a penny, so they gave me five hundred pounds.'

'*How* much? Good heavens.'

'I reckon you could say they loved that dog. They were over the moon they'd found her. I'd been waiting for you to come in. I nearly clocked Justin for charging you last time you were here. So I think a shampoo and blow-dry is on the cards, don't you?'

Gill had almost finished her hair when he asked her if she'd thought about the dog ringcraft classes Justin had suggested.

'There you are again, Gill. I honestly don't think I could even contemplate the expense of dog classes and shows.'

'Pop along – just to see. Justin and I take one every week in the Community Centre here.'

An hour later Thomasine tripped out of the salon feeling the confidence that a decent hairstyle gives a woman. But she was also walking on air, boosted with reassurances that the home-catering venture was a great idea, plus a booking for dinner for six next week at Gill and Justin's, with the menu already worked out. Best of all, she had a name for her business: Thomasine's Treats, they'd suggested. She quite liked it, but wanted to ponder it a bit longer. They had also given her the phone number of their printer.

Once home, she prepared as much of the food as she could and cling-filmed the containers and put them in baskets which she covered with gingham tea towels. She had time for a hurried bath. She was doubtful what to wear, but eventually opted for jeans and a T-shirt, since she'd be hidden away in the kitchen. But then she flapped at the thought she might be expected to serve the food and instead changed into a black skirt with a white shirt and a silk paisley waistcoat. She made a mental note to buy some large white pinafores. Gill, thinking ahead, had pinned her long hair up in a full, but neat, French pleat.

'You don't want your hair dangling all over the food now, do you?' he'd said when she had told him she hated herself with her hair up. Now, looking in the mirror, she decided he was right. Done his way, it suited her, made her face look thinner, made her look more 'grown up' somehow.

34

Wimpole was all of a dither.

'I wish you'd consulted me about this, Oliver. What if she can't cook?'

'I'm sure she can. Thomasine looks like a woman who can.'

'What does that nonsense mean?'

'She has a sensual look about her, not a puritan one – people like that can usually cook,' Oliver explained.

'I've never heard such a load of old cobblers in my life. What's she doing?'

'I left it to her.'

'What if Rudolph doesn't like it? He's a fussy eater.'

'Then Rudie will have to go without. Remember what Nanny used to say.' He wagged his forefinger at her and smiled affectionately. She did not respond.

'It's not good enough at all! And I don't like her name. My aunt's cat was called Thomasine, and a nasty, spiteful creature she was.'

'Wimpole, why don't you go and lay the table and keep your mind off things,' he suggested patiently.

While Wimpole clattered about in the dining room, Oliver lit the fire in the drawing room. He stood at the window while he waited to see if it would draw. He looked out on the garden, where October was already

344

making its mark with fallen leaves and fading, bruised roses. It was an odd thing, but he felt Wimpole was not only nervous, like any bride in the run-up to her wedding, but more than that, as if she was frightened of something. Wimpole was never scared of anything. It was distinctly strange.

The fire drawing satisfactorily, and Slipper like a shadow trotting along behind, he went into the kitchen to find Thomasine already at work.

'I hope you don't mind me letting myself in, but the back door was open,' she said. 'And I've brought my dog with me. Once she's explored she'll sleep. Is that all right?'

'That's fine by me. Hullo, old girl.' He bent down and patted the puppy. 'You know, my grandfather had one of these.'

'Everybody's grandfather did.' Thomasine was laughing and he liked the effect.

'I've been lighting a fire. It's really chilly this evening. Duck! Lovely.' He washed his hands at the sink. 'Anything I can do to help?'

'I hope everything's under control. I'll yell if I get into a muddle.'

'Don't be nervous. It'll be fine.' He patted her shoulder and she felt a rush of pleasure, and then told herself to pull herself together.

'Fancy a drink?'

'I'd better not. I don't want to ruin your dinner.'

'Just a little one,' he insisted.

He sat at the end of the pine table and watched her preparing the food. He liked watching her; despite her nervousness she moved in an assured, smooth way. He liked her hair pulled back from her face, he had not realised what fine bones she had, nor that her eyes were so large. How he'd love to unpin her hair and see it fall heavily onto her shoulders . . .

'You look deep in thought. Any problems?'

'I was thinking how very attractive you are.'

'Me?' She laughed, self-consciously touching her hair as if checking it was still in place.

'Sorry, that was rude of me.' He too felt embarrassed, astonished that he'd had the nerve to speak out.

'Don't be – sorry, I mean,' she said softly and almost held her breath at her own temerity. Then the telephone rang and the spell was broken.

When Oliver went to take his bath she was relieved, since she hated anyone watching her cook. But, at the same time, she was aware she wished he'd stayed. This was very odd – hadn't she disliked him when she first met him, thinking him too smooth for comfort? One lunch and she liked him, and even more so tonight. It was dangerous ground – ground which was likely to shift at any moment. He'd that predatory ex-wife whom she'd no desire to cross swords with, she'd a disapproving daughter – what on earth was she thinking about? Go back to your celibate life, Thomasine, you don't need the complications of a man. Still, she thought as she began to make her sauce, she liked his dog.

When everything was under control in the kitchen, she checked the dining room. It looked a picture. Oliver owned some spectacular silver, which reflected in the highly-polished surface of the long refectory table. She admired the fine set of Jacobean chairs, so right for this room. The napkins were finest damask, the candles were the creamiest-coloured wax and the flowers, button chrysanthemums in bronze and yellow, were prettily arranged, she wondered by whom.

'Checking my handiwork?'

Thomasine turned to see Wimpole, smartly dressed in a blue wool dress and a little light make-up, standing in the doorway. She wondered how long she'd been there.

'It's a lovely room. The table looks great. Did you do the flowers? They're gorgeous.'

'What you cooking?'

'Duck with –'

'Not greasy, I hope.'

'I hope not too. It shouldn't be. I always –'

'I should have been consulted.'

'I'm sorry? Oliver told me to do whatever I wanted.'

'Well, he never should have. And it's Mr Hawksmoor to you.' Wimpole marched from the room, leaving a perplexed Thomasine, who'd never been treated like a servant before. She'd only met Wimpole once before and she'd seemed pleasant enough then.

With everything checked again, and on time, she finally allowed herself to sit down at the kitchen table and enjoy the drink Oliver had poured her. She began to list in her head the order of cooking the vegetables, but the thoughts slid away to be replaced by wondering what it would feel like to kiss Oliver. She covered her face with her hands as if to blot out the image. If she put the potatoes on –

And yet . . . what would it be like to lie in a man's arms – Oliver's arms! If he made love to her, would it be the same as Robert or different? Different, she was almost sure. Almost, for that was the problem; having known only one man sexually in her life, she could not be totally sure.

Silly thoughts, silly ideas. He was flirting, that was all, and she was no better than a mooning teenager. From outside she was vaguely aware of the sound of a motor.

'He's here,' Oliver popped his head around the kitchen door.

'You don't want to eat yet, though?'

'No, I was telling you to come and join us.'

'You're inviting me?'

'Of course, who else? You're the fourth, didn't you realise?'

'Well, no.' She looked down at her skirt, smoothing her baggy blouse. 'I'm not dressed . . .'

'You look fine to me, and Wimpole's not sporting her tiara! Come on.' He held his hand out to her and half dragged her across the hall into the drawing room.

Rudolph Adams was a large man, and looked out of

place in the pretty drawing room. He stood clutching his cap to him as if trying to make himself smaller, as if afraid of breaking things. He was very fit looking, tanned with piercing blue eyes, and although Thomasine found the eyes rather cold, she could understand Wimpole finding him attractive. As she shook his hand she was aware of Wimpole watching her suspiciously. She made Thomasine think of a small bird, with her sharp black eyes and tiny frame.

They all sat down while Oliver fussed over the drinks tray. Slipper advanced into the room, sniffing at their feet. Thomasine saw how Rudolph lifted his feet as the dog approached.

'Have you met our latest addition?' Wimpole asked, bending down and scooping up the puppy.

'Put that down, Wimpole, it's unhygienic,' Rudolph ordered, and to Oliver's astonishment Wimpole obeyed.

Despite the difficulty of being both guest and cook, the meal progressed well. In future, though, Thomasine vowed to be one or the other, it would be easier. The food was eaten with relish, and Rudolph had two helpings of everything. Wimpole had changed from the sharp virago Thomasine had met before the meal, and was pleasant again. Had something upset her, or had she been nervous about the evening and that had passed? Or perhaps it was the excellent wine that had softened her up.

There was a new phenomenon in Thomasine's life. Just as when she had been pregnant every other woman seemed to be too, now she'd acquired a dog, every conversation at some point or other turned to that subject.

'You let your dog *sleep* with you?' Rudolph asked her with a shocked expression.

'Why, yes. I like to hear her snoring in the night.' She felt she sounded as if she were making excuses, which was quite ridiculous since she could sleep with a puma if she wanted to. 'Where do your dogs sleep?'

'In the kennels, of course.'

'But they're gun dogs,' Oliver intervened. 'That's different. Bandage, even if he didn't sleep with me, was close by in the dressing room.'

'Sophia allowed that?'

'Sophia had to lump it. I could never marry a woman who wouldn't share me with a dog.' He laughed at this, but Thomasine noticed Rudolph didn't, and she found herself thinking how glad she was she'd admitted the truth about Nova.

'Have you told Thomasine about that great Newfoundland you nearly lumbered us with?' Wimpole asked. 'The one that lived in Baskerville Terrace.'

'Not much point now when you've let slip the punch line,' Oliver said, and proceeded to launch into a long, involved and funny story about the dog.

Everyone laughed except Rudolph, who sat po-faced and not amused at all.

Later, the dinner at an end, Wimpole offered to help clear up, but Thomasine would not hear of it.

'No, that's my job,' she insisted, collecting the glasses onto a tray as the others made their way to the drawing room for brandies. 'I'll bring the coffee in.'

'You ought to marry her, you know, Oliver, before someone else snaps her up,' said Wimpole, very tipsily.

Thomasine stood rooted to the spot. She knew she often blushed, but never like this!

When she took the coffee in she quickly put the tray on the table, bolted back into the safety of the kitchen and began to attack the washing up. Heavens! How awful! Wimpole had spoilt everything now. Spoilt what? What was there to spoil? A bit of flirtation, that was all, hadn't she decided anyhow not to get involved? Such a change in the woman – it was as if there were two of her. Or was there such a change? Maybe Wimpole had said it on purpose, one to embarrass her and two to make Oliver run to the hills as men invariably did when *marriage* was mentioned.

'Sorry you were so embarrassed.' Oliver had walked in so quietly she hadn't heard him. 'She was very drunk, you know.'

'I realised that.' She did not look up from scouring the pans.

'You could leave that for Grace to do in the morning.'

'And have her say I'm a slovenly cook – no thank you.'

'Would it matter what she said?'

'Yes, to me, if I'm to be a professional,' she said primly. On guard.

'I'll help you.'

'No. I can manage. You go back to your guests.'

'I felt like a gooseberry in there, I'd much rather wash up with you.'

'It's all done.'

'Then have a brandy with me, here.'

'I've got to drive, even if it's only a couple of miles.'

'Coffee then?' She looked at him now and saw he was pleading with her. Treacherously, she found her heart liked that.

'Just coffee and then I must be going. I've put Nova in the car.'

'You shouldn't have done that. It's cold out there.'

'She's got her blanket.' But already he was rushing out of the kitchen to return a moment later with a very appreciative bulldog, whom Slipper welcomed ecstatically, as if she'd never seen her before.

'I worry for Slipper. I think she might be thick.'

'Shush – not in front of her. It's not fair.' Thomasine put her finger to her lips and wondered if, perhaps, she wasn't a bit tipsy too.

They sat at the pine table with their coffee and, just as proud mothers watch their toddlers play, Thomasine and Oliver watched their puppies.

'Rudolph doesn't seem to like dogs very much, does he?' she ventured.

'No, and come to think, Bandage was never that keen on him. It's worrying. Normally I never take to people

350

who don't like dogs, or whom my dogs don't like. I've tried telling myself it's stupid, but it's never worked out – they've always let me down. Yet I've always liked Rudie well enough. Odd.'

'Does Wimpole like them?'

'Very much.'

'Then maybe he'll take to them for her, or pretend he does.'

'Pretending doesn't work – my wife pretended for years, and look where that got us.'

Thomasine was surprised to be invited to Wimpole's wedding a week later. She rather hoped that Oliver had instigated it, but it was irrelevant since she could not go. She had Gill and Justin's dinner party to attend to, and sensing that they were both probably good cooks, she dared not risk taking the afternoon off.

So she missed seeing Wimpole and Rudie wed in the little church in Middle Shilling, Wimpole, dressed in a cream velvet suit, looking younger than anyone had ever seen before. And she missed the cool atmosphere between Ben and Oliver that no fluttering on Cora's part could mend. She did not see Eveleigh turn her back on the Lucketts, nor note her leaving early. She was spared seeing Beth cling to Jim like ivy, which caused much gossip. But best of all, she did not have to see Sophia vamping Oliver, which caused even more gossip.

She would have regretted not seeing Slipper, resplendent in a white satin bow.

November

35

'But, Alan, your cover's blown, it could be dangerous for you to return to that pub. They put you into hospital once. They'll do it again.' Alan listened politely to his superior officer.

'But that was five months ago. And we never knew for sure why they bashed me up, did we?'

'True.'

'I mean, we don't *know* it was them. Or that bloke Vic might have thought I was chatting up his girlfriend, Vicky. It might have had nothing to do with the dogs.'

'But it might have had everything to do with the dogs.'

'If he has suspicions, my turning up after all this time, like I've been away, will surely allay them. If I go back to The Locomotive, what am I saying to him? *No hard feelings, mate.* Now, *if* he thinks I'm from the police or the RSPCA – well, the last thing he'll expect is me showing my face again.'

The boss looked doubtful. Alan ploughed on, determined to return to Morristown. 'Isn't this the first whiff you've had about the fighting in ages? I know it's not enough to send someone in officially, but the point is I'm going there anyway, to look for a cottage. And who else have you got to send?'

Alan knew he'd got his boss there. The whole office, it seemed, was out on assignment. Alan himself had only just got back from a trip to Spain checking out Spanish abattoirs and the movement of British sheep – and neither had been a pleasant occupation. He stood, sending up a silent prayer that his boss would listen to him. In the months away he'd found that, although he'd tried, he couldn't shake the memory of Kimberley. He wanted to see her. He'd overreacted when she was cagey about giving him her phone number and address. Perhaps her parents were difficult. He'd been a fool. He should have understood, especially when his own mother had been so possessive. He'd be an even bigger fool not to try to find her, not when she occupied his dreams in a way no other girl ever had.

'All right. But no heroics. You promise?'

'Thanks, sir,' Alan grinned.

The consensus of opinion amongst his team was that he was brave, but bonkers. Alan just shrugged and smiled broadly. He wasn't going to 'explain about Kimberley, nor that whilst in Spain he thought often of the fighting dogs and felt he'd let them down. They were all in the RSPCA because of a love of animals, but it wasn't something they verbalised. It was not a good idea to get too emotionally involved, they'd been told, but how the hell not to was beyond Alan's understanding.

He booked into a pleasant B&B late Friday afternoon, leaving himself just enough time to visit a couple of estate agents and collect details on cottages for sale in the area. He browsed through them as he ate a hamburger in the local MacDonald's in the large shopping precinct in Morristown.

For all his brave talk, he felt his heart thudding as he walked towards The Locomotive. But it was too late now. He made himself push the door open, and stepped into the smoky fug of the public bar.

Alan smelled the heavy perfume she wore before he heard her speak. 'Long time no see.'

'Hullo, Vicky. How's you?' he said, trying to sound normal but afraid that his nervousness made him sound like a robot.

'Where have you been? I thought you'd got fed up with us.' Vicky smiled up at him; he wished she wouldn't look at him like that, so blatantly sexual. 'You're ever so brown.'

'I've been to Spain.'

'Lucky old you. We didn't go away this year. Oh look, there he is. Vic, over here. Look who's back.' Vicky waved at the looming figure of Vic standing in the doorway, seeming, to Alan, to have doubled in size.

'Thought you'd pissed off,' Vic said, as he slipped the money for his pint across the bar. Alan had, in the circumstances, to admire his composure.

'I went away on a job. And I've been in Spain. But before all that, I was mugged. Went to hospital.'

'You never were.' Vicky looked so concerned that if Alan had not known better, he'd have thought it was the first she'd heard of it. 'Was you badly hurt?'

'Bit of concussion. Bruising mainly.'

'Did you see the bleeders?'

'No, more's the pity. I'd have given them what for if I had.' Alan banged one first into the palm of the other.

'I bet you would too,' Vicky said admiringly, and Vic shuffled his feet, fingering his beer glass, but still managing to look remarkably controlled.

'How's things, Vic? Seen those kids with the bull terrier again?' Alan, feeling he had nothing to lose, came straight out with it.

'Why you ask?' Vic glared at Alan.

'I liked the look of the dog. Just curious.'

'Curiosity killed the cat.'

'Lucky I'm not a cat then, isn't it?' Alan laughed, though he shivered inside. Hadn't Vic said that to him once before? 'I just wondered if they wanted to sell it, I might be interested in buying.'

'They already have – sold it, I mean. Bloody useless mutt it was too. No balls.'

'Who to?'

'Don't know his name.' Vic looked deep into his beer

glass and Alan knew he was lying. However, he could think of no way to prolong the conversation without being too suspicious. More alarmingly, no other topic of conversation presented itself to him either. The way Vicky was continuing to eye him, he was afraid she was going to start flirting with him again. The last thing he needed was another beating from Vic.

'You got wheels?' Vic suddenly asked.

'Yeah. Why?'

'Interested in changing them?'

'Not at the moment. You selling?'

'Might be.'

'What?'

'Whatever's your fancy.' Vic grinned. Now why would he do that, tantamount to admitting he stole cars to order? Was he being tested, was Vic watching his reaction?

'I'll keep that in mind – next time, perhaps.'

'Have you got a nice car then?' Vicky asked him, undulating her hips very suggestively as she spoke.

'It's all right.' He avoided giving the make.

'Vic's got a bike and a cruddy van, haven't you, Vic? I keep telling him he ought to get a nice warm car, but he won't give up on his bike, will you, Vic?'

Vic ignored her, and Alan thought, oh dear, she's coming on too strong. 'My bird wouldn't like me to have a bike. Says a helmet would mess up her hair.'

'You got a girl?' Vicky looked downhearted.

'You don't want to let a girl tell you what's what. I wouldn't.' Vic looked – Alan didn't think it was his imagination – pleased.

'Anything for a quiet life, that's me.' Alan smiled and looked sheepish all at the same time. 'Same again?'

Their drinks ordered, he carried them towards their table and saw another man had joined the group – older, tougher, not someone he'd care to meddle with, he thought, seeing the cold blue eyes which stared intently at him in an unfriendly way as he placed the glasses on the table. He strained to hear what Vic and the man were saying, but all he heard was the word 'acre', or it could have been 'baker'.

'I'm off then.'

'Don't go on my account,' Alan said politely, reluctantly getting to his feet to let the man pass.

'I'm not,' the stranger said coldly.

'He's a friendly cove.' He laughed to show he did not care as he watched him go.

'He's all right,' Vic said, non-committally.

'What did you say his name was?'

'I didn't,' Vic replied sharply, picked up his pint and slurped noisily at it. Instinct told Alan he'd just met one of the dog-fighting cartel. He could just imagine Don's reaction if he went into the office and claimed he'd met one of the ringleaders. 'What makes you so sure?' Dan would be certain to ask. 'I feel it. It's instinctive,' would be all he could answer. Dan would nearly die laughing. 'Instinct! Go and get me facts!' he'd order. But Alan knew, he didn't know why, he just did. He wasn't going to give up now; after all, he was doing this in his own time.

'Penny for them?' Vicky was smiling at him.

'Don't want to bore you.'

'You'd never bore me.' Vicky slyly glanced from Alan to her boyfriend. Vic was staring at him in such an aggressive way that Alan decided he'd best make himself scarce.

'I must be off.' He stood up. 'See you both around.' He emphasised the *both*, hoping Vic noticed.

'Don't hurry back,' Vic snarled in reply.

Once outside the pub, he decided he'd made his last visit here. Vicky and her flirting were too dangerous, and in any case, Vic was too cagey to let anything useful drop. He'd be better off following him discreetly and see where that led him; Vic was too nasty a bit of work to get buddy-buddy with. He must have been mad coming here again, maybe the bang on the head had given him a death wish or something.

He strode on through the cold night until he reached his car, parked behind Tesco, and got in. He gunned the engine, eased the car out of the car park, and doubled back to the street in which The Locomotive pub was. He parked four cars away, doused his lights, switched off the engine and sat and waited, hoping Vic hadn't left in the meanwhile. Hopefully he would be in his van, he'd never keep up with the bike.

His heart sank when, after he'd waited nearly an hour, Vic and Vicky appeared, both carrying crash helmets. Another night, he thought, as he watched Vicky hoist her long leg over the pannier and admired her rear as she did so. The engine of the bike roared, but rather than speeding away, Vic drove up the road at a sedate speed. Alan followed, keeping a safe distance. From the way he handled the motorbike, Vic must be smarting from a speeding ticket.

The bike stopped and Vicky got off, hurled the helmet at Vic and shouted something at him that Alan, stopped a good way back, could not catch. She flounced off into the labyrinth of the Forest Glade estate, pausing before she turned a corner to give Vic a V sign.

It was not so easy keeping up with him as they left the city, for Vic weaved his way in and out of the traffic. He seemed to have thrown his previous caution to the winds, and drove far too fast along the by-pass. But it was dark and once off the fast road and on the country lanes, with no other traffic about, Alan, even from some way behind, could still see his lights.

Then suddenly there was total blackness and Alan cursed that he'd missed him. Coming round a bend he nearly had a fit as he saw Vic waiting by a gate, looking menacing astride his bike, his large black visored helmet on, watching the road, obviously checking if he was being followed.

There was nothing for it but to press on and hope he did not see who was driving. Alan put his foot down and shot past the opening. He looked in his mirror once he was past to see Vic starting up his bike. Now what, Alan thought, heart sinking. But the lights did not follow him. Instead Vic seemed to be crossing a ploughed field judging by the beams of light bouncing up and down.

Alan went round the last bend and slowed down. He had not the foggiest idea where he was – some sleuth you are, he told himself. Fifty yards further on he came to a crossroads and a signpost. One arrow pointed to Shillingham, one to The Shillings and the road he had just come along was signed to Connicstown. He repeated the name several times to get it in to his head and made for Shillingham. He knew his way back to Morristown from there.

Jim was asleep, on his own, when the call came. It was a very distressed Eveleigh – one of her dogs was ill and in great pain. He was immediately awake for, of all his clients, Eveleigh was the least likely to call at such an ungodly hour unless it was critical.

It was a bitterly cold night, and as he often did when called out, Jim pulled his cords over his pyjama bottoms and a sweater over his top – it saved time when, and if, he eventually climbed back into bed. Within fifteen minutes he was pulling up outside Eveleigh's. He went straight round the back to where he could see a light shining in one of the kennels. As he walked, he could hear the restlessness of the other dogs as they moved agitatedly on their bedding, snuffling at the doors to be let out. A couple of them were barking; not the full, normal, deep-throated bark, but a more experimental, uncertain bark, as if the dogs were clearing their throats.

'What have we here then?'

Eveleigh, kneeling beside a large St Bernard bitch, looked up at Jim, her face streaked with tears, her long hair – uncoiled from its normal bun – spiked with straw. On her lap lay the dog's huge head. Its mouth was lathered with froth and Eveleigh's dressing gown was soaked with saliva. The dog's eyes were rolled up. She looked at Jim and shook her head sadly.

Nonetheless, Jim took out his stethoscope and listened hard, but there was nothing. 'Eveleigh, I'm sorry.' He put his hand out and took hold of hers and squeezed it, trying to comfort her. 'It isn't one of your champions, is it?' The dog looked so bedraggled, its hair damp with sweat, not like the normal spruce appearance of Eveleigh's dogs, that it was impossible to identify which one it was.

'No. Thank goodness – Lohengrin's kennel is further down – I padlocked it. You can never be too careful – not these days. Brünnhilde, well, she's a bit of a favourite and she was sleeping with me. This was Isolde – she was a brood bitch.'

'How old?'

'Seven. A sweet dog.'

'She's not pregnant?'

'No. She could have had one more litter. But I thought she's done me proud in the past, let her have an early retirement.' She managed to smile.

'What happened?'

'I heard intruders. My little King Charles woke me – the St Bernards never hear anything, they sleep too deeply. But Coco heard. By the time I got down here, they'd gone and poor Isolde had been poisoned.'

'Poison? You sure?'

'Just look at her, Jim.'

'But it could be something else. An epileptic fit. A seizure, heart . . .'

'No. She was screaming with pain when I found her. She was doubled up in agony.'

'The bastards! Have you called the police?'

'Just you. I had to get back to her.'

'Of course. I think you should phone them, you know. This is very serious. There's nothing more we can do for Isolde, and the less we disturb here the better. Come on, Evie, let's make some tea.' He held his hand out to her.

Gently, Eveleigh lowered Isolde's heavy head on the straw. She leaned over and kissed her before allowing Jim to haul her to her feet. 'The last person to call me Evie was my husband.'

'I'm sorry. I didn't think.'

'No, please. I like it.' She walked in front of him out into the open. 'It's all right, my darlings. Nothing to worry about, go back to sleep,' she called to her snuffling, agitated brood.

Jim was not a person who easily lost his temper, but he did an hour later. One of the investigating policemen had already upset Eveleigh by querying if she had put rat poison down which the dog had inadvertently eaten. But worse was to come when, although not saying it outright, the man's train of thought became all too obvious.

'I mean,' he said, sipping at the tea Eveleigh had given him, 'I should think it costs a bob or two to put down a big dog like that.'

Eveleigh stood speechless, clutching the teapot to her as if, if she let go, she might hit the officer.

'That's a diabolical accusation,' Jim shouted.

'I wasn't aware I was accusing Mrs Brenton of anything, sir.' The 'sir' was added after an almost imperceptible – and insolent – pause.

'I can assure you that there isn't a more caring breeder in the whole country than Mrs Brenton.'

'And you're her vet, I gather.'

'Yes. What's that got to do with it?'

'Quite a bit, I should think. For a start, you would say that of a client, wouldn't you? A valuable client, no doubt.'

'Are you trying to suggest that *I* had something to do with this?'

'I'm not implying anything – sir. Just doing my job.'

'I've a good mind to report you for insolence.'

'You must do as you wish – sir.'

Again that pause, which was so irritating, and yet impossible to prove intentional. Eveleigh caught hold of Jim's sleeve and tugged it, gaining his attention.

'The officer has to ask all manner of questions, Jim, if we're to get to the bottom of this.'

'Thank you, Mrs Brenton. Now, all these strange happenings – the unordered deliveries. You didn't think to call us in sooner? Now, why was that, Mrs Brenton?'

'I didn't want to make a fuss,' she answered lamely.

'I see. Is there anything else we should know?' The policeman sounded bored.

'There were the phone calls.'

'What phone calls?' Jim asked.

'Didn't Mrs Brenton think to tell you either – sir?'

'I knew you'd worry, Jim. There was nothing you could do about it, was there?'

'What sort of calls?' Jim demanded.

'They were threatening my dogs.'

'Oh, Eveleigh. Why didn't you tell someone? We could have mounted a watch system or something.'

'I hoped it would stop. I'd almost decided to take up the offer to sell.' Eveleigh lifted her chin and clenched her hands at her sides. She was obviously fighting back tears, and Jim could not but admire her courage.

'And let them win?'

'I couldn't put the dogs at risk.'

364

'And where would you have gone?'

'I thought about Scotland. In the Highlands, perhaps, an isolated croft somewhere.'

'Oh, poor Eveleigh.' He put his arm about her shoulder. She turned and, despite the presence of the policeman, buried her head in his chest, allowing herself the luxury of tears.

36

The news of the break-in at the kennels swept excitedly through the villages. Police cars were not often seen in the lanes thereabouts, so that the presence of two at the same time, parked outside Eveleigh's, fuelled the rumours to an hysterical degree.

In the village shop Thomasine heard a whispered tale that Eveleigh had been found by the postman in one of the dog kennels with her throat cut. She did not stop to do her shopping, but drove home, feeling sick with horror and close to tears at the thought that Eveleigh was dead.

The telephone was ringing as she entered the house. She heard Eveleigh's voice on the other end with such a sense of relief that her legs felt suddenly wobbly and she had to sit down quickly.

'I'm so happy to hear you,' she gabbled. 'They said in the shop you were dead!'

'Oh these villages! They're unbelievable. No, I'm fine; sadly my dog, Isolde, died in the night. We had intruders.'

Thomasine then realised how low Eveleigh sounded, and kicked herself for not picking up on it sooner. 'I really am so dreadfully sorry about poor Isolde. She was such a gentle dog. I wonder –' She paused, not sure if she had enough nerve to offer. 'I wonder, I've got my painting of Isolde if you would like it, I'd –'

'That's why I'm calling you. I wondered if I could buy it from you – a souvenir of a dear dog.'

'I don't want you to buy it! I'm happy for you to have it.'

An hour later Thomasine delivered the painting. Inevitably they argued about it, since Eveleigh was adamant she should pay and Thomasine was equally adamant she should not. Eveleigh looked grey with worry and exhausted.

'Are your other dogs all right? Is there anything I can do to help?' Thomasine asked, and as she did, she realised how much she had changed. There would have been a time when she would never have thought to help out with dogs. 'After all, it's only a question of size, isn't it?' she said, mirroring her thoughts.

'How kind, but Kimberley is coping well. I bless the day she came, she's so willing.'

'Then let me make you some coffee, Eveleigh. You look washed out.' When she returned from the kitchen with the tray, it was in time to let Oliver in. 'Hullo,' she said, feeling ridiculously shy.

'Is Eveleigh in. . . ?'

'Oliver, in here,' Eveleigh called from the sitting room.

'Jim phoned. Eveleigh, why didn't you tell us? We might have been able to help.'

'It was my problem, Oliver. I've never seen the point in burdening people, and I've been on my own so long now that I don't think to turn to others.'

'It's called friendship, Eveleigh. That's what we're here for, surely, to help each other out at times like this.'

'That's kind, Oliver, that's just what dear Gill and Justin said to me. But, oh dear, who would have thought it would come to this?'

'Was it poison, as Jim fears?'

'We shall know later today. Jim normally would have

done the post-mortem, but the police insisted poor Isolde was taken to the vet at Morristown.'

'Whatever for?'

'I think they suspect us – well, me, of killing the dog, and they're afraid Jim is covering up for me.'

'You are joking, aren't you?' Oliver said, and Thomasine realised it was the first time she'd seen him serious.

'Unfortunately, no.'

'Is it another breeder, jealous of your success?' Thomasine asked.

'I find that so difficult to grasp. Dog people love dogs, we live for them. Who could be so cruel?'

'There are nutters in all walks of life, Eveleigh.'

'I know, but I'd rather not think so. Jim thinks it's far more likely to do with the land – some big businessman trying to scare me.'

Eveleigh told her all about the letters, the strange deliveries and the phone calls. Thomasine in turn was distressed that Eveleigh hadn't told any of them the full story.

'I do hope it's no one you know. That, in a way, would make it doubly bad.'

'Well, at least it's not Ben. That would have been too awful.'

'Ben Luckett?' Thomasine asked with surprise.

'He owned the land originally, but he's sold it.'

'What's to be done now?' Oliver asked. 'You know, in some ways the police involvement might be the best thing – it might scare them off.' He was about to add 'for the time being', but managed to stop himself in time.

'I'm glad you've got Kimberley here,' Thomasine said. 'It would be worrying if you were completely alone.'

'You need better security.'

'I've arranged that already, Oliver. A locksmith is coming to fit mortice locks on all the kennel doors – they'll be safe at night. And Mr Gurton, the electrician, is out there now putting up those lights that switch on if something crosses their beam – or something like that!'

Eveleigh waved her hand in the air vaguely, a sure indication of her fatigue. 'And Jim has been a tower of strength. He's offered to move in until all this blows over – he can get his calls re-routed.'

'That is kind.'

'Oh, I don't think I could possibly take him up on it. He's such a busy man.'

An hour later Oliver and Thomasine stood by their cars in the November chill.

'How's business?'

'It's unbelievable. I can't thank you enough for getting me started. I haven't even advertised yet, but already I've got two lunches booked and I've had a couple of enquiries about Christmas parties.'

'Brilliant. I think you should get a green van with *Thomasine's Treats* in gold lettering on the side.'

'I'm coming round to that name too. Why green?'

'Because it's my favourite colour. Why else?' He grinned. 'Who are the bookings?'

'Some people called Hetherington, they live over near Conniestown – I've my hairdresser to thank for them. And, oddly enough, your father-in-law. Cora phoned and asked if it was true I was doing it and could I do a lunch for ten tomorrow. Apparently the two Filipino servants he had walked out and left him in the lurch. Did you mention me? Do I have you to thank for that?' She smiled at him.

'Not guilty. Tell you what, though. You could do us all a favour. Try and manoeuvre it so that you tell Cora about the dog poisoning when Ben's in the room. Watch his reaction.'

'Oh, Oliver, surely not? Eveleigh said he'd sold the land, so it can't be him.'

'It's easy enough to say, isn't it? Doesn't mean he has.'

'I can't believe that. Ben is such a kind man and he adores dogs.'

'So did Hitler.'

'Oh, Oliver, you know what I mean.' She playfully

368

pushed him and then felt bashful at displaying such familiarity.

'I don't mean Ben administered the poison himself. Good Lor' no – he would never do his own dirty work. And I'm not saying he ordered it. More likely he's told someone to get rid of the kennels and has left it up to them how they do it. That's why I want you to watch his expression.'

'But this land can't be *that* important to him. He's loaded, isn't he?'

'Was. My adorable wife – soon to be ex, hurrah,' he added hurriedly, in case Thomasine misinterpreted his use of 'adorable', 'let slip that Daddy was a wee bit stretched, thanks to the Lloyd's débâcle. If that's so, then he's got to raise money and fast. Planning permission on that land is of the utmost importance, therefore, and poor Eveleigh is in the way. I know Ben Luckett. He's ruthless. This could get even nastier.'

Despite the success of the dinner she had cooked for Oliver, Thomasine still felt the same degree of nervousness as she unpacked her car and carried the boxes into Cora's kitchen. She had more to unload this time, for working at Oliver's had taught her that strange kitchens were as hard to find one's way around as any maze. Then she had wasted valuable time searching for the right saucepan, a balloon whisk, a sharper knife, so this time she had brought more of her own equipment. She was early too, another lesson learnt – she wanted to check out how the cooker worked, if it was an Aga, what alternatives were available – she had put a Baby Belling in the boot, just in case there was no back-up; she'd been caught out cooking on Agas before. You had to know about Agas.

Of course Cora's kitchen was the one she need not have worried about – it was a cook's dream.

'Shame I don't do more in it then, isn't it?' Cora laughed as she responded to Thomasine's compliments on the immaculate, custom-built, colour co-ordinated, equipment-packed kitchen. Of course there *was* an Aga, but backed up by a double built-in oven, and both Halogen and gas hobs.

'You could rent this fridge out as a bedsit,' Thomasine said when Cora opened the double doors of the huge Whirlpool refrigerator. Saucepans, when not neatly stacked on their own pyramid-shaped stands, dangled from a large batterie de cuisine, and on the marble-topped work surface was a full set of Sabatier knives.

'My char will help you, and she'll do the washing up and the floors.' Cora's scarlet, thin-strapped sandals tapped at the faded antique terracotta tiled floor which alone looked as if it had cost more than most people's kitchens. If she hadn't known better, Thomasine might have thought that Cora was pointing out the floor on purpose.

'I didn't know I was to have help. I assumed I'd be doing the washing up. If so, I'm probably charging you too much,' Thomasine said, frowning with uncertainty.

'What a sweet thing you are! Of course I shall pay you what we agreed. My char would be here in any case.'

'Well, if you're sure.' Thomasine began to unpack her boxes of food. 'I do hope you'll like the menu I've chosen.'

'Of course we will.' Cora eyed the food. 'Oh dear, didn't I tell you? Ben loathes mushrooms, and the vicar's wife only eats feather or fish.'

'Well, no, you didn't. Sorry,' said Thomasine, her heart already racing. The mushrooms were no problem, she'd just leave them out, but a Beef Wellington was decidedly not from a feathered nor scaly creature. Yet she had no alternative to fall back on. She there and then made the resolve in future to clear all menus with her client, whatever the client said.

Thomasine looked at her watch with an agitated expression. 'I might have time to pop out to Shillingham and buy some chicken breasts and do one en croute just for the vicar's wife.'

'Why not do ten, then we'll have an either or?' Cora suggested, smiling brightly at such an ideal but simple solution. 'A far better idea. There's a whole box of chicken breasts in the freezer.' She swung open the freezer section of the fridge.

'Yes, of course,' Thomasine agreed reluctantly; she'd wanted only to use fresh food in her business. She was glad now, though, that, given the extra work, she had not insisted on lowering the price.

She was placing the meat in the microwave to defrost – against all her principles – when the door swung open and in stalked Sophia. 'My, my, Cora told me you were the new cook and I said it's just not possible,' Sophia said in her husky drawl, and, despite her smile, looking down her nose at her, or so it seemed to Thomasine.

'It's very possible. I'm here.' She managed to smile back, and wondered why on earth she always felt at such a disadvantage with Sophia. She should loathe her for her ability to make her feel like this; instead she found she felt a sneaking admiration.

'What on earth for?'

'I need the money,' Thomasine replied honestly.

'Your ex looked well enough heeled when I saw him last, and if his bride wasn't in a Versace jacket, I'll eat my hat. Even if she looked a mite ludicrous. Somehow the jacket and pregnancy didn't go together.'

'Really?' Thomasine said with as little interest as she could muster, while a lump appeared in her chest. Of what? Anger? Pain? She was not sure which; as small as a pea, it rapidly began to take on the dimensions of a sizeable rock. 'You know them, do you?' She could not resist a smidgeon of self-congratulation at how cool she sounded, especially since her whole world seemed to have slanted off-kilter at the roundabout way she had learnt Robert's wife was pregnant.

'I've known Chantal for years. Absolute sweetie – divine château, but of course you know that.'

'No, I don't. I've never been there.'

'Well, take my word, it's ravishing. I mean who she doesn't know isn't worth bothering with.'

'Well, that cuts me out,' Cora said. Thomasine could have kissed her and instantly forgave her the mushrooms and the vicar's wife's preferences.

'Me too.' She even found herself laughing.

'I suppose you knew she was pregnant?' Sophia asked, sounding offhand, but hitting the spot with stiletto-like technique.

'Oh really, Sophia! I'm sure Thomasine knows all this, but it's the last thing she wants to talk about – ex-husbands and their wives are boring.'

'Thomasine's isn't, he's dishy as hell.'

'Yours isn't so bad either,' Thomasine said with spirit.

'There is a difference though – Oliver isn't my ex.' She picked up a stick of carrot and waved it in the air before popping it in her mouth. 'And, *entre nous*, I doubt if he ever will be – an ex, I mean.' And with that she smartly left the room, the swing door flapping open and shut long after she'd gone.

'She's got a hope!' said Cora. 'The last thing Oliver wants is that bitch back in his life.'

Thomasine looked at Cora in surprise, and, she realised, gratitude.

'She's a spoilt brat, always has been. I wish to God some idiot would come and take her on – she's spending far too much time here for my comfort. Still, I'm holding you up. I'd better be . . .' But before she finished the sentence Ben entered through the noisy flapping door, a silver tray with three glasses and a bottle of champagne on it.

'I thought the cook might like a small life enhancer,' he boomed genially.

Thomasine glanced at her watch again. It was far too

early, but she had no intention of offending her host by pointing this out to him, so she accepted with a smile.

'Have you met our prospective new MP, the guest of honour at this lunch?' he asked Thomasine.

'No. I didn't even know we were to have a new one.'

'Old Johns fell off his perch a couple of weeks back. This bloke's his replacement.'

'You hope he'll be. I think this by-election could be interesting,' Cora said.

'Look at her, Thomasine – designer clothes, diamonds, spends more on manicures than the average family spends on food, and she calls herself a socialist.'

'You are what you're born, no point in changing.'

'There's every point. With my taxes . . .' Ben was beginning to wind himself up, no doubt as Cora intended, as he angrily tore at the wire around the cork.

'Maybe I should talk to this new candidate about Eveleigh's poor dog.' Thomasine not only wanted to defuse the situation, but also to do Oliver's bidding, and this seemed a good opportunity.

'What poor dog?' Cora asked with interest.

'Didn't you know? One of Eveleigh's dogs has been poisoned . . .'

It was Thomasine's turn not to finish her sentence for at that point, on that word, Ben dropped the bottle of champagne, which exploded sending shards of glass and fountains of wine all over the kitchen. For a split second Thomasine saw horror on his face.

'Ben, you clumsy bugger, you can clear it up.'

'It slipped right out of my hand.'

'Poisoned? What, rat poison?' Cora asked.

'An accident, of course?' Ben looked more than anxious.

'No. The dog's been taken away for an autopsy, but it looks deliberate.'

'Who on earth could do a thing like that? Horrible. Ben, you must do something.'

'What the hell am I supposed to do?'

'Go and see her. Try and sort out this kennel business for her once and for all.'

'It could be anyone, anything. Eveleigh's very successful with her dogs – it's probably another jealous breeder,' Ben said as he swept the glass up.

'I can see another breeder wanting to hurt Eveleigh, but not her dogs, surely? They'd be dog lovers.'

'I suppose it's like anything else, you'll even find fanatics in the dog world, people who'd stop at nothing.' Thomasine said this to make Ben feel more relaxed, and observing him from the corner of her eye she saw that it had worked – his shoulders visibly lost the rigid set they'd had ever since Thomasine had dropped her bombshell. She was certain now that Ben knew far more than he was letting on, though she was pleased she could report back to Oliver that he'd obviously known nothing about the dog being killed; his shock was genuine.

'Spot on, Thomasine. I'll get another bottle.'

'If it's for me, Ben, please don't bother, I'm rapidly getting behind here, I must get on.'

'Yes, come on, Ben, let's leave Thomasine alone to do lunch – no cook likes to be watched.' Cora ushered Ben out through the flapping door. Before she could begin to work Thomasine had to mop the floor where the spilled champagne was already becoming tacky.

Once back into the soothing routine of peeling and chopping, she allowed herself to think. Not of Ben and the dog, she was certain in her mind about that. No, she thought about her husband. As she diced her onions and garlic the knife sliced rapidly through the crisp, white vegetables, its motion dictated by the anger she felt. How could he firstly up and marry and not even let her know, and secondly not warn her about the pregnancy, have her find out from others? How thoughtless, how unkind – how bloody rude! And the creep, she'd wanted other children, begged him for them, and he'd refused.

Well, she was glad she had now – at least that was one less link with him.

The knife paused in mid-air. She liked this reaction. A couple of months back she'd have been wallowing in hurt feelings and dashed dreams. That had been an uncomfortable time, a useless, demeaning way to feel. This anger was far better. The cause of the anger was much more satisfactory – not that he was married, but because he had such filthy manners.

Her satisfaction, however, wouldn't help Nadine. She would be truly hurt, no doubt she would regard it as rejection. Oh, hell. She thought of the moods and dramas Nadine could make out of this news, and she did not fancy the prospect at all.

Still, she'd think about that later, good food never materialised from a worried, distracted cook. She'd think of other things.

Oliver. Just thinking his name made a smile appear on her face. But what had Sophia meant about him? Did she mean they were getting back together? Oh no! She would hate that. She felt her spirits drop like an express lift. She hadn't, up until now, really faced the truth – she was more than a little fond of Oliver. What she was feeling was, she was pretty sure, the beginnings of falling in love.

37

Despite Alan's snooping and two more garbled and muffled telephone calls, he and his colleagues were no further on in their search for the Morristown dog-fighting cartel. The informant had said nothing specific, regardless of the gentle coaxing of the inspector. They all agreed that both calls were from the same person. One only had to listen to the taped voice to hear the upset and, most thought, fear in it. They had worked out the scenario that Fred, as they had dubbed him, had probably just attended such a fight; was sickened by what he saw, wanted it stopped, but once in contact with the RSPCA, lost his bottle and could not quite bring himself to name names. Whether that was from the fear of being beaten up or from a misplaced sense of loyalty was anybody's guess.

Alan, like the others in the office, had listened to the tape over and over again in the hope that in a pub, in a shop, they might just hear the voice again. The only other clue was the background noise of a television playing and a bird, a budgerigar, chirping in the background. Noises which would be common in half the homes on the Forest Glade estate.

Alan was also frustrated that, although his house hunting had brought him to Shillingham on several Saturdays, he'd never again met Kimberley. His social life was looking up and he had even been on a couple of dates, but he hadn't been able to get involved; it was Kimberley he wanted. As he drove again, a Phil Collins tape playing, he liked to think about her and make up imaginary conversations of what he'd say to her if he ever found her again.

It was Friday and Alan was en route to Shillingham again, booked into his bed and breakfast for the weekend. His trip was twofold. He was to pick up, from an estate agent, the keys of a possible property situated in a wood above Middle Shilling. It was within his price range, and he was keen to buy. The money from the sale of his mother's house was in the bank, but it bothered him lying there. He did not trust himself not to raid it and buy himself an exotic holiday or an expensive car, and he knew the sum could so easily be chipped away.

For a while he sang along to *In The Air Tonight*, but soon fell back to thinking. If he bought this cottage, what would he do with it? If he let it the extra money would certainly come in handy, but would being a landlord prove to be a hassle? Could he afford to keep it just for weekends? Whichever way, he'd have somewhere to retire to. At that thought he laughed out loud. What a notion, it was something he couldn't even imagine.

He supposed a day might come when he'd want to leave the Special Branch. It was difficult to imagine, since being in the Special Branch rapidly became a way of life hard to give up, especially when hot on the trail of something important. Then, the adrenalin never stopped pumping and one lived on a perpetual high.

'You'll get too old for it one day,' he told himself. And one day you'll get married and have to settle down, he also said to himself, which brought his thoughts full circle back to Kimberley.

He would also use his time in Shillingham to visit the local vets. He was probably on a hiding to nothing. He knew that invariably the dog-fighting fraternity, afraid a vet might report them to the police, chose to treat any dogs hurt in a fight themselves.

Still, it was worth a try. He might learn if any vets in the area had been burgled – if saline solution and drips were taken as well as medicines it was often an indication that dog fighters were involved, he thought as he parked his car.

The new veterinary practice had nothing untoward to report. He liked the young couple running it on sight. It was a husband and wife team – it was surprising how often it was – and they were as proud as punch of the new facility they had created, sinking all their savings and a frightening bank loan into it. Still, they told him, business was good and word got put around. The other local vet, a Jim Varley, had been good enough to pop in and welcome them and had no hard feelings. He had even suggested they did a night-call and weekend roster between them.

Alan, though he liked them, thought he'd never get away and for a good fifteen minutes was backing towards the door. He emerged onto the pavement, looked up and saw Kimberley on the other side of the road. His heart seemed to somersault.

'Kimberley,' he shouted. And without looking, he plunged into the road and raced towards her. 'Kimberley!'

'Hullo, Alan,' she said, not pausing.

'I never thought I'd see you again!' He fell into step beside her.

'Well, whose fault is that?' She stopped walking and stood rigid, her emotions a raging mixture of joy at seeing him, aching with longing for him, perplexity and hurt at his cavalier behaviour towards her.

'Kimberley. I'm sorry. I was a fool. You don't know how often I regretted losing my temper – I've paid for it.' He grabbed her hand and held it tight, as if fearing to lose her a second time. 'But it's not Saturday!'

'No. I don't come in on Saturdays any more.' She still sounded distant, but she did not pull her hand away.

'I know,' he said.

'How do you know?'

'Because I've come looking for you.'

'That's nice.' She looked away shyly, but was unable to stop a huge smile wreathing her face.

'Coffee?' he asked, hopeful now.

'Um . . . Nice.' They made for The Copper Kettle and the Conco machine.

Once settled at the table in the window, coffee and cake ordered, neither was quite sure what to say to each other. Alan thought she had been pleased he'd been looking for her, but on the other hand, he didn't want to move too fast and frighten her away. And Kimberley, unused to being searched for by young men, was unsure how to proceed. Showing too much interest in him might frighten him away, too little and he could lose interest. But where the middle ground lay, that elusive area which might, just might, lead to happiness, was a mystery to her. Kimberley was on new territory.

'You look very pretty,' Alan blurted out, and could have bitten his tongue off for rushing.

'So do you –' she giggled. 'Handsome, I mean, not pretty.' And she giggled some more, and hated herself for being so gauche. She looked at the paper napkin on her lap with great interest, as if she'd never seen one before.

'Nothing bent about me,' Alan laughed and held his hand limply in the air and knew he wasn't being funny.

'What are you doing here on a Friday?' she asked, and he could have kissed her for moving on to safe ground.

'I'm looking at a house tomorrow.' Experience taught him not to mention the vet.

'You won't find many houses for sale at the vet's,' she said, quite pleased with her joke, but then blushing furiously as she realised she'd given the game away, that she'd seen him before he'd seen her.

'Oh that. I just popped in . . .' He purposely dropped his napkin on the floor and bent down to retrieve it, giving himself time to think of a reply. 'I wanted to know if they knew of any kittens wanting homes.' He congratulated himself on that response.

'And did they?'

'No.'

'Just as well. You shouldn't really get one until you're settled in your new home. Moving cats about confuses them.'

'That's true. I just need something to love.' He put his head on one side and smiled at her – he couldn't let such an opportunity slip by.

'Oh,' she mumbled, and began to pleat the gingham tablecloth into neat folds. Half of her hoped that remark was a sign to her, the other half telling her not to be so stupid.

'And what have you been doing?'

'I've got a job,' she said with the pride of the newly employed. 'In a kennels. St Bernards, they're wonderful. The owner's teaching me all she knows. And I've got a little flat, all my own. It's lovely. And I've been shopping and bought this lamp for it. It's the exact blue I wanted.' This was the longest speech that Kimberley had ever made to anyone in her life, and she was so surprised at herself that she did not notice Alan relax in his chair with an almost inaudible sigh of relief.

'Do you like the job?'

'Other than Isolde dying.' And Kimberley told him of the poisoned dog.

'Bastards! People like that should be hanged.'

'And drawn and quartered,' Kimberley agreed with him, and decided conversation wasn't so difficult after all.

'I'm glad you like dogs.'

'I'm glad you do too.' She smiled but this time she looked at him as she did so.

'You wouldn't fancy going to the cinema, maybe having a curry, say tonight?'

'There's no late bus to the Shillings. I don't know if I could.'

'I'll come and pick you up. Remember I've got a car. Then maybe you could show me the dogs – I'd like that,' he said, and the professional in him registered that he could check the kennels out at the same time, all on the q.t.

Alan gave her a lift back to the kennels, but she didn't invite him in, she didn't like to, not without checking with Mrs Brenton first. In the excitement of meeting Alan, she had completely forgotten to buy the instant coffee that Eveleigh had asked her to get, since it was much cheaper in Shillingham than in the corner shop.

'I'm so sorry. I don't know what got into me,' she apologised to a far from annoyed Eveleigh, remembering the scene there would have been with her mother if she had forgotten something.

'Oh, it's no matter.'

'I can pop to the village shop.'

'Would you? Perhaps you could get me a loaf too.'

Taking the old bicycle she'd seen in a shed, and which Eveleigh had given her permission to ride, she raced into Middle Shilling. She was seriously puzzled when she saw Alan emerge from Mr Varley's and stand talking to him for a moment in the lane. Why? What was he about? She ducked round the back of the shop so that he didn't see her. The last thing she wanted was to embarrass him. All the same, she thought, as she pedalled back to the kennels, two vets in one day when he'd agreed a kitten was a bad idea – very mysterious.

Her bicycle wobbled dangerously when, as she passed the Old School House, a window flew open and a voice shouted her name. She stopped in the lane, legs either side of the bicycle, and peered up at a bedroom window.

'Nadine!'

'Hang on, I'll come down.' And a few seconds later Nadine cannoned out of her front door. 'Am I pleased to see you! I hate everyone here. There's no one to talk to. I've been keeping a look out for you. What do you get up to?'

'I'm working. How long have you been here?'

'Too long!'

'Why didn't you look for me?'

'Too depressed, I suppose. I mean – that school is gross.'

'A bit different from what you're used to, I expect.' Kimberley smiled, imagining how the others would find Nadine not to their taste at all. 'I live just up the road from here, at the kennels.'

'No! That's brill. Come in. Let's talk.'

'I have to get back.'

'When then?'

'I've a date tonight,' she said, her face glowing with pride. 'How about tomorrow evening, after work?'

'Brill!' Nadine waved her away.

Kimberley grinned broadly for the rest of the ride back. She'd a job, a flat of her own, perhaps a boyfriend, and her friend back. She couldn't remember when she'd last been so happy.

Nadine was restless and bored. She wondered now if she'd made the right choice in coming to Middle Shilling. Perhaps she could have weathered her father's and Chantal's sloppiness, and her stepmother's relentless nagging. She missed London with a miserable, sodden ache. She needed her friends. Every night she went to bed fed up, and each morning woke with the situation uncured by sleep. She even missed her old school and longed to be back there.

She knew her mother was trying to make things better for her, but for some reason her concern made Nadine feel an almost uncontrollable rage towards Thomasine. She wanted to blame her for everything that was wrong, but hadn't yet worked out how to do so.

To make matters worse, although she wanted to be left alone, Nadine resented the time her mother devoted to her new career. Thomasine was obviously overjoyed with her new-found independence and success, which fuelled her daughter's resentment. Why should she be happy when Nadine wasn't? And her mother was so patient with her that there were days Nadine wanted to kick her.

She loved the little dog Nova, loved to hold her, smell her, kiss her broadening head. While at the same time hating the dog, wishing it was not there and wanting to crush it to death. To add insult to injury, her mother seemed, somehow, to be aware of this and always took the dog with her, which merely made Nadine feel she was not trusted. Which hurt even more.

Nadine was convinced she was totally unloved.

She'd been here well over a month, she'd tried to settle in, but the countryside was so boring. She'd sussed out the local kids and found she had nothing in common with them, and she knew she never would. Kimberley was her last hope, but she feared even she might only want to talk about her new fellow – boring.

Still, maybe things were about to get better. Last Saturday she'd been wandering listlessly about the Cromwell Cross – the huge indoor shopping centre in Morristown – when she'd spied a group demonstrating outside a pet shop. They did not look like the pink-cheeked, smiling, sweet-smelling, concerned mums and grannies she'd demonstrated with over the calves.

They were dirty, scruffy and lank-haired. They were earring and nose-studded. They were abusive. They smelt. But that did not matter, they had a cause. They were the FAA – Freedom for All Animals, as their banner proclaimed, even if the graphics were on the amateurish side.

She approached them and stated her credentials, with which they were not nearly as impressed as she hoped. 'Bunny huggers!' they spat out dismissively.

She apologised for the kindly women. Agreed they were useless. Said it was all a dead loss – and felt like St Peter with her denial of them. But she smothered that notion and asked if she could join them.

They were wary, said no decisions could be made that easily; they had security to think about and she might be a plant. She agreed and gave them her address, her phone number and fifty pounds she'd saved for new jeans and a sweater. They promised to set up a meeting for her with their leader, 'Cracker Barrel'. They promised he would phone.

All week she'd waited restlessly for the telephone call that would haul her out of this boredom. The call that would make her a crusader again. Tonight she just knew it would come.

'Hullo. Is this the Ruskie? I was given your number to ring by the Hopper.'

'The Ruskie? I'm sorry, there's no one here of that name.' She felt her spirits sink.

'Code names, idiot! I'm the Cracker Barrel. Lines could be bugged.'

'Oh, you are. Oh, how wonderful!' And at the idea of a telephone tap she felt so excited she could barely get the words out.

'I gather you want some action?'

'Please.'

'You got transport?'

'No.'

'Pity. Do you know Morristown? In the bowling alley, next Friday evening at eight.' The telephone went dead.

Nadine was bubbling with excitement as she replaced the receiver. She loved the drama, the use of code names, the carefully chosen words. The very thought that someone might be listening to the call thrilled her. She loved the sheer unexpectedness of it all. What would tomorrow be about? A hunt, factory farming, live export of animals, a handy laboratory to smash up?

Until now her activities had all been pretty amateurish stuff, but with the FAA she was moving into another league. The FAA were dedicated to any means, violent if need be, and the very thought of them made her feel sick with excitement. She'd feared they would think she was too young and might be a liability. But she'd known what she was doing in the Cromwell Cross when she'd handed over her money and had hinted there was plenty more where that came from. So what if she'd bought herself in? The how didn't matter at all. Now she had a real purpose in life.

'Who was that?' Thomasine appeared in the kitchen doorway holding her flour-covered hands high. 'Anyone for me?'

'No. It was a friend. We're going bowling next week.'

'That's nice.' Thomasine returned to her pastry making and did not see Nadine poke her tongue out at her before picking up the phone to ask Kimberley if she fancied going bowling next Friday – she didn't feel brave enough to go alone. Kimberley found her infuriatingly mysterious about who she was to meet there. 'It's to do with a good cause,' was all she would say.

'But how will we get there?' Kimberley asked.

'My mum will take us. If not, we'll get a taxi. I'll pay.' Then she raced to her room to choose her clothes for the meeting, even though it was nearly a week away.

She couldn't look like them. It took ages to get one's clothes as degraded as that. So she settled on black jeans, black sweater and her leather jacket, which wasn't really enough for this cold weather, but it would have to do. She wanted to look slick, mysterious. A bit like the *Black Magic* man.

Kimberley had read about cloud nine: tonight she had climbed upon it. Alan had arrived early to pick her up from the kennels.

'Sorry I'm early. I couldn't wait to see you again,' he said as he got into the driver's seat and she curled her toes inside her shoes from the sheer joy of hearing him say such things.

He looked so smart in his pressed jeans, she wondered if he always ironed them, she'd never met anyone who did that before. The lack of nice things to wear had never bothered her before, but it did now. She hoped he wouldn't realise how cheaply she was dressed. In the market she'd bought a loose-knit, fawn jumper for a tenner, and the new black leggings she wore had only cost a couple of pounds. She still hadn't been able to afford the Doc Martens she yearned for, and was making do with a pair of high-ankled black trainers from Bata. She'd pass, for the time being. But clothes would be high on her list of priorities now; the bits and bobs for the flat would have to wait.

'You sure you're warm enough? You've no coat,' he asked, turning the heater up higher.

'I don't feel the cold,' she lied, not wanting him to know she couldn't afford a new coat and was too ashamed to wear her old duffel.

'I've a Barbour in the back. You'd better wear that. You are a silly, you'll catch your death of cold at this rate.'

In the darkness of the car she smiled and enjoyed his concern for her – a new experience.

They drove to Morristown. 'Fancy a drink? We're too early for the second house.'

'Lovely.'

He parked the car in the multi-storey, as near to the exit as he could get. 'Less chance of being vandalised.'

'It's a super car.' She looked at the red Golf with admiration.

'I decided to treat myself.'

'My, my. A new car and a new house! You must be loaded.'

'My mother left me some loot,' he explained, and she felt dreadful, afraid he'd think she'd been prying.

'I shouldn't have said that, I'm sorry.'

'Don't be daft. I don't mind.'

Her heart jolted when he took hold of her hand and, as they walked along, she felt it was somehow the most natural thing in the world to be doing. He looked down at her and she smiled. He squeezed her hand.

'This pub's a bit rough, do you mind?' He had stopped in front of The Locomotive.

'Not when I'm with you,' she said, and he was almost overwhelmed with pride and his need to care for her.

It was like passing through a thick curtain of noise as they went into the saloon bar. At the far side, pint in hand, Alan saw Vic. He waved, and making way for her, pushed through the crowd and introduced her. Kimberley felt so proud he wanted her to meet his friends. Alan was hoping that by turning up with the girl he'd boasted about, he would make Vic less suspicious of him.

'What you fancy?' he asked.

'Malibu and pineapple juice would be lovely.'

'I'll get these, Alan,' said Vic, turning to the barman. 'How's tricks?'

'Oh, so-so. This and that. You know how it is,' he said nonsensically.

'Too bloody right I do. Swings and roundabouts, isn't it, mate?' Vic replied and Alan agreed.

'This is Kimberley.'

'How d'ya do,' Vic said.

Kimberley turned to speak to him and, with horror, saw Butch and Greaser grinning at her from a table where they sat with a very blonde girl. She nodded, but as imperceptibly as she could; she didn't want Alan to remember she knew them.

'Join us,' Vic offered.

'No, ta, mate. We're just off to the flicks. We don't want to get too comfortable,' Alan said. Letting them see him with a girl was one thing, he didn't want to get too involved.

'Suit yourself,' said Vic, moving back to the table with his drinks, and Alan wondered if he'd offended him.

'Those lads were with you the first time we met in Shillingham, weren't they?' God, he thought, his memory must be going – of course that's where he'd seen them. It had taken Kimberley to trigger his memory. 'Friends of yours?'

'No, I know them, that's all,' she said, colouring. 'From school,' she added hurriedly, and then wished she hadn't for she didn't want to remind him how young she was.

Alan quickly downed his drink as she sipped hers. 'Shall we get going?'

'Sure.' She quickly drank the rest of hers and to her mortification burped. She covered her mouth, horrified, but he only laughed.

'See you, Vic.' He waved.

'Bye, Kim,' Butch called out. 'Where do you get to these days? Aren't we good enough for you?'

'Don't be silly.' Her face was as red as a geranium as she let Alan lead the way.

'Don't you like them any more?' he asked as they began to walk towards the cinema.

'Who? Butch and Greaser? They're all right. I just got bored hanging about with them.'

'They don't seem your type. Too rough by far.'

'I didn't have many friends; I suppose I used them for lack of anyone else,' she said, realising that being offhand about them might be misinterpreted. 'I was lonely,' she added for good measure.

'I know all about that.' And he took hold of her hand and squeezed it, which made her feel all right again. 'Nice dog he had.'

'Did he?' she said, feeling flustered. 'What's the film?' she asked, to get away from the dangerous subject of Butch and Bandage, now languishing in her father's shed, scarred and battered. She shivered.

'You cold?'

'No, I'm fine.'

In the cinema he put his arm about her and kissed her, and then some more. She let him put his hand under the big, baggy jumper. She wriggled in her seat from the almost excruciating pleasure of his hand searching for her breast, which he gently caressed through her brassiere. She'd no idea what the film was about.

She was in a daze of sexual excitement and budding love as they walked out and he took her for a Chinese. Over the meal they talked non-stop about everything, it seemed. She'd lost all her shyness, and as she wanted to know all about him, she did not mind letting him know the little there was to tell about herself. She kept quiet about the dogs, of course, but how she longed to tell him, to confide in him and ask him what she should do. The mention of Bandage earlier had upset her, made her think about the poor dog, renewing her determination to rescue him. But how?

He kissed her in the car outside Eveleigh's, but to her disappointment he didn't fondle her. She hadn't wanted to come home. She wished there had been somewhere they could go and be alone, for she wanted them to 'do it'. She was sorely disappointed that they hadn't, but was too young and too shy to know how to suggest that they did.

38

The previous afternoon, when she had returned from the Lucketts', Thomasine had tried to telephone Oliver to tell him of her conclusions about Ben, but his telephone was out of order. Although she had reported it, it was still not ringing in the morning so, taking her courage in both hands, she drove round to his house. As she approached Bishop's End the excitement she felt was unsought, but appeared unstemmable. She parked around the back and rang the back-door bell, and was surprised when Wimpole answered it and, somewhat grudgingly, invited her into the kitchen.

'I love this room,' Thomasine said, sitting at the pine table while Wimpole made the coffee.

'Herself wasn't much good, but at least she knew how to do up a house.'

'Sophia you mean?'

'Who else? Still, you're right about this kitchen, like an illustration in that tarty magazine she works for – when she feels like it. Pity she couldn't cook.'

'I saw her yesterday. She hinted she and Oliver were getting back together.' Thomasine was pleased with the lack of interest she managed to put into her voice, making it sound like a passing comment.

Wimpole banged her cup down on the table. 'Over my dead body!' she declared. 'And that's just wishful thinking on her part. I reckon it hasn't worked out for her as well as she thought it would, being on her own, and she wants him back. But the best thing that ever happened to Oliver was the day she walked out – even if it did mean losing his dog. Which reminds me.' Wimpole leapt up from the table with an agility which belied her years. She quickly walked to the back door, put her head out and bellowed 'Slipper'. The puppy came scurrying in. 'He gets so neurotic about this mutt, he's so scared it'll run away like the other one. My hubbie's having to build a new fence to keep it in – at least that's what the idle bugger's supposed to be doing.'

Thomasine began to laugh at this, thinking she was joking, until she glanced up and saw the bitter expression on Wimpole's face. She realised she was not joking, and stopped the laughter immediately. Wimpole, fussing with the dog's water bowl, did not appear to notice.

'Thomasine, what a wonderful surprise!' Oliver said the moment he entered the kitchen. 'I wondered where my coffee had got to, why didn't you tell me Thomasine was here, Wimpole?'

'Because you said you didn't want to be disturbed – getting precious about his writing is our Oliver, just like his Aunt Phoebe.'

'I meant don't bother me with boring things. Of course I want to be interrupted when it's Thomasine.' Oliver smiled at her and Thomasine, to her annoyance, felt embarrassed and very gauche and wished she didn't want him to mean it quite so much.

'I bet you say that to all the girls,' she retorted, and immediately regretted it, since it made her sound even more gauche, like some pick-up in a discotheque.

'He doesn't. He means it,' Wimpole added.

'How's the book going?' Thomasine asked, not just out of interest, but to get the conversation back on safer ground.

'A bit hit and miss.'

'It's wonderful. I couldn't put it down and can't wait

to see what happens next,' Wimpole declared, sounding for all the world like his mother, her voice dripping with pride.

'I'd love to read it. That is if you don't mind. If you want.'

'I'd take that as an honour. I'd value your opinion.'

'I'm off to dust.' Wimpole stood up. 'See you later, Thomasine.'

'Grace came yesterday,' Oliver said.

'She's all right on floors, that woman, but she's blind to anything higher than a skirting board.'

'You never approve of anybody in my life, Wimpole.'

'Yes I do. She'll do.' Wimpole nodded in Thomasine's direction and smartly left the kitchen.

'Gracious. Whatever next!' Thomasine laughed nervously.

'I rather tend to agree,' Oliver said softly, so softly that Thomasine wasn't sure if she'd heard right.

'I came to tell you about Ben. I tried to call you. Did you know your telephone was out of order?' She spoke briskly, to cover her confusion and the moment, if moment there had been, slipped away.

'And?'

'He was shocked rigid about the dog, even dropped a full bottle of champagne. I'm sure he knew nothing about it, but . . . I think he's involved. Perhaps he told someone to make Eveleigh's life difficult and they've gone too far.'

'Like old Henry the something or other. "Who'll do the business on this wretched priest?" and poor Becket got bumped off.'

'Something like that.' She smiled. 'What do we do?'

'Ben's not a bad man – greedy maybe. We should be able to reason with him.'

'You sound rather doubtful.'

'I've never had any dealings with him over business and money. He might be different where the filthy lucre is concerned.'

'What if we blackmail him – tell him that we'll go to the tabloids if he doesn't lay off? His shareholders wouldn't like that sort of exposure,' Thomasine suggested.

'He hasn't got any – his companies are all his own, at least as far as I know. Of course, if we were right and the tabloids printed it, he could say goodbye to his knighthood. However, if we were wrong, I can tell you I wouldn't fancy being sued for libel by Ben – and he'd have every right to.'

'Would Sophia help?' She was shocked at how much she disliked even using her name in case it made him think of her.

'Sophia? You have to be joking. Sophia is only interested in one thing – herself. If she thought we were going to make Ben out of pocket, she'd work against us, not for us. In any case, she hates dogs.'

'Is Ben scared of anybody or anything?' Thomasine felt wonderfully pleased with his response. He apparently loathed Sophia. Wimpole had been right, any thought of reconciliation was obviously in Sophia's mind alone.

'Losing Cora – he's always been scared that because she's so much younger one day she'd do a flit. Bloody hell, yes – Cora! If we could get her to work for us . . . Brilliant thinking, Thomasine.'

'I didn't do anything – you thought it through.'

'How about you, me, Jim and Eveleigh talking to her, all together? That's the best way.' He poured them more coffee. 'How's the cooking going?'

'Better than I hoped. I had another enquiry this morning. In fact, I've written a bit of blurb to put in a brochure, I'd like you to look at it before I take it to the printers.' She opened her handbag and took out the piece of paper on which was the final draft of her idea – the wastepaper basket was full to overflowing with the rejected attempts.

Oliver felt in his pocket for a pair of spectacles which

he slipped on in order to read her effort. She watched him as he concentrated on the paper and she thought how well the half-lenses suited him.

'That's very good. Excellent. And I see you've kept "Thomasine's Treats" – it's snappy, memorable. Have you thought about the van? I see it in dark racing green.' He sketched the shape of a van expansively in the air with his hand.

'It'll be some time before I can afford a van – I've masses of equipment to get first.'

'You need a partner.'

She looked away abruptly. He spoke in that soft, smooth tone again, and she wasn't sure if he meant it or was teasing her. She picked up her bag from the floor.

'I'm off to Shillingham. Anything you need?' she asked automatically. Life in the country had taught her one thing; whoever was making a journey into town always offered to shop for friends.

'Lunch,' he answered shortly.

'Lunch – you mean food?'

'No. I mean may I take you out to lunch?'

'How long is this going to go on?' Beth asked as Jim stood, his hand on the back door, looking as if he was longing to escape.

'What?' he asked, knowing full well what she meant.

'You know damn well. How long are you going to be shacked up at Eveleigh's?'

'Don't be ridiculous. I'm not shacked up. I'm helping her out. When this blows over I'll come back.'

'It's not very professional.'

'I don't understand.'

'Well – your messages and things,' Beth said lamely, clutching at straws.

'I don't see the problem. My night calls are re-routed. I'm here in time for surgery. You take the daytime messages just as before.'

'You're being a shit, Jim,' she spat out.

'I beg your pardon?' He stepped back into the kitchen with the weary expression of one who knows what is coming and is already tired of it.

'You know exactly what I mean. How could you treat me like this? One minute you're in bed with me, the next it's Eveleigh.'

'Eveleigh! Have you gone totally mad, Beth? What the hell are you going on about now?'

'You're as thick as thieves with her, you always have been. So why haven't you done something about her before? Why involve me and then do this to me?' She was shouting now, her normally pleasant face twisted with an anger he had never dreamt her capable of.

'Beth! I don't know what the hell you mean – Eveleigh's a friend. She's got a problem with intruders and I'm helping her sort it out.'

'Pull the other one. And in any case, don't I have problems? What do I do if my husband turns up? Why aren't you looking after me?'

'I'm sorry if you jumped to the wrong conclusion. You said yourself you'd stopped worrying about your husband. When you've come to your senses maybe you'll feel like saying sorry.' He turned to go.

'Sorry! Me say sorry? It's you who should be apologising. First you seduce me and then you treat me like this. How dare you do this to me!' And she leapt at him and began to pummel his back.

He turned slowly, deliberately, grabbed her hands and held them tight. 'Now, you listen to me, Beth. I did not seduce you. It was you who climbed into my bed, remember?'

'You didn't push me away.'

'No, I know, and now I regret I didn't.'

Beth's face seemed to dissolve in front of him. As she absorbed his words her mouth turned down, her eyes filled with tears which gushed down her cheeks, even her body slumped. 'Please don't say that.' She stepped back and held her hands up, palms turned towards him as if warding him off, or pushing the words away from her. 'Don't spoil it.'

'Oh, Beth, there's nothing to spoil.'

'Yes there is – you love me. I love you.'

'I don't, Beth. I'm sorry, but I don't love you.'

'You will. I'll make you love me.'

'It doesn't work that way. I wish I did love you, it would make everything so much easier. But I can't make myself, if it's not there. I should have made you leave me that first night, or got up and moved away myself. I should never have let it happen again and again after that. I've been wrong. I'm sorry, Beth. Deeply sorry.'

'But you enjoyed being in bed with me – you couldn't have faked that.'

'That's true. I did enjoy it. But it doesn't make it right.' He paused, looking at her, at the sadness in her face, and hated himself. He took a deep breath. 'It was sex, Beth. I'd hoped that was all it was for you too.' He loathed hurting her, but knew he had to.

'You used me – you fucking bastard!'

'Yes, I used you and I'm ashamed I did. I said I'm sorry. It won't happen again.' And he turned abruptly, walked out of the kitchen slamming the door shut behind him, not wanting to see her face, witness her distress and to know he was the cause of it.

Eveleigh was round the back of the kennels bedding the dogs down, with the kennel girl helping her. Solemnly Kimberley shook his hand, after wiping hers down the side of her trousers first.

'Can you see to the last two, Kimberley, while I get Mr Varley a drink?'

Kimberley was happy to be left on her own. In the time she had worked here the dogs had become her life, and the last two, Lohengrin and Brünnhilde, champions both, were her favourites. There was something about the evening routine that was different to the rest of the day. The dogs had been exercised and were tired. They'd been fed and there was a sleepy contentment about them with the daytime friskiness gone. They were more affectionate, more malleable. Each and every one enjoyed a good hug before they were bedded down for the night.

These two and Parsifal had been moved closer to the house to be in earshot, for on them were pinned Eveleigh's hopes for Crufts next March. It was still four months away but, as Eveleigh was fond of saying, the preparations for Crufts were ongoing and never-ending. Although there were new locks on all the night-time kennels, these three had even larger padlocks on their doors and Eveleigh had instructed Kimberley to string tin cans on a trip wire, hidden by sacking, across the opening of each kennel.

Content that all was safe and secure, Kimberley knocked on the sitting-room door to tell Eveleigh she was out for the evening. She took her bicycle and made for Nadine's house, where she had been invited to supper, thinking she was glad that Mr Varley had arrived early. She didn't like to leave Eveleigh on her own. She thought they made a nice couple. She didn't usually think like this, she supposed it was because she was in love herself and wanted everyone else to be.

Eveleigh, seeing the drawn expression on Jim's face, poured him an extra large whisky. 'Get that down you. You look as if you need it. Hard day?'

'You could say that. But I'm not on call – the Shillingham vets are on this weekend.'

'It must be odd for you, after all these years, to have free evenings.'

'It's bliss.' Jim stretched in the comfortable armchair

and put his feet out and rested them on Parsifal, who was sprawled, all eighteen stone of him, on the rug in front of the fire. 'Is this a precaution?'

'Yes and no. It's his turn for a treat.' She looked sheepish. 'I've not completely made up my mind between Lohengrin and Parsifal for Crufts. Brünnhilde, yes, she's the best bitch I've ever had.'

'Lohengrin's a fine dog,' said Jim, who nursed a soft spot for him.

'I know, I know. But maybe he's too young. Parsifal here is that little bit steadier but still I have a feeling about Lohengein – here.' She put her hand on her breast.

'Didn't Lohengrin get best male last year?'

'No, that was Siegdried and it was several years ago. Of course I thought he should have been Best of Breed. I nearly pulled out of Crufts this year, with all the unpleasantness, and then I thought why? That would be silly – that would almost prove me guilty, wouldn't it? And Jill is judging. It should be interesting.'

'I'd like to come with you if I can arrange it. I've never been to Crufts.'

'Then you should go. It's quite a spectacle, you know. That would be fun.' And then, as if thinking she had shown too much pleasure, changed the subject. 'I got steak in for supper, if that will do you? I'm not much of a cook, but I can grill a steak without too much mishap.'

'It sounds wonderful. And I've got a bottle of wine in the car.'

Jim had not meant to say anything to Eveleigh about Beth, it wouldn't be fair. But he did. Maybe it was the wine, the warmth from the fire, the relaxed atmosphere, or a combination of them all that lulled him into a state where it seemed the most natural thing to be doing. Once he'd finished talking it seemed an age before Eveleigh spoke.

'You're an honest man, Jim. Perhaps too honest. You

could have gone on indefinitely with her, couldn't you? It wasn't very clever of you, but we all know about men's weaknesses, don't we?'

Jim looked up with alarm, but when he saw the smile on her face he realised she was teasing him, that she understood. It had suddenly become very important to him that she of all people didn't think too badly of him.

39

There had been a time when Kimberley had daydreamed of what a whole day spent with someone she loved might be like. The reality was not to be a let-down.

Alan called for her on Saturday morning. Shyly, Kimberley introduced him to Eveleigh. 'Alan wondered if he could see the dogs, Mrs Brenton?'

'You like dogs, Mr Farmingham?'

'Yes, I do. But I work so I can't have one.'

'I wish more felt like you. A lonely dog becomes a troubled dog. But please do, Kimberley. Show your friend the kennels.'

They walked outside, Kimberley clutching her jumper to her, too proud still to put on her old coat.

'She seems very nice, but a bit distracted.'

'It's the worry over the dogs that's doing it.'

'I hope you're safe here.'

Her smile burst wide and full of happiness. 'Yes. The vet comes and sleeps over.'

'Lucky vet.'

'This is Brünnhilde.' She stopped in front of the bitch's kennel. 'They're named after characters in Wagner's operas. Mrs Brenton's husband loved his music and she's kept the tradition on.'

The dog lumbered to her feet and trotted over to the wire, curiosity conquering her urge to sleep. She placed one very large and dirty paw on the fence, as if in greeting.

'She likes you. She only does that to selected people. What have you been doing, Brünnhilde? Just look at your feet. And I washed them this morning. You have to watch their feet, make sure the fur doesn't bundle up hard between their toes.'

'She's a lovely dog.'

'She's a champion. Her puppies will sell for hundreds and hundreds. Champion Brünnhilde Rhinemaiden Starpoint of Oakleigh, that's her real name.'

'What makes her a champion?'

'Well, see her height, she's tall – the taller the better, but she hasn't lost her correct proportions. She's got a lovely short muzzle, nice and square at the end. And she holds her tail beautifully, not curled up over her back. And her head . . . it's right.' She trailed off here, for she could not remember what else Eveleigh had taught her.

'You know a lot!' He grinned at her.

'I don't. I know nothing. But Mrs Brenton's teaching me.'

'Do you want to do this for ever?'

'Yes. I love it. I thought I wanted to work in a bank – but after this, no thanks.'

'These kennels are a treat.'

'Lovely, aren't they. In summer the dogs have flower baskets – cute, isn't it? And their inside kennels are all heated, you know. It costs a fortune,' Kimberley informed him proudly. Alan wished all dogs were so lucky.

He drove across to a pub by the river the other side of Morristown. Alan had booked them a table by the window so she was able to watch the river and the swans. She wished she'd been smarter, everyone else was. She carefully noted what people were wearing so that next time she came here she could look like them. It was a casual smartness, she noticed; jeans were clean and pressed, as were the T-shirts, and she saw that lots of the women wore navy blazers and lovely scarves. She vowed she would look like that as soon as she could afford it.

She enjoyed the roast beef and the wine, even though she normally drank beer and had never tasted red wine before. But her greatest pleasure was finding out more about him. She had wondered if, the other night, they had talked themselves dry, but they hadn't. And today he seemed to want to tell her even more personal things.

'My dad left one night. He went out to buy some cigarettes and never came back.'

'He wasn't – ?' She paused; it hardly seemed polite to ask if he was dead.

'Murdered? Killed? Not as far as we know. He just disappeared off the face of the earth.'

'Did you look for him?'

'The Salvation Army tried and, of course, the police, but he'd done a runner and that was that.'

'Poor you, and your poor mum.' Her sympathy for him was sharply balanced by thoughts of how wonderful it would have been if her own father had chosen to disappear.

'I think she might have been one of the reasons he went – she nagged, d'you know what I mean?'

'Not really.' It was an honest answer. She didn't; her mother would never have had the courage to nag anyone.

'So he went AWOL. I had to get out too, she was doing the same to me – nagging all day long, possessive, smothering me.'

'You mean with love?'

'Yes.'

'But that must be nice.'

'It can be destructive too. I thought it was best for both of us if I left – I hoped she would make friends, find new interests. But she never did. Then she died and we'd never made it up. I'll always regret that.'

'I've never been loved,' she said sadly, and he longed to take her in his arms there and then.

'I love you,' he said simply.

She looked at him nervously, her eyes full of tears which she brushed awkwardly away. 'Please don't say things you don't mean,' she said with dignity.

He put his hand quickly across the table and took hold of hers. 'But I do mean it.'

'You don't know me, or anything about me.'

'I don't need to. It's the truth. I knew it would be like this. I always felt that one day I'd meet someone and I would be certain. That first day I was pretty sure – now I'm completely. And I know why now. I want to protect you. I need you to need me.'

'I want to be loved so badly,' she said, so quietly that he had to lean forward to catch her words.

It was crowded and noisy in the popular pub, but where they sat it was as if there was an oasis of complete silence. He still held her hand as they looked at each other, and their expressions said more than any words.

Kimberley felt safe with him. For the first time in her life she knew she was with someone who really did love her. 'I can't believe this is happening to me,' she said.

'Me neither, but it is.' And then he leant over and kissed her gently on the lips.

They drove through the country lanes back to the Shillings, and with the aid of a map looked for the cottage he was to view.

The car bumped up an unmade and overgrown driveway with woodland on either side. Kimberley didn't want the journey to end, didn't want to get out of the safe cocoon of the car, didn't want to meet and have to talk to anyone.

The drive opened out into a clearing which was full of brambles and overgrown shrubs and trees. In the middle was a small, brick-built house.

'The agent calls it a cottage, doesn't look much like

one to me. Come on, I picked up the keys.' He dug in his pocket and waved a bunch of keys at her.

'Is it all right?'

'It's empty.'

It was a two-bedroomed, two-living-roomed cottage with a built-on scullery for a kitchen. It was musty and damp with a lingering smell of cats.

'It's pretty grim, isn't it?' Alan said, disappointed by the estate agent's description.

'It's certainly been badly neglected. But – I don't know, I don't know anything about houses, but if it was painted and had some pretty wallpaper it could be nice.'

'Do you really think so?' He brightened up.

'And you could make this back room into a kitchen-living room – paint it white and yellow, a happy colour, with matching curtains. And then the old kitchen could be the bathroom.' Her face was flushed with excitement as she spoke.

'It's all I can afford without taking a mortgage. Everything round here is so expensive. You really think we could make it habitable?'

'Without a doubt,' she said, her heart having lurched when he said 'we'.

He wrenched open the front door with difficulty, since the hinges appeared to be rusted. 'If we cleared all this and planted a lawn –'

'It would be nigh on perfect.' She clasped her hands together to stop herself from waving them around. 'Absolutely perfect,' she repeated, and knew that her dreams were taking her over, ignoring sense and reason. But she couldn't control them.

They went up the stairs to inspect the bedrooms again.

'Which one should we have?'

'Oh, this one,' she said. 'It's bigger and it's got a built-in wardrobe and –' But at that point Alan's arms were about her and his lips on her and all thoughts of interior decoration were forgotten in the thrill of his hands searching her body, finding her breasts, playing with her

402

nipples, drawing her along with him as he hardened, as his body pressed close to hers. Without pausing in their kiss they both bent down and were kneeling on the floor, and then lying side by side. They removed their clothes with a desperation fuelled by longing. Alan bundled his jacket into a makeshift pillow for her head and she lay back upon it and opened her legs invitingly to him. 'I love you,' she mouthed as he lay on top of her and gently entered her. Her body rose slowly towards his and his bore down upon her until they were rocking in unison and the thrusts he made became more powerful and demanding and the two of them clawed at each other with relief.

'Kim? We've got it!' Alan's voice was bubbling with excitement over the telephone.

'Got what?' she asked, although she knew the answer, she just wanted to hear him say it.

'The house. The seller's accepted my offer. Oh, Kim, isn't it exciting? We've got our house! We can begin planning. I'll be back on Friday. We'll go and see it again.'

'Lovely!' she said, feeling she was moving in a dream; terrified she might at any moment awaken. She pulled herself together sufficiently to explain about going bowling with Nadine. 'We can all go,' he said before he disconnected the call. She stood leaning against the kitchen wall, cradling the telephone to her as if by holding the instrument she was holding him.

'You look as if you've had good news,' said Eveleigh as she bustled past, carrying a stack of stainless-steel feeding bowls.

'Oh, I have, I have.' And Kimberley followed her out to the kennels, and while they worked she told Eveleigh about the lunch and the house and the way he said 'we'. 'And he says he loves me,' she concluded.

'I'm so pleased for you.' Eveleigh smiled at the girl. Over the weeks, she had become fond of Kimberley. With no children of her own, and unsure how to deal with the young, she had worried whether they would get on. She need not have. Kimberley had responded to her kind concern for her, relaxing visibly, yet appearing to find it difficult to believe she was safe and cared for. Eveleigh never pried, but allowed Kimberley to tell her what she wanted her to know and when. She reminded Eveleigh of some rescued greyhounds who had virtually given up on ever finding kindness from man, and were acquiescent and stunned when they did.

'But do be careful, my dear,' she ventured.

'Of what?' Kimberley leant on the broom with which she had been sweeping out the kennel run.

'When you want very much to be loved it's possible to mistake other emotions for love,' Eveleigh said, hoping Kimberley would realise she spoke from concern for her.

Kimberley frowned. 'I thought of that, honestly, but I'm sure Alan's speaking the truth. He's so straight, he hasn't time for messing about, I'm certain.'

'Well, let's hope you're right. But forewarned is forearmed.' Eveleigh collected the last of the water bowls to soak and scrub clean.

'Can I use your phone when I've finished here – just a quick call?'

'I'm fully aware you *can* use the telephone, Kimberley. *May* you? Of course.'

Kimberley looked after Eveleigh as she walked back to the house and shrugged her shoulders, not understanding what she meant. When she had finished sweeping the kennels she called Nadine to tell her she and Alan would pick her up at seven thirty on Friday.

'I don't want to go bowling with *him*,' Nadine said. 'You said you'd come.'

'I'm sorry, but I didn't know.'

'Traitor! Well, just give me a lift. We'll meet up after.' Nadine thought Cracker Barrel would not mind her appearing with another girl, but another man might anger him. She couldn't take the risk.

*

On Friday evening in the back of the car Nadine could barely control her excitement, but she was infuriatingly mysterious. Kimberley, concerned for her, warned her how dangerous Morristown could be, especially at night.

'Don't fuss. You sound like my mother. Don't forget I'm used to London, this dump's nothing compared to that.' They dropped her outside the bowling alley and she waved them off as if impatient to see them gone.

'What's all the mystery?' Alan asked as they drew away. 'Drugs?'

'I don't think so. I think it might be something to do with animals.'

'Animals?' Alan crashed the gears with a grating noise.

'She's potty about them. She got expelled for demonstrating about the export of live calves. She was on TV,' Kimberley said proudly. 'I think she might be meeting up with some group of –' She waved her fingers in the air, searching for the words. 'You know, what are they called?'

'Animal rights activists?'

'Yes, that's it! Bit of a mouthful, isn't it?'

'Do you know which one?'

'No idea. Heavens, I'm not even sure that's what she's doing. Why are you so interested?' she asked warily. She realised she was jealous – a new emotion, something she'd never felt before. That must mean she was in love. She smiled in the darkness of the car.

'I hope she wasn't carrying a bomb!' he joked, sidestepping her question, telling himself he must be more cautious. 'Curry do you?' He pulled up outside an Indian restaurant.

'Alan, you needn't keep spending money on me like this.'

'I like to.' He put his hand on the nape of her neck as he spoke, and she forgot all about Nadine and what she might be up to.

They waited a good fifteen minutes in the car outside the bowling alley, even though they'd arrived at ten on the dot as arranged. Not that they minded. They made good use of the time. A rapping on the window made them jump guiltily apart. It was Nadine, alone, and tense with anticipation.

'Nice time?' Kimberley looked over her shoulder and saw Nadine's eyes glistening with excitement, and momentarily wondered if Alan had been right about the drugs.

'Sure thing. I won.'

'You went bowling?' Alan asked.

'That's what one normally does at a bowling alley,' Nadine said sarcastically. She disliked Alan, but had refrained from saying so to Kimberley, not yet, not while she needed help with transport. 'I met a friend.'

'From school?' Kimberley asked.

'Not likely!' Nadine snorted and lit a cigarette.

'I didn't know you smoked.'

'You don't know everything about me,' Nadine replied, adopting an air of mystery, but she couldn't keep it up and giggled instead. 'Oh, it's no good, I've got to tell someone or I'll burst. You swear not to tell a living soul?' She refused to continue until the others had agreed. 'This group's the real thing. We're going to raid a dog fight, beat the bastards up.' She flopped back on the car seat, a triumphant expression on her face.

'How? When?' Alan asked quickly.

'Next week, on Saturday.'

'Where?'

'I don't know. I expect they move the venue – a different place each time. Why are you so interested? You're not one of *them*, are you?' She was worried now.

'Don't be silly.' For Alan the realisation that, through Nadine, they might, after all this time, be about to crack down on the local dog fighting was almost too much to contain.

'Dog fighting's for sickos,' said Kimberley, aware that her palms were damp from sweat, her heart racing. Would her father be involved? Would Bandage be one of the dogs? She shivered, even though the heater was on.

'You cold?' Alan asked.

'No – I was thinking about the poor dogs.'

Alan pulled the car into a lay-by and stopped the engine. He swung round in his seat. 'Do you think this is wise, Nadine? It could be rough. You could get hurt.'

'I don't mind. I don't mind if I get killed, if we stop the cruelty.'

'That wouldn't do much good,' Alan said reasonably. 'What would your mother have to say?'

'Oh, don't you start! I had enough trouble back there with Cracker Barrel, he said I was too young as well. Creep. I told him what's what.'

'Cracker Barrel? What a name!' Kimberley laughed.

'We have to have aliases – the fuzz you know. I'm Ruskie – Nadine/Ruskie, get it?'

'Doesn't sound Russian to me. It's French, isn't it?' asked Kimberley.

'From the Russian, of course,' Nadine snapped back, sounding affronted.

'How many will be going?' Alan relentlessly continued.

'I don't know. I've only just joined this group of the FAA.'

'What's that when it's home?'

'Freedom for All Animals,' Alan volunteered. 'Isn't it?' He hurriedly asked.

'You seem to know an awful lot, Alan.' Nadine leant forward, her arms on the back of the seat in front.

'I read an article about the FAA in one of the Sundays.'

'You're not the only one loves animals, Alan does too, don't you, darling?' Kimberley said defensively, but felt awkward using the endearment. She never had before, and it was strange to hear herself say it, as if she were using a word from a foreign language. 'Why don't you leave it to the RSPCA to deal with? Phone them up and tell them, Nadine.'

'You must be joking! What good would that load of wankers do?'

'That's hardly fair,' Alan said as calmly as he could.

'They get bogged down with trying to placate all sides. They don't take a strong enough stance.'

'Don't go around trying to kill people, you mean. What about that scientist whose car was blown up last month?' Alan could feel his anger growing.

'He deserved it, the way he treated animals – vivisectionist creep!'

'So that humans could live,' Kimberley said quietly.

'Not if it means creatures suffer. In any case, there's no proof. Maybe the car just happened to catch fire.'

'Or pigs might fly.' Kimberley heard Alan mutter under his breath.

'If you feel like this, Nadine, then you must never take any medicines, in case they've been tested on animals,' Kimberley reasoned.

'I can't undo what's been done. I'm talking about the future – no more testing.'

'So it's all right to let kids die of cancer, that's fine by you, is it?'

'Why you being so horrible to me?' Nadine said sulkily.

'It's true what Alan's saying, and why have you got make-up on?'

'I only wear stuff not tested on animals.'

'How convenient. How do you think it was ever decided that such and such an ingredient was safe to slap on your face? Somewhere along the line it was tested,' Alan argued logically.

'Not recently.' Nadine was beginning to feel deflated. 'Whose side are you on? I thought Kimberley said you loved animals too?'

'I do, but, in my personal opinion, there has to be a balance. If controlled experiments on animals means a kid can live, we have to do it, with as much humanity as possible.'

'You're a barbarian!' Nadine's voice exploded with anger.

'I don't go round planting bombs under people's cars. Burn buildings down, putting other lives at risk.'

'No, you're too much of a wimp to do anything like that, aren't you?'

Alan opened his mouth to defend himself, but stopped just in time. 'Oh, what's the use!' he said instead, and restarted the engine.

'I wish you two wouldn't row,' Kimberley said quietly. 'I'd like us all to be friends.' In response there was a loud snort from the seat behind her.

40

Because Cora was away, it was over a week before Oliver could arrange a meeting with her. After much debate, he and Thomasine had decided it would be better if Eveleigh and Jim weren't present, that too many of them might appear intimidating.

Oliver shaved with particular care this morning, not because he was off to meet Cora, but rather because he'd be seeing Thomasine.

'That dog's piddled again,' Wimpole greeted him as he entered the kitchen.

'She's only a puppy.'

'Well, I'm not clearing it up and that's flat. I'm not a lavatory attendant,' Wimpole huffed.

'Have I ever asked you to?' Oliver commented patiently, and would have liked to add that since this was no longer her home it wasn't any of her business. And come to that why, now she was married, was she spending so much time here? Often, like this morning, she let herself in and was pottering about before he was up. Still, what was the point, he didn't want to hurt her feelings and make her feel unwanted. He went to the laundry room, Slipper padding along behind him, to collect a mop and a bucket of disinfected water. 'You get us both into trouble, Slipper. You've got to pull your socks up and get this peeing sorted out. Garden, girl, that's your loo.' The small dog sat on the floor and listened to Oliver, her head first on one side then the other. Oliver chucked her under her chin and the dog rolled onto its back, kicking its four legs in the air with joy. 'Old Bandage used to do that, you know.' His voice was tinged with the sadness he always felt when thinking of his lost pet.

'It's the first sign of madness, talking to yourself,' Wimpole said as he returned.

'I was not talking to myself. I was in conversation with my pooch.'

'Even madder.' Wimpole sniffed dismissively. 'You ought to rub her nose in it, give her a slap. That'll stop it.'

'It would do no good whatsoever. If you can't discipline a dog without hitting it, you shouldn't have it in the first place.'

'Discipline! My arse.'

'What's got in to you, Wimpole? You're in a real grump this morning. Anything wrong?' Oliver asked, not criticising but concerned. When Wimpole burst into tears he wasn't prepared for it. 'Oh, Wimpole love, sit down, do. Are you tired? You shouldn't bother coming here, you must have enough to do at your own house. I can manage. Oh, good God!' He looked panic-stricken as Wimpole's wails became louder. He'd never seen her cry, ever, and was at a total loss. He stood beside her chair pouring her tea, patting her shoulder, running his hand through his hair and generally flapping.

'I wish it was like what it used to be!' Wimpole eventually said through her sobs.

'Wish what was like what it used to be?' he repeated

inanely, and shook his head in bewilderment at his ungrammatical sentence.

'Like then. Not now.' Wimpole gulped for air.

'Aren't you happy, Wimpole?'

'Of course I'm not bloody happy. I wouldn't be wailing if I was, would I?'

'I suppose not. Is there anything I can do?'

'Not a lot. It's my own fault. As my mum used to say – you made your bed, now lie in it.'

'I've never understood what that means. I mean, if you make my bed, does that mean you have to lie on that one, or what?' he babbled from sheer embarrassment.

'Sometimes, Oliver, I think you're completely thick,' Wimpole said snappily, pushed her chair back and rushed from the room.

She's doing too much looking after me and Rudie, Oliver thought as he fetched the plate of scrambled eggs she had made him, sitting warm on the top of the Aga. He should have thought. He didn't know why she did, he hadn't asked her to. But the first morning back from her honeymoon she'd arrived long before he was up, and it had just sort of continued. She'd carried on as she had before the wedding, sorting him out generally. He'd been selfish not noticing how tired she must be with a husband to care and cook for. He must put a stop to it.

He jumped up at the sound of a knock on the back door and immediately kicked the bucket of sudsy water flying. 'Oh shit!' he exclaimed as the door was opened tentatively and Thomasine poked her head round.

'Morning,' she said, but immediately burst into laughter at the sight of Oliver standing in a spreading pool of water, the bottom of his trousers soaked and Slipper skidding around the puddles, rump waggling, wondering if this was some new game.

'Hi! Sorry!' He shrugged expressively, picked up the mop and began to limit the damage.

'I'll do that – you go and change,' she volunteered. When most of the water was back in its bucket she put the kettle on and cleared the table as she waited for it to boil.

'Can anything else go wrong?' Oliver said, grinning as he came back into the kitchen in dry trousers. 'What a start to the day! The dog peed, Wimpole bawled her eyes out, and I nearly drowned.'

'Wimpole? What's wrong?' she asked, as she set the teapot onto the pine table and got mugs from the dresser.

'She suddenly burst into tears and said she hated "now". All that had happened was the puppy had messed, and I cleared that up.'

'That doesn't sound like Wimpole.'

'We had a minor disagreement about house training dogs, that was all. Then I asked her if anything was wrong and hey presto – Niagara Falls had a competitor.'

'She's had a row with her husband.'

'No, it's more than that. I mean – she cried.'

'Women do.'

'Not Wimpole.' He was frowning as he spoke. He found he hated the idea of Thomasine crying.

'It must be one hell of an adjustment, getting married for the first time at her age. I've had it the other way around – sorting my life out after a divorce. It's hard. But then you know, don't you?' She looked at him enquiringly.

'No, I don't. If anything I can't remember when I was last so happy.' As he spoke he found he didn't like what her words implied. She must love her husband if she was finding it so hard to build a new life.

'You don't miss Sophia at all?'

'Missed my dog – never her. I suppose I didn't love her any more. You obviously loved your fellow, though.'

'Do you know, that's the odd thing. I thought I did, but now I'm sure I didn't. I was in love with what being with him meant – a family, security, my home. It took me time to realise, but I was grieving for a way of life, not for him.'

'Hell! You don't know how happy hearing that makes me. I thought you were still mooning over him.' He referred to Robert with loathing. Anybody, anything, which made Thomasine unhappy filled him full of hatred.

'You are sweet, Oliver.' She wished he would do something – take her hand, kiss her, not just say nice things and then not follow them up. She did not know where she stood with him and feared it was just his innate charm talking. 'I don't think I like Rudolph very much,' she said.

'Don't you? Why?' He wished she hadn't changed the subject. Whenever he plucked up the courage to let her know how he felt, she was off on another tack, like a startled doe.

'He looks a hard man to me, and he seems to have no sense of humour – and that's always a bad sign.'

'Like people not smoking or drinking. You find yourself wondering what their hidden vice is.'

She laughed. 'Yes, I suppose you do – but less with smoking these days. Have you given up yet?' She smiled at him.

'I thought I'd give it a whirl on Monday.'

'Oliver, it's always *Monday* with you.'

'It's a good day to start things.'

'Or not, as the case may be. Should we be going?'

'Yes, sure. I told Cora we'd be there around ten, so we've plenty of time. I'll just shut Slipper in the laundry room.'

'Will Ben be here?' Thomasine asked as they drew up outside the Lucketts' house.

'No. I asked Cora that. Quite intrigued, she is. Oh no!' he moaned as Sophia appeared at the front door.

'My, what a pleasant surprise. The two of you,' Sophia said pointedly as they approached her. 'Cora's all agog and so am I. Come in, do.'

'I've come to see Cora – privately, if you don't mind,'

Oliver said as Sophia showed them into the drawing room.

'Then Thomasine can join me for coffee and a chat.'

'No, Thomasine's with me.'

'How cosy for you both.' Sophia smiled – dangerously, Thomasine thought. 'I'll tell Cora you're here.' She left the door ajar.

'I don't think she likes me,' Thomasine whispered, for she had the uncomfortable feeling that Sophia might be listening at the other side of the door.

'She'd loathe any woman who happened to be with me,' he said in a louder than normal tone, easily heard beyond the room.

'Does she want you back?'

'God forbid,' he said with feeling. 'It's more a case of she doesn't want anyone else to have me. I mean, have you been going out with Jim Varley?'

'Me? No.'

'There you go – proves my point. Sophia told me you were.'

'Why on earth should she say I was with Jim?'

'To put the kybosh on me trying anything on with you.'

'You're joking!'

'Oh no, I never joke where Sophia's concerned.'

'But Jim's got Beth – you should have known that.'

'No, because he'd told me there was nothing going on there, that she was his housekeeper pure and simple.' Jim hadn't at all, but what the hell, thought Oliver, all's fair . . .

'Poor Beth. She loves him.'

'Does she? Good God, I don't think Jim knows that. Cora –' His face lit up with pleasure and he kissed his stepmother-in-law enthusiastically on the cheek.

The atmosphere in the room was not so pleasant five minutes later, after Oliver had explained why they were there.

'I can't believe you can accuse my Ben of having a dog

414

killed. He loves dogs, you know he does. How dare you come here, spreading lies like this,' Cora said angrily, jumping up from her chair as if she had sat on a bee and standing, tiny but belligerent, on the hearthrug.

'I didn't say he did. You're not listening to me, Cora. I think it was a case of someone acting a little too enthusiastically.'

'It amounts to the same thing.'

'Hardly. Look, all I want you to do is to ask him to lay off Eveleigh and her dogs.'

'Why can't she move?'

'Why should she?'

'It would save a lot of hassle if she did.'

'Why can't Ben buy land elsewhere?'

'Land's not that easy to get around here, as well you know.'

'Tell him I'll buy it off him.'

'With planning permission?'

'Don't be daft, Cora. It would be worth a fortune with planning permission – if he gets it, which I seriously doubt. No, tell him I'll pay him what he paid plus all his legal expenses up to date. I can't do fairer than that.'

'Yes you can. You can mind your own sodding business.'

'Cora, love!'

'Don't Cora love me. Ben's my husband and I stand by him whatever he decides to do. And I don't go behind his back on anything. You might be a sneak, Oliver, but I'm not. I'm shocked by you. I never thought you were a devious bastard, but you are, just like the rest.'

'Cora, please. I don't want to fall out with you.'

'Then you should have thought this out. I'd be obliged if you left now. And preferably never came back – and that goes for you too, Thomasine. Even if you haven't said anything, you're obviously in cahoots.'

'Right, if that's how you want it to be, Cora. But you won't win, I'll promise you that.' And so saying, Oliver walked quickly across the room and Thomasine hurriedly followed him.

'Thanks for the coffee,' she said to Cora as she went, and decided that was about the silliest contribution she could have made.

As they crossed the hall they were greeted by a slow handclap from Sophia, sitting on the stairs.

'Well done, Oliver. Not quite the little diplomat you thought you were, are you?' They both chose to ignore her.

'Wow! That was tough,' said Thomasine, settling into Oliver's car.

'Not quite what we expected.'

'Bully for her though, he is her husband. Loyalty is important.'

'Even when he's wrong?'

'Probably even more so when he is,' she said sagely.

They drove along in silence for a while, both wondering what to do now for Eveleigh and her dogs.

'Now what do we do?' Oliver eventually said. 'I don't really fancy the tabloids.'

'Couldn't you talk to Ben?'

'I thought of that ages ago, but Business Ben is a totally different kettle of fish from Friend Ben. I doubt if he'd listen.'

'Not even to your generous offer?'

'Not coming from me. He might have done if it had been Cora.'

'I'd hoped to keep this from Nadine, my daughter. But if we went to the papers she'd learn about it from them. She'll end up picketing Ben somehow or other. She's heavily into animal causes. She even got expelled because of them.'

'Doing what?'

'Demonstrating. I'm not sure, but I think she's in with those FAA people.'

'I hope not, they're a load of loonies.'

416

'I can't be sure, but I was cleaning her room and found some literature of theirs.'

'Then I should try and wean her off them, if I were you. They're subversive and violent.' She shivered at his words. 'They are, no doubt, watched by the police – who have probably got huge files on them all. It could make life difficult for her when she grows up.'

'I don't think that's reason enough to ask her to stop. You can't talk to the young on those terms. She believes passionately in any animal group's causes; fear of the law and the future won't stop her.' She sighed deeply.

They lapsed into silence again as Oliver negotiated the narrow country lanes.

'How about getting her involved in the legitimate side of animal welfare?'

'How?'

'Talk to Eveleigh. Get her interested in that side of the dog world. Start showing your dog – get her to do the showing.'

'Nadine! You don't know her. She thinks all pet ownership should be banned. She thinks it's demeaning to the animals. She probably regards Crufts with as much loathing as a feminist regards the Miss World Competition.'

'Lord, you have got a problem then. Is it my imagination, or wasn't life a hell of a lot simpler once?'

'Much. And especially for parents.'

'Thank God I never was one,' he said with feeling.

With Jim definitely out of the picture, and Thomasine's explanations of her feelings for her ex-husband, Oliver felt free to ask Thomasine out to dinner that evening.

They drove to a quiet restaurant in Morristown, where they enjoyed a good meal. On the way back Oliver suggested they stop at his house for a coffee and brandy. Thomasine, who had left a sulking Nadine at home and Nova playing with Slipper at Oliver's, readily agreed.

One brandy became two as they explained themselves to each other. A kiss was the natural progression, and then another. Both of them, having lived without sex for so long, had mistakenly told themselves it was not necessary for them, that they could live without it – which they could, until those kisses released the pent-up feelings, freed the need lying fallow in both of them.

Oliver's mouth on her nipple shocked her body into remembered anticipation. Both of them felt they would explode from the frustrations that neither, until now, had been aware of. Frantically they tore at each other's clothes, desperate for the touch of skin on skin, for him to be inside her.

Their passion accelerated with a speed that over-whelmed them. As he began to enter her, she paused for a second and thought 'This is unwise', but need over-came reason in a millisecond and their bodies joined with abandon. As they came they both called out their love for each other.

They flopped back on the rug in front of the fire, exhausted, covered in their mingled sweat, and looked at each other with amazed expressions.

'I meant it. I love you,' he said, as he traced the outline of her mouth with a finger that smelt of her.

'I love you too,' she said softly, those words she'd never thought she'd say again.

Saying the words made them want each other again. To hold, to feel, to kiss, to explore. Quietly, sensuously this time, they made love. Joyous, languorous giving of love. And, this time, unbeknown to both of them, Oliver's heartfelt relief that he'd never been a parent had already come to an end.

December

41

Jim slept at Eveleigh's for almost two weeks. After the first, it was apparent that his presence was not entirely necessary; not a peep had been heard at night, apart from the odd prowling fox and startled rabbit. But he stayed on because he was enjoying himself, for Eveleigh was good company. Until he arrived at Oakleigh Kennels he had not been aware of how tired he was, or how tense. The stress of living with Beth, the consequences of his wrongdoing, were far greater than he had realised.

The evenings spent with Eveleigh were some of the most contented he'd enjoyed in ages. They had far more in common than either of them had known before. They both liked George Shearing and early Stan Kenton music. Together they did *The Times* crossword puzzle. Both were avid Dick Francis readers. They liked plain, wholesome food, especially steamed puddings with custard, were partial to a malt, and would rather have claret than burgundy. Neither could imagine living in a city, and would prefer to be dead than do so. And, above all, they had their passion for animals, especially dogs.

'We're like a couple of old slippers, aren't we?' said Jim one night, stretching comfortably in an easy chair in front of the large fire, which they were sharing tonight with Brünnhilde.

'Who'd somehow got separated.'

'Then found each other again.'

'Exactly.' Eveleigh felt contentment too, having resigned herself to never finding it again.

At night, in the spare room, Jim found he was conscious of Eveleigh in hers, just along the corridor, and her close proximity sometimes made it difficult for him to sleep – but he'd learnt his lesson and did nothing. He valued his friendship with her far too much to risk it over sex.

Eveleigh, in her room, often could not sleep either, and found herself thinking of Jim and what he was like without his clothes on. Often she wished she could be brazen as Beth had been and go along to his room and climb into bed beside him. She cuddled whichever St Bernard was sharing her bed instead.

He could not stay here indefinitely. With no intruders, they began to wonder if perhaps they had overreacted. And Jim knew he could not keep up his resolve not to touch her if he stayed much longer. If he was to build a relationship with Eveleigh, he had to do it properly and court her as she deserved. He respected her too much for anything else.

As she saw him off on the last morning, Eveleigh stood at her kitchen window and wondered what was wrong with her. Why hadn't he made love to her?

As soon as he entered his house, Jim wished he hadn't been so honourable and was back at the kennels. The atmosphere was heavy with indignation, hurt, and ruffled feelings. Even Harry had stopped speaking to him. He scurried into his surgery to escape the oppressive atmosphere. Sitting at his desk, he wondered how long he would have to lurk in there away from the main house. It was then that it struck him what a ludicrous situation his lack of control had landed him in.

As he berated himself for a bastard, a voice inside him, small at first but rapidly growing, clamoured to be heard. This was unfair. It wasn't *all* his fault. Beth had started the whole catastrophic sexual adventure – his sin was his weakness. They were not married, nor had the subject ever been addressed, and yet Beth was behaving like a disgruntled wife. And it was his house, after all, that he was being made to feel uncomfortable in. And to add insult to injury, although he was still paying her wages, she had to all intents gone on strike; his laundry remained undone and the house was uncleaned.

He had to tell her to go!

Each morning he resolved that he would talk to Beth that evening, tell her she must find somewhere else to work, that she could remain here until she did. Such resolutions were easy to make, but by evening he could not do it and would hole up in his study pretending nothing was going on. Since she no longer cooked for him, he ate at the pub and in the morning made himself coffee with the kettle in the surgery. He didn't even have to use the kitchen door, but let himself in by the patients' entrance. He hadn't set foot in his kitchen for days.

If relations in the house were at an impasse, Jim and the new veterinary practice in Shillingham had shaken down into a mutually beneficial relationship, where Jim had to be on night call one week in three and every third weekend. For the first time in his professional life he could plan ahead. He could even accept invitations to dinner in the knowledge that he wouldn't be interrupted and have to go rushing out into the night. How pleasant it would have been if he and Ann had had such freedom! Such thinking got him nowhere, he told himself as he drove along the winding road towards the Walters' farm, where a cow with mastitis awaited him. And Ann, if she could have, would have told him to stop being a fool, to stop thinking about what might have been, and to get on with his life without her.

As he approached the entrance to the farm he realised he was back to his normal good spirits. Nowadays, as soon as he left the house he felt slightly happier, and the further away he drove the better he felt.

Chris Walters was waiting for him in his immaculate yard. Coming here was always a pleasure, not just because he liked Chris and his wife Fee, but because it was all so ordered, the creatures well cared for. It was a mixed farm, part animal, part arable – not so common these days, with large-scale farming the norm. Chris's farm had a few of everything. Jim often said it was a dry-land ark. They'd cattle and pigs, goats and chickens, ducks and geese, horses, ponies, dogs and cats, and Chris's latest venture, a herd of deer for venison.

Chris was not that type of farmer who, resenting Jim's fee, called the vet out too late. Chris called at the first sign of trouble, and so the cow's mastitis, caught early, was soon treated and the cow happily settled.

'Time for a drink?' Chris offered.

Jim looked doubtfully at his watch. 'I'm running late.'

'There's something Fee and I want to talk to you about. It might be serious.'

'In that case –' Jim followed Chris to the back door, where they slipped off their wellingtons, and stepped over a sleeping St Bernard blocking the passageway.

'It's something about St Bernards – they always have to obstruct your passage. Buttercup there is for ever sprawled across the doorway.'

'Protecting the pack, no doubt.'

'Really. You think so? Asleep!' Chris laughed as, in stockinged feet, they entered the chaotic, but welcoming, kitchen. Two golden retrievers sauntered over to inspect the visitor, but upon realising it was Jim, painful memories surfaced and they scurried quickly under the kitchen table and watched him with suspicious eyes, bodies taut and prepared for instant flight.

'It must be awful when you love dogs to have them run away from you,' Fee said as she put glasses and a bottle of whisky on the table for them.

'Not all dogs remember. Some have no recollection of me treating them at all and only react on the surgery doorstep.'

'But mine are the most intelligent dogs I've ever met,' Fee said proudly, and Jim smiled to himself. How many times had he heard that? 'How's Beth?'

'She's all right.' He realised he looked sheepish, as if his guilt was stamped on his face for all to see.

'I called her up the other day, she sounded a bit odd.'

'Did she?'

'Yes – I wanted some of her dried flowers and she was quite sharp with me.'

Jim could understand if Fee felt affronted, since it was she who'd found the job for Beth in the first place. 'It's her husband – he's out of prison and she's a bit windy about him finding her.' He congratulated himself at such a brilliant explanation.

'Beth? A husband? You're joking. Beth's never been married.'

'No? Are you sure?'

'Certain. I've known her since schooldays. My mum knows hers – she'd have said if there'd been a wedding.'

'I must have heard it wrong. So, what was it you wanted to tell me?' He had to change the subject, he felt so angry and so puzzled. Why should Beth have lied to him?

'You'd better tell him, Fee. It was you who heard it.'

'It's just a worry, Jim. We've got no proof – nothing like that. And this is strictly between us.' As Fee spoke she looked constantly at her husband, as if for encouragement. 'It's difficult. He's not the easiest of people.'

'Who isn't? Don't worry, I won't repeat anything said within these four walls.'

'Do you ever get called to the smallholding off Conniestown Lane? Primrose Acre, it's called.'

Jim thought a while before answering. 'No. I'm pretty sure I've never been there. They grow vegetables, don't they? Sometimes in summer you see a stall on the roadside with strawberries for sale.'

Jim sipped at the whisky Chris had handed him and wished they'd get on with it, he'd be late at Oliver's at this rate. 'What seems to be the problem?'

'On odd nights my dogs here have gone mad howling, and once in the daytime. They don't normally do that, they're very calm dogs, as you know. At first we thought it was a fox they could smell and we checked the chickens, but we've lost none. Then one night the dogs were down here howling and pacing and I was upstairs. I looked out of the window – and I noticed over at Primrose Acre – you can see it from the bedroom, it's too far away to see from the yard – well, I saw some cars parked, and that in itself is unusual. And when I opened the window I could hear men cheering and shouting. And in a lull, I don't think I imagined it, I'm sure I heard dogs growling and snarling.'

'Aren't you a bit far away to hear anything?'

'Fee's got ears like a bat. She hears my car when I'm still on the road. I admit when she called me I couldn't hear a bloody thing. But if Fee says she heard it, she did. And it would explain the weird behaviour of Romulus and Remus here.' He bent down and patted his retrievers who, evidently having decided that Jim hadn't come to see them, had inched forward on their bellies, tongues lolling, to be more part of the scene. 'Look at them, nosy buggers, can't bear to be left out of anything.'

'So, you think that there are organised dog fights going on over there?'

'I didn't say that, exactly, Jim,' Fee said quickly.

'No. But it's what you think?'

Miserably, Fee nodded her head.

'Would you mind if I mentioned this to the RSPCA?'

'Why Fee's so worried, Jim, about all this going further is, if she's right we want it stopped, who wouldn't? But if she's mistaken, what then? I wanted to go and look, but she begged me not to.'

'You don't know this man. He's evil. He'd kill you.'

Both men laughed at her concern. 'I mean it,' she said defiantly.

'We are both worried. If she's slandering him he could sue, and we can't afford that sort of hassle. Times are hard.'

'I understand, honestly,' Jim told Fee. 'I wouldn't even mention you by name to them. Just that someone had seen something suspicious and told me in passing. I've already had a visit from an inspector, asking if I've

426

treated any dogs wounded in fights or had any equipment stolen. This could be the lead they're waiting for.'

'In that case I think you should, don't you, Fee?' She agreed. She was smiling now that the responsibility was shifting to someone else.

'Is there a pattern to it?'

'We've racked our brains on that. Not really. But it's nearly always a Saturday.'

As soon as he was back in the surgery Jim dialled the number the young RSPCA inspector had left him, but there was no reply. He dickered with calling the usual number but decided against. Perhaps the young man was part of the Special Branch, and it was a case of the utmost secrecy with one section not knowing what the other was up to.

He bathed and changed and was coming down the stairs as Beth came up them.

'Jim, I think Castille's ill.'

'How ill?'

'I think she must be dying.'

Jim bounded down the remaining stairs two at a time. As he approached her basket, Castille looked up with the blank look of a dog in pain. As soon as she realised who it was, her tail thumped against the side of her basket; not her normal tattoo of welcome but a rather weary, half-hearted thump or two.

'What is it, my old love?' Jim bent down beside her and ran his hand along her flank, then felt her bloated stomach. Her normal breathing was interrupted by a sharp intake of breath as his fingers felt a distinct lump. He hardly needed the thermometer to tell her temperature was far too high. She panted from dehydration; her breath smelt foetid.

'How long has she been like this?'

'Only a couple of days.'

'She couldn't get like this in a couple of days. Has she been eating, drinking?'

'Not much.'

'And you didn't tell me?'

'You're hardly ever here. And in any case, you've not shown any interest in the dog. Don't blame me.'

He looked up at her from the dog, his hand still absentmindedly stroking her, calming her. 'You did this on purpose, didn't you? You're punishing me through the dog.' He spoke in a calm way, almost emotionless, as if the shock had destroyed all feeling. But this very calmness made him sound more frightening.

'Don't be silly. I thought she'd get better. She's been ill before.'

Jim ran through all the possibilities – there was only one. The dog had a growth in its groin large enough to feel, tight as a ball. He could relieve the fluid that had built up. He could give her antibiotics for the fever. He could give analgesics for the pain. But for what? The tumour would continue to grow, the pain increase, the dosages with it. Jim knew what he had to do.

He walked stony-faced into his surgery. As he prepared the syringe his fingers trembled and he dropped it twice before he was able to fill it.

He returned to his dog. Once again the head lifted, the tail weakly thumped. He'd done what he despised in others – he'd cruelly neglected his own dog. He'd been so involved with his own problems he hadn't noticed her deteriorating. Beth should have told him sooner, but it did not alter the fact he himself should have been aware of it.

'I'm sorry, Castille,' he said, his voice thick with emotion as he took her paw gently in his hand and searched for a vein. The dog did not even whimper as he inserted the needle, but licked his hand as if knowing he was helping her. He pushed the plunger slowly. 'I love you, Castille. I couldn't let you suffer. Forgive me . . .' As he spoke, the fluid seeped into the dog and painlessly she drifted away; his only consolation was the relaxed expression on the dog's face as death claimed her.

Jim remained some time kneeling in front of the dog. He wished Beth would go. He wanted to be alone with Castille. Wanted to cry, to mourn for her. He looked up.

'Oh, Jim. I'm sorry. I'd no idea.' Beth stood looking with horror at the dead dog.

He ignored her. 'Amtie,' he called the little King Charles who was cowering under the table, sensing the events unfolding in front of her. 'Come on, Amtie. You must say goodbye too.' He put out his hand to encourage her. Jim believed that dogs should be allowed to acknowledge the death of their companions and grieve too. The little dog padded over to Jim and stood as close to him as she could. He put his arm round her. 'See. Nothing to be scared of. Castille's at rest now.' And the little King Charles sniffed at Castille, looked at Jim, and then padded back to her basket.

Jim bent down and lifted Castille, heavy in death. Beth opened the door into the hall and then into the surgery.

'Are you going to bury her now?'

'No. I'll do that in the morning.' He laid the dog on a bench and covered her with her blanket from the basket, pushing the material round her as if to keep her warm. He stood, his head bowed. He'd fought the tears long enough; as they seeped from his eyes, he acknowledged grief had won.

'Are you staying in now?' He thought he detected the sound of hope in her voice.

'No, I'm going out.'

'To Eveleigh's?'

He didn't bother to reply, couldn't find the energy to question her over her phantom husband. He got his handkerchief out from his pocket and wiped at his eyes.

'Of course dear Eveleigh will understand, won't she? You can cry on her shoulder, can't you?'

'What on earth are you going on about?' said Jim wearily.

'Look at you. A grown man crying your eyes out. It's only a dog.'

He swung round and looked at her, his expression passing quickly from sadness to anger. 'How little you know, Beth, how little.' Beth looked away from him, aware she'd said too much and now he never would forgive her.

42

Jim did not speak of Castille's death at Oliver's dinner party: he doubted he could have talked about it without breaking down, and did not feel he had the right to lumber them with his sorrow. But he was very quiet, and once or twice Oliver and Thomasine exchanged puzzled glances. Eveleigh blamed herself for his silence, certain he was annoyed at being so obviously paired off with her and wondering if, now he was back with Beth, he regretted confiding such intimate details to her as he had, and was now drawing away from her. Eveleigh had, in the past, often found this was the outcome when secrets were shared.

Oliver and Thomasine tried their hardest to rescue the evening. The plan had been to discuss where and what to do next over Eveleigh's kennels. But looking at his guests' sombre faces, Oliver doubted if this evening was the best time to make plans – Jim and Eveleigh's hearts did not seem to be in it. Maybe he'd made a mistake, maybe he should have invited Beth too. It was a puzzle, one never knew where one was with people.

Thomasine was so full of happiness she felt she would burst if she could not let some of it bubble free. She was amazed and stunned at how she felt and wanted to tell everyone, wanted the world to know. So far she had told her dog and had hinted to her mother, but Di hadn't been listening, or else the hint was too subtle, for she had nattered on with no comment. Instinct had told her to be wary of telling Nadine, for her daughter, she knew, would have to be made privy to this information in gentle doses.

Still, she thought, Jim and Eveleigh would soon become aware of the way she and Oliver looked at each other, constantly touching each other. But they didn't. The evening creaked on with silences becoming more frequent and longer each time. She had hoped to discuss the animal movement that Nadine was involved in with Jim, to try and find out more, but decided that this evening was not the best time for that either.

Jim was drinking heavily, which puzzled them all. Oliver had opened a third bottle of wine with serious misgivings, and had virtually decided to forgo the port, but Thomasine, after she had put the Stilton on the table, missed Oliver's signals and placed the port decanter and glasses beside it. When Oliver mumbled that perhaps they'd had enough without the port, Jim, for the first time that evening, showed animation as he strongly disagreed with his host.

'He shouldn't drive,' Thomasine said half an hour later when, to everyone's consternation, Jim fell asleep sitting bolt upright at the table.

'I do hope he's not on call,' Eveleigh fretted.

'How about some strong coffee?' Oliver suggested. 'Do you know what's wrong, Eveleigh? He seems to have been a bit off colour for the past few weeks.'

'I've no idea,' she replied, in such a tight-lipped manner that Oliver was pretty certain she knew something.

It was finally decided that Eveleigh would drive Jim home and Oliver would return Jim's car in the morning. Thomasine was relieved at this; if Oliver had driven him back she would have found it necessary to leave too. They were too early into their relationship to assume he'd want her to stay.

Oliver helped a stumbling Jim into the car and they both waved his guests away into the night.

'Phew – what a sticky evening, wasn't it?' Oliver said with feeling as the tail lights disappeared around the curve in the drive, and he put his arm about Thomasine.

'Do you know what was wrong? Was it us?'

'Something with Jim, and something Eveleigh knew about, I think.'

'She's potty about him, of course.'

'Who?' Oliver stopped dead in his tracks from surprise.

'Eveleigh, of course,' she laughed at his astonished expression.

'Well, I never. Old Eveleigh!'

'She's not *that* old. And she's rather attractive in an understated way. She's got a fab figure. Don't tell me you've never noticed?'

'To be honest, I hadn't. She's always bundled up in tweeds and Barbours.' He grinned at her. 'Where're you going?'

'To clear the table and load the dishwasher.'

'No you're not. Grace'll be in in the morning. Come here.'

'What are you paying me for then?' she said archly, but her heart was racing with anticipation.

The cold air revived Jim dramatically. He sat up, rubbed his face with his hands, looked around and saw Eveleigh beside him. 'Oh shit! I'm sorry.'

'That's all right, Jim. We thought it best you didn't drive, the police might be about.'

'I don't know what got into me. What must Oliver and Thomasine think?'

'Probably that you're overworked and stressed,' she said kindly. The car lurched as Eveleigh swung it around a sharp bend. It was as if the jolt made Jim's memory, until now damped down by alcohol, return in a rush.

432

They were soon at Jim's, and Eveleigh carefully negotiated the gateway and stopped in the yard.

'Here you are, safe as houses,' she said, turning to him with a bright smile. 'Jim! Oh, Jim, what is it?' He was sitting rigid, facing front, staring with unseeing eyes out of the windscreen, tears gushing down his cheeks. 'Is there something I can do? Do you want to tell me?'

'It's Castille –' He stopped. Speech was hard, as if he had a rock in his throat.

'Your crossbreed? Has something happened? Is she ill? Is she –' At this Jim covered his face with his hands and a sob escaped, an anguished, ugly sound for he had tried to choke it back. 'Oh, Jim. My poor Jim.' She put her arm around him and pulled him towards her so that his head lay on her breast. She stroked his hair gently. 'I understand. Grieve, Jim. Let it out,' she said softly.

It was as if her permission released him, for now he cried in earnest with no attempt to control it. For minutes he cried as she held him close.

The tears subsided. He lay still a second and then sat up, pushing his hair back from his forehead, fumbling for his handkerchief, blowing his nose, dabbing his eyes.

'What must you think of me? I'm sorry. Blubbing like that, whatever next!' He tried to laugh.

'I grieve with you, Jim. There's nothing so hard as losing an old companion like that. And doubly hard for you if you had to –' She found she couldn't quite put into words 'destroy her'. Jim nodded bleakly. 'It's bad enough having to make the decision to call you to put one of my dogs to sleep, and still, every time it happens, no matter how ill the dog, I feel a murderess. I can't imagine how sad and guilty you must be feeling.'

'She'd had a good innings. She was fourteen.' He said this as if it could help, but it didn't.

'She was Ann's, wasn't she? So you've also lost a link with the past.'

'How did you understand that?' He looked at her with surprise.

433

'You forget Coco, my little King Charles – she was my husband's. I know he touched the furniture, sat on the chairs, but sometimes, when I stroke her, it's different. It's like, as my hands touch where he once touched, it's as if I can feel him.'

'Someone said to me "It's only a dog." That upset me more, somehow.'

'Only people who've never been loved by a dog can spout such rubbish. I've found that in some ways losing a dog is harder than losing a person. All that devotion, that undemanding love. I never cried when my mother died, but I mourned for months for a dog that died shortly afterwards. In some people's eyes that must make me a monster, I suppose. But I got more from my relationship with the dog than I ever got from my mother.' She patted his hand. 'Don't feel guilty about it, Jim. Grieve – it's a very real grief you are facing.'

Jim had never heard Eveleigh tell so much of herself. 'You're a friend in a million,' he said. 'Maybe Castille will be reincarnated as a nice person.'

'On no!' Eveleigh looked quite shocked. 'I've always thought the Buddhists got it seriously wrong presuming that the human form was the highest level of attainment. No, no. I think if a human lives a good life, then, with luck, they'll come back as a dog – far more suitable.'

Jim looked at her and saw she was smiling. He laughed a real laugh this time. 'Eveleigh, my darling, you're a tonic.' And he leant over and kissed her full on the mouth, and then opened the door quickly, leapt out and shot across the yard to the house so as not to see her face. The door slammed shut.

Eveleigh sat in the car for a moment, her fingers touching where his lips had been. Mixed emotions sped across her face; shock, disbelief and happiness succeeded one another in milli-seconds.

From an upstairs window, Beth, her face twisted with anger, watched.

When Alan returned to the office in Horsham he found a message from Jim. 'Ten-thirty, my place?' he read, and Jim's name; that was all. Such terseness and discretion must mean Jim had information so important he could not risk it over the phone. He set out immediately to drive to Middle Shilling.

'You do understand that the friend who told me about Primrose Acre has no proof?'

'You're not prepared to tell me who told you this?'

'I promised not to. You must understand, Tom White is an unpleasant character and many hereabouts are afraid of him.'

'White, you said?' Alan did not write the name down, since notebooks could get lost.

'You know him?'

'No,' he replied, but he wondered if Kimberley, with the same name, did.

'We'll look into it. Thanks, Mr Varley, for tipping us off.'

'It's not much, but it is the only thing I've heard.'

'Any lead, we're grateful.' He didn't like to ask Jim if he thought it was possible for a human to hear over that distance, even at night. He also refrained from pointing out that it was rare for a fight to be held on premises which were someone's home. Normally buildings used for fights were such that the owner could disassociate himself and claim he knew nothing – like very isolated barns or disused factories. Not someone's backyard. It seemed implausible, but on the other hand Nadine had been adamant a fight was to take place this coming Saturday . . .

After seeing him off, Jim reluctantly returned to the surgery and his waiting clients. His depression was worse this morning; he still had to bury Castille, he still hadn't seen Beth, and he had a murderous hangover.

Alan rang the doorbell of Eveleigh's house several

times, but no one answered. He walked around the side of the house with the diffident step of one who's not sure whether he should proceed further or not.

As he neared the back he heard the noise of chain link rattling, as if the dogs were hurling themselves at their fencing. He quickened his step, aware that he was hearing sounds of great agitation.

'Here you! Who are you?' he shouted loudly as, turning the corner into the yard, he saw a man huddled over the entrance to one of the kennels halfway along the building. The man looked up, grabbed the bag at his feet, and began to run. The dogs, hysterical by now, barked and growled and leapt, frustrated by the fence that prevented them reaching the intruder as he hurtled past them towards the open fields beyond.

Alan gave chase. The man had scrambled through the bushes which marked Eveleigh's boundary. When Alan reached it he leapt over. He was gaining ground easily: evidently the man was older and slower than him.

Alan was within an arm's length of grabbing him when his foot caught in a rabbit hole and he crashed face down, the wind forced out of him in an animal grunt. All he could do was lie there, fighting to catch his breath, as the intruder loped away across the field. As he got to his feet he heard a car door slam, a powerful engine start up, and saw a flash of a dark car, black or dark grey, he was not sure. But its make and number remained a mystery.

Gingerly, he tried his foot on the ground. It was sore, but no great damage had been done. He limped back across the field towards the kennels and arrived just as Eveleigh appeared, her expression anxious, alerted by the cacophony from her dogs. At the sight of him she looked warily to left and right and backed towards one of the kennels. 'Alan?' she said, puzzled, but with her hand resting on the bolt ready to spring Wotan, one of her largest dogs, if necessary.

'Mrs Brenton – please don't be afraid of me. I think I interrupted an intruder. At least, when I shouted, he scarpered. I don't even know why I yelled, there was something furtive about the way he moved that made me. And Kimberley had told me about your losing a dog.'

'Thank God you turned up, Alan.'

'I was in the area and I hoped you wouldn't mind me popping in on Kimberley.'

'Where was he? Which kennel?'

'This one.' Alan walked towards the middle of the run and stopped before one gate.

'That's Lo Lo. Oh my God.' From her pocket Eveleigh took a key and unlocked the padlock. 'I've had to put these on each kennel. Shocking!' Lohengrin jumped up in welcome, placing his front paws on her shoulders and enthusiastically licking her face. Alan stepped back smartly as the dog shook his head and a spray of slobber headed in his direction. Eveleigh pushed the dog down and opened his mouth, smelt his breath and ran her hands along his sides. 'He seems all right, but I'd better call Jim Varley.'

'Look at these.' Alan had tripped over a pair of wire-cutters which had fallen into the grass. 'I won't touch them, they could be evidence.'

'Then you think I should call the police? They were most unpleasant last time, and did bugger all. I've got to think. Leave the cutters for the moment. Can I offer you a coffee?' She began to walk back to the house.

'Hell! I've just thought. Do you think Kimberley is safe?' He began to quicken his pace.

'She'll be fine. One of my dogs has an ear infection, she's taken her to the vet's – I try to call him out as little as possible.' It would have been so easy this morning to call Jim in to see the dog. She'd wanted to, but sense had prevailed. After his outburst of grief last night it would be better if he chose when he came here, rather than be summoned by her and put in a difficult position.

'I've just come from there. I didn't see her.'

'That's odd.' Eveleigh looked even more worried as she unlocked the back door.

'This means I can never leave the kennels, not for a moment!' Eveleigh said as she put the kettle on the Rayburn. Angrily she spooned instant coffee into two mugs. 'I had to inspect the home of some people who want one of my puppies – see if it was suitable.'

'Do you always do that?'

'I've been caught out before. Years ago I sold a dog to a couple who claimed they'd got two acres. It transpired they lived in a flat in a high-rise – I ask you! Of course the dog was impossible, poor dear, cooped up and knocking things over – St Bernards need a lot of sea room. So they brought it back. Since then, whenever possible, I check them out. You can't be too sure.' The kettle boiled and she added water to the mugs and was fussing about with milk and sugar when the door opened.

'Alan! What are you doing here?' Kimberley looked anxiously at her employer, unsure how she'd react to boyfriends calling in the middle of the day.

'He saved yet another dog, my dear. Thank goodness he came when he did. Coffee?' She collected a mug as she filled Kimberley in on the latest events.

'How can people be so cruel?'

'That's not all. On my way back from inspecting the new people – they're fine by the way, Kimberley, the puppy will be safe with them – I met a friend of mine – Fee Walters, they farm over near Conniestown. She told me she's almost certain that dog fights take place near her, she feels certain there's to be another on Saturday. I wish I'd a machine gun, I'd go myself and kill the bastards.'

'Saturday?' Kimberley felt her stomach clench and her pulse race.

'I must phone Jim.' Eveleigh crossed the kitchen to the telephone. Alan took the opportunity to search for Kimberley's hand and squeeze it.

'I have to go,' he whispered so as not to disturb Eveleigh. His heart had lurched at her casual mention of the dog fight. So now he knew who was involved. He'd have to get back to the office, talk to his boss. Information was coming in too thick and fast to be ignored. He prayed this Fee woman didn't blab to many more people.

'See you tonight?' Kimberley whispered back.

Alan looked at his watch. If he drove like a bat out of hell he could see Don and still make it back. Hopefully he'd be put on the assignment, and then he wouldn't have to rush back and forth.

'Sure thing. What do you fancy, cinema? Hamburger?'

'Nice pub, I want to talk.' She wondered what had made her say that. He'd think it odd.

43

'I didn't come to live with you to be neglected like this,' Nadine said sulkily as she buttered some toast for an extraordinarily late breakfast. Thomasine was wiping Nova clean. They had been for an early morning walk and it had rained so hard in the night that Nova's underside was soaked from the grass and her paws were muddy. Thomasine rubbed the dog vigorously with a towel. As Nadine spoke she concentrated harder on the dog and chose to ignore her daughter, or rather to try to, for from past experience she knew the girl was trying to wind her up.

'Look at you. What a mess,' Thomasine talked to the dog as she fussed over her, obviously to Nova's satisfaction for every time she stopped rubbing, the dog headbutted her arm to start again. 'You'd never win at Crufts looking like this, would you?' She bent down and kissed the wide, flat top of the bulldog's skull.

'You think more of that dog than you do of me.' Nadine's lower lip protruded in a petulant pout.

'Don't be silly.' Thomasine still did not look up.

'I'm not. You are. Just listen to you – it's gross. To get your attention I'd have to turn into a flaming bulldog, wouldn't I?' Nadine pushed her chair back, its legs grating noisily on the quarry-tiled floor.

'No, that won't be necessary.' Thomasine laughed as she finally looked at her daughter, but judging by her sour expression the joke was completely lost on her. She stood up. 'What's the matter, Nadine? I can't believe you're jealous of a dog. That's ridiculous.'

'Is it? You're never here with me, but you take her with you everywhere. You talk to her and you never talk to me.'

'That's not true. I spent hours with you yesterday talking about your school work and your options. What else do you expect of me?'

'You just think of yourself. You don't worry about me – if you did you wouldn't be out until all hours, leaving me alone here.'

'For God's sake, Nadine, at your age! I didn't think you still needed a babysitter.'

'I get lonely. I need company too. If I had a car I could get out and about, meet my friends.'

'How often do I have to tell you I can't afford to buy you a car? It's all a struggle at the moment.'

'Ask Dad to help.'

'No.' Thomasine swung round, away from her.

'Why not?'

'Because I don't want to.'

'So I have to suffer because of your pride?'

'Look, Nadine, can't we talk this through like two sensible adults? What's the problem? Tell me and I'll see if I can do something. Come on.' Thomasine sat down at the table and took hold of her daughter's hand. Nadine looked fixedly at the table and said nothing. 'Please, Nadine. Talk to me. I don't want to go on with this endless carping.'

'No one loves me!' Nadine burst out, and began to cry.

'That's not true. I love you, so does your father – whatever you think.'

'No you don't. No one does. I've no friends.'

'There's that nice girl Kimberley. You said you liked her.'

'She's got a boyfriend. She's got no time for me any more.' She continued to sob.

'You'll meet someone, one day.'

'No I won't. How can I, living in a dump like this?' Nadine snapped back, the tears immediately stopped. 'It's all right for you to talk. You've got a bloke to screw you.'

Thomasine gasped. Her hand seemed to take on a life of its own. It flashed across the table and slapped Nadine across the face.

'How dare you hit me!' Nadine had jumped to her feet, holding her reddening cheek.

'I'm sorry, I shouldn't have done that.'

'Too right you shouldn't.'

In the basket Nova sat shivering from head to toe. Her large eyes watched the two women with an expression almost of terror. She panted noisily. Thomasine squatted down and scooped the dog into her arms, making soothing, mewing noises, holding her tightly.

'See. What have I said all along? It's the dog, not me.'

'Is it any wonder? She just wants to love me, she asks for nothing in return. It's simple, this love, uncomplicated, undemanding.'

'Oh, stuff you and that thing.' Nadine banged noisily out of the kitchen.

Nova began to lick Thomasine's face gently with her long, pink tongue. She buried her face in the soft, furry ruff at the dog's neck and allowed herself to cry.

All day Kimberley had been preoccupied. She kept forgetting things and dropping things. Worst of all, she failed to shut one of the kennel gates properly and allowed Wotan to escape. It took her ages to persuade the great brute to go back into his kennel.

'What is the matter?' Eveleigh finally asked her.

'Nothing. Honest. That intruder upset me.' She hoped this would placate her boss.

'Understandable. And all those questions from the police – such suspicious people. But let's hope they can trace where those wire-cutters came from and who bought them.'

'Probably Texas Homecare, and we'll never know.'

'We've got to hope, Kimberley.'

'Has Alan phoned?' she asked, in a tone which, she hoped, implied only minor interest.

'Yes. He went to the police direct and left them with a sketchy description of the man. He seems a nice young man.' Her smile was a small, sly one as she glanced at her kennel maid.

'Yes.' Kimberley blushed. She felt tongue-tied. 'There's just one thing –' She paused. 'Alan invited me out tonight, but I won't go if you're frightened to be left alone.'

'Me, frightened? Good gracious, no. I've dug out my husband's old shotgun – just in case. I've also decided that I'm going to bring all the dogs into the house, to be on the safe side.'

'All of them?' Kimberley looked aghast.

'Yes. It'll be a bit of a squash, but at least we'll get some sleep.'

The rest of the day dragged by for Kimberley. She longed to see Alan again, for when she was with him she could forget the worry that was gnawing at her. The talk of dog fights made her concern for Bandage increase. She hated herself for her futile indecision so far. She wondered endlessly whether she should confide in Alan and tell him everything – about the fights, the puppy farm. How wonderful it would be to unburden herself.

442

She tried to imagine how it would feel to be rid of the guilt which she seemed doomed to cart about with her.

But what could Alan do? Wouldn't she be lumbering him with her problems, and was that fair?

She tucked her new white shirt into the waistband of her equally new black skirt and studied herself in the mirror. She worried whether her legs were good enough for such a short skirt, at the same time wishing she'd had enough money to buy herself new shoes. Was it her imagination or did she look different, more assured? Was she standing straighter, prouder, or was it simply that, unused as she was to wearing skirts, of course she looked different. She pinched her cheeks to give them more colour – she hadn't any blusher. Perhaps she would confide in him after all. She couldn't go on like this, not sleeping, always this gnawing guilt. Yes, she'd already told him she wanted to talk to him; perhaps subconsciously she had been preparing the way.

'Love your legs!' Alan said the minute he saw her in the skirt. 'Sexy.'

They did not go to the pub. Instead they went to the new house.

'But it isn't yours yet.' She looked about her nervously.

'Soon will be, so does it matter if we jump the gun by a week or so?'

'How are we going to get in?'

'There's a broken pane of glass in the back door. I noticed it when we came before. Here, take this.' From the boot of his car he took two tartan rugs which he handed her. Then he delved back and came up with two Tesco carrier bags. 'Supper,' he explained.

The second carrier bag contained paper, wood and firelighters, not food. Kimberley stood clutching her coat tightly about her.

'Don't want you catching cold,' he said as he laid a fire in the small sitting-room grate. He put a match to it and was rewarded by a belch of acrid smoke. He flapped his hands in front of his face ineffectually.

'Here. Let me.' Kimberley took a piece of newspaper, scrunched it into a ball, lit it and stuffed it up the chimney.

'It'll catch fire.' He tried to stop her.

'No, it'll warm the chimney. It's cold, that's why it's smoking. See? That's better, isn't it?'

He'd thought of everything, even remembered the corkscrew for the wine, which they drank from paper cups. There was a knife to cut the quiche, and paper napkins to wipe their fingers, and candles to see each other.

'Strawberries? At this time of year. You're mad!' She pushed him affectionately.

'Only the best for you.'

'This is the most romantic night of my life,' she said, sighing with contentment, settling into his arms as they lay down on the rug he'd laid on the dusty floor.

As he began to make love to her, she discovered just how wonderful, how tender, how complete making real love could be. And she understood that when 'in love', lust changed, became a wondrous, tender thing. She was learning how wonderful it was to give as well as to receive. When Alan was inside her and she felt his weight upon her she wished it would never end. It made her feel lost when it did, and she felt such an intense loneliness that she had to fight hard not to cry and it puzzled her how, in the midst of such happiness, she could feel so sad.

'So, you wanted to talk. What about?' He was propped upon one elbow looking down at her, stroking the soft skin of her breasts.

'No. What gave you that idea?'

'You did.'

'Can't think what I meant.' She didn't want to lie to him and felt a twinge of guilt, but it was only the smallest of lies. She did not want the outside world with all its pain and nastiness to spoil this time with each other. She'd tell him another time, she promised herself.

But her wish was not to be granted. 'Have you seen anything of Nadine?' he asked.

'No. She phoned asking to see me tonight, but I said no. I felt bad about it since I think she was crying.'

'She struck me as too tough a nut for that. Odd, wasn't it? Two lots talking about a dog fight in such a short space of time.'

'I suppose so,' she said, reluctant for this line of conversation to continue.

'If you see her and she says anything, you'll let me know, won't you?'

'Why?' She sat up, clutching the rug around her. 'You interested in dog fights?'

'Might be,' he said nonchalantly.

'I'd hate that.'

'Then I'm not interested.' He grinned at her.

'I'm glad.' She settled back into the crook of his arm, but the mood had changed, she felt worried again. Restless.

'I suppose we should be going soon,' she heard him say.

'Would you do me a favour?' she asked abruptly. Knowing suddenly what she must do. 'I've got to pick something up and it's miles out in the sticks.'

'Sure. But isn't it a bit late? It's gone midnight.'

'No. They'll still be up,' she said vaguely.

As they approached Primrose Acre, Alan felt there was something familiar about the lane they were in. He couldn't be sure, but he thought he was close to where Vic had stood in a gateway the night he had followed him. Still, these lanes all looked the same in the dark.

'Where the hell are we? Is this near Conniestown?'

'It's miles over that way,' she answered quickly. 'Can you stop here?'

'But there's nothing here.'

'This is it.' As the car came to a halt she already had the door open. 'Wait here.'

'I'll come with you.'

'No, please. It wouldn't be a good idea. These people, they wouldn't approve. They wouldn't like the idea of me with a boyfriend.'

'Who?'

'Just people. I won't be long.' And she'd gone, and though he peered through the window he could not see her. He settled down to wait, a niggling worry at the back of his mind that something wasn't right.

It was as well she didn't have new shoes on, she thought, as she ran across the ploughed field that ran beside the rutted driveway. She stumbled several times and forced herself to slow down, otherwise she might fall and hurt herself and then she risked being found. There were no lights in the house, but she hadn't expected any.

At the yard, she tiptoed across the cobbles. She was hoping that the dogs, since they knew her, would not bark. So when a deep growling began, rising by the second towards a bark, she nearly jumped out of her skin.

'Shush, it's me. Don't be silly,' she whispered as she opened the shed door, but to no avail. The dog continued, but what was worse, the others joined in, making an unholy chorus. 'Bandage. It's me. I've come to get you.' She felt her way across the shed to Bandage's bed. She put her hand out to calm the growling creature. There was a noise like a trap shutting sharply, and Kimberley yelped with pain as the dog's teeth closed on her outstretched hand. Her yell made the dog release her. She put her hand between her legs, whistling with the pain. She couldn't believe that Bandage would do that to her.

Across the shed she found the bench where her father kept the dog bowls, and where she knew there should be a torch. She switched it on and swung the beam, and where Bandage should be she saw a strange dog, hackles up, his mouth in the rictus of a snarl, his teeth flashing ominously in the light. She walked down the other side of the barn checking each pen as she went. The two pit bulls she knew were barking noisily. There was another new dog, a Rottweiler, she thought. In the last pen, his back to her, standing in the corner, was Bandage, his head down, his shoulders hunched with dejection. Poor Bandage, she should not have delayed. She should have come for him weeks ago.

'What the fuck's going on!' The barn door banged open. Just in time, Kimberley threw herself down on the filthy floor and cowered behind a large sack of feed. As she dived she had the presence of mind to click the torch off.

'Stop that fucking racket, you filthy sods.' She heard her father kick the wooden partition, but the barking continued. Then she heard a sickening thud and the scream of a wounded animal. 'Shut your bloody mouths. Understood?' her father bellowed at the dogs, and from the ensuing silence she could imagine the dogs cowering with terror as she once had, as her mother still did.

She longed to have the courage to jump out and hit him herself, but reason prevailed. It wasn't until she heard the door slam again that she realised she had been holding her breath from sheer terror.

She stayed where she was for a good five minutes. She listened to the agitation of the dogs, willed them to calm down. She peered around the sack, and gingerly put on the torch. On the sack was a length of rope. She grabbed it, opened the barricade into Bandage's pen and before he had time to react, had the rope around his neck and was pulling it hard.

She had moved so swiftly, so silently, the other dogs had not recovered their senses. But now they had, and the barking and growling began again. Bandage wouldn't budge. She pulled, she pushed, but he stood in his despondent position as if he did not hear her.

'Forgive me, Bandage, it's the only way,' she said, and kicked him hard in the rump and then he moved, jerking her out of the barn, across the yard, into the field. She flopped down on the earth behind the hedge – just in time, as the kitchen door opened and, through the vegatation, she could see the silhouette of her father against the light. This time he had his gun in his hand. She pulled Bandage to her, hugging him tight, whispering words to him, praying he wouldn't bark too.

She waited, crouched in the field, until her father had entered the barn again. Then she was on her feet, urging Bandage forward. She wanted to run as fast as she could back to the safety of the car before her father pursued her, but Bandage was limping and their progress was slow.

'Where the hell have you been? I was worried sick,' Alan said as she stumbled up to the car.

She opened the back door and with difficulty man-handled the heavy dog into the car and leapt in beside it. Alan swung round in the seat. 'What on earth – ? What the hell have you got there?'

'Drive, for Christ's sake, drive!'

From the side window she could see a light bobbing across the field towards them, she could hear her father shouting. 'Go! Go!' She banged the back of the seat with a clenched fist.

Alan, seeing the light himself, put the car into gear and they lurched forward. He drove in silence for a few minutes, and then, checking there was nothing behind him, pulled into a lay-by.

'What's going on, Kimberley? Who does the dog belong to?'

'Me,' she lied.

'But . . .'

'Please,' she begged him. 'Get me home.'

He drove, not knowing what to say. His mind was in a

turmoil. It was a bull terrier in the back. It had wounds –
healed, but fighting wounds, he was sure. A moment
later he stopped at the crossroads, saw the sign to
Conniestown, and knew that was where Vic had lurked
that night. Was that Primrose Acre? And if so, what was
Kimberley's connection with it? It was her dog, she'd
said. Did that mean she was involved? His hands held
the wheel tight.

He pulled up outside the kennels, and turned round to
see Kimberley, her arms about the dog, crying.

'Kim,' he said. 'Talk to me.'

'I can't.'

'Is it really your dog?'

'No. I lied. I was frightened you might make me take it
back. I rescued it.'

Relief flowed through him as if his veins were full of
molasses. 'Oh, Kimberley, I love you. You don't know
how happy you've just made me.' And Kimberley
looked at him, puzzled, not understanding his reaction
one little bit.

44

Jim stopped his car on the hill behind the Shillings,
climbed out and looked down at the villages still asleep
beneath him. The houses were covered in a soft mist, as if
in the night a cloud of chiffon had floated down and
buried them. Only the roofs of the taller houses protruded, and here and there was the smoke from the
newly-lit fires of the early risers. It was cold, but the air
was sharp, not damp, and he looked up at the sky in the
juvenile hope that snow might be threatening, but saw
the sun breaking through. Jim leaned against the warm
bonnet of his Land Rover, lit a cigarette, and waited for
the village to wake from its night-time slumber.

Below him the mist peeled back, as if the villages were sloughing off a skin. The sun shone – it was going to be a wonderful day, one of those rare bonus days that winter occasionally presented. Ann would have loved a day like this.

As the thought entered his mind, he was already steeling himself for the sense of loss and longing which always followed. Only it didn't. He gingerly tried again; imagined Ann, on her horse, as he'd seen her that day . . . He smiled to himself. He was thinking about Ann as he did about his father, his mother, his best friend killed in a car crash. 'Have you gone?' he said aloud to her spirit, and there was no reply. He waited for sadness and felt only a strange, calm happiness. 'Of course,' he said, as if he finally understood something.

He'd made a decision, he hoped wisely.

Bandage had lain all night, his head resting on his paws, his eyes wide open, alert to every sound, to any danger, in a miasma of scent – dog and bitch scent which overpowered everything else. When morning came, he stood. He walked the confines of the strange kennel he was in, sniffing at the smell of dog. Several times he inspected the perimeter, his nose snuffling, smelling. He stopped abruptly. He lifted his snout and stood rigid, his nostrils moving slowly like a miniature bellows. He ran to the end of the kennel, pounded up the length and, straining the muscles of his hind quarters, sprang powerfully up and soared over the wire mesh. He landed heavily the other side and lay quiet a moment. Then, his breath regained, he was running, his snout close to the ground, across the yard, along the side of the house, out into the lane, his concentration total.

Thomasine had been up since five. She doubted if she had had more than a couple of hours' sleep, and then it had been fitful slumber – tossing and turning, jolting awake several times, with her heart racing and an awful feeling of premonition.

She had finally given up trying and got up. Nova had not appreciated her rising so early and had looked at her resentfully before burrowing under the duvet and settling down for an uninterrupted snooze.

Maybe Nadine was right about the dog, perhaps she was being stupid about her, treating her, she supposed, rather like a child. But then, it was something she could not seem to help. She loved the dog with an intensity which had surprised her. She had fallen for Luna, but nothing could have prepared her for the way she now felt about Nova.

She sat at the kitchen table, a mug of tea in front of her, and felt depression pressing in on her from all sides. She thought she'd been fortunate and had found a new happiness with Oliver. But it was a happiness which could not be, not with Nadine as angry as she was. If she stayed with Oliver and kept the dog, her daughter's misery and sense of isolation would only increase. But if she gave Oliver up and sold Nova, then her own unhappiness would be incalculable.

She heard a familiar thumping noise – Nova negotiating the stairs. Nova did not walk down stairs like a sane dog, but instead slid down them by placing her front legs on the tread and letting the rest of her slide down behind her – quite terrifying when she'd first seen her do it, but she was used to it by now.

She let the dog out for a pee. She bent down to pick up her water bowl to refill it and found herself clutching the sink as a wave of dizziness hit her, followed sharply by a need to rush to the loo. She wasn't sick, she just felt it. She sat on the lavatory lid waiting for the feeling to subside. How odd. She was never ill. Perhaps it was stress, worrying about Nadine. Or perhaps it was the chicken that she'd only half eaten last night. That was probably it, she decided, and immediately felt better for finding a solution. She sluiced her face with cold water and felt better still.

By the time she returned to the kitchen, Nova was hurling herself at the back door to be let in. When the door opened she strutted in, angry discontent at being kept waiting in every movement. 'You're a tyrant, Nova.' Thomasine bent and patted the creature which had so quickly and cleverly dominated her. 'Biscuits?'

The dog settled with her breakfast, Thomasine made herself another mug of tea and realised that it was her fourth so far that morning. Still, she supposed it would do her less harm than coffee. She resumed her seat at the kitchen table and went back to fretting over what was best for her to do. She had to resolve something, that was for sure. Then with a jolt she sat upright. *She* had to resolve it. Why her? Why did it always have to be Thomasine who resolved things?

How many times in her life had she apologised when she hadn't been in the wrong? How often had she cooked one meal when she would have preferred another? How often had she done things she wasn't interested in, gone to places she didn't want to visit, just to keep the peace? How many times had she backed down for others?

She had never been allowed to be herself: first there was her domineering mother, then her selfish husband, now her tyrant daughter – at that she managed to smile – and tyrant dog. Why was she so weak? That was it, she'd conned herself over the years to believe that her acquiescence was a form of strength, when all along it had been a weakness.

It hadn't mattered so much before, and she hadn't needed to analyse it because she'd believed she was happy doing it. Now she had touched real happiness, and she was supposed to let it slip because her daughter wanted all her attention. For how long? One more year, and she'd see her only when it suited Nadine to come home from university, or whatever she was going to do.

Years of aloneness stretched ahead if she allowed Nadine to have her way.

She knew now why Nadine was so anti the dog and Oliver – she didn't want Thomasine dissipating her energies on anyone or anything else. Probably it was Oliver she objected to the most, and Nova was being used as a substitute – she didn't want the inconvenience of her mother with a new man. It wasn't jealousy which was motivating her, as Thomasine had first presumed. No, she didn't want the disruption. Just as her own mother had never allowed her to bring friends home for tea, because of the mess and noise they might have made. Just as her husband had objected to her getting a job, in case he might have to fend for himself too much.

'Simple, when you can see the wood despite the trees, Nova.' The dog stood on its hind legs, using its pleading expression to be picked up. 'You're getting too fat,' she said as she did so, and Nova settled her rump content-edly on Thomasine's lap, her front paws on the table, and looked arrogantly about the kitchen, rather like a ship's figurehead.

Absentmindedly Thomasine stroked the dog's pelt. She could feel herself calming down; she invariably did when she sat like this, stroking her pet.

She loved Nadine, nothing could ever take that away, and there were many things about her she liked. Her generosity. Her passionate concerns. Whether it was raising money for Romanian orphans, joining motor-way protesters, tying herself to a tree which the local coun-cil had designated unsafe, or, as now, protesting against the export of live animals, Nadine's feelings were genuine. She was quite capable of sacrificing all she had for others. And yet – oh the moods, the tantrums, they made her so tired! Maybe later, maybe when she was older and less obsessed with herself, she'd be easier to know.

'Maybe,' Thomasine said sadly.

*

When one St Bernard stirred, they all stirred. Loud had been the snorting, farting and snuffling which had, Kimberley was sure, rocked the house during the night. She eased herself out of her bed – one dog lay across the bottom and one beside her – tiptoed into her small living room, where another lay on the sofa, and had to step over the sleeping form of a large male dog, who had chosen to sleep across the kitchen doorway as if guarding the contents.

Before she had finished dressing they were all awake and inquisitively inspecting their new surroundings. As she leapt to save an ornament sent flying by one swishing tail, she appreciated why Eveleigh insisted on inspecting any new homes to make sure they had a large enough turning circle for one of her dogs.

The St Bernards flounced down the stairs in front of her as she ushered them into the yard and across to their kennels. All the other kennels were occupied and swept, so Eveleigh must have been up for some time. She assumed she must have seen Bandage. She was not concerned. She had decided to tell Eveleigh she and Alan had found him straying on the road. She knew her employer well enough to know she would make no fuss.

She had, before sleeping, laid her plans. As soon as she'd finished her morning's work she was going to take Bandage where he belonged, back to Mr Hawksmoor and Bishop's End. She could let him free in the garden, then hide in a bush and watch and wait to make sure his owner found him. She couldn't give him to him direct, he might ask too many questions.

She made her way along to the end kennel where, last night, she had locked Bandage. It was empty.

In the kitchen she found Eveleigh making breakfast. 'Mrs Brenton, you haven't seen a bull terrier this morning?'

'No. Should I have?'

'It was a stray I found. I locked it up, it must have

jumped out. It doesn't matter,' she said, not meaning it. It mattered a lot.

Alan's day was going to be a busy one. He had had to hare back to Horsham to consult with the Chief Inspector. After such a slow and frustrating start on this particular enquiry, everything seemed suddenly to be rushing to a conclusion. When the snippets of gossip, the little information they had gleaned, were jigsawed together and cemented with this latest information, including the dog Kimberley had rescued, they all agreed there was enough to justify Alan moving to the area for the run-up to Saturday. They had suspicions enough to approach the local police, who would decide whether to launch an operation against Primrose Acre.

The main problem they faced was lack of time. They hadn't been able to familiarise themselves with the premises, do recces, observe, at leisure from a distance, the comings and goings. They did not have time to work by the book. Instead, they were studying Ordnance Survey maps to decide who should be where and who would move in from which direction. Alan always loved this stage – this was when the excitement began, when the adrenalin began to pump.

Oliver had worked half the night on his book. He was glad he had it to concentrate on. He'd been put out last night when Thomasine had rung to cancel their date. She'd sounded odd on the telephone and when he'd asked her what was wrong she had, infuriatingly, replied 'nothing'. Oliver loathed it when women said that. He knew from experience with Sophia that, on the contrary, it meant that everything was wrong, or something catastrophic had happened, or was likely to happen.

'*Nothing*, my arse,' he'd muttered to himself as he'd replaced the receiver. He'd found some cheese skulking in the refrigerator and helped himself to a large wedge of Brie and, with a pile of Bath Oliver biscuits and a new

Pinot Noir he wanted to try, he'd settled to work. As the fire crackled, as Slipper snoozed and farted, Oliver decided he was content with his life. Why complicate it with a woman who said 'nothing', he told himself.

What with the work, the bottle of wine and the brandy he'd drunk to reward himself for a good night's effort, Oliver woke late and in a sorry state. Thank God it wasn't one of Grace's mornings, he thought as he pulled his bedroom curtains and was blinded by the unexpected sunshine. 'Oh, no, it's a lovely day,' he moaned, for good weather always made him feel worse, as if he was being punished further. Hangovers were best nurtured by miserable, rainy days which were in tune with the pain of the sufferer, he thought as he let Slipper out the back door.

Filling the kettle was a head-splitting effort, and when it boiled and the whistle blew, Oliver thought his head had finally broken in two.

'Do you have to make so much bloody noise?' he said angrily as he opened the back door to Slipper's scratching. 'Shut up!' he said, for he dared not shout because of what it might do to what remained of his brain. The dog, of course, took no notice of a spoken command and continued to bark, jumping up and down on the spot like a demented jack-in-the-box. 'Come in, won't you, it's bloody cold.' He held the door wide, but the dog continued to bark, and then, sure it had Oliver's attention, ran up the yard, then back, and then up again. 'Slipper, will you come in, it's cold enough to freeze the balls off a brass monkey. *Slipper.*' He ventured a yell, and immediately regretted it. In answer the dog ran to him and then back again, barking furiously all the while. 'What is it? Have you found something?' Oliver stepped back into the kitchen and across to the passageway where his Barbour hung. He slipped on his wellies, not easy with bare feet, put the jacket over his dressing gown and hoped he wouldn't bump into anybody.

'Come on then, Slipper, what is it?' he said wearily,

reaching the step. Slinking across the yard, its belly almost scraping the ground in an effort to ingratiate itself, was a black dog. Slipper ran round and round it in delirious, yapping, circles.

Oliver stepped down. He looked at the dog, which averted his eyes. Its tail was hidden between its legs. Half of an ear was ripped off, there was a gash on one front leg, its hackles were up, but from fear, not aggression. Oliver took another step, his heart racing. He could barely breathe. He wanted to believe; he didn't dare. He knelt down on the cobbled yard.

'Bandage,' he said softly. 'Bandage, is it you?' He put a hand out towards the battered dog. In his daydreams Bandage, should he ever return, always came back as the dog who'd left. He should have been bounding across the yard, flinging himself at Oliver, drowning him in licks for kisses. But this dog cringed when he put his hand out. This dog hung his head as if in shame. This dog was a cur.

'Bandage. It is you, isn't it? Oh my poor old boy, who's done this to you?' Oliver was sitting now, oblivious to the cold of the damp cobbles, his hangover miraculously cured on the instant. He talked gently, softly, encouraging the dog to slink closer to him. He grabbed hold of Slipper, whose antics were not helping the progress. 'Come on, old boy. I love you.'

The dog was close enough now that if he leaned right over he could stroke him. But it cowered from his touch as if stung, leapt back and stood away from him, head down, shivering, watching warily, prepared at any moment for flight. Oliver sat there for a good half hour, patiently talking, willing the dog to trust him, to move closer. Inch by inch, he shuffled nearer to him.

Finally, from somewhere, the dog found the courage to stand close to him. Gingerly he put his hand out. The dog sniffed it and momentarily, his tail twitched. Oliver touched him, all the time talking, welcoming him, telling him how much he'd been missed, how much he was loved. Oliver ached to hug him, but knew he must be patient and do nothing to startle him.

His patience was rewarded. The dog suddenly squatted on the floor, laid his head in Oliver's lap and howled. It was a chilling sound, for the howl spoke of loneliness, fear and pain – or so Oliver thought. He threw caution to the wind and bent down and bundled the dog into his arms and hugged him tight, as if he'd never let him go. 'If I find who did this to you, Bandage, I'll kill him, I'll bloody well kill him.'

45

'What do you think, Jim?' Oliver asked anxiously. He had been watching Jim for the last ten minutes painstakingly examining Bandage, who lay patient but scared on the newspaper which Oliver had laid on the kitchen table.

'You wouldn't know it was the same dog, would you? He's had all the stuffing knocked out of him, poor old dog.' Jim patted the dog's head. Bandage wagged his tail, but tentatively, as if he wasn't sure if he should.

'He's so frightened. Bandage wasn't scared of anything – well, almost, he hated thunder and rolled-up newspapers.' Bandage licked Oliver's hand. 'Sorry, Bandage, fancy talking about you in the past tense, it won't do, will it?'

Jim stood up and stepped back, surveying his patient. 'He's lousy, you realise. He's half starved. He's weak from a combination of that and exhaustion. He's got worms. And his front leg's a bit iffy – I don't like the smell of it at all.'

'What, gangrene?' Oliver said with mounting horror. 'What about his ear?'

'That's healed. Don't worry – I think we've probably

caught the leg wound in time. Even if we hadn't, dogs get around amazingly well on three legs.'

'I'd hate that.'

'Better than putting him down, though. These are old dog bites, you realise. The sore on his leg is from a deep cut – probably made by something metal, a spade perhaps. It was obviously left untreated.'

'He's been used for fighting, hasn't he?' Oliver felt sick at the idea.

'He might have been at the beginning. But not recently. He's not been up to scratch for some time. Fighting dogs are kept as fit as fleas, they have to be to fight. The odd thing about the bastards who go in for this business is that they look after their dogs. There can be a lot of money tied up in bets and challenges, so they feed them well. He's just too starved and unfit to be any use in the ring and, as we can see, he lacks aggression.'

'If they tried to make him fight he wouldn't, he's the least aggressive dog I've ever had.'

'They have ways and means, you know. They make them aggressive, teasing the poor brutes. They get their blood up throwing live cats in with them – nice friendly actions like that.'

'What on earth for?'

'To get them to taste blood, the theory being once they have they'll want more.'

'If he wouldn't fight why did they keep him so long?'

'Stud, I should think. He was, and could be again, a fine dog. He didn't need to be well fed to mate.'

'So it hasn't been all bad then, Bandage?' He smiled at the dog who, as time ticked by, was becoming more and more relaxed with them.

From his bag Jim took a pile of bottles and packages. He injected the dog with antibiotics for the wounds. He had medicated shampoo for him, flea powder and worming pills. He produced a bottle of white liquid which, he promised Oliver, could clear up the patches of eczema he had.

'Eczema? Like a human?'

'Dogs can suffer stress too. Imagine what his life has been like for the past few months – first he's stolen, and he feels lost and homesick; then he's made to do something he doesn't want to do – fight; then, it appears, he runs away to find you. A human would have had a nervous breakdown with that lot. He's going to need a lot of TLC, and you'll have to watch him with Slipper. Territory and position are all that matter to dogs. We used to think that probably all they thought about all day long was food and sex. It isn't. It's guarding their territory and thinking, "I'm top dog and how do I stay so?" or "I want to be top dog, how can I push him out of the position?" '

'Restless life. I wonder where he's been.'

'Judging by his paws, not far away. If he'd walked a long way I'd have expected to see some damage, or at least hardening of the pads, but his are fine.' Jim began to repack his bag. 'He's more than likely to have been nearer than either of us know.' He paused. 'This is strictly between us, but do you know anything about a Tom White – has a smallholding over near Connies-town? No? Well, the rumour is he might have been staging dog fights over there.'

'Here? But . . .'

'I know, you presumed it was a pastime of inner city louts? You'd be surprised.'

'Bastards!'

'My feelings exactly. Still, must get going.' Jim hauled his heavy bag off the table and Oliver saw him out.

He returned to the kitchen. 'Bath first or breakfast, Bandage? Which do you think?'

The dog sat down, ignoring Slipper, and looked up at Oliver, his tail thudding on the kitchen floor, his eyes, for the first time, showing interest in Oliver and his surroundings. But just then an RAF plane flew over low, and Bandage scampered under the table, shaking and panting loudly.

'Let's do the bath later, old friend. Let's find you something to eat, get you settled.' Oliver continued to talk to the dog as he prepared him a bowl of food.

Kimberley bumped into Nadine in the post office. She was scared and depressed at losing Bandage and she didn't really want to talk to anyone, but Nadine persisted and she found herself accepting an invitation to go back to Nadine's for coffee, from where she telephoned Eveleigh to check she did not mind her being late back.

'Why did you do that?' Nadine asked.

'It seemed the polite thing to do.'

'Right Goody Two-Shoes, aren't you?' Nadine plonked the mug of coffee and a packet of Jaffa cakes onto the table and took a bottle of milk from the fridge. 'Help yourself,' she said to Kimberley as she selected a CD to put into the slick black player at the other side of the room. What it must be like to be so rich, Kimberley thought, for she knew from previous visits that there was another player in the sitting room and Nadine had her own in her room. All she possessed was a small radio which, since it had seen better days, was getting harder to tune.

'What's that?' she asked as loud music poured into the room.

'It's Marion's latest.'

'Oh yes?' She tried to sound knowledgeable.

'They're American punk – Orange County.' Nadine rattled off, tapping her heavy Timberland boots to the noise, and moving her mouth as if she were chewing gum, even though she wasn't. Kimberley eyed the boots and wanted them, wondering if they were 'it' now and Doc Martens passé.

'Nice,' said Kimberley, not understanding what Nadine was talking about and not liking to say she preferred Country and Western herself.

Nova, who had been snoozing on Thomasine's bed, managed to find the energy to come and investigate who the visitor might be. 'I love this dog. Just look at her face, it's almost human.' She patted Nova, whose rump swayed back and forth from pleasure.

'I hate it. It's ugly. Gross!'

'She's not ugly. She's beautiful. I thought you liked animals.'

'In their place. I don't think dogs should be owned. It's undignified. It's abusive. It should be banned.'

Kimberley laughed. 'What a daft idea. And what would you do with all the dogs? Kill them?'

'Of course not.' Nadine flicked her hair back with annoyance. 'We'd allow those in ownership to die out and ban any future ownership. Breeding would stop.'

'Oh yeah, and who's going to tell the dogs that?'

'You're being thick on purpose.'

'But what would be the point?'

'The point is you'd give the animals back their dignity.'

'Not much use if they're becoming extinct.'

'And the world would be a healthier place. Do you know how much urine and faeces dogs dump each day in this country?'

'No, but I'm sure you're going to tell me,' she grinned.

'You sound just like my mother!' As Nadine scowled in response, Kimberley wondered why she was bothering with her. She had Alan now, she didn't need anyone else. Then she stopped such thoughts, feeling ashamed of them. Maybe she didn't need Nadine, but maybe Nadine needed her. There was a restlessness, a vacancy in her expression, which struck an echo from her own past. She must try and be patient with her.

'You can laugh, it's serious. Why don't you come and meet my group? We need people like you. People who care about animals.'

'But I wouldn't want dogs banned. I like dogs.' As if to confirm this she fussed over Nova.

'There's masses of other things. We demonstrate against vivisection. And fur coats, and the horses, sheep and calves shipped abroad live. And dog fighting.' She breathlessly listed the group's causes.

'Yes, you mentioned the dog fighting the other day.' She studied her nails. It still bothered her that Alan was interested, but he had asked her to find out and she'd do anything for him.

'It's definitely on. This Saturday. Why don't you come? It's going to be wild.'

'Where is it?'

'We're meeting at the crossroads outside Connies-town, you know, that village between here and Morris-town.'

'I meant where's the fight?' She was aware her heartbeat had quickened.

'I don't know. We're not told things like that until the last minute – security is very tight,' she said proudly. 'It's on some smallholding or something. Don't your parents live out that way? Didn't my mum drive you there?'

'That's right, but it's not a smallholding,' she said quickly, which was true – it might have been a small-holding once, but her father had not worked it as such for ages.

'You see, you should come. You could help us, you know the area.'

'I've got a date on Saturday.'

'With Alan?'

'Yes.' Kimberley smiled; she liked to hear his name being used by others.

'You slept with him yet?'

'None of your business!' She blushed furiously.

'Then you have.' Nadine giggled. 'What's it like? Did it hurt?'

Kimberley was saved from having to answer by Thomasine appearing through the back door, laden with Sainsbury's carrier bags. Nova threw herself into an hysterical, welcoming, hurling ball of fur.

'Hullo, Kimberley. How are you?' Thomasine smiled, pleased to see the girl, hoping that if the friendship was on again her daughter might prove easier to handle.

At sight of her mother Nadine's face set again into a scowl. Kimberley offered to help with the shopping, while Nadine sprawled, rather ostentatiously, on her chair.

'Come on, Kimberley. Let's go somewhere private where we're not being spied on.'

Kimberley glanced from daughter to mother and saw Thomasine's shoulders slump. 'I've got to be getting back to work,' she said, not wishing to get involved; she liked Thomasine too much to side with her daughter.

'Please yourself,' Nadine said sulkily, but she followed Kimberley out into the garden. 'Some friend you are, siding with the enemy.'

'I think your mother's lovely. I wish she was mine.'

'You're welcome to her.'

'Oh, Nadine, you don't mean that.'

'I do. She'd rather have that bloody dog than me.'

'If you're always like this, I don't blame her,' Kimberley said sharply, quickly mounted her bicycle and pedalled away before Nadine could even think of an answer.

She pedalled furiously down the main street and when she saw her aunt outside the shop began to wave, but when she saw she was talking to Oliver the bicycle wobbled as she almost lost control.

'I didn't realise I could have that sort of effect on a

beautiful young woman,' Oliver smiled at her as she stopped. Kimberley looked at him blankly, not understanding Oliver was jokingly flirting with her.

'Guess what, Kimberley, Mr Hawksmoor's dog's returned. Isn't that wonderful?'

'Really? That's good. How?' She thought she'd better add.

'Turned up in the garden this morning,' Oliver explained, and wondered why she looked so shifty.

'You must be really happy . . . Got to go.' She got back on to her bicycle.

Oliver watched her cycle away.

'Tell me, Grace, do you know a Tom White?'

'And why would you be asking?'

'The same name – that's all.'

'He's my brother-in-law,' Grace replied, tight-lipped.

'Is that so?' Oliver, having elicited this information, didn't know quite how to proceed, and wished he'd thought it out before opening his big mouth. 'Does he keep dogs?' he blurted out, thinking he'd got nothing to lose.

'I wouldn't know. Mr White and me never socialised with that side of the family,' Grace said with dignity.

'Ah, yes. Well. I see,' he replied in the time-honoured way of one who didn't see anything. They parted, Oliver to drive into Shillingham to get some extra vitamins for Bandage, and Grace to her home where she immediately picked up the phone, called the kennels and asked to speak to Kimberley.

'It's just he looked really fishy when he asked me about the dogs, Kimberley. As you know, I've not much time for your dad and what he gets up to, but when all's said and done, he is blood, and so I thought I'd best mention it.'

'Thanks,' she said, replacing the receiver. She stood leaning against the table, feeling sick.

'Not bad news?' asked Eveleigh as she walked past.

'No, nothing,' she replied. It was all too close for comfort. First there had been Eveleigh's friend telling her about dog fights near Conniestown. Then Nadine and the way she talked, it could only be her father's place. Now Mr Hawksmoor asking questions. What on earth was she to do?

46

Thomasine had to get out of the house. The atmosphere which Nadine was creating was getting her down, despite her resolution to ride the storm.

Nova was leaping up and down with excitement, yapping her high-pitched bark, which always sounded so surprising, coming from a bulldog. 'How do you know? I haven't even said *W.A.L.K!*' She spelled it out, and Nova hurled herself on the floor, rolled onto her back and turned round and round on the carpet, four legs flailing the air. 'You're a witch, Nova.' She bent down to clip on the lead.

She walked on the hills behind Middle Shilling. Nova enjoyed rootling in the copse, putting up a rabbit, snuffling about in the leaves, getting covered in mud. Thomasine climbed to the summit of the hill and looked down at the villages below her.

Far away beyond the church tower, beyond Badger's Wood the other side of the river, she pinpointed where Oliver's house must be. Was the smoke rising from those trees his chimney's smoke? She wished he were here. In such a short time he had become all-important to her. Thoughts of him filled her waking hours, and her sleep was dotted with dreams of him. Her body now, just thinking about him, told her of its aching longing. She might have fine thoughts of giving him up, putting duty first, as she had yesterday, but she knew she deceived herself. So much for her new-found independence, her self-sufficiency.

She knew as she stood there, the breeze whipping at her jacket, her cheeks reddening from its sharpness, that she could never let him go. Knowing this made her feel elated, full of courage, able to deal with any problems. Somehow she would work it all out; somewhere she would find the patience to deal with her daughter.

As she descended the hill these feelings of euphoria escaped her, and she imagined them fleeing back up to the top of the hill like a huge bundle of tangleweed. And the nearer the village she got, the less resolute she felt.

With Nova safely back on the lead, they trudged along the road back to The Old School House.

'If ever I saw a depressed walk, yours is it.' Oliver had pulled up beside her. 'Problem?'

'Don't even ask, I might feel impelled to tell you.' Her heart flipped wondrously at the sight of him.

'Fancy cooking me an omelette?'

'It's about time you learnt.' She looked at him, at the fullness of his lips, the laughter lines at his eyes, and longed to touch him, to curl up in bed with him, to have him inside her. Just thinking about it, she felt aroused. She moved her body almost imperceptibly from one foot to the other. He looked up at her, recognised the desire in her eyes, and touched her hand, which leant on the open car window.

'Come home with me,' he said, his voice husky.

'I can't. Look at me, look at Nova.'

'I don't mind a bit of mud.'

'You will.'

He climbed out of the car, and as he leant over to open the back door his body pressed suggestively against hers. In unison they laughed with delight, knowing what the other was thinking.

'Up you get, Nova.' Oliver helped the short-legged

bulldog into the car as Thomasine climbed into the front seat.

'You seem in a good mood,' she said as he joined her.

'I wasn't when I got up. I don't like being stood up.' He looked sternly at her.

'Oliver, I said I was sorry. I just couldn't make it.'

'Don't I deserve an explanation?'

'I didn't want to bother you, it's my problem and it's so predictable, I suppose. It's my daughter – it would seem she doesn't approve of us . . .'

They sat in the car in the middle of the village while she told him about Nadine.

'You don't sound too certain how you feel.'

'It's very confusing, that's why. I love her, and yet it gets so difficult at times. I want to throttle her and then I hate myself for my reaction. One thing, though, I'm determined that she's not going to dictate how I live my life.'

'Poor kid, she must be confused too. Look at the changes in her life so far. The divorce, a new stepmother, and a pregnant one too, a new home, a new school. And now us. One would be enough.'

'She *is* seventeen,' she said with a tinge of exasperation.

'So? What difference does age make? Seven, seventeen or twenty-seven – it must still hurt like hell to watch your parents split, deal with the confusion and have to face the sort of insecurity you're left with.'

'Please don't say that, Oliver. I feel bad enough about her as it is. And to be jealous of my dog!' She shook her head, still disbelieving.

'I doubt if she really is. She's too intelligent for that. More likely she's seen you dote on Nova and to get noticed by you she pretends to hate the dog.'

'How do you know all this? You talk like a parent.'

'No, a child. It happened to me too. I was a classic case, I blamed myself for my parents' divorce. I thought it was something I'd done, that they didn't like me any

468

more. I was left with a great gaping hole in my life and I never felt safe again. Then we drifted apart, my mother and me – I suppose I hated her for a time and she, sensing that, withdrew from me. I guess it's something you never get over totally.'

She put out her hand and touched him. 'Thanks.'

'Now let's get this show on the road. I've got a big surprise for you.'

'What? I hate surprises.'

'You'll love this one.'

Five minutes later they entered his driveway. 'Oh no! I wanted an omelette and to take you to bed – look, bloody Wimpole and hubbie, what a time to choose.'

Thomasine began to laugh, but stopped abruptly, her face draining of colour. Standing on the driveway was a large, black Mercedes with a half-remembered number plate. The 'A' on it seemed to enlarge and jump out at her, so that she closed her eyes, as if to make it stop, overwhelmed by the certainty that this was the car from which Luna had been thrown back in March. But then sense took hold and asked her how she knew, and logic pointed out she could not accuse every black car with an 'A' in the number. But she hadn't, that was the point; in all those months she'd never once thought she had seen the car. Not until today.

Thomasine took a deep breath – so what if intuition thought this was the car? What could she do about it? Who'd believe her? And, in any case, did she want to mention it to Oliver? No. It would not be a good idea, he loved Wimpole. She might be driving a wedge between Oliver and his old nanny if she told him her suspicions.

'You all right, you've gone pale?'

'It's nothing,' she smiled wanly. There's that bloody word again, he thought as he opened the front door for her.

Wimpole appeared in the hall at the sound of their entry.

'What a happy day, Oliver. The vet was over to see

one of Ben's nags and he told us. See, I always told you that old mutt would find you again. You can't keep a good dog down, don't they say?' She whooped with pleasure as she stood on tiptoe to kiss him. 'And Thomasine too, there's a nice surprise,' she said archly. They entered the kitchen, Thomasine and Nova last.

Nova, upon smelling dog, raced in front of Thomasine, but no sooner had she entered the kitchen than she stopped abruptly, skidding on the tiles. She stood rigid a second, then turned and cowered behind Thomasine's legs.

Rudolph was sitting at the kitchen table, a mug of coffee in front of him, grinning broadly at Bandage, who was standing in the corner of the room facing the wall, his tail curved between his legs, his flanks shaking.

'Look at that silly bugger.' He pointed at Bandage and laughed as he did so.

'What did you do to him?' Oliver demanded.

'Me? I ain't done nothing.'

'You must have. Just look at the poor creature.' Oliver looked angry.

'He just pissed off into the corner and sulked.' Rudolph looked put out, but more by Oliver's reaction than the dog's. He stood up and crossed to the kitchen sink. From beneath the kitchen table came a low growl. They all looked down – Slipper lay, head between her forepaws, teeth displayed, her body taut as if prepared for fight or flight.

'Bandage wasn't there when I was in here,' Wimpole said, looking anxiously from Oliver to her husband and back again. 'Oh, shut up, Slipper, do!'

'Bandage only does that when he's upset.' Oliver stalked across the kitchen to his dog and hunched down beside him. He began to stroke him, talking softly. The trembling stopped, his tail switched a minute degree.

Rudolph remained standing at the sink, staring impassively out of the kitchen window as if the whole business was of no interest to him. Thomasine stared at his back, willing him to turn and look at her, hoping she would be able to read in his eyes that it was he who had thrown Luna into the road.

Slowly Oliver coaxed the dog further into the room. Bandage walked stealthily, lifting one paw into the air and pausing, glancing nervously about him, before placing it down on the floor again. His ears were pinned back, his lips slightly curled up over his teeth in a rigid grimace. But at each step his confidence appeared to grow until he was in the middle of the room – and then Rudolph turned from the window and looked at him with an expression of distaste. The dog barked once, a high, frightened, sharp bark, and dived under the table and curled up, making himself as small as possible beside Slipper, who jumped to her feet and stood guard, her hackles up and growling louder – a slow, deep, rumbling growl.

'It would appear that my dogs don't like you very much, Rudie,' Oliver said, and Thomasine hoped he never had cause to speak to her like that, his tone was so chilling.

'Rudolph loves dogs,' Wimpole said staunchly.

'Quite honestly, Wimpole, I think it would be better for the dogs if Rudolph waited for you outside in the car.'

'Well, really, Oliver. Can't the dogs wait outside?'

'No. I don't want Bandage frightened further and Rudolph's obviously upsetting him.'

'Don't let my presence interfere with such an important dog. Bloody hell, whatever next,' Rudolph said, and without any farewells, he stamped from the room, which made the dogs jump.

'I never thought I'd hear you of all people being so rude, Oliver. You don't know where he's been, what's happened to him to make him like that. It's not Rudolph's fault.' She sounded angrily defensive.

'Look at him now.' Bandage had wriggled out from under the table on his stomach. He stood up and was busily sniffing at Wimpole's feet, his tail wagging and, reassured, moved on to Thomasine, his tail waving back and forth like a metronome, his hackles down, his face relaxed. He, Nova and Slipper had a good introductory sniff. 'See, he's not afraid of anyone else. But he was frightened witless when we came in. Odd, isn't it, that he was only afraid when Rudolph was present?'

'I don't think I like what you're implying, Oliver.'

'And I don't like what I'm thinking.'

Wimpole was looking with a concentrated expression at the floor, and Thomasine realised she had not seen her look anyone in the eye since they had entered the kitchen.

'What's going on, Wimpole?' Oliver asked in a gentle voice. 'Tell me.'

'I don't know what you're wittering on about.'

'I think you do, Wimpole,' he said, even softer.

'I'd better go.'

'If you change your mind – if you think you can talk – phone, I'll come and collect you.'

'I shouldn't hold your breath, then,' Wimpole replied, sounding sassy even though she looked oddly dejected. She slammed the door as she left.

'What on earth was that about?' Thomasine asked as she sat on a chair, as aware as the dogs that the atmosphere in the room had completely changed.

'Thomasine, it might sound daft, but I trust my dogs' judgement where people are concerned. Bandage here has never been wrong once. If he doesn't like someone, sooner or later they turn out to be duff. He never liked Rudie, for sure, but he didn't behave like this. What we've just witnessed in Bandage was sheer terror. Why? Has he been involved with Bandage's disappearance? Is he involved in the fighting . . .'

'I wonder . . .' she began, and debated whether to tell him about Rudolph's car, but decided not to. She'd no evidence, it wouldn't be fair. 'Still, Bandage is back, and

472

you must be so happy,' she said instead. 'Will it put Slipper's nose out of joint?'

'Jim said to watch them. It might have been more difficult if she was a dog, but as a bitch – oh, I'm sure she'll be happy to cede him the position of pack leader. As it should be.' He was grinning now.

'So long as only dogs stay such male chauvinists.'

He grabbed hold of her and pulled her onto his lap. 'Don't you want me to dominate you? Lord it over you? Be brutal with you?'

'No thanks. Just equals suits me fine.' She laughed, happy that his mood had changed.

'Thank God for that; being macho is an exhausting occupation.'

They made love, not in bed as he had planned, but in the Great Hall, where he had lit the fire. They never got round to having the omelette.

'Alan? Jim Varley here. Thought I'd better report to you an odd thing. Do you know Oliver Hawksmoor? No? Well, it's by the by, but his dog, which has been missing for at least nine months, turned up this morning. Bull terrier, scars all over it, undernourished. It's been used for fighting or I'll eat my hat.'

'Any clues to where it's been?'

'No, except not far. His paws were in too good a condition for a marathon hike.'

'Thanks. Mr Varley, we might be needing you. We're sure now that there's a dog fight on Saturday evening.'

'Saturday you say? I'll keep that free then – for the wounded. Bit like *Casualty*, isn't it?' He replaced the receiver and turned round to find Beth standing at the bottom of the stairs, a sullen-faced Harry behind her.

'Hullo. You made me jump,' he said, feeling gauche. Had she overheard him? Still, the conversation would have meant nothing to her. This was it, he told himself, now. Do it – say it.

'Jim, I'm leaving.' Beth announced calmly.

'I don't want to go! Uncle Jim, stop her,' Harry wailed, and kicked at his mother, clipping her shin.

'You little bastard.' She swung round and pushed Harry back towards the stairs. 'Now shut up!'

'Look, Beth, don't carry on like this. We made a mistake. . .'

'No, you're wrong there, Jim. I made the mistake – I thought you were a gentleman, but you're as big a lying pig as the rest of them.'

'I've not lied to you. Not as you've lied to me.'

'Oh yes, and what does that mean?'

He paused, thinking what was the point, and then an image of Castille's fever-racked body flashed in front of him. 'The husband that doesn't exist, for one.'

She looked away from him for a split second, as if collecting her thoughts. 'I don't know what you mean,' she said.

'Why did you tell me that sob story – was it to soften me up? Were you scared I was angry with you and wanting me to feel sorry for you? Well, I did – more fool me. But it was a trap that didn't work, did it – come the end.'

'A trap? Me trap you? What for? Half the time you stink of animals and disinfectant – it gives me the shudders. And you're boring, Jim Varley, so bloody boring – in and out of bed,' she finished on a spiteful but triumphant note.

The doorbell rang.

'That's for me.' She pushed past him.

Ben Luckett stood on the doorstep.

'Hi, Ben. Can I help you?' Jim stepped forward, trying a smile on for size.

'Come to pick the little lady up,' Ben said over-heartily. 'Cora felt too embarrassed to come.'

'Sorry?' Jim said, nonplussed.

'Didn't she say? Oh, Beth's coming to work for us. Cora and she arranged it.'

'I didn't even know Beth knew you.'

'Yes, she's been coming to the house for yonks doing those dead flower thingummy-bobs. She burst into tears, told Cora what had happened, and here we are – we're taking her on. Cora's a bit ruffled about it, bit anti you – you know, female solidarity, that sort of crap. I can't say I blame you.'

Jim opened his mouth to defend himself, but shut it again.

'I'll give her a hand with her bags,' he said instead.

It was harder saying goodbye to Harry than he had realised it would be. He hugged the boy close and wiped Harry's damp face with his own hanky. 'I'll still see you, Harry – we'll work something out.'

'It won't be the same.'

'Harry, get into this Range Rover, now,' Beth ordered, thin-lipped with spite. Had he done this to her? The new job had certainly given her the confidence to show exactly what she thought of him.

The sound of the phone ringing gave him the perfect excuse to slip away. A cow with a prolapsed uterus, just the thing to get him out of the lonely house for the evening, and to keep his mind off his confused feelings of guilt.

47

On Saturday morning, Kimberley's face was wan from sleeplessness. Tossing and turning through the night hours had given her no solution to her problems. When she saw Alan this evening, what would she do? She could imagine herself confessing to him about her father, but would he be glad, want to meet him, become involved in the fighting? Or was it a front, and would he be disgusted with her for not acting sooner? Which was the real Alan? If he wanted to see the dogs fight, would she feel the same about him?

Eveleigh called her from the yard to the telephone.

'Kim, love, I'm sorry. I can't see you this evening, something's come up,' she heard Alan say.

The long 'oh' with which she responded was full of suspicion. Alan felt a heel; he knew how insecure she was and he loathed to hurt her.

'I wouldn't have done this in a million years – I wanted to see you so badly.'

His voice was sincere, and gave her the courage to ask what had come up.

'Work. I've got to work this evening.'

'Come round when you've finished.'

'I might be at it half the night.'

'Half the night?' The suspicion deepened.

'It's God's honest truth.' He paused a moment. 'Have you seen Nadine?'

'Yes.' Her heart felt as if it would burst.

'Did she tell you – you know –'

'What?' Her mouth was dry.

'Where her lot are meeting on Saturday.'

This was her chance, she could tell him now, all her fears, she could share them, make things better for herself.

'No, she didn't say,' she finally said. How could she tell a living soul her father's dreadful secret?

'Ah, well. I'll see you tomorrow.'

'Fine. Take care.' She hung onto the receiver, loath to lose contact with him, but also worried at how he kept on about Nadine. Why?

Alan was standing in front of the blackboards at Morristown Police Headquarters. He'd drawn the lay-out of Primrose Acre on one board. Maps of the region were pinned on the other. The room was crowded with members of the RSPCA as well as police.

He was edgy. He wasn't too happy at the lack of

surveillance and knew the others would rapidly be agreeing with him.

'As you can see, given the exposed nature of the property, we've had to use these Ordnance Survey maps rather than staking it out. Using binoculars, we're pretty sure these outhouses are all there is. And this one –' Alan used the wooden pointer '– this long shed is the closest to the Walters' farm, the most likely place for the noise to have come from, so we think that's where the fight will be.'

'Why is the surveillance so poor?' one of the senior policemen demanded.

'Lack of time.'

'Then if it's so iffy, why don't we leave the raid this time? Use Saturday night to suss it out, take the car numbers, identify the punters and go in next time?' the same police inspector asked.

'There might not be a next time,' Alan's Chief Inspector patiently explained. 'These rings are not run by amateurs, you know. Their security is top notch. They only release the venue of the fight to their followers at the last possible moment. They're invariably one step ahead of us.'

'How do you know it's here?'

'We don't.'

'Then what the hell is all this laid on for?' the police inspector said in exasperation, looking round the crowded room.

'We've had odd rumours of dog fighting hereabouts for over a year. It started in a small way – garages, back rooms, that sort of thing – but then it got bigger. They got wind of us some time back and packed up for months – moved up to the Midlands, we think. We want, obviously, to catch as many as possible. As you know, it's an offence to attend a fight, let alone organise one. Our mole reckoned that a really big one, with punters coming from as far away as London and the

Midlands, with big money involved, was about to take place. He didn't know where, just that it was soon. We'd suspicions about a couple of places, and then young Alan here got wind of Primrose Acre.' To Alan's acute embarrassment everyone looked at him.

'And who's your informant?'

'This is Alan's show,' Don said, waving his hand, deferring to Alan.

'I haven't met him, sir. But from his voice I'd say he's a young chap. My theory is he attended a fight once, hated it, and contacted us. The trouble is, whoever he is, he's pretty lowly in the hierarchy, so that although he knows when there's to be a fight, he's not one who's privy to it until the last minute. He sounds scared, really scared, and, unfortunately, this last call he sounded ratty with us, like he was ready to give up. Also, one of the local vets got onto us. A bull terrier which had been missing for months returned home: in his opinion it had been used for fighting, and in this vicinity. I have also been informed that the Freedom for All Animals brigade are on to something this weekend.'

'Oh bugger me – not that lot.'

'I'd hoped I might find out where they're meeting – to stop them. But unfortunately I haven't.'

'It's mad not having cased the farm. Surely you could have done more?'

'Not really.' Alan realised, from the attitude of this particular policeman, who would be blamed if it all went wrong. 'I drove around and walked a bit, but as you can see from this plan, it's impossible to size it up properly, the house is too exposed. It's ideal for their purposes, however. Flat fields surround it, you can see any cars on the road from the house, and no one could approach without being seen. Their lookouts will have it easy.'

'I think you should go in, Bob.' The Chief Superintendent, who had been quietly listening, stood up. They

478

were in luck; unbeknown to them, this policeman bred boxers as a hobby. 'We don't want to prolong the dogs' suffering, do we?'

At these words from his senior officer, the police inspector acquiesced, even though he muttered to himself. The wheels were in motion, a search warrant application was being made, they had the necessary police back-up. The two teams would work in unison. They were almost home and dry.

When darkness fell they climbed into the horsebox, which they often used like a Trojan Horse on country operations. For who, in the country, would give a horsebox a second glance? Inside the vehicle the tension and excitement was relieved by some pretty lame jokes.

Alan had visited the Walters that morning, and persuaded them to allow their yard to be used as an ops centre. He assured them he'd learnt from sources other than Jim that Primrose Acre was involved. Chris and Fee had, as requested, pulled the curtains of the farmhouse. The yard light was out and their dogs firmly locked inside the house. One by one the men climbed out of the horsebox and moved across the ploughed field, hidden by the night, keeping to the cover of the hedgerows. Without incident they took up their pre-arranged positions and settled down to wait.

Alan peered about him in the darkness. It was perfect. It was a moonless night, and he could barely see Andy in position just twelve feet away from him. The whole smallholding was completely ringed by men. But he felt sick with worry. All this organisation, men and overtime, and if no one turned up, he'd be to blame, he was sure of that.

Kimberley paced up and down her room. Her agitation was twofold now. To the worry of what was possibly about to happen to her father, and Nadine's friends on their raid, was added the fear that Alan had met someone else, someone he preferred to her. Why else, after all he had said, would he cancel their date?

She couldn't cope with this burden of worry, which increased rather than diminished as time ticked by. She kissed goodbye to the St Bernards she'd moved, for safety, into her sitting room. She did not want to bother Eveleigh by telling her she was going out, and so she slipped unnoticed into the yard and pushed her bicycle to the road. In her haste, confused with her concerns, she had forgotten the light was broken. She wondered whether to turn back, but decided it did not matter; she knew the roads well, and there would be little traffic at night.

Despite Oliver's understanding attitude, inspiring Thomasine yesterday to try again and be more patient with her daughter, they had had another momentous row. She could not even remember what had triggered this one; they all seemed to be melting into one. The upshot was the same though: they were not speaking to each other. Thomasine decided that rather than risk being rebuffed if she tried to say goodbye, she would leave a note on the kitchen table to explain she was dining at Oliver's.

Nadine, skulking in her room, smiled to herself as she heard her mother's car leave. At least she needn't creep out now. Dressed from head to toe in black, her hair stuffed up under a black beret and with black sunglasses on, she paused in front of the mirror and admired how like an SAS soldier she looked. In the kitchen she raided the tea caddy where her mother kept spare cash, just in case she needed it. Soon she was on her bicycle, pedalling furiously towards her rendezvous with the other members of Freedom for All Animals. She was excited, not just because they were about to go into action, but also at the prospect of meeting new people, amongst whom might be someone who would like her, perhaps even love her.

Jim was at Oliver's when Thomasine arrived. Worried about the wound on Bandage's leg, he'd decided to call in to check it out.

'I think he'll be all right, Oliver. We caught the wound in time. I'll give him another shot. I must say, he looks better for his bath.' He patted Bandage. 'Smart rascal, aren't you?' Bandage responded to the fuss, tail wagging and gently head-butting Jim's leg. 'He's a great deal more relaxed. Looks as if he's going to trust us after all. Maybe it won't be the long haul I feared.'

'I was afraid he'd need *counselling*, like the rest of the world,' Oliver smiled. 'Stay for supper,' he invited reluctantly.

'No thanks. You don't need me around,' he teased. 'In any case, I've a dinner appointment at Eveleigh's.'

'Good on you. Seeing a lot of her, aren't you?' It was Oliver's turn to tease.

'Not that much,' Jim said, puzzled, as Oliver showed him to the door.

'See you tomorrow?'

'Maybe, I'm not making any promises. There's . . .' He stopped abruptly, remembering in time to be discreet. 'I might be very busy tonight and tomorrow, I'm expecting a load of casualties. I'd best be off,' he mumbled, and virtually bolted out of the door.

Oliver looked thoughtful as he returned to the kitchen, where Thomasine was cooking their dinner. He replenished his and Thomasine's drinks. Something devious was afoot. How could he know in advance he was going to have a load of casualties, unless . . . 'Here you are, sweetheart.' He handed the glass to Thomasine.

An hour later they got the closest they'd ever been to a row when he pushed his plate away, barely touched.

'What's the matter, don't you like it?'

'I'm not hungry.'

'You've barely spoken. I feel like the hired help, and a not very successful one at that.' She took his plate and threw his food into the trash can noisily, marking her displeasure.

'I'm sorry, Thomasine. It's just there's something at the back of my mind I can't shake off. Jim triggered it. He said he was expecting loads of casualties. How could he possibly know?'

'Perhaps he's psychic –' She began to laugh and stopped. 'Nadine!' she said, clutching at her throat. 'Oh my God, what's she up to? She's been too secretive lately – more so than usual. She gets odd calls and never says who from. And that FAA business bothers me. What's there around here, any laboratories?'

'Not that I know of. I did wonder, what with Bandage and odd things Jim's let slip, if there was an illegal fight planned, something like that.'

'That's just the sort of thing they'd go for. Oh my God!'

'Give her a bell. Check she's safe.'

Thomasine's heart began to thud with foreboding as she listened to her telephone ringing and ringing unanswered. 'She's not there,' she said bleakly. 'Did Jim tell you where?'

'No. But the other day he was asking me about a Tom White, who lives over near some friends of mine – he asked if I knew him. I don't. But I asked Grace and she was very offhand. You don't think – ?'

'At Primrose Acre? Kimberley's dad?' Thomasine's face was ashen. She grabbed at Oliver's sleeve. 'I've got to go there. He's dangerous, he threatened us with a gun. Oh my God, she could be killed!'

'I'll come with you. Leave Nova here with my two dogs. I'll get my torch,' he said, and wished he had a gun.

Nadine's legs felt like jelly by the time she reached the crossroads for Conniestown and a small waiting group of people. She might be only seventeen, but she was not particularly fit, for exercise and organised games were of no interest to her.

No one leapt forward to welcome her – not like the other groups she'd been with. Nor did she see the friendly faces of the middle-aged and elderly women, along with the gentle hippies, who had been so in evidence when she had been demonstrating against the export of live sheep and calves. This lot looked rough and aggressive. Like her, they were dressed in black from head to toe, but they wore leather and heavy buckled boots she'd die for. She smiled at them, but there was no response. She was already keyed up for the attack, it didn't help to find she was beginning to feel nervous of the others. She laid down her bicycle in the ditch.

'When do we get going?' she asked the man standing beside her in as friendly a tone as she could muster.

'I dunno,' he answered, flicking the blade of a Stanley knife open and shut menacingly as he did so.

'Seen Cracker Barrel around?'

'Don't be bleeding wet.'

'It's cold, isn't it?' she said to the man on her other side, hugging herself and jumping up and down.

'What did you fucking well expect?'

'Sorry I spoke,' she said, a spurt of anger at his rudeness giving her momentary courage. If it had not been too juvenile, she would have liked to poke her tongue out at him.

'You didn't say nothing about birds coming along, Gr – '

'Shut your bleeding mouth. No names, get it!' His lips were pink against the black of his knitted balaclava. Those and his brown eyes were all that were visible.

'She's got the camcorder, nitwit. We need her.'

Nadine stayed silent. Her stomach felt as if it was turning to water – she'd completely forgotten to bring the video camera. She decided to say nothing, it might be safer, her lapse would not endear her to them. She'd think up some excuse later. If there was a fight, and looking at this lot she thought it more likely, she could say it got broken.

48

'It's just along here.' Thomasine leant forward in her seat, peering into the deep darkness for the turning. 'Look there, see the lights.' She pointed excitedly over the fields.

'Shit! Stupid sod, no lights,' Oliver cursed as he swung the car violently to the right to overtake a cyclist. Ahead of him a minibus, without signalling, swung across the road, entered a driveway. It was going far too fast to turn and so it rocked dangerously. Oliver stood on his brakes. 'That driver's insane. We'll let it go.'

'But, Oliver, we don't have time.'

'You won't be much help to her dead, will you? A minute won't make much difference.' He spoke sharply, not cross with her, but with the lunatic driver ahead. As he stopped the car the cyclist with no lights overtook them and, also making no signals, turned into the same lane.

'Psst, Alan. Something's coming.'

The minibus hurtled at full throttle up the rutted drive, the passengers bouncing about like corks in a barrel. Nadine, lighter than the men, was thrown all ways until her head banged on the metal roof and she slumped back onto the seat, lights flashing before her eyes. She moaned, but the men were too excited to take any notice of her. She rubbed her head, beginning to wish she hadn't come, wishing she was at home with her mother. Seeing the coshes and the knuckledusters appearing in the hands of the others, she started to feel seriously afraid.

The members of the RSPCA and their police companions bent double as they raced across the furrowed field. Adrenalin flooding their systems made them move faster and be more alert. At the same time as the minibus juddered to a halt, the doors crashed open and the demonstrators tumbled out, they ran almost silently into the yard.

There was no point in stealth now. The demonstrators, swinging round, had seen them; knives, clubs and cans of mace were raised menacingly as, with an unholy roar, rage blinding them to the policemen's uniforms, they hurled themselves into action. There was the sickening sound of flesh meeting flesh, animal like grunts, thuds as some fell onto the cobbles.

'Police!' a voice shouted, but no one took notice as the fight continued. Nadine stood, frozen with fear, in the doorway of the bus, and sharply stepped back.

'Alan, the shed! Over there – second along!' Above the racket he heard Andy yell.

Oliver's car screeched to a halt. At the sight of the mêlée he was out of his car in a flash, Thomasine beside him.

'Christ, women too! You cruel bitch!' screamed a man as he hurtled towards Thomasine. 'Call yourself a fucking woman!' Oliver jumped between them, his arms up, his body swaying in front of a terrified Thomasine. The man continued to run towards them. Oliver, fist clenched, swung his right arm and hit him square on the jaw. He sprawled at their feet. Oliver looked at his fist with astonishment, as if the hand, unaided by him, had done the dirty work.

Alan and the others in his team were running towards the shed. Alan grabbed hold of the door catch, pulled with all his might as the others raced past him into the darkened interior. A flashlight swept the walls. Andy flicked on the lights.

They stood rooted to the spot. The shed was empty.

There were no dogs. No spectators. No blood. No gore. No pain.

A few bales of straw were piled one on top of the other in tiers which might have been for spectators to sit on, but might also have been only a straw store.

'Shit! Shit! Shit!' Alan banged one huge fist into the palm of the other. 'He was tipped off. But how? By whom?'

He felt washed with despair at the failure of their efforts. The adrenalin was still pumping, flowing through his body, and the flight-or-fight surge was rapidly converted into anger, made worse by frustration at the outcome.

As one, he and his colleagues swung out into the yard. The fighting had ceased; a semblance of order was returning. The police had begun to take control of the demonstrators, who were now identified for what they were, and not participants in any dog fight.

Tom White stood on his doorstep, a smile on his face – a smile Alan longed to wipe off once and for all. 'Nothing there, sir,' Alan reported to his Chief Inspector. 'They must have been warned.'

'Get him. Arrest that bastard!' The man Oliver had knocked down was back on his feet. He waved a fist at Tom White, threatening. 'He has fighting dogs. I've seen them. I've seen him train them. There must be proof – some sign in there.'

'It's no use,' said Alan, almost certain that here was the informer, but for the man's safety he said nothing. 'We have to catch them with the dog fight in progress. The floor could be covered in canine blood, it wouldn't do us any good.'

Tom White stood impassive, his wife hovering behind him, the irritating smile still on his face.

'The puppies. He's a puppy farmer. You should see the conditions. This way.' The young man turned on his heel, the others followed. They opened the door of the second barn. The stench made them reel back. They covered their mouths with their hands.

'Where's the bloody light?' a voice called out.

'Gentlemen, let me be of assistance.' Tom White calmly walked through them and switched on the light.

The pens were in place, the cages piled one on top of the other. Of the dogs and puppies there was no sign.

'As you can see, I used to do a bit of breeding – no great amount. Puppy farming!' Tom snorted. 'What gave you that idea?' He laughed. 'I gave it up ages ago – not a good enough earner.' He smiled again, and Alan was not alone in wanting to hit him – hard.

From outside came a commotion. Oliver was angrily explaining, or trying to explain, that he was not interested in dog fights and never had been, and they had no right to arrest him, to a police constable who was more interested in picking his teeth than listening to Oliver's pleas.

'Please, will somebody listen. We were looking for my daughter,' Thomasine was nearly in tears from a combination of fear and frustration. 'Her name's Nadine.'

'I know Nadine.' Alan stepped forward.

'Is anyone a doctor?' a voice called from the darkness. 'There's an unconscious girl over here.'

'Nadine!' Thomasine cried, and was swept along by the others towards the bus.

Nadine was lying half in and half out of the bus. A police constable was slapping her hands, trying to rouse her. She groaned. Thomasine was quickly at her side. Slowly Nadine sat up, rubbing her head, looking around her with an exaggeratedly puzzled expression.

'What happened?' she said weakly. 'Where am I?'

'You were knocked unconscious,' the policeman explained.

'We must call an ambulance.' Thomasine looked about anxiously.

'Mum! What are you doing here?' Nadine spoke in a normal voice. But then, as if suddenly remembering, she put her hand back on her head and groaned again. 'Did we get them?' she asked, a pathetic catch in her voice.

Oliver, released by the police, watched her closely and wondered.

'Were you unconscious?' Thomasine asked anxiously.

'I don't know. I think I might have been.' Nadine looked away from her.

'You all right, Ruskie?' One of the demonstrators stepped forward.

'Cracker Barrel? Did we get them?'

'Nah. Bugger all here.'

'Oh no!' Nadine began to cry. She cried from pent-up fear, from disappointment, from all the confusion which beset her. She felt something trickle on her forehead. She brushed at it and looked at her hand. 'I'm bleeding!'

Thomasine dabbed at the blood.

'Let me. We're trained in first aid.' One of the policemen knelt down and looked at her head with the beam of his torch. 'I think it's only superficial – head wounds always bleed, they look far worse than they are, but I think we should radio for an ambulance.'

'I'll drive her, it'll be faster.' Oliver stepped forward.

'Mum, I'm scared.'

'She's under arrest.'

'Please, Officer.' Thomasine looked at the senior policeman with appeal.

'It would seem there have been some crossed wires here. We all had the same goal, even if your daughter and her friends went about it in the wrong way. Best get her seen to.'

Oliver picked Nadine up and carried her to his car, Thomasine in hot pursuit. The group around the minibus began to break up.

*

'I wish I could get my hands on the bastards who warned him. I'd kill them,' Andy muttered as they walked back towards the horsebox.

'Me too,' said Alan, falling into step beside him and suddenly feeling exhausted. A slight figure materialised from the shadow of the barn.

'Alan!'

'Kimberley. What on earth?' His face lit up with pleasure at the sight of her.

'Hullo, Kimberley. Long time no see.'

'Greaser?'

'I've been waiting to get your old man for ages – bastard!' He spat onto the ground with distaste. 'Ginger's here too.'

'Your father?' Alan looked at her with horror. 'Tom White's your father?' He stepped back from her – he had to, for fear he might hit her if he stepped towards her. What a fool he'd been! Of course it all fitted in now – the dog she'd rescued, her name. He'd allowed love to deaden reason. 'I thought you felt like me. That you loved animals too.'

'Alan, I do. What have I done?' She stepped forward, putting her hand out to touch him.

'Done? You've let that creep, your father, get away with murder. You warned him – it had to be you!' And Alan pushed her away from him and, feeling his heart was breaking, stalked off into the night.

The Casualty Officer insisted Nadine was kept in hospital overnight, a routine measure for cases of mild concussion, they reassured Thomasine. The cut on her head was superficial and required no stitches, only a plaster.

On the drive back Oliver said little, giving Thomasine time to think. She was shocked at how easily her equilibrium had taken a knock. How could she have thought she would forge ahead with her life, that Nadine would have to put up with it or go back to her father? It was impossible to separate oneself from one's child so simply. Nadine was part of her and always would be. Nadine could have died if things had been worse at Primrose Acre, and they would not even have said goodbye. Then how much happiness could she have had, with that legacy of guilt and pain?

Oliver drove the car into the driveway of Bishop's End. 'The dogs must think we've deserted them. Poor old things,' Oliver said as he unlocked the door and they heard the barking and scrabbling from the kitchen. 'Poor Thomasine, you look done in.'

'I am tired,' she said wearily, pushing back her hair from her face with a gesture which implied it was almost too much effort.

'Have a brandy.'

'No, I'd better not get too comfortable or I won't want to go.'

'Then don't,' he said softly. They opened the kitchen door and allowed the three dogs to welcome them back enthusiastically. Oliver put his arm about her. 'Stay here tonight.'

'I could, couldn't I? Even my dog's here,' she smiled through her exhaustion. How often she'd wished she could sleep with him for a whole night, wake in the morning to feel him close beside her. It hadn't been possible with Nadine at home, a Nadine who monitored her movements with the moral severity of a nun. And now she was so tired that the idea of making love was the last thing she wanted.

'Just to sleep, curled up like spoons. What do you think? You're too tired for anything else.' He kissed her cheek gently. She looked at him tenderly.

'It's almost as if you know what I'm thinking.'

'I wish I did – then I'd know.'

'Know what?'

He stroked her hair and leant his head against hers, and when he spoke it was so muffled that she told him she had not caught what he said.

'I'm frightened you might have made a bargain with God.' He looked at the floor as he spoke, as if afraid of what response he might see in her eyes. 'You know, before you knew that Nadine was all right, you might have promised God to ditch me if He saved her. And now you feel you're stuck with it.'

Thomasine clasped her hand over her mouth and looked at him with horror-filled eyes. 'What have I said?' he asked anxiously.

'The truth.' She sighed. 'Only, oh God, I'm so ashamed of myself, I couldn't do it! I reckoned I should. *Please God, if you let Nadine live I'll give up Oliver.* It was so simple, but when it came to it, I couldn't make the promise. I couldn't face losing you! I feel dreadful about it. What sort of mother am I?' And what must you think of me, she thought, but did not say it, afraid what his answer might be.

Gently he cradled her face in his hands and stood looking at her for what seemed an age.

'I love you, Thomasine. Like I've never loved anyone before. When I'm free – will you marry me?'

On top of everything else this was almost too much for Thomasine, who felt she was about to cry from happiness. 'Oh, please,' she said in a whisper, which wasn't exactly what she had intended; they were not the words she had practised, those times she'd fantasised when alone in bed and waiting for sleep.

'Oh, my darling, I'm sorry. You've had a bastard of a night and then I'm so stupid, I spring this on you.'

Afraid he hadn't heard her correctly, she pulled herself together with a shake of the head. 'I couldn't think of anyone I'd rather spend the rest of my life with,' she said, which she thought sounded a lot better. Evidently Oliver did too, for he hugged her so tight, as if afraid she was about to escape from him. Miraculously, Thomasine found that all her exhaustion had disappeared in a flash, and sleep was the last thing on her mind.

The dawn was fast approaching when, snuggled close

in the crook of his arm, squashed close together in the narrow space that three deeply sleeping dogs occupying the rest of the bed allowed, he whispered in her ear. 'If you had made a promise to God, what would you have given up?'

She giggled. 'Don't be shocked. I did make a bargain – not much of one, but other than you, it was the only thing I could think of giving up which I didn't want to. Gin!' she replied.

Kimberley had hardly slept. Her pillow was damp from tears. She felt bereft, empty. She saw her dreams fading, as insubstantial as the morning mist. She cuddled up to Sieglinde, whose large head with its tender expression rose from the pillow they shared. With hooded eyes she looked at Kimberley, and then her long, pink tongue appeared and licked her face, as if licking her tears away.

'Sieglinde, what am I to do?' She nuzzled the ruff of hair at the dog's neck, the softest part of her, and drew comfort from the closeness and warmth of the huge dog.

If everyone believed as Alan did, that she had warned her father, how long could she expect to keep this job? How could she expect Eveleigh, with her passion for dogs, to retain her with suspicion like that hanging over her? And as if losing Alan wasn't enough, she would lose Nadine too – another one with passionate views about dogs. Alan, Nadine, Eveleigh, the dogs, it would be too much – she might just as well be dead.

Everything was so unfair. Last night her father, thinking her one of the demonstrators, had slapped her face so hard her head had rocked back and forth on her neck. He had accused her of informing on him and would not believe that she hadn't. Worse, her mother agreed with him and hit her too, and spat at her, telling her she never wanted to see her again.

Damp from her own tears, squashed by the huge dogs, Kimberley gave up. She might just as well be up and working as lying here feeling sorry for herself. If she was doing something, then maybe she could put her misery aside, if only for the time being.

Eveleigh found her scrubbing out the kennels. Not the normal daily cleaning, when the runs were sluiced and the kennels mopped, but on her knees with a scrubbing brush, frantically attacking every inch, the scent of disinfectant heavy in the air.

'My dear Kimberley, what are you doing?' Eveleigh stepped back with horror when Kimberley looked up at her, and she saw her swollen, discoloured face. 'Oh, my poor child, who's done this to you? Let me help.' She put out her hand and Kimberley grabbed at it. Eveleigh helped pull her to her feet. 'I think we've got to talk.'

'The dogs' feeds,' Kimberley said, with difficulty through swollen lips, stuttering her words between sobs, which Eveleigh's concern had reactivated.

'They can wait. It won't hurt them, just this once.' Eveleigh led Kimberley into the kitchen. She sat her down on a chair and, before asking her to explain anything, collected a bowl of warm water, cotton-wool balls and some witch-hazel. 'Such a pretty face,' she tutted as she worked, bathing the girl gently, soothing the bruises. Then she made a pot of tea and, despite the hour, added a large tot of whisky to it. 'Peps you up fast,' she explained to a doubtful Kimberley. 'Soothes the hurt inside. Now, I want to know, Kimberley. Did Alan do this to you?'

'Oh no. Not Alan. It was my father . . .'

Eveleigh sat silent as Kimberley, at first with difficulty, but eventually in a torrent of words, told of her father, the dogs, the puppies, her shame, and finally explained the events of the previous evening. 'I went there . . . I'm not even sure why . . . And Alan blames me . . .' Her voice finally trailed off, the sorry tale told.

Eveleigh sat for a moment looking with rapt attention at her hands, as if they held the key. Kimberley slumped in the chair, exhausted now, docilely awaiting her fate.

'I've never heard such a load of codswallop in my life!

493

What a dreadful situation. The choices you faced would've taxed anyone! Look at the number of wives and mothers who know their man is a rapist or murderer, and can't bring themselves to phone the police. It's the same sort of dilemma.'

Kimberley managed a wan smile at the way Eveleigh equated murder with cruelty to dogs. She would, she thought.

'But I knew about his activities and I eventually knew they were wrong – the puppy farming, the dog fighting – and I did nothing. I'm guilty by association. I should have stopped him.'

'How? You were a child. Just one look at your face shows what a violent person you were having to deal with. As soon as you could escape, you did.'

'Yes, but I left the animals to their fate.'

'I don't think you could be expected to shop your own father.'

'But it's not as if I loved him.'

'Perhaps not, but one has a sense of duty, even if misplaced. And the poor dogs. There was nothing there, you said?'

'Not one dog. It was as if they'd never been, it was as if I'd imagined it all.'

'I wonder where they've been taken – does your father have a close friend who might have helped him out?'

'He knows no one – not in that way.'

'Still, it's put a nice, neat finish to his activities, hasn't it? The RSPCA are sure to keep a sharp eye on him now – he wouldn't dare start up again, would he?'

'What if he moves away? And what about the dogs and puppies?'

'Ah well, my dear, that doesn't bear thinking about.' Eveleigh shook her head sadly.

Alan had not slept either. He could not think of a time when he'd been so depressed. The nature of his work

494

often led him to disappointment, but his failure was made worse by Kimberley's involvement.

He could never forgive her – never. Would he continue with buying the house now? If he didn't complete the purchase he'd lose his deposit, but could he ever live there with the memory of his happy times with Kimberley, and having to be constantly reminded of her duplicity? Could he face the house aware that the joy he'd known there was lost to him for ever?

He thought he had known her, he'd been convinced he'd found his soulmate. How wrong could one be? It was beyond his comprehension that anyone could behave as she had. He'd been trained not to get too involved; part of his job, when undercover, was to be able to witness cruelty to the animals he loved and not by a blink to show his distress, his anger at man's insensitivity to living creatures. But this time he was not dispassionate – his anger against Kimberley was total.

He had other painful memories too. The dressing-down he'd received from the police inspector was far worse than he'd anticipated. He was left feeling demoralised, unprofessional – a fool!

Lost as he was in these dark thoughts, he jumped when the telephone rang.

'It's on again.' He heard Andy say.

'You're joking!'

'Nah. Sorry to interrupt your Sunday lie-in, but I've just heard from Don. It's on this morning, so you'd best get your skates on.'

'You sure this isn't another wild goose chase?'

'No. Your Deep Throat friend has come clean. He's a Graham Garner – known as Greaser.'

'Why should he suddenly allow us to know who he is?' Alan asked suspiciously.

'He was one of the FAA people last night. Says he's pretty sure Tom White didn't see him and that when he met up with his mate last night he was falling about laughing at their cleverness in shifting the dogs. This mate – a creep called Butch – hasn't got a dog, but follows the fights. Greaser said he'd like to go next time and Butch told him where the dogs are and the venue. Just like that! If they cancel this fight they won't have time to move the puppies and bitches.'

'They had time enough last time.'

'The joint's already staked out. The fuzz have got it surrounded – anyone can get in, but no one gets out without their say so.'

'Even so –' Alan was still doubtful, his depression making sure he only saw the darkest side of things this morning.

'Don thinks it more than likely. He reckons the bastards have been lulled into a false sense of security. After last night's cock-up, they think we're off with our tails between our legs and the coast is clear. Clever, really, when you thing about it. And I suppose with creeps coming from London and the Midlands they've had to lay on something.'

'Devious sods. When and where's the briefing?'

'Morristown. Nine-thirty. I've put the vet on stand-by. Ta ra.'

Alan quickly showered and changed. He was glad this had happened – he needed something to keep his mind off Kimberley.

49

Oliver offered to take Thomasine to the hospital to collect Nadine, but she declined. 'I need to talk to her by myself,' she said, her face set in a determined line.

'Don't be too hard on her.'

'She could have been killed.'

'But she wasn't, was she? Are you going to tell her

about us getting married?' He smiled, somewhat sheep-ishly, as he spoke.

'I don't know – where Nadine's concerned, it's best to play it by ear.' She stood on tiptoe to kiss him goodbye. 'I still can't believe it's true. That you love me.'

'Join the club.' He kissed the tip of her nose and held the car door open for her.

In the kitchen he put the kettle on for coffee, and he wandered back into the hall, Bandage, Slipper and Nova padding along behind him with nails clicking like castanets on the wooden floor.

The telephone rang shrilly. He paused before picking up the receiver. It was an odd thing, but he knew it was bad news before he even picked it up.

'Hullo –' he said, tentatively.

'Oliver – you said if I wanted to talk – you said you'd collect me. Oh, Oliver – come quick.'

'Wimpole, what is it?'

'I can't talk. Not now. He'll hear.' And the line went dead. Oliver was in his car in a flash and en route for Wimpole's cottage.

Nadine appeared to be no worse off for her ordeal. In fact she was more cheerful than she had been in months. She apparently liked the nurses, for Thomasine, as she entered the ward, found her sitting on her bed, fully dressed, laughing and joking with a circle of admiring young women. She stopped laughing at sight of her mother.

'I've come to take you home, Nadine,' she said, feeling suddenly awkward, as if she had walked in uninvited on someone's private party.

'Mrs Lambert, we think your daughter is so brave. Anything could have happened to her last night,' a plump nurse gushed.

'I'm proud of her too,' Thomasine replied. 'Very proud,' she emphasised. She looked at Nadine, who smiled slightly in response.

On the drive back to the house they talked of the

weather, the nurses, the number of magpies they saw, all inconsequential matters, in silent accord to delay discussion of weightier subjects until they were home.

'Where's Nova?' Nadine asked immediately they entered the house and no dog came scurrying to meet them.

'Oliver's looking after her for me.' Immediately she wished she hadn't said that. She should have thought to cover up where she'd been all night, and returned the dog before going to the hospital.

'Oh yes!' Nadine said knowingly, and began picking over the fruit in the bowl in a desultory manner, as if not sure if she wanted to eat anything or not. 'Did you mean it?' She swung round and faced her mother.

'What?'

'That you're proud of me.'

'Yes. I am. *Very*.' Thomasine paused, unsure how to continue. 'But that doesn't mean that I'm happy about what you did. I thought I was going to pass out with fear.'

Nadine grinned broadly with pride. 'I didn't think you'd care what I did.'

'I can't imagine why. I really do love you, Nadine, whatever you think.'

'I've made it hard for you at times, haven't I? To love me, I mean.'

'Sometimes.' Thomasine felt that if she'd been standing she'd be reeling with shock.

'I don't know why I do it, you know. Half the time I don't want to – it just happens.'

'You know, I think it will be happening less now. Once you acknowledge something like that, then you're halfway to solving it. At least in my experience.'

'You've been very patient. I mean, what with Dad being such a shit –'

'Nadine!' Thomasine tried to look shocked, but instead failed and found she was laughing.

498

'It's true. We both have been. Mind you, Chantal was the biggest shit of all.'

'Just because I laughed you needn't think that gives you *carte blanche* to swear like that.'

'It's true though, isn't it? How's Oliver?'

Thomasine put her hand to her head, amazed. 'What's changed, Nadine? I'm almost afraid to believe this is happening – you'll be saying you love Nova next.'

'I do – well, a bit. I still think she's ugly. No, it was last night. I mean, if I had been killed – banging my head like that, the doc said I could have. Well, if I had, you'd have been left all alone. That's unreasonable, isn't it? And you'd be left with nothing resolved, just bad feelings. And I wouldn't want you to remember me like that – hateful, selfish – gross!' She grinned at her use of the last word.

'Don't even talk about dying!'

'And I was scared last night – it was different from any other demo I'd been on. It was a raid, and really violent. I didn't like most of those people, I think some of them were more interested in the chance of a fight than the dogs. And when I saw you and Oliver – it was the best moment I'd had in years. And I realised how much I loved you, and, well, that's it really.'

'Oliver is very nice you know, and he cares about you too. And, well –' She paused, still uncertain this conversation was real, but Nadine had to be told. 'He's asked me to marry him, and I said yes.'

'That's brill! Where will we live?' Nadine said, with barely a pause.

'I don't know, we haven't talked about that, he only asked me last night.'

'Ah ha, I see – up to hanky-panky as soon as my back's turned,' Nadine grinned mischievously. Thomasine pretended to hit her.

'Cheeky! Which do you think you'd prefer?'

'His place. It's bigger than here. And I'm sorry I called you names – I was confused.'

'I understand. I'd forgotten already,' she fibbed. She stood up. 'That's settled, then. What do you fancy for lunch?' And she found herself marvelling that in the midst of such momentous discussions and decisions she should think of stomachs, but that, no doubt, was what being a mother was all about.

'Thing is, Mum, I really will try – to be better, I mean. I might not manage it all the time. I expect I'll have the odd gross day.'

'What a relief!' she laughed.

'What's funny?'

'You are, my darling. Oh, how I love you! Now I know you *really* mean it.' She ruffled Nadine's hair which, judging by the violent way she jerked her head away, did not go down well. And then, as if realising her reaction, she ruffled it herself and grinned broadly at her mother.

'What about Kimberley, Mum?' she asked abruptly.

'What about her?'

'I'm just so shocked. That was her father's place, you realise. She must have known what was going on there – and never told. I don't think I ever want to see her again – ever.'

'Don't decide anything until you've talked to her. You don't know what went on in her life – maybe she was terrified of her father. There's not a lot you can do about anything, no matter how you feel, if you're threatened by the sort of violence that we've never known. Be understanding, Nadine.'

'Oh hell! Haven't I been nice enough for one day!'

'Why, oh why didn't you come and tell me?' Oliver, sitting at the table in Rudolph's cottage, pushed his hand through his hair in a gesture of frustration.

'Tell you what? That I'd made the biggest mistake of my life?'

'I'll be honest, I was surprised when you said you were getting married – it wasn't just my own confusion. I wondered why, at –' He stopped abruptly.

'At my age? Was that what you were going to say? Cheeky!'

'Well, yes. I should have asked you outright.'

'Would I have known the answer? Oh, I took a fancy to him – he can be very nice. But I think, at the back of my mind, I felt that it wasn't fair to you to have me as a liability for the rest of my life.'

'You were never that, Wimpole.'

'But you didn't know what was ahead of you, did you? You might have met someone who wouldn't put up with me – and then where would I be? I suppose I was trying to carve out my own security – and a right mess I've landed myself in.' She put her fingers up and gingerly experimented with touching her swollen lips. 'My old mum always used to say that my mouth would get me into trouble one day – all lip, she used to call me. She was right. It must look as fat as an elephant's.' And she laughed, but Oliver realised it was not from humour but to cover up the unimaginable pain she must be feeling.

'When did you realise it was not going to work?'

'If I'm honest, I had me doubts before we even waddled up the aisle. He could be right as rain and then suddenly – whoosh – he'd be in a temper for no apparent reason. He's a violent sod. Then on that honeymoon . . .' She shuddered. 'Well, it wasn't nice, not nice at all. I said to him, I'm not having none of this, and that's when he whopped me the first time.'

Oliver, presuming she was referring to sex, had to cover his mouth with a hand so that she could not see his half smile. Instead he accepted a second cup of tea, suggested she try drinking hers with a straw, and he promised to buy her some when she said she didn't have any. 'So where is he now?'

'Gone out, and I hope he never comes back.'

'You're coming home with me.'

'I hoped you'd say that.'

'See, Bandage was right again. He didn't like Rudolph one little bit, did he? So why did you hit you this time?'

501

'Because I said I'd go to the police and report him, and he said –' She stopped, looked about the small cottage room as if afraid Rudolph was still there and would hear her, and then began again. 'And he said if I snitched on him he'd bloody kill me. And I said he hadn't got the balls to do that – which was stupid of me, but by then I was in a rare old temper – and then he hit me. Then I called you and then he came back and I rang off, and I'm so scared. You see, he could, I know now he's quite capable of killing me.' The words had tumbled out of her in a panic-stricken rush.

'What on earth has he done that he'd kill you rather than let you tell?'

'It's the dogs.'

'What dogs?'

'The fighting dogs. Out the back.' She gestured with her head in that direction. 'In the kennels, he breeds them.'

As the realisation of what she was saying dawned on him, his anger hardened and grew until he felt as if there was nothing in him but this fury. 'Bandage, did he have anything to do with Bandage's disappearance?'

'No, but a friend of his did. He laughed. He thought it was funny. He said the stupid dog remembered him. I should have told you, I know. I didn't know what to do, which way to turn.' Wimpole began to cry, silently, as she saw the expression on Oliver's face. 'Oliver, be careful –' She put her hand out as if to restrain him but he shook her away.

'How long have you known?' he asked stiffly, not sure if he could control his fury with her either.

'Since I moved here.' She spoke barely louder than a whisper, as if that could minimise her shame.

'You have to tell me everything you know – *now.*'

The cold tone of his voice made her clutch her throat at the fear that she could lose him too. He sat opposite her, listening to her sorry tale, his face becoming stonier with every word. He had thought he was full of anger

502

before, but that was nothing to the rage which was beginning to boil up within him at the appalling story she was relating. He stood up abruptly, pushing his chair back so that it fell with a clatter to the floor. He did not bend to pick it up, for he was deaf and blind to everything but his new and desperate need to avenge.

'Oliver, he's mad –' Wimpole too was on her feet. But he did not hear her, did not see her hand outstretched to delay him, and forgot his promise to take her with him. He rushed from the room and out into his car.

The narrow roads which criss-crossed Ben Luckett's estate, of necessity, slowed Oliver's driving until he was banging the steering wheel with frustration at his speed. The stupid woman, she had wasted so much time, why could she not have told him the minute he arrived, he muttered to himself. Without stopping he swung the car through the gates and once on the main road was able to put his foot down. He drove fast, too fast.

He was delayed further by a large horsebox lumbering along in front of him. He hit his horn and flashed his lights, but the vehicle blocked him. He inched out and saw a short stretch of straight road where only a maniac would overtake. He pulled out, pushed his foot down hard, and prayed. A car was approaching, on collision course. He took a deep breath and forced an extra smidgeon of speed from his car, snaked in front of the horsebox at too acute an angle, almost clipping its fender and, fighting to control the car, careered towards his destination.

By the time he arrived at the house of his father-in-law, he was drenched in sweat, his heart was racing, he was dry-mouthed from nerves, his system flooded with adrenalin and his blood pressure sky high. He ran up the steps to the front door, not bothering to ring the bell but pushing the door open and stalking in. He called out, but nobody anwered. He searched in the drawing room, dining room, in the study, in the kitchen, but the house was deserted. He stood still, the only sound his beating heart. Now what? Suddenly he stiffened as he heard a roar of men's voices. He crossed to the den – a huge room with a full-size billiard table. At the far end was a double-glazed sliding door which led into the indoor swimming pool. He grabbed hold of the handle and slid it to one side.

The noise was deafening. A crowd of men, shouting and baying, were perched on the edge of the empty pool. They were so engrossed that they did not hear the door slide back, the sound of Oliver's footfall on the tiled surround, nor his exclamation of horror. They were totally oblivious to his shout of 'you cruel bastards!'

He stood on the edge of the pool and looked down on to a scene from hell. The bottom of the pool was covered in stained sawdust. A red line had been drawn dividing the arena into two halves. It was a suitable colour, given the amount of blood splattering the pale blue tiles of the pool. The men were screaming and shouting, some abuse and others encouragement. Standing at the deep end Ben Luckett momentarily looked up, his eyes ablaze with excitement, a dribble of saliva trickling down his chin as he salivated from pleasure at the spectacle of two dogs, terrifyingly silent compared to the men, tearing each other to shreds for the entertainment of their owners.

'Sport! You bloody call this sport! You sub-human bastards!' Oliver screamed at them as he leapt into what would normally be the shallow end of the pool. He ran, slithering and sliding on the blood and saliva, towards the dogs. His only thought was to separate them. He was a third of the way along when a man jumped down, landing heavily on top of him, and rolled him roughly on to the floor.

'Mind your own fucking business.' He recognised Rudolph's snarl. Oliver, despite Rudolph's considerable weight, scrabbled to his feet and, heaving with all his might, threw Rudolph onto his back. He had the satisfaction of hearing an animal-like grunt escape from Rudolph. He didn't stand a hope in hell, was his last

504

conscious thought, as a pile of bodies, like a rugger scrum, fell on top of him. The wind whistled out of his crushed lungs and all he could feel was pain until, mercifully, everything turned to darkness.

He lost the darkness, and wanted the comfort of it back. Hot, searing pain arched through him, as if his whole body was broken. All there was in the universe was pain . . . In the distance, a long way from him, he began to hear a great roaring, drumming noise . . . As he tumbled through the tunnel from unconsciousness to consciousness, accompanied by the agony, the noises separated, became clearer. They were coming closer. And then they were all around him. Shouting, screaming, roaring. He heard the thud but could not yet see as men toppled over into the pool, slamming down onto the hard tiles, grunting, groaning. He heard the sound of dogs barking – ferocious, alarmed, violent dogs. He could not as yet tell that the barking was not from the dogs he had tried to save, for they were oblivious to everything but their fight, their laboured breathing adding to the general cacophony.

He felt the pressure on his body ease as one by one the men were removed from him. He lay flat, still winded, trying to breathe normally. His mouth was full of sawdust, the salt taste of blood on his tongue. Gingerly, he sat up, and winced as what felt like a dozen sharp knives stabbed inside his chest. He shook his head and looked around him. The swimming pool was a heaving mass of fighting men, human blood mingling with that of the dogs. They skidded and fell on the ever-spreading crimson pools. In their midst, teeth firmly rooted in each other's flesh, ignoring the mayhem around them, the dogs continued their ominously silent struggle as men fought and fell on all sides.

Oliver slumped against the side of the pool, for a moment enjoying the cool feeling of the tiles against his cheek. Two men in uniforms he did not recognise stealthily approached the dogs, holding wooden staves with wedged ends. Expertly they rammed the wedges into the dogs' mouths and, with muscles bulging at the strength needed to prise the determined jaws apart, freed them from their cruel dance of death.

Oliver yelled in agony as he was yanked to his feet, his arm painfully twisted behind his back. 'Hang on a minute, I'm bloody hurt,' he managed to say, but after that he did not seem to be able to hack through the muddle in his head to find the right words to stop them clipping on a pair of handcuffs. He was left standing, propped up against the side of the pool.

Now he could see Rudolph sprawled unconscious on his back on the bottom of the pool, covered in blood, his mouth open. Ben, purple with rage, his eyes bulging alarmingly, was in handcuffs too. The place was a mêlée of police, police dogs and RSPCA inspectors as they rounded up the spectators.

'This way.' A young policeman pulled at Oliver, another pushed him in the back and someone, he wasn't fast enough to see who, kicked him in the shins.

'Not again!' he sighed. 'I'm not one of them. I was trying to break the bloody fight up,' Oliver protested, but the effort of saying all that was almost too much for him. He felt himself sway as if his legs had been drained of blood and sinew.

'Oh yes, sir? That's what they all say.' And the policeman unceremoniously shoved Oliver up the steps of the pool. 'You're coming along with me.'

50

It was chaos at the police station. The duty sergeant had given up trying to keep his temper and was shouting for some semblance of order as he attempted to process the sudden influx of customers.

Oliver looked up. One large fair-haired man was swinging his fist at an only slightly smaller one.

'You fucking creep, I knew you were a plant! I bloody knew!' Vic shouted.

Alan put up his hand and grabbed hold of Vic's wrist. 'Sorry about that, mate. But animals come first in my book.'

'You slime. I should have fucking killed you when I had the chance,' Vic shouted as two burly coppers restrained him. 'How do you sleep at night being a ponce!'

'And how well do you sleep, Vic, after torturing defenceless animals? You're sub-human, you are.' And he swung on his heel and ducked into one of the interview rooms to prevent himself from smashing his fist into Vic's face. It would only give him momentary satisfaction and would be followed by a lot of problems he could do without.

Oliver had given up trying to explain he wasn't one of *them*, and sat philosophically on a bench awaiting his turn. He hugged his chest to ease the pain slightly. Conscious of someone sitting down beside him, he shuffled his rear along the seat, and looked up to see Ben Luckett, perspiring profusely.

'Hullo, Ben. Come here often?'

'Don't you ever take anything seriously? Do you always have to behave like a facetious twit?'

'If I didn't make a joke of it, perhaps I wouldn't be able to control myself. Then I'd do what I really want to do, and you wouldn't ever see the light of day again, Ben.'

'Who are you kidding? See me shaking in my boots?'

'You are in a bit of a spot now, though, aren't you? No knighthood -- oh dear no, not the way the Queen feels about dogs.' Oliver laughed quietly. 'And think of all the money you invested dreaming of the old "Arise, Si Benjamin" routine.'

'You shit!'

'No, Ben. You've got it wrong. You're the shit,

and that cruel bastard Rudie over there. What a nice pair you make. Got Rudie to do the dirty work, did you?' It was like casting a fly, he decided, getting Ben to spill the beans – not too fast, gently does it, he told himself.

'I don't know what you mean.'

'Don't you? If I say Eveleigh Brenton? Ring a bell?'

'Eveleigh? You know I know her.' Ben shrugged.

'Dogs. St Bernards in particular. One of them dead. Get my drift?'

'Oliver, I despair of you. No wonder Sophia wanted to ditch you.'

'Tell you what, Ben, I'm in a bit of a quandary here. I mean, I know you and Rudie did it. I'd just like to hear you say it.'

'You mean you've no proof. Bad luck, Oliver.' Ben threw back his head to laugh, and Oliver saw his back teeth were rotten and full of metal fillings whilst his front teeth shone white and perfect.

'Actually, Ben, I know an amazing amount. You should believe me.' Thanks to Wimpole, he was only lying a little.

'You don't fool me,' Ben counter-bluffed.

'That's a shame – for you, I mean. You see, I haven't been seen by our friendly coppers yet. It's not going to be that difficult to explain to them that I'm not one of your merry band. To show my appreciation of their courtesy and fulsome apologies – you know, to show I harbour no hard feelings – then I think I should drop in their shell-likes all I know about you, Rudie and the poisoned dog, don't you? Then you really would be looking at a prison sentence, Ben. On the other hand, if you tell me what I want to hear, if you do what I want you to – then I could be persuaded to forget it.' He touched his lips with his index finger.

'What do you want to know?' Ben asked with the resignation of the pragmatist.

'Well, for starters . . .'

An hour later Oliver accidentally compounded his

508

problems in the interview room. The officer asked him if he minded a member of the RSPCA being present. He was not entirely sure, but he thought the man sitting opposite him was the same young man who, last night at Primrose Acre, had said he knew Nadine – Kimberley's boyfriend.

'I do know Kimberley White,' he said, cheerfully offering her name as his credentials. 'She'll vouch for me, I'm sure.'

Alan paled. He stood abruptly, pushed his chair back, mumbled an excuse to the policeman and stalked from the room. He was still so angry over Kimberley, and hurt too. He could not be certain that in the presence of that creep he could maintain the professional detachment that was expected of him. Better by far to leave the interview.

Without Alan to vouch for him, it took Oliver three long hours of frustration, controlled temper, cajoling and apology to be believed and to get out of the police station. To add insult to injury, he had to get a taxi home from Morristown, since his car was still at Ben's.

He had hoped Thomasine would be there, but only the dogs welcomed him. He decided to have a bath to soothe his aching limbs and get rid of the smell of blood and the police cells. He had just lowered himself into the tub when the telephone rang.

'Where have you been? I've been worried sick.'

'It's a long story. Got a week?'

'I thought I'd better let you know that Nadine is being angelic and approves of us – can you imagine!'

'Can I come round?'

'I think you should. I've got Wimpole here, she's in a dreadful state. Would you bring Nova with you, please?'

'Hullo, Oliver!' Nadine was grinning broadly as she opened the door.

'How's the head?' he smiled back at her.

'Better than your mush. What happened?'

'I had an argument with a man about a dog.' He bent

down to unclip Nova's lead; the effort made him wince from the pain in his chest.

'Are you all right? You look funny,' Nadine enquired with unusual concern.

'I'm a bit sore – it's nothing,' he replied, thinking how brave he was.

'They're all through in the kitchen.'

'All' was Thomasine, Eveleigh and an agitated Wimpole who, from her red-rimmed eyes, had been crying hard, and at sight of Oliver looked as if she might quite easily start again.

'Wimpole, love, don't . . .' He realised that all his anger with her had evaporated.

'Don't even say it or I will,' she answered, blowing noisily into a man-sized handkerchief. 'I thought you'd never speak to me again.'

'Don't be silly.'

'What happened? We've been worried sick,' said Thomasine, standing on tiptoe for a kiss.

'Did you see Jim?' asked an equally anxious Eveleigh.

'Sorry, no. But it was such chaos.' He explained, at length, about the dog fight in the swimming pool, toning down the gory bits in deference to his audience.

'And Rudolph?' Wimpole asked, and Oliver wondered if he'd imagined it or was her voice tinged with sadness? If so, he hoped it was for what might have been and not for the man.

'He's in the clink with Ben. But knowing Ben's luck, they'll be out by nightfall.'

'Did you find out about, you know?' Wimpole asked, looking anxiously at the other women.

'What? That you'd overheard Rudie on the phone, presumably to Ben, saying he'd seen to the dog?' Oliver put it baldly, working on the principle that it would all have to come out eventually. It was probably better to do it straight away.

'Oh, no!' Eveleigh said.

'I managed to prise the lot out of Ben. It was as we

suspected, Thomasine. He'd said to Rudie that he wished someone would get rid of Eveleigh and her dogs for him. Rudie obliged – just as well he didn't try to get rid of you, Eveleigh. Ben swears he didn't know anything about it until you told him, Thomasine, and I'm inclined to believe him. He did lie, he hasn't sold the land – that was to divert our suspicions, Eveleigh.'

'But did my Isolde have to die? Such inhumanity.'

'Do we know who tipped them off about the fight at Primrose Acre?' Thomasine asked to divert Eveleigh's trend of thought.

'Yes, Beth.'

'Beth!' Thomasine and Eveleigh chorused together.

'Inadvertently. Ben overheard her talking to Cora, something about she hadn't asked Jim for some money owing to her in her rush to get out. Cora said she would run her over to pick it up on Saturday evening and Beth said there was no point, that Jim was expecting to be busy. Ben put two and two together – hey presto, all the dogs were moved.'

'Cora knew nothing about this, did she?' Thomasine asked anxiously, worried that if she had then she would never trust her judgement of people ever again.

'Not a dicky bird. Ben packed Cora and Sophia off to Paris for a weekend of shopping armed with his credit cards. And what's more he shipped Beth out too, Harry as well. They were sent to Euro-Disney via the tunnel. Treats that he knew they were unlikely to refuse.'

'Did you tell the police all this?' Thomasine asked.

'No.'

'Why on earth not?'

'The snippet of conversation Wimpole heard was not proof, it said nothing really. What dog? It could be any dog. Wimpole didn't like the way Rudie said he'd "seen to" the dog. She said it made her go chilly inside, didn't you, Wimpole? But she might have been imagining it. He could have meant he'd sprayed it with flea powder, or changed its feed. So I did a deal with Ben – if he was straight with me then I wouldn't tell the police.'

'But I don't understand why you had to make the deal,' Thomasine said.

'If Oliver hadn't forced it out of him then I would never have been able to relax, not knowing if it was him or, as the police thought, a jealous breeder. I would have always been looking over my shoulder – never sure. Isn't that it, Oliver?' Eveleigh asked. Oliver nodded. 'And was absolutely everything him?'

'The lot. The rumours, the gravel, insurance people – everything. Rudie helped him again there but he also used other people who owed him favours – even from your dog world, Eveleigh. He was like a Chicago gangster calling in his markers. I jotted down their names, if you want them.'

Eveleigh shuddered. 'I'd rather not know.'

'Very wise of you. Don't forget, he might have coerced them. You'd never know with a character like him.'

'But of course, none of this helps me with the Kennel Club. If they continue to believe the rumour-mongers then I'm finished as a breeder.'

'All taken care of, Eveleigh. He's agreed to write to them explaining he did it as a joke that got out of hand. He's willing to grovel for you – on the understanding we never tell about Isolde.'

'But how do you know you can trust him to do this for Eveleigh?'

'Simple. Unless she gets an acknowledgement from the Kennel Club that all has been explained and that she is no longer under suspicion, my bargain with Ben is null and void and I toddle off to the nick and tell them all. We've got him tied in knots.' He started to laugh, but stopped abruptly since it hurt his chest too much.

'Oliver, you've gone white, are you sure there's nothing wrong?' Eveleigh fussed.

'It's only my ribs; they took a bit of a lambasting.'

'You're going to the hospital,' Thomasine insisted.

'I'll go and see the doc –'

'Hospital,' Thomasine said firmly.

'God, woman, you're so bossy – I love it.'

'Oliver, I don't know if I shall ever be able to repay you.'

'No need, Eveleigh, it was my pleasure.'

'I think you should still shaft him.' Nadine spoke for the first time.

'No. I gave my word.'

'I could,' she said defiantly.

'Nadine, no! You don't understand what you would be up against,' Thomasine admonished.

'But to kill a dog?'

'Nadine, it's dreadful, I know. After all, it was my dog, but please, you'd not be doing me a favour. If you break Oliver's promise Ben might return to the attack. The dogs are my only concern. I suggest that we tell no one outside this room – and that includes Jim. I think it might put him in an intolerable position professionally.'

Nadine was obviously thinking, weighing up the pros and cons. 'Well, all right then, but for the sake of the dogs only.' She was quite taken back by the adults' approval of her decision, unused as she was to it.

'What made you telephone Oliver this morning, Wimpole?' Thomasine asked, suddenly aware that the older woman had been sitting in the corner of the room, saying nothing.

'I –' She looked over at Oliver as if asking for help.

'You'd seen some dogs about, hadn't you, Wimpole, and didn't like the look of them. She thought they were pit bulls.' Wimpole smiled at him, grateful that he was not about to tell them that she had known full well what dogs were bred in Ben Luckett's kennels and had an even shrewder idea about the dog fight, though even she hadn't known it was to be held in Ben's swimming pool.

'Why was the fight in the swimming pool? Imagine the expence of emptying and then having to fill it. That I don't understand,' said Eveleigh.

'It's an ideal place, easy to sluice the blood away when it's all over.'

'Oh never!' Eveleigh wished she hadn't asked.

'Ben'll be off to Spain, I bet you. He'll want to escape the scandal. No knighthood for him now.' Oliver once again felt a degree of satisfaction at that.

'There's just one thing, Oliver. How can you guarantee that the person who buys the land off Ben won't do the same to Eveleigh?'

'I can guarantee that totally, Thomasine. You see, I'm buying the land.'

'*I love you*,' Thomasine mouthed at him just as the telephone rang. 'It's for you, Eveleigh.' She handed over the instrument.

'Jim, what a lovely surprise.' As she spoke Oliver and Thomasine looked at each other knowingly. But the joke faded as they listened to Eveleigh's voice becoming serious, noted the absence of any smile. 'That's horrendous!' she said, replacing the telephone. 'I've got to go up to Ben's.'

Twenty minutes later they drove up to the back of Ben Luckett's house in convoy, Thomasine driving Oliver, with Eveleigh following in her cumbersome Bentley. Nadine had been persuaded to stay behind.

They found Jim and a gaggle of police and RSPCA men in a barn beyond the stables. As they approached, Jim looked up, his face set in a rigid expression. 'Bless you, Eveleigh, I thought we could rely on you.' He looked more tired than any of them had ever seen him before.

Thomasine grabbed hold of Oliver's hand for support at the sight that awaited them. In boxes, crates, behind wire netting, were dogs of every breed. Dogs, bitches, puppies – lice-ridden, with suppurating sores and no spirit shining in their eyes, no tails awag, like normal dogs. They cowered in fear, backing away from the hands that were trying to treat them, as though unused to anything but cruelty.

'Tom White?' Thomasine asked.

'We assume so.'

'The poor creatures.' Thomasine sank on one knee to pick up a puppy – a Yorkshire Terrier, she thought, but its hair was so encrusted with filth it was difficult to tell.

'How many?' Oliver asked.

'We've counted sixty so far, and then there are the pit bulls.' Jim nodded to a corner of the barn where five dogs sat in separate cages, one covered in blood from recent wounds. Four others, scarred but not bleeding, sat and watched them with wary eyes.

'The whole thing's odd. The RSPCA inspector told me that normally only two dogs are brought to a venue to be matched, but this time they presumably planned three fights. They'd obviously only had time for one. I had to destroy the other dog -- it was past help. This one will mend, I hope. Those others must have been the next acts in the cabaret,' he said bitterly.

'Still, they bagged the lot,' Oliver said with satisfaction.

'Yes, we were lucky. Normally Ben would have been conveniently away for the day. They were obviously so confident that there would be no raid, he took the risk. And to think I liked him and thought he cared for animals. Unbelievable.' Jim shook his head.

'Man's best friend! That's a laugh, isn't it? When you see how we abuse them?' Eveleigh said. 'How many dogs do you want me to take?'

'The inspector will tell you. It's very good of you, Evie.' He put out his hand to touch her, and then, realising it was covered in blood, snatched it back. Eveleigh put up her own hand and touched his cheek.

'You look so tired,' she said softly.

Alan had been sent from the police station back to the Lucketts' to help the hard-pressed uniformed inspectors. 'Excuse me,' said Eveleigh to the others upon seeing him. 'Alan, may I have a word?'

'I heard you're helping, taking a load of the dogs until

we can find homes for them. That's good of you, Mrs Brenton.'

'It's nothing of the sort. I feel privileged to be asked to help.'

'That's nice. Still, you might have them for some time – the puppies will be easy enough to rehouse, but the bitches – that's another story.'

'I doubt if some of them ever will be. They're too traumatised ever to settle in a normal family. But it's not the dogs I want to talk to you about. It's –'

'Kimberley? I'd rather not talk about her, if you don't mind, Mrs Brenton.'

'But you must, Alan. The poor child is distraught.'

'So she should be after what she's allowed to happen.'

'But, Alan, she's only a child. What could she have done? Have you no compassion?'

'For the dogs – yes. For her – not a scrap. Excuse me, Mrs Brenton, I've work to do.' And he turned and walked away from her.

January

51

Christmas came and went. As a forest takes time to recover from a great storm, so Shillingham and the Shillings took time to recover from the awful events at Ben Luckett's.

People divided neatly into two groups. The largest said they'd always had their suspicions about Ben, always knew he was up to no good. 'You only had to look at his eyes,' was a common phrase. They were not surprised. The other group, smaller by far, evinced astonishment that such a 'nice' man should have been involved in such appalling cruelty; some even said they were sure there must have been a mistake. Unfortunately for Ben, this group lacked both the weight of numbers and the verbosity of the majority, who appeared also to be rather enjoying Ben's downfall.

Ben did not face the fine of two thousand pounds, or six months in jail, that was the maximum punishment in law. (At this information, 'Pathetic,' or 'It should be life,' were frequently repeated.) Ben, as Oliver had predicted, had scarpered to Spain as soon as he was out of police custody. 'At least he can watch the bullfights,' Eveleigh was heard to say acidly.

Ben's financial affairs were in a more fragile state than anyone had realised. So Cora, left to deal with a mountain of debts and the forced sale of her home by the bank, received much sympathy and understanding. But Oliver remembered the stand she'd taken when he'd asked her to help over the kennels, and knew he would never feel the same about her again, and Eveleigh herself harboured serious doubts that Cora was entirely ignorant of her husband's activities. Eveleigh knew that if ever she had to choose between a husband and dogs, she would have no crisis of loyalty; she would not hesitate to turn him in.

Sophia was too mortified to return home, ever, which suited Thomasine very well.

The loss of Ben as an employer was felt deeply in the community. The receivers had pared the remaining employees down to a skeleton staff, just enough to keep the estate ticking over. It reflected in the local shops' takings, of course, so redundancies were inevitable. Both Grace White's sons faced being laid off from the home farm, unless a buyer could be found quickly – unlikely, with the market in such a parlous state. Beth was looking for a new job, difficult with a young son. And Rudie had moved away, no one knew where.

Oliver had cracked two ribs in the fight, but there was no question of him lying on a sofa while Thomasine nursed him tenderly, especially as she had been with him when the doctor told him to 'carry on as before'. Instead he opted for a fine line in stoicism, and was rewarded with much admiration for his courage. His purchase of the land assured the safety of Eveleigh's kennels. She, in turn, hired the land back from him for more space to exercise her dogs.

Thomasine and Oliver, to the detriment of Thomasine's Treats, saw each other every day, their relationship intensifying until it seemed that they had no need of anyone or anything else. This was not strictly true: Thomasine was always conscious of Nadine, but since she had met a young RSPCA inspector who worked locally, her daughter was in love, happy and, most importantly, happy for her mother too. And without doubt both Thomasine and Oliver needed their dogs.

Tom White and his wife were ostracised. No stall-holder would buy his vegetables, and when they wanted to shop they had to travel to the anonymity of Morristown. He had not only to face charges in relation to the dog fighting; the RSPCA were prosecuting him for causing unnecessary suffering to the dogs on his puppy farm. They hoped he would be banned for life from keeping animals, but knowing the unpredictability of the courts, they had prepared themselves for less.

Alan continued with his purchase of the house. He did not plan to live there but to rent it out instead. He was glad when he was assigned to a group monitoring the export of live sheep, trailing convoys across Europe to check the animals were rested and watered, as EEC laws required, on the long journey to their final destination. He was busy and deeply involved in the work, which was necessary, but could be dangerous. He thought often of Kimberley, but with anger and bitterness.

Kimberley had always worked hard but now, as if in atonement for her father's sins and her own cowardice, she laboured for the dogs' welfare in such a way that Eveleigh was concerned for her.

'You need time off, Kimberley.'

'I need to do it, Mrs Brenton. I won't rest until each dog that came from Primrose Acre has been loved back to health.'

Eveleigh did not say what she feared – that that day would never come. The puppies had been no problem, and good homes were easily found for them, especially when the media picked up on the horrifying tale. The mature bitches were another matter. Jim Varley could cure their ills and Kimberley and Eveleigh could nurse their poor, undernourished and skinny bodies back to health, but Eveleigh doubted if all of them would ever recover their spirits completely, if their fear of man would ever be replaced by trust.

Of these bitches, Eveleigh took a King Charles into her house as a companion for the ageing Coco; Oliver adopted an Old English Sheepdog and Thomasine a Yorkshire Terrier; Gill and Justin welcomed a miniature poodle. The RSPCA, Jim Varley and Eveleigh decided that the remaining eight, too nervous to risk placing with families, would be better off spayed and cared for by her in the kennels, until the day they died. The same decisions, hard though they were, had to be repeated at the dog refuge and at Fee Walters', where the other Tom White dogs had been taken.

Jim often dined at Eveleigh's and she had, on the odd occasion, dined at his house, albeit doing the cooking herself. Jim had also taken her out to dinner in Shillingham, and they had attended a couple of dog shows together. Their relationship had settled into a comfortable cosiness in which Jim thought he'd never been happier, but with which Eveleigh was less content.

Thomasine emerged from the doctor's surgery feeling stunned. It was not possible! She went straight to The Copper Kettle, and ordered a coffee.

She was pregnant!

She had gone to the doctor because she thought herself menopausal. She had been content with that idea. She wanted no more children, Nadine was enough for anyone! And how good to start this new life with Oliver with no concerns about contraception. So she had thought.

She ordered another cup of coffee and, to comfort herself, a large slab of chocolate cake. How to tell Oliver? She wanted to marry him, but how would she feel if, in the future, in the midst of a row, he should turn to her and say 'I only married you because of the baby'? She did not want that.

And Nadine! She blanched at the thought of having to tell her daughter she was pregnant. She could imagine how horrified she would be – what seventeen-year-old wanted to be seen with a pregnant forty-three-year-old – heavens no, she'd be forty-four in a month – mother?

She could, of course, as the doctor had hinted, get rid

of it. Have an abortion. All neat and tidy, Oliver need not even know. A night in London – she was going shopping, she could tell him, staying with her mother – Oh dear God! Her mother. She could just imagine the furore when she told her. She ordered another cup of coffee and was halfway through it when she realised she was late for her hair appointment.

'Well, what a to-do it's all been, hasn't it?' Gill said as he fussed over her hair. 'Our poor little Sandie, she looks so scared all the time. Our Sadie's been a saint with her. She and Sukie are busy teaching her how to be a dog.'

'That's nice. Yes, my fiancé's dogs and mine are the same with the two we adopted. They're very protective too.'

'We could learn a lot from dogs, I always say. They're certainly kinder to each other than we are. What's awful is Justin and I didn't know it went on – puppy farming, I mean.'

'Me neither. Though I must admit that sometimes I'd see adverts for puppies listing half a dozen breeds and I thought, that's odd, one breeder breeding so many different dogs. I know now.'

'What, that they're a puppy farmer's?'

'That or an agent's. I tell everyone, beware of adverts like that.'

'At our class we're getting the message across. Thought any more about coming?'

'I might – we have five dogs between us now. They're quite a handful.'

'You come along. Bring your fiancé. I tell you, it's a laugh a minute.'

On the way back home Thomasine practised half a dozen scenarios of how to break the news to Oliver, and hadn't opted for the right one by the time she reached The Old School House.

'There's a message for you from Oliver. He wants you to pop over – soon as poss,' Nadine said, as she helped unload the bags from the car. Thomasine was still adjusting to having a helpful daughter. She always thanked her extravagantly, but she'd schooled herself not to be surprised if, overnight, the monster Nadine returned.

The groceries unpacked, she drove straight over to Oliver's to find an agitated Wimpole in the kitchen, cleaning silver. 'You made me jump!' She dropped a fork on to the floor.

'Sorry. Where's Oliver?'

'In Phoebe's Hall, where else?' Wimpole replied, and knocked the bottle of silver polish flying. Thomasine bent to pick it up.

'Wimpole, I've been meaning to ask you and I always forget – did Rudolph ever say anything to you about having a bulldog?'

'A bulldog? No, I can't say I remember him mentioning one. Why?'

'Oh, just a thought.' Thomasine would have loved to know if it had been from Rudolph's car that Luna had been slung all those months ago. And was it Rudolph, in a roundabout way, she had to thank for getting to know dogs – Luna and Nova in particular? But she supposed she'd never know now. As another fork clattered to the floor she thought perhaps the subject of Rudolph and dogs was upsetting Wimpole, so she went in search of Oliver.

'What's wrong with Wimpole?' Thomasine asked, kissing the top of Oliver's head as he bent over his work. 'She seems in a bit of a state.'

'She's been evicted.'

'She's what?'

'Well, not exactly, but the estate's been sold and she's got to get out of her cottage by the end of March.'

'Poor Wimpole. Then what?' she asked, but already knew the answer.

'That's what I wanted to talk to you about –'

'It's all right by me.'

'You don't know what I was going to suggest.'

'I imagine you were going to say she'd come here to live.'

'Well, you're wrong. I wouldn't presume such a thing, not when we're getting married. We are still, I hope?'

'Please.' She pursed her lips for a kiss, and then remembered. A shiver raced through her.

'What's the matter?'

'Nothing.'

'My darling Thomasine. Please, do me a favour. Please don't ever say "nothing". In my experience it always means all hell's about to break loose.'

'I'm pregnant,' she burst out, not at all in the way she had intended. She stood in the middle of the room, her arms limply at her side, looking at her shoes and realising she was slightly pigeon-toed, but not wanting to look at him, anything but that.

She heard him cross the room, felt him take hold of her face in his hands, but she kept her eyes closed.

'Look at me.'

'I can't.'

'Please.' He bent forward and kissed both eyelids gently.

'I didn't mean to tell you like this,' she mumbled.

'It's the most wonderful news I ever heard.'

'You don't have to say that.'

'I know. I'm just telling you it is. Look at me, my darling. See my face.'

Gingerly, she opened her eyes. His face was so close to hers that she had to step back before she could see his smile, his eyes which glinted with something suspiciously like tears. 'I never thought to hear wonderful

525

news like this, ever. I'd resigned myself to never being a dad. Now this.' He spread his hands in jubilation.

'I can't marry you,' she said. 'At least, not yet.'

'You what?' He stepped towards her, and she reversed away from him. 'But you said –'

'I know, but this changes everything.' She placed her hands either side of her flat stomach. 'Now you feel you have to marry me, and I couldn't bear that.'

'I loved you enough half an hour ago to want to marry you. What's changed?'

'You probably think you love me more now.'

'I do.'

'But you don't. It's the thought of the baby that has made you say that.'

'God preserve me from women's logic.' He put his hand to his head.

'You needn't be so bloody patronising,' she flared up from confused emotions.

'Darling, I'm not. Believe me – I'm only a man, for God's sake.' He shrugged and experimented with a laugh, but she did not respond to it. 'Look, Thomasine, I can't help loving you more with this news. I can't say I'm sorry that I want to look after you even more – there'll be more to look after.' It was a weak joke and neither of them smiled.

'Don't you see? I want you to want *me*. To marry *me*.'

'Then what do we do? I was going to suggest Wimpole moved into your house and I rented it off you, and you and Nadine came here. So pat.'

'I have to have the baby first. Then if you want to marry me, we can.'

'What the hell's the difference?'

'It's simple. I'm not making you, you see. You'll never be able to say you only married me for the sake of the child.'

'But I never would!' he protested.

'Yes, you would. One day down the line. In a row it would be useful ammunition.'

'I do think, dear Thomasine, you're off your trolley.'

'I don't think so. I'm being very sane. I'm protecting our relationship.'

'I can't see it.'

'You will, one day.'

52

Kimberley was a constant source of worry to Eveleigh. She had always been a quiet girl, but now she rarely spoke. She did her work in the same conscientious way, and, if anything, appeared to love the dogs even more. It was just that as each week passed, and there was no note, no call from Alan, she slipped further into herself and deeper into depression, in the face of which Eveleigh felt helpless.

Snow had arrived with a vengeance. For two days the kennels had been cut off from the village by the bitter January storms. The new arrivals preferred the warmth of their night-time kennels, and burrowed into the clean straw. Not so the St Bernards. As the first snowflakes fell a mighty rustling and panting and excited agitation rippled from kennel to kennel.

'I do believe the snow triggers some deep buried memory of their ancestors in the Swiss mountains,' Eveleigh was convinced. 'You wait and see,' she said to a sombre-faced Kimberley as she prepared to release the dogs.

With a rush the great dogs were snuffling and sniffling through the snow, finding the deepest parts, hurling themselves shoulder-high into the drifts, rolling in it, eating it, creating snowstorms of their own, the snow flying from their paws as they dug holes in it for no apparent purpose. 'Come on, sweeties.' Eveleigh opened the gate into the pristine, snow-covered paddock, where the dogs went wild. 'Aren't they having fun?'

'They're all like puppies,' Kimberley replied, and for the first time in weeks she was smiling.

They followed the dogs into the field. It was Kimberley who threw the first snowball, which sent the St Bernards into paroxysms of joy as they tried to catch it in their large jaws.

'Sieglinde, no!' Eveleigh shouted, laughing, as the dog jumped up and knocked her to the ground, whereupon she started frantically burrowing in the snow and half burying her. 'Siggy, you've got it wrong. You silly dog, you're supposed to rescue me, not bury me.' Eveleigh was still laughing as she began to scramble to her feet, but Wotan, joining in the fun, pushed her from behind, and she shouted in pain as her ankle twisted beneath her.

'Are you all right?' Kimberley struggled through the deep snow towards her.

'It's my stupid ankle, it's doubled up. I can't get my boot off . . .' She stopped speaking as she and Kimberley watched the white snow turning red with alarming speed.

Kimberley brushed at the snow frantically, having to push the heavy, inquisitive dogs out of the way. Eveleigh's right foot was facing the wrong way. A bone protruded above the top of her ankle boot. Ashen-faced, she looked at Eveleigh.

'Does it hurt?'

'Oddly, no.' Eveleigh looked at her ankle with fascination. 'Perhaps we should stop the bleeding,' she suggested diffidently. Kimberley took off her belt and tied it tightly around Eveleigh's shin. It worked, the bleeding slowed.

'I'll go and phone for help.' She took off her anorak and put it round Eveleigh's shoulders, and ran. Half a dozen St Bernards, thinking it a game, joined her, but Sieglinde and Wotan stood guard over Eveleigh.

Kimberley dialled for an ambulance. She then tried Jim Varley, but got the answer machine, so she phoned the only other family she knew and Nadine answered.

'I'm not speaking to you,' she said immediately.

'Please, Nadine. This is an emergency. I need your mother . . . '

Grudgingly, Nadine called Thomasine.

Her calls finished, Kimberley grabbed a blanket, had the presence of mind to fill a hot-water bottle and raced back to Eveleigh, who was still sitting in the snow looking grey and shivering uncontrollably.

It took the ambulance and Thomasine nearly half an hour to battle through the snow to the kennels. There they found Eveleigh sitting up, wedged between two St Bernards and leaning on a third as if she were sitting in a living, furry, armchair. She was wrapped in blankets and, in the circumstances, reasonably cheerful and very calm about the situation.

'I couldn't stop her shivering, then I thought the warmth of the dogs might help.'

'Undoubtedly you and the dogs saved her. Shock can be a killer.'

'She'll be all right, won't she, Mrs Lambert?'

'Surely she will, but I doubt if she'll make Crufts this year.'

As soon as Jim Varley received the message that Eveleigh had been taken to the casualty department in Morristown, he was in his car and racing to see her. He had a long wait. Eveleigh's fracture was so severe that surgery was required. But eventually, when she recovered consciousness, it was to find Jim sitting beside her bed, holding her hand.

'Jim . . . ' she croaked.

'Eveleigh! God, what a scare you gave me.'

'I've only broken my ankle,' she said with difficulty, still muzzy from the drugs in her system.

'Only? When I got here and they explained to me –

God, if it hadn't been for Kimberley . . . I could have lost you! I've been so slow, so stupid. It was staring me in the face and I didn't see it.'

'See what?' She waved her hand vaguely at him.

'That I love you.'

'That's nice,' she said softly, before drifting back to sleep.

Eveleigh was the first to admit that she was not an easy patient. Apart from the odd cold, she had never known a day's illness. And now, feeling fit but immobilised by her broken ankle, the inactivity was almost too much for her to cope with.

Kimberley cared for her during the day with a patience Eveleigh thought she would never be able to repay, especially when half the time she was being irascible with her. Jim had moved back into the house so that Eveleigh should not be alone at night. His presence did not stop her short, sharp bursts of irritation, but he was patiently amused by them.

Her food was wrong, the house too hot or too cold, the weather annoying. Incapable of resting, she'd sit on a chair manoeuvring the hoover around a room Kimberley had already cleaned. Most of all she fretted about her dogs and the care they were getting.

'Eveleigh, honestly, you're working yourself into a state over nothing. Kimberley is managing beautifully. That girl's a godsend.'

Jim meant well, but this only gave Eveleigh another source of worry – she began to fear the dogs would switch allegiance to Kimberley, love her instead of herself. She worried that, unless she got moving quickly, she would never get back on to the old footing with them.

Everyone put this uncharacteristic behaviour down to her enforced immobility. Certainly she found this irksome, but if the truth were told, what was upsetting Eveleigh the most was Jim. At night, when she lay on the bed which Kimberley and Jim had carried downstairs and put up in the rarely used dining room, and she heard Jim above her moving about in the spare room, she could have cried from pent-up emotion and frustration. Why didn't he come to her? Why didn't he make love to her?

Eveleigh received a constant supply of visitors. Gill and Justin brought Sadie, Sukie and Sandie, and offered to do her hair. But Eveleigh brusquely rejected the offer. 'What does it matter how I look?'

'My, my, we're not our usual sunny self today, now are we?' When even the antics of their poodles failed to amuse her they opted to leave.

'We've got to do something, Jim. She's going to get stuck in this doom if not, people can, you know.' Fee Walters, who had come to visit her, spoke to Jim outside the house as she was getting into her car.

'Fee, I just don't know what to do. We just can't seem to chivvy her along.'

'Well, somehow or other she's going to have to go to Crufts – otherwise she'll be a crabby old so-and-so for ever,' Fee advised. 'That's our last hope with her.'

Friends from the dog world made the journey, far from easy given the atrocious weather, to see her. But Jim began to think they did more harm than good. Their endless chatter about Crufts was pushing Eveleigh further away from them all as the realisation that she would not be showing her dogs finally sank in.

Nadine, in her new role, ran errands and played canasta with her. She even, at Eveleigh's request to be understanding, re-made friends with Kimberley. Oliver made her laugh, but the person she most looked forward to seeing was Thomasine.

Eveleigh had never had a friend other than her Reggie, and certainly she had never sought a female one. But Thomasine was different. Thomasine was how Eveleigh would like to be. She was open and said what she thought, something Eveleigh found difficult to do. And while attractive, it was in an unconcerned way – how she looked and what she wore were of minor importance to Thomasine, for Eveleigh could never have made friends with a fashion plate. And, most importantly, Thomasine did not gossip, nor did she pry. Eveleigh could not have put up with either.

Eveleigh had never confided in a soul. There had been times when she had thought what a comfort it might be, but she was incapable of doing so. Until she got to know Thomasine and thought she might perhaps risk it, almost certain that Thomasine wouldn't say a word, not even to Oliver.

' . . . You see, Thomasine, he told me he loved me. At least I think he did, but I wasn't totally out of the anaesthetic, so I might have dreamt it,' she found herself saying one afternoon when the two of them were alone. She had been right, confiding was a great comfort.

'And you want him to have said it?'

'Well, yes. Very much so. But what do I do? I mean he's kissed me once, that's all.'

'Maybe he's scared to. Maybe that's why he only said it when he knew you'd be all woozy. Has he ever told you anything in the past that he might think stands in the way of you building a relationship?'

'Of course! Yes,' Eveleigh said, more animated than she had been in days. It had to be Beth. He'd confided in her his shame at sleeping with the woman; did he think she now despised him as much as he despised himself? 'Thomasine, you're so clever,' she said, but she did not. explain further, and her assessment of Thomasine was correct. Thomasine did not ask but, sensing this particular conversation was at an end, asked her if she fancied more tea.

'I'd prefer a gin and tonic.'

'You're getting better.' Thomasine smiled at her as she stood up to prepare the drinks. 'I've something to tell you,' she said, resettling herself in the armchair and resting her feet on Brünnhilde's broad back.

'I thought several weeks ago that you had.'

'So? What?'

'I think you're going to tell me you're pregnant.'

Thomasine looked astonished. 'How do you know? I only found out myself last week.'

'I just knew – there was a look about you. I can't explain.'

'You're a witch, Eveleigh. Or is it being a breeder?' She laughed at this notion.

'Maybe it is.'

Despite Eveleigh's determination to get back on her feet, her ankle did not feel the same way. She could move on crutches now but, with the snow still lying, she was unable to venture outside. And there was no way she could put any weight on her foot. Using the crutches tired her and her frustration with herself as she pushed herself to the limit was enormous. The doctor patiently explained that there was no way she would be fit enough to trundle her dogs around Crufts – just over a month away.

'You could get someone else to do it for you,' Oliver suggested.

'Who?'

'Maybe Thomasine could help.'

'What if Brünnhilde pulls her over, in her condition?'

Oliver looked sharply at Thomasine. 'I didn't tell her, she guessed.'

'Thank goodness someone else knows. Talk to her, Eveleigh. Try and get her to see sense. She says she won't marry me.'

'Thomasine?' Eveleigh looked surprised.

'I will marry him. When it's born. Not before.'

'Eveleigh, I'm potty about her. Please persuade her.'

'I can't make her, Oliver. That's her decision.'

'You must have an opinion.'

'Yes, but I doubt if she wants to hear it.'

'Eveleigh, you can be the most frustrating person on

this planet.' Oliver was virtually jumping up and down with annoyance.

'What about Crufts?' Thomasine asked, pointedly.

'There's Kimberley.'

'But she's so young.' Eveleigh frowned. 'It takes a long time to learn how to show a dog to the best advantage.'

'She's quick. She'd learn. She knows the dogs.'

'But, Oliver, she'd be up against the most professional handlers in the world.'

'Is there someone else you trust who would show for you?'

'No.'

'There you are then – it's Kimberley.'

The problem was that Kimberley did not share Oliver's confidence in her when he later put the proposition. 'I'd make a mess of it, and Mrs Brenton would be so angry with me.'

'There's no one else, Kimberley.'

'She did mention it. I said I'd think about it.'

'There's not a lot of time to think, Kimberley. Look, even if you don't manage to get up to Crufts standard, it'll give Mrs Brenton something to think about. You'll be doing us all a favour – this boredom of hers is getting a bit of a pain.' He spoke with so huge a grin that she did not feel disloyal when agreeing with him. 'And, after all, it's only like taking a dog for "walkies", isn't it?'

It wasn't. It was far more complicated than that.

February

53

Eveleigh had finally decided which two dogs to enter for Crufts, Brünnhilde and Lohengrin. Of the two, Kimberley liked Brünnhilde the most. But it was the male dog on which Eveleigh pinned her greatest hopes.

Kimberley had already attended a couple of Gill and Justin's ringcraft classes with a puppy Eveleigh had kept from her most recent litter. Despite all her experience of showing dogs, she still liked her puppies to gain the knowledge of how to perform in a show-ring, and get used to strange dogs at the classes which Gill had taken over.

Brünnhilde's session passed without incident as she behaved beautifully, but Lohengrin evidently sensed Kimberley's nervousness immediately, pulling on his lead, rolling on his back and finally tripping her up. Kimberley was quickly reduced to tears.

Thomasine had driven them to the community hall in Shillingham, and was sitting on the sidelines with Eveleigh. 'He's too much for her,' she said, as the large dog deftly walked in front of Kimberley, tripping the girl yet again.

'He's showing off. He knows he's in control. She's so nervous it's transmitting to him – down the lead like an electricity conductor,' Eveleigh said in a voice which sounded partly disappointed but also as if this was exactly what she had expected.

'What are you going to do?'

'If we're going to show at all, then I'm afraid it will have to be Brünnhilde. We'll never get Lohengrin to stop being so silly with her now – he's enjoying all the attention far too much.'

'They look the same to me. Brünnhilde's slightly smaller. So why do you think Lohengrin's better?'

'It's not so much that he's better formed than Brünnhilde, it's just he's got such a personality. She's very sweet, but she never shines in quite the same way. He loves the ring, people watching him – he performs. It makes him stand out – a judge can't ignore him. You're seeing the downside here – he just can't stop clowning. Gill, love, you'll never get him to shift that way – bribe him, it's all we can do,' she called to Gill, who was losing the battle of wills to get Lohengrin to move from the centre of the small ring they'd marked out with tape on the wooden floor. The dog was sprawled right across the walkway, preventing anyone else moving.

Gill dug in his pocket and produced a titbit, waving it at the dog. Like magic, Lohengrin rolled over and was up in a trice, trotting along behind Gill sniffing at his hand.

'What a bad boy!' said Gill, returning him. 'I'm surprised at one of yours, Eveleigh. I said to Justin, I thought all Eveleigh's dogs were perfect, I said.'

'Not always. Lohengrin is going through an adolescent phase. They often do, and on top of that it's having an inexperienced handler – he knows it, so he plays up.'

'Right big show-off, aren't you.' Gill tweaked Lohengrin's ear. 'But Brünnhilde's a dream. Kimberley can manage her.' He smiled kindly at Kimberley, who was trying not to show how useless she felt.

'But not well. She's all over the place with her. The dog doesn't stand a chance.'

Thomasine pulled a face at Gill over the top of Eveleigh's head and squeezed Kimberley's hand tight. 'Still, we've got two more of your classes, Gill.'

'I'm afraid not. The council's closing us down. Not tickety-boo at all.'

'But, Gill, why?' Thomasine asked.

'This hall is used by a play group – say no more!'

'The anti-dog lobby?'

'Exactly, Eveleigh. Someone complained it was unhygienic and Bob's your uncle – we're out.'

'But you clean it well, surely?'

'Justin and I scrub our little fingers to the bone after every session. I tell you, you wouldn't find a dog hair in here, with the gallons of disinfectant we use.'

'First the parks. Now this,' Eveleigh said.

'It'll be the streets next. They'll have flying squads zooming about arresting OAPs with their pooches on a lead. The prisons will be full!'

'I get so upset. It's irresponsible dog owners who have brought about this state of affairs.' Eveleigh looked so depressed that Thomasine could personally have killed all the anti-dog lobby, who probably all looked like her sister Abigail. 'Well, we can forget Crufts then. That's for sure.'

'Why, we've got this far? Tell you what. I'll come over after work and help Kimberley. Would you like that?' Gill volunteered.

'It's out of the question, Gill.'

'Yes please,' said Kimberley without thinking, and ignoring Eveleigh.

'There's no point . . . '

'See you Wednesday evening.' Gill rushed off before Eveleigh could object further.

Oliver was not at the disastrous class. He'd driven to London to see Sophia. He'd decided not to tell Thomasine, but Wimpole, a much subdued Wimpole, knew where he'd gone.

'What a pleasant surprise,' Sophia welcomed him. 'Come in, do. I've been meaning to call you. Drink?'

'Thanks.' Oliver appeared to be studying the paintings on the wall, but was, in fact, collecting his thoughts, trying to work out the best way to approach her. He'd practised all the way up in the car, but now, faced with her, all his plans and intentions seemed doomed to failure. He could have asked a reasonable woman straight out, but Sophia was unlikely ever to be open to reason. If he should ask for a divorce he'd guarantee she'd say 'no' on principle.

'How're Slipper and Bandage?'

'Marvellous. Thanks.' He took the whisky she handed him. 'They get on like a house on fire. Daft expression that, when you think about it, isn't it?'

'Sorry?'

'Who wants a house on fire? . . . Never mind. How's Ben?'

'Getting fat.'

'And Cora?'

'I haven't seen her for weeks. Learning Spanish. She joined Daddy. They've a divine villa.'

'How did he manage that?'

'Manage what?'

'Are you being obtuse on purpose? He's supposed to be bankrupt, remember?'

'Am I likely to forget? They bought it ten years ago and put it in Cora's name, so it's safe from the creditors.'

'I didn't know.'

'Neither did Cora.' She laughed, and, though he grinned, Oliver was convinced there was something dodgy about the transaction. 'It was great of you to buy that land. I never thanked you.'

'Anything for dear old Eveleigh.'

'Has she snared Jim yet?'

'I don't think that's quite the right word to use. Let's just say their relationship is moving along satisfactorily.'

'And you and the so *sweet* Thomasine?'

'I see her from time to time,' he said guardedly, afraid to tell her the truth.

'You should shack up with her,' Sophia interrupted. 'After all, you've *so* much in common – dogs, I mean. Perhaps you could breed – dogs, I mean. Still, I'm glad you came. I've been meaning to call you – talk about something important.'

'And what's that?'

'Darling, don't be upset, will you? Promise you won't be cross?' She pouted prettily at him.

'I can't promise till I know what it is.'

'Well . . . ' Sophia, with infuriating slowness, trailed her finger round the top of her glass, making it ring. 'Pretty noise, isn't it? I want a divorce, Oliver.'

Oliver choked on his drink, delving in his pocket for a handkerchief to mop up the whisky he'd spilt.

'There, I knew you'd be upset. Oh dear, I should have been more subtle about it. I'm sorry, Oliver, to tell you so brutally, but I've fallen in love – you have to know.'

'Who with?' He was glad he'd choked on the whisky, it disguised his voice so it was difficult to know if he was happy, sad or angry.

'He's sweet. You'll love him. Filthy rich.'

'That's nice for you.'

'So you won't have to give me so much money now.'

'That's nice for me.' He felt stunned. Was this Sophia? 'Well . . . I can only wish you happiness, Sophia.'

'Oh, how sweet of you. How dear. Another drink?'

'No. I must be going. It's getting late.'

'Did you come for anything in particular?'

'Not really, I was just in the area,' he lied, as his heart sang.

Outside the house, at last, he could not resist doing a jig in the middle of the road to an audience of one stray, but very puzzled, dog.

Kimberley's patience with Eveleigh knew no bounds. Several times a day she pounded round the ring they had contrived from hay bales, thankful that the thaw was over and that the weather, for late February, was dry. Brünnhilde shared her patience as she good-naturedly padded round with her.

'Your stride's too long –'

'Too short –'

'Pull her head up –'

'Push her head down –'

'Don't crowd the dog –'

'Too fast –'

'Too slow –'

She took all the criticisms in good part, even managing to smile as she did, so determined not to let Eveleigh pull her down and take away the little confidence she was building. Away from Eveleigh, Jim, Thomasine and Nadine attempted to boost Kimberley's belief in herself.

For nearly a month Kimberley had been learning to show the dog, not only walking and running, but stationary too. How to show the dog to her best advantage, to note the line, to place the feet, to groom the all-important flowing tail, to ensure Brünnhilde's total confidence in her. All this besides her duties in the kennels.

Crufts was now two weeks away and tension was rising.

'There won't be a dog at Crufts who doesn't love to show. It's up to you, Kimberley, to get that something extra out of Brünnhilde,' Eveleigh said for the umpteenth time.

Kimberley dropped Brünnhilde's lead and stood in the middle of the makeshift ring. 'What the hell do you think I'm trying to do!' she shouted, before running blindly to the house, leaving Nadine to catch Brünnhilde.

'Well! Really!' Eveleigh exclaimed.

'Really! Exactly! She's doing her best and what appreciation do you show her?' Nadine advanced on Eveleigh, who was sitting in the wheelchair she had reluctantly adopted. 'She's worked off her feet, and now this! You don't even say thank you to her. And I'll tell you something – she wants Brünnhilde to win more than anything else, just to repay you for all you've done for her. More fool her, I say.' Nadine stood glaring belligerently down at Eveleigh, the resin cast supporting her ankle propped up in front of her.

'Am I that impossible?'

'Gross.'

'It means so much.'

'To her too.'

'I must apologise.'

'I should jolly well think so.' Nadine pushed Eveleigh back to the house, Brünnhilde in tow.

Jim carried a tray, with a small silver bowl of snowdrops and Eveleigh's omelette, into the sitting room, where she sat in a chair by the fire, her ankle on a footstool in front of her, her other foot resting comfortably on Brünnhilde, whose large body covered most of the hearthrug.

'You are so kind to me,' she smiled up at him.

'It's my pleasure. Though you must be getting fed up with omelettes,' he joked as he uncorked a bottle of white wine and poured her a glass.

'My, this is good,' she said after she had tasted it. She looked across at Jim sitting in the chair opposite and felt how right they were together, how comfortable and content she felt with him. If only he would say something – if only she had the courage to act on Thomasine's advice. But then she was so afraid she had dreamt the tender scene in the hospital. How she loved him, how she longed for him. She pushed her hair back from her face and, without realising, sighed.

'Anything wrong?' Jim asked, looking up from his own food.

'Nothing –' she began. 'The dogs, Crufts, Kimberley, everything –' she sighed again. She drank a quick gulp of wine. 'No, that's not true. It's – Forgive me, Jim, but I have to speak.' She closed her eyes, shutting the sight of him away, afraid what she might see on his face. 'Jim, I love you!' Her hands were clenched now in tight fists. She felt mortified. What had got into her?

She felt her hand being lifted, was aware of his breath on her knuckles, felt his lips brush her skin.

'Eveleigh! My darling. I love you too. I've been afraid to say –'

543

'I thought you did once – in the hospital.' Still she sat with her eyes tightly closed.

'Look at me, Eveleigh, please.'

'I can't, I'm too embarrassed.'

'You must.'

Gingerly, she peeped out. He was so close to her, smiling so gently at her.

'You weren't fully *compos mentis* when I told you. It was a bit of a cheat. And I was afraid too. After Beth – I didn't know what you thought of me.'

'I admired you for telling me. I tried to understand how you'd got into such a pickle, but then, I'm a woman, so I couldn't grasp it totally. But in any case, after what that woman did over the dogs – well!'

'Dear Eveleigh,' he smiled. 'We'd make a good team, you and me.'

'And think of the vet's bills I'd save.'

Jim leaned over and kissed her. Brünnhilde opened one eye, lifted her head, watched them a moment, and then sank back into the serious business of sleeping. If Eveleigh had not been so occupied she would have been convinced her dog was smiling.

March

54

Four days before they left for the show Kimberley, with Nadine as assistant and Eveleigh supervising, began the long preparations for Brünnhilde to look her best.

They bathed her in the large footbath Eveleigh had had installed, soaping her and giggling furiously as the dog shook herself, spraying water from her thick pelt, soaking them to the skin. They rough-dried her with towels in front of the fire, and then with a hairdryer as they brushed out her long hair, which Brünnhilde particularly liked. They had to pay extra attention to the long fur around her paws and on her chin to get them as white as possible, though total whiteness would never be achieved. Jim had trimmed her toenails, since Kimberley was afraid to do them. They brushed her with a wire brush to remove all the loose hair, fluffing her tail up. Her ears were cleaned, her eyes, the folds of skin on her face, her teeth. Brünnhilde looked wonderful. Until it was time to leave for Crufts she would live in the house, fussed and cosseted.

Thomasine decided that without doubt she had been fortunate to meet Oliver. He cared about Nadine and felt a responsibility towards her, which she had barely dreamed was a possibility. She constantly told him how grateful and relieved she was.

'You don't have to keep thanking me, Thomasine. You're a package deal, you and your daughter. I wouldn't have asked you to marry me if I didn't want Nadine too.'

'She's not the easiest child –'

'She's not a child, sweety. She's a young woman.'

'Is that where I've gone wrong?'

'Maybe.'

He had involved Nadine in all their decisions. Where to live, which room she wanted, how she wanted it decorated.

'It's perfect as it is, Oliver,' Nadine said. Thomasine struggled to hide her astonishment as Nadine accepted the flower-sprigged wallpapered room with its looped and swagged matching chintz curtains.

He'd accompanied them to a parent-teacher evening at the school, where the reports on Nadine had made Thomasine's heart sink. But on the way home, when Oliver talked to her, her unbelieving ears heard Nadine agree she'd been a fool and would work harder in future.

No longer was there a problem over the dogs, her clothes, her untidy room. She'd even eaten meat. Before her eyes Nadine was changing.

The move from The School House to Bishop's End was accomplished in stages, but now the final boxes had gone and the furniture van had today moved the pieces of furniture Thomasine wanted to keep. Wimpole would be moving into their old home the following day.

By evening they were all tired. 'Let's go to the flicks and have a Chinese?' Oliver suggested. Thomasine, having reached the point where she was convinced they would never be straight again, happily agreed. As they drove home, half listening to Nadine and Oliver talking, she felt, strangely, that they were a complete family in a way she had never experienced with Robert.

'We've got to decide on music. After what to watch on TV families fall out over music more than anything else,' Oliver said wisely, as if he'd been a parent all his adult life.

They argued good-naturedly about what cassettes could be played in the car. The final agreement was that all classical and modern rock music were banned. They settled on the safe middle ground of Pink Floyd, Status Quo and the odd Beatle recording, which all three liked.

'It'll be compromise all the way now, I suppose,' Nadine said from the back.

'You can play whatever you want in your room, just don't inflict it on us,' Oliver answered.

'Some compromise!'

'It is. Your modern stuff in your room. Classical in my work room. Mix, as now, in the drawing room. What could be fairer?'

'What about the kitchen?'

'Country and Western.' Thomasine turned and smiled at her daughter.

'And in the nursery?' Nadine asked slyly.

Thomasine's and Oliver's jaws both dropped open, and eyes widened in unison, like a formation dance duo. Thomasine, who at four months still barely showed, had been putting off telling Nadine.

'You should have told me, then you needn't look so gob-smacked,' Nadine said, trying not to shriek with mirth at their expressions.

'How long have you known? Who told you?'

'I guessed. You've been whispering and secretive – I was right, wasn't I?'

'I didn't know how to tell you,' Thomasine confessed.

'Quite easy, you just do.'

'I didn't want to upset you.'

'Why should I be upset?'

'Well . . . you know . . . '

'You weren't afraid I'd be jealous, were you? Mum, that's gross! Of course I wouldn't be – jealous of a baby, whatever next? I'm grown up now.'

'Of course you are, and I was stupid. I'm sorry.' But Thomasine did not yet possess Oliver's confidence in a changed Nadine; she still remembered her jealousy over the dogs. Such a person could easily be jealous of a baby.

'When are you getting hitched?'

Oliver glanced sideways at Thomasine. 'After the baby's born.'

'You what?' Nadine leant forward. 'That's dreadful.

Why? Your divorce will be through in time, Oliver. You've got to get married.'

'Don't lecture me, it's your mum who's the problem. You tell her.' And Oliver could have sung with happiness, knowing Nadine would be relentless in her onslaught on Thomasine's objections. He couldn't have hoped for a better ally.

'I do hope the dogs are all right – Nova and the puppies are quite capable of chewing the house down by now.'

'Don't change the subject,' Nadine and Oliver shouted in unison.

Nadine was in bed. The dogs, a snoring, twitching, scratching bunch, were sprawled in front of the fire. Thomasine and Oliver sat curled up together on the sofa, enjoying the peace and each other.

'Just look at Slipper.' Oliver pointed to where Slipper, lying close to Bandage, had one of her paws on him, as if she were holding him.

'They're wonderful, and to think a year ago I didn't give dogs a thought.'

'It was delayed development, that was all. You were so nice already, the dogs had to follow.'

Thomasine threw back her head and laughed with delight. Oliver leant over and took hold of her hand.

'I love you so much. Please, please marry me.'

She stopped laughing and gazed at him for what seemed an age. He had such a dear face, such a kind face, she thought. And how she loved his smile. How she loved him.

'Am I being stupid?'

'Very.'

'As if you weren't enough, now, I suppose, Nadine will never let up either. You wear me down.'

'I mean to. Is that a "yes"?'

'I think it must be.' She smiled at him as he sat, still holding her hand. 'What's the matter?' she asked, suddenly concerned, for it looked as if his eyes had filled with tears.

'Sorry!' Self-consciously he put up his hand to wipe his eyes. 'It's just, I've never wanted anything so badly in my whole life as I want to marry and love you.'

'My darling,' she sighed, and leant to kiss him as Oliver produced a ring from his pocket and quickly slipped it on Thomasine's finger before she changed her mind.

They set off for Crufts very early on a bleak March morning in convoy. Oliver, with Thomasine and Nadine, went first. Brünnhilde sat on a clean blanket in the back of Eveleigh's Bentley with Kimberley. The window, despite the cold was, of necessity, slightly open, for Brünnhilde was panting with excitement as if she knew where she was going. Without the fresh air the other windows of the car would quickly steam up. A far happier, non-irascible Eveleigh sat beside Jim, who was driving the large car.

'I do hope Grace and Wimpole manage,' Eveleigh said. 'I hope we haven't asked them to do too much.'

'Eveleigh! Stop worrying!'

'Oh, Mrs Brenton, I mixed the other dogs' feeds and made endless lists for them.'

'I'm being silly, aren't I?' Eveleigh smiled at them.

'Yes,' they replied in unison.

At sight of the huge Exhibition Centre and the crowds in Birmingham, Kimberley wanted to run. 'It's enormous!' she exclaimed, standing outside the car, the wind whipping across the open plaza, fluffing Brünnhilde's fur. Kimberley pulled her coat tight, and waited while Jim unloaded Eveleigh's wheelchair. Then, pushing Eveleigh and holding on to the dog, she moved towards the dogs' entrance where, having shown their exhibitors card, they were allowed in.

It was Sunday, the final day of Crufts, and the

working dogs judging day. Their documents had been sent to them by post; now they had to match their number with those on the dogs' benches. An official of the Kennel Club, a friend of Eveleigh's, saw how difficult it was for Kimberley to manage both chair and dog, and stepped in and pushed Eveleigh.

'I was so glad that unfortunate business was cleared up, Eveleigh. Scandalous! That someone could pull it off,' he said.

'Ben Luckett had contacts everywhere, people who owed him a favour – even in our dog world.'

'I never believed any of it, you know. Nor did any member I spoke to, not of you, Eveleigh, you've done so much for dogs.'

'Thank you,' Eveleigh smiled modestly.

'You got the letter?'

'From the Chairman of the Disciplinary Sub-Committee? Oh, yes. I'm going to frame it,' she laughed, managing expertly to cover up the hurt she had felt and the intense relief when the letter came.

Kimberley was walking alongside them as they entered the first great hall, already crowded with people and dogs, even though the general public would not be allowed in until ten. From the ceiling above each ring hung its number: they were looking for ring number 19, for close by it would be the St Bernard benches. They crossed the first hall, past the stalls being set up where anything a dog would ever need could be bought, from food to blankets, from kennels to figurines, from oil paintings to jewellery in the shape of every dog represented, and even one for a pet crematorium. They passed the Guide Dogs for the Blind stall, the Retired Greyhound Trust, HM Customs and Excise with their search dogs. They kept stopping as they progressed through the second exhibition hall as people rushed up to speak to Eveleigh and wish her well.

At last they reached the St Bernard section. There were the rows of numbered wooden benches, each with a partition, and they finally found theirs. Brünnhilde had a good sniff and jumped up with no bidding, then sat down and with wise eyes surveyed the scene.

Eveleigh was being greeted on all sides by fellow St Bernard breeders, glad to see her here, happy that all the unpleasantness had been resolved. She tried not to think that it was a pity they had not spoken up for her when she needed them, but managed, instead, to smile her thanks and keep her counsel.

Dogs were being put on the benches. Some were placidly clambering up themselves, the more nervous or the novices having to be pushed, pulled and hauled onto their seats. Benching chains were clipped on to a holding ring for security but, looking at the number of St Bernards already overwhelmed by a great need for sleep, they seemed to be unnecessary. Brünnhilde greeted the dogs either side of her before curling up for a snooze herself. More than twenty thousand dogs were judged over the four days of Crufts, and today a good five thousand of them were settling into position. It was amazing, Kimberley thought, that the humans were making more noise than the dogs.

Jim arrived with the bags, and Kimberley was soon occupied unpacking Brünnhilde's grooming kit, filling her water bowl, shoving her blanket under her for comfort. She then sat beside her, as if guarding her, constantly brushing her just to keep busy and to keep her nerves at bay while Brünnhilde snored contentedly.

'It's unbelievably clean, especially when you think this is the last day. I thought it would whiff something awful of dog,' Oliver said, as he and Thomasine joined them at the St Bernard benches.

'And did you see the dog loos! Amazing!' Nadine was failing in her plan to look nonchalant, swept along like everyone else by the atmosphere of mounting excitement.

'And the dogs are all so good. Just look at them sitting

there so patiently. Nova would have caused a riot by now.'

'They're used to it. Most of these dogs have been doing shows since they were puppies,' Eveleigh explained.

'Kimberley, here are your clothes.' Thomasine held out the zippered plastic dress bag she'd brought with her, since there had been too much risk of it being crushed in Eveleigh's Bentley.

'Should I put it on now?' Kimberley asked, incapable of making any decision herself.

'You might as well – we've an hour, but by the time you've titivated yourself . . . '

'I'll come with you, Kimberley,' Nadine offered, and they wandered off together.

'Any chance of seeing Gill and Justin?' Thomasine asked.

'Probably not. Poodles are in the Utility Group, and they were shown yesterday. We can find out if they won.'

'Then the bulldogs were yesterday too? Oh, what a shame, I hoped to see some.'

'You must go to the Kennel Club's Discover Dogs exhibition, Thomasine. You'll find examples of every breed of dog shown here over the four days of the competition.'

After her experiences the previous year, Eveleigh was determined that Brünnhilde should not be left for one minute alone on the bench, just in case. She and Jim took the first turn, and Thomasine and Oliver took the opportunity to see the dogs.

Each breed had its own section, and they walked up and down the aisles lined either side with the wooden benches on which sat the pick of every breed in the country.

'I want them all,' Thomasine said, as they ambled by admiring the boxers. In contrast to the St Bernards, none of these dogs slept, but sat bolt upright, eyes darting each

and every way, excitedly alert. The Rottweilers sat as if
on duty and watched them pass with wary eyes.
Alsatians with beautiful expressions, pricked-up ears,
tails pluming behind them, slunk by, obediently close to
their masters. They met Alaskan Malamutes with intelligent eyes and coarse, oily coats, magnificent mastiffs and
Newfoundlands. Norwegian, Finnish, Swedish and
French dogs of whose existence they'd been, until now,
ignorant. Desperate-to-please Dobermans, elegant
Danes, spotted Dalmatians; sheep dogs, cattle dogs,
water dogs; hairy dogs and strange, half-bald Portu-
guese water dogs; push-me-pull-you dogs. Tall, short,
thin, large – Thomasine thought she must be in paradise.
In the Discovering Dogs section they found two bulldogs
and, adorable as they were, Thomasine was convinced
that Nova was better.

Kimberley changed in the ladies' into beige trousers,
cotton blouse and matching flat suede pumps.
   'God, that's so ugh! What on earth made you buy
that!' Nadine said, without thinking, and then, since she
was still in 'nice' mode, apologised.
   'I quite like it. Mrs Brenton bought it for me, she
insisted. She says smart dogs deserve smart handlers.'
She was putting on a light make-up, concentrating on
brushing on her mascara. 'I don't usually wear this
colour, but she wanted a colour for Brünnhilde to stand
out against – give her a better outline. This works well
with her reddish-brown bits.'
   'You nervous?'
   'Terrified.'
   'You'll be fine. Bet you win. Hang on, you've got a bit
of hair sticking out.' She reached up and pushed the
offending strand back into the band which was holding
Kimberley's blonde hair in a pony tail. 'You look great.'
She hugged her friend.
   'Thanks. Shall we get a coffee? Do you think we've got
time?'

They dawdled on their way to one of the many cafés, looking at the things to buy. Kimberley bought a poster of a St Bernard and Nadine one of a bulldog – 'for my mum, not me,' she insisted. They were looking at costume jewellery, all dog-related.

'Kimberley?'

She swung round. She felt the blood rush from her face to be replaced rapidly and redly. 'Alan,' she spoke in a whisper. 'Ooops,' said Nadine.

'You look lovely.' He meant it, then wished he hadn't said it.

'And you look so smart.' She glanced quickly, but admiringly, at him. 'In uniform.'

'I'm on duty at the RSPCA stand.' He'd missed her, but until he saw her he had not realised how much. And upon seeing her again the old longing flooded back and, mysteriously, the bitterness had disappeared.

'No more Special Branch?'

'Got the sack?' asked Nadine, feeling remarkably left out of things. In any case, she'd never really liked him – too nosey by far.

'Can we talk, Kimberley?' He ignored Nadine.

'I can't . . . '

'I see. Sorry I asked.' She saw the anger in him flare. Why did they always have to have these misunderstandings?

'You don't understand. I'm showing a dog in fifteen minutes.'

'After?'

'If you like,' she said simply, and turned quickly on her heel, knowing she was blushing again and furious with herself for doing so.

'What a creep. Why do you give him the time of day after the way he treated you?'

'You didn't want to speak to me, either,' she said heatedly, not liking to hear him criticised.

'That's different. I changed my mind, didn't I?'

'But you were here, and God knows where he's been.'

She said this with concern, for he had looked tired and much thinner than three months ago.

Kimberley stood at the entrance to the ring with the line of St Bernard bitches for the post-graduate class, Brünnhilde standing patiently beside her. Her heart was racing, her mouth was dry, she wanted to pee, she felt sick and she couldn't imagine what she was doing here.

Someone gave an order and the line moved forward as the dogs and their handlers entered the ring. Kimberley was aware of the crowd, several deep, clustered around the edge of the ring, but she did not look up. *Concentrate on your dog,* she remembered Eveleigh's instructions. She checked for the neatly folded Jiffy cloth she'd put in her waistband to mop up any slobber from Brünnhilde's generous mouth.

She patted Brünnhilde with short, sharp, nervous pats. The dog jerked her head and looked up to her, a puzzled expression on her large gentle face. 'Sorry, Brünnhilde. I'm fine. Don't worry about me. Who's a beautiful girl then . . . ' She spoke gently, as instructed – *Talk to the dog.* She dared to glance about her, but something seemed to be wrong with her vision, for she could make out no individual face, everything was a blur.

Watch the judge. Where was the judge? Down the line, she need not check Brünnhilde's position yet. Or should she? Better. She bent down and aligned Brünnhilde's front legs, checking that her large, arched feet were neatly together.

'How old?'

The voice made her jump. 'Sorry? Um . . . ' Her mind was a total blank as she looked at the woman judge with blind panic.

'How old is she?' the woman repeated patiently.

'Three,' Kimberley managed to say.

Brünnhilde stood stoically as the woman felt her body beneath the thick, long pelt. She checked her ears, her eyes, her tail, her teeth. Ran her hands down her thick legs. Checking for faults, for deformities, for what? Kimberley's mind shrieked and she saw that Brünnhilde's feet were not in line, and she bent down, worrying how long they'd been like this.

'If you would take her round, please.' The judge sketched in the air the route she was to follow.

'Good girl, Brünnhilde. Good girl . . .' She tugged gently on the lead as Eveleigh had taught her and Brünnhilde shook herself, but to her relief no slobber flew, and ponderously, then more easily, she began to move in an unhurried, smooth motion, Kimberley running alongside. Brünnhilde's tail flowed behind her, the feathered fur spreading as she moved faster. And it suddenly all felt so right as she ran in step with her and they appeared to move as one. Just as Eveleigh had said, *as if you're ballroom dancing.*

Five bitches were selected and Brünnhilde was one, though it took a whisper from another woman to tell her. Then all five were inspected and they stood in line again. Everything seemed to take an age as the judge paced up and down the row looking carefully at each dog, checking a second time, then a third and then a fourth.

The judge stood back, deep in concentration, looking up and down the line. Dramatically she lifted her arm and pointed straight at Brünnhilde. The crowd went wild. Brünnhilde jumped up at Kimberley. The only person who did not know that Brünnhilde was Best Bitch in her class was Kimberley. The woman beside her told her to go and stand by the board she had not even seen brought into the ring. People were congratulating her, kissing her and she had a rosette pinned on her.

The welcome from the others was tumultuous.

'I couldn't have done it better myself,' Eveleigh beamed at her, clutching her hand.

'You were great,' said Nadine.

'I couldn't breathe,' said Thomasine.

'You both brought a lump to my throat,' said Oliver.

'Well done,' said Jim.

'Hullo, Kimberley,' said Alan.

Kimberley sat with Alan having a coffee, still flushed with triumph, still so excited she could barely sit down.

'I missed you, Kim.'

'Me too.'

'I'm sorry.'

'Me too.'

'I should have believed in you.'

'There was a lot to believe.' She looked away from him, loathing to think of that time, the shame, of those poor dogs. Then she was aware of his hand searching for hers.

'Eveleigh told me you'd not gone to warn your father. That you'd gone to make sure it was stopped.'

'Something like that. I'm not even sure any more what I was doing. But why didn't you tell me what you did? That hurt me,' she found the courage to say.

'It's difficult, Kimberley. I wanted to tell you – often. But . . .'

'You didn't trust me.'

'In this job it's often best not to say anything. If I had told you what I was about you'd have been put in a spot – Be honest. What would you have done?'

'I don't know, that's the honest truth. I understand in a way. I nearly told you about my father. I don't know how many times.'

'But you didn't.'

'No, and I hated myself that I didn't. If I had, we'd never have had our falling out – all these lonely months.'

'It's been hell, hasn't it? When I saw you just now in the ring, I loved you so much, I wanted to tell everyone.'

'Please . . . I couldn't bear it if . . .'

'We won't this time. I promise. I bought the house, it's mine. There's the chance of a transfer to Morristown –

559

uniform branch. I've looked into it, I can apply – if you want me to.'

'But won't you miss your work in the Special Branch?'

'I can adjust. I'd rather be with you.'

'I don't want you to stop doing what you like. It would be better if you waited to move.'

'But then the place will have gone.'

'There'll be other chances. Honest, it's better this way. I'll move to Horsham. I don't mind.' But she did, she felt a lump in her throat at the thought of not being with the St Bernards. 'You look tired, and thinner.'

'I've been tracking sheep being driven down through France to Spain. There was a bit of an altercation,' he grinned. 'My foot got in the way – got run over!'

'You might have been killed!' Her eyes were round with horror at the very idea.

'But I wasn't. And I'm back. My foot's fine. I only told you to make you feel sorry for me. I love you, Kimberley, will you marry me?'

She could not believe what was happening to her – drinking coffee from polystyrene mugs, here in this crowded hall, surrounded by people and dogs. She smiled; the dogs seemed appropriate. She was suddenly full of such delirious happiness – no bleak future, never again unloved, someone to care for her. 'I'd like that.'

'Kimberley!'

She looked up from their entwined hands. It was Oliver.

'Sorry to interrupt, but Eveleigh's throwing a wobbly, convinced you've done a runner. You're needed – it's time for the Best St Bernard Bitch to be chosen.'

'I'm going to faint. I know I am.' Thomasine was fanning herself with her programme. Brünnhilde had, after a gruelling session in the ring, been chosen Best Bitch. The wait for the selection of the Best of Breed, when she would compete against the Best Dog, seemed

560

endless. If Thomasine had felt tense before, it was as nothing to now.

Brünnhilde won! She was chosen as the Best St Bernard and now had to move on to the selection of the Best of Group, which would be judged in the main ring and where she would be up against the best of each breed of working dog. If Brünnhilde emerged Best of Group, then she'd be in the final with the dogs from the other five groups.

Brünnhilde seemed to be aware that she'd done well, but this did not stop her catching up on some much needed sleep after so much excitement. Her great head lolled on her legs, her paws hung limply over the side of the bench and she wiffled contentedly.

'Wonderful, isn't it, the atmosphere here?' Oliver said to Thomasine as they sat on the folding chairs Jim had brought, guarding Brünnhilde while Eveleigh and Jim grabbed a bite to eat.

'Dog people are so nice. They must catch it from the dogs.'

'Shall we do this – show our brood?'

'I'd really like that – bet my Nova wins more than your Slipper.'

'Poor Bandage, he'll never be smart enough again.'

'But you've got him back, that's the most important thing.'

'And I've got you. Bliss!' He leant back in the chair and immediately toppled over, but the clatter didn't even wake Brünnhilde.

Brünnhilde was Best in Group!

The excitement in the St Bernard section had reached an uncontrollable level. Old rivalries were forgotten, ambitions were buried, everyone wanted Brünnhilde to become Best in Show – if she did, then she would be the first St Bernard to win the honour since 1974.

'It's all too much!' Eveleigh was frantically fanning her face. 'Where is the child?'

'Don't worry, she's with that nice RSPCA Inspector. They look as if they're floating on air – and I don't think it's all down to Brünnhilde.' Jim was having a great day. He'd met up with colleagues he'd not seen for years. He was already loaded down with samples from the animal-food manufacturers who wanted him to try their new products – for whelping bitches, for puppies, for adult dogs, old dogs, fat dogs. 'It's amazing! There's a diet for each and every dog, I wish I'd come here years ago.'

'I wish you had too.'

'Happy?' he asked.

'Totally,' she replied. She clutched the arms of her chair with her work-roughened hands. She felt a strange elation, the excitement she supposed. She suddenly realised that the fear had disappeared. Ahead of her stretched a happy future; she had a companion for life, loneliness was banished.

If Kimberley had thought everything tense before, it was as nothing compared to this. The huge hall was buzzing with excited anticipation. The atmosphere was charged as if with electricity. The stands around the main ring were packed, the tickets sold months ago – just for this, for her and Brünnhilde. She shivered. It didn't bear thinking about.

'Are you cold?' the woman beside her asked.

'Excited,' she replied, and hoped Eveleigh hadn't seen. *Speak to no one but the dog and the judge*, was another of her instructions.

Brünnhilde sat down, her tongue lolling. She was hot. Kimberley was hot. Thank goodness she'd taken Eveleigh's advice and dressed in cotton; already she could feel sweat trickling down her spine.

She wanted a drink. She looked around her at the blazing lights. Of course, television, but such a thought only made her stomach contract. I'm going to faint, she thought, and took deep breaths. Her throat was so dry she could barely swallow. Was she ill?

Brünnhilde nudged her. 'Sorry, sweety, I haven't been talking to you. It's all right. I'm all right.' Of course she was. Alan was out there somewhere watching, he'd begged, bribed, and cajoled his way in. She was going to be married. Have babies. Puppies. Oh God, she was so happy.

She tweaked at her waistband, suddenly remembering Eveleigh's warning that this judge liked *a neat dog and a neat handler*. She was aware the woman beside her was shaking. At least she wasn't doing that. Just look how she was transmitting her nervousness – her dog, a Weimaraner, sleek and grey-beige, was already pulling on the lead. At least she wasn't doing that!

The judge looked so severe. A bright red rose in his buttonhole. He was a famous breeder of Rottweilers, Eveleigh had told her, thank goodness there wasn't one in the ring. As she talked to Brünnhilde, steadying her all the time, she watched him. He didn't once smile and he was working his mouth all the time, sucking in his cheeks, licking his lips as if he had toothache. 'Please God, don't let him have toothache,' she said aloud, as if to Brünnhilde.

'I beg your pardon?' said the finalist the other side, a white bull terrier attached to her lead.

'Nothing,' Kimberley said, feeling foolish and thinking that Bandage, but for his poor scars, was a finer dog than this one.

They lined up. The announcer called their names. The final six were the bull terrier, best from the Terrier Group, a beagle from the Hound Group, the gundog, the Weimaraner, a Pekinese in the Toy Group, a German Spitz for Utility, and Brünnhilde for the Working Dogs.

The judging finally began. The beagle performed perfectly, face alert as he trotted neatly and precisely around. The Weimaraner looked frightened and nearly tripped up his handler, but his gunmetal coat gleamed with health and excellence. The German Spitz was an exuberant happy pile of white fur, obviously having the time of its life. The terrier behaved impeccably, and then it was the turn of the Pekinese, which moved smartly like a hairy hovercraft on the green carpeted ring. So large for such a little dog.

Brünnhilde was last. After her examination, the longest, most thorough yet, she and Kimberley moved out into the ring. The roar from the audience soared to the rafters. Since Brünnhilde was representative of the working dogs, and this was their day, she had the unfair advantage of stands packed with working-dog enthusiasts, cheering, egging them on.

Round they went, Brünnhilde with head and tail held high, lolloping rhythmically along, taking control, showing Kimberley how it should be done. And Kimberley realised she was enjoying herself as she hadn't done before, she could have happily run round the ring for hours, she felt so at ease.

When they halted she hugged Brünnhilde with all her might, and dared to look into the crowd and saw them all – Eveleigh, Jim, Thomasine, Nadine and, best of all, Alan, waving, thumbs up, shouting encouragement at her.

Then she bent to the task in hand. Making Brünnhilde stand tall and straight, showing off her line to perfection. Talking constantly, sensing Brünnhilde had had enough, that she wanted to crash down and sleep, and knowing, if she did, she'd never get her back up again.

It took an age, an awful nail-biting, saliva-drying, heart-pumping age.

The judge waved for the stands to be brought in. The attendants, smart in black and white, strode in carrying the numbers, the all-important numbers one and two. And the cup was there, and Kimberley felt sick again, and she was sure she was going to fall.

The judge walked back and forth, reversed from the line, studied them unsmilingly – and then his left hand pointed dramatically, followed in a millisecond by his right and he was pointing at her. The roar of the crowd was deafening and she and Brünnhilde ran forward, Brünnhilde jumping up and down in excitement, knowing she'd done well. Rolling on the floor in a whirling mass of fur.

'Reserve Best in Show! It's beyond my wildest dreams,' Eveleigh was saying once the cups had been awarded, the congratulations made, the photographs taken, the kissing calmed down and the tears mopped up.

'I thought I'd won,' Kimberley was downcast. 'I thought he pointed at us first, not the Pekinese.'

'My dear girl, you don't know what you achieved today. People show all their lives with this dream and never attain it. I'm so proud of you both.'

'Honest?'

'Pleased as pleased can be.'

And Brünnhilde barked once, long and loud, as if she was too.